WITHDRAWN

☑ **W9-BXL-689**

GAYLORD M

IN THE PRESENCE OF
HORSES

Barbara Dimmick

IN THE PRESENCE OF HORSES

WHEELER
PUBLISHING, INC.
ROCKLAND, MA

★ AN AMERICAN COMPANY ★

Published in Large Print by arrangement with Doubleday, a division of Random House, Inc., in the United States and Canada

Wheeler Large Print Book Series.

Set in 16 pt Plantin.

Library of Congress Cataloging-in-Publication Data

Dimmick, Barbara, 1954-
   In the presence of horses / Barbara Dimmick.
     p. (large print) cm.(Wheeler large print book series)
   ISBN 1-56895-860-9 (softcover)
   1. Lehigh River Valley (Pa.)—Fiction. 2. Women horse owners—
Fiction. 3. Horses—Diseases—Fiction. 4. Bethlehem (Pa.)—Fiction.
5. Pennsylvania—Fiction. 6. Horse farms—Fiction. 7. Orphans—Fiction.
8. Farmers—Fiction. 9. Large type books. I. Title. II. Series

[PS3554.I4379 I58   2000]
813'.54—dc21
                                                00-022865
                                                               CIP

For Andrea, who lured me back into the saddle

And for T.A.B.—all these years later

Part One

chapter one

A true black horse carries not a single hair of brown. What most folks call black is usually bay or seal. But this colt was a true black— true black with a white, cockeyed blaze and four elegant white stockings. Everything else was wrong. He was three years old, coming four. By now his growth should have evened out; he should have been taller at the shoulders than at the rump. He wasn't.

"You'd be riding downhill with every stride," I remarked.

The owner was somewhere in his thirties. He stood a good five, six inches taller than I, and the cuffs of his muddy golf jacket did not cover his wide, pale wrists. His fine blond hair, although longish in the back, had begun to recede, leaving a high vulnerable forehead. Across his nose, rimless glasses rested at a very slight angle; one lens seemed askew. His name was Pierce. He and I had just finished turning the horses out, and with the last of the halters still in hand, we were leaning against the paddock rails. A tall chestnut mare gave a squeal, then flipped up her hooves and bucked across the paddock. The others snorted and cantered after her. The black trotted like mad to keep up. Pierce followed his every move with such intensity that I almost regretted my remark about the horse's conformation.

"Allie meant to start him this spring," he said, his voice flat. "She gave him the extra year."

I didn't know who Allie was and I didn't ask.

Pierce studied the horse a while longer, then looked at his watch. It was seven-fifteen, and my interview had consisted of coming to the little farm with its snug barn and haphazard fences and helping him with the chores. We'd started at five-thirty. He told me he taught media arts and communication at the local high school, that he had practically no time for the horses, and that I'd be more or less on my own until classes got out in June. Then he'd see if he could help.

The six horses wheeled away from us. The morning was brisk, and the grass was wet on their hooves. We'd hayed and grained and watered them, Pierce explaining the routine, showing me everything he could think of and telling me things I'd known since I was a girl, which told me he hadn't known them all that long himself.

The horses cantered past us, then swept through the gate that led out toward a pasture. The black kept up at an industrious trot. From the rear I could see that his hocks were set at an odd angle and that, with each stride, the left one gave a funny hitch. His rump, though, was knotted and tough. I supposed it was from how hard he had to work just to get from one place to another.

"He's got muscles anyway," I said.

"Allie always liked him," Pierce said. "From the minute he was born. His name is Twister."

I could see him staring at the horse. The halter hung quietly in his hand.

"How about you, Natalie? Any thoughts?"

"Depends on what you have planned."

"Get him going. That's what Allie wanted." He turned then, sketched a hasty sign of the cross, gave me a weird grin. "Wishes of the dead," he said, and I could not tell whether he was about to start sobbing or cracking one-liners.

We stood there a while longer, shifting from foot to foot in the morning chill and staring at the horse. So, I thought, Allie was dead. Whoever she was. Pierce offered no explanation, and I guessed that was all right: I had no real wish to hear the story. Anyway, it was obvious the black horse would break down. Those hocks.

I wondered if it was wise to stay, even for a little while. Earlier he'd said the riding lessons started the Saturday before Memorial Day, then ran weekends until school got out and switched to five mornings a week during the summer. I had no wish to teach; it would do nothing to keep up my skills. But did that mean I shouldn't stay just long enough to get my feet under me again?

I looked up at the sky, at the blue breaking over the fat, low, familiar Pennsylvania hills. How close was I to Bethlehem? Eighty miles? I'd been coming in from Ohio and I had not wanted the job I'd looked at south of Pittsburgh—too many rich kids in the barn, not enough good horses. Then I'd stopped in at a breeding farm in the Laurel Highlands,

5

but they'd filled their job the day before. And so I had tiptoed further east.

In the end, Pierce didn't really offer me the job; he just seemed to assume I'd take it. He rushed down the lane to the house, and twenty minutes later came back out wearing a black suit with a boxy cut and a magenta tie. For some reason, I had expected something different, less exotic. Say corduroys, or tweeds. His hair was slicked back, but even from the doorway of the barn, I could tell he had a slight cowlick that would free itself by the beginning of second period. His Toyota wagon rattled down the farm lane and swung right, back toward the town of Shipville. I wondered if he was sweet to his students, or cruel.

I stood a while longer thinking. There were twenty-three acres, and a little one-bedroom efficiency over the garage I could have, unless I wanted to look for a better place. I hadn't even seen it yet, but I didn't care. I'd been living over barns—or garages or equipment sheds—for twenty years.

Out at my truck, I opened the passenger door and chose a saddle. I traveled with three: different tree widths, different depths of seats, different styles. I could blend in anywhere and could probably fit a saddle to any horse that came along. Here, where the owner knew so little, I'd opt for my favorite, my Kieffer—a hand-sewn German saddle with a deep seat. For some reason, I thought this choice would have pleased my Aunt Vee. A tall slender woman, Vee never got on a horse without breeches and boots, gloves and a proper jacket. Her saddle had been a well-oiled Stübben, which must have been too damn big for her: I'd been small for eleven but she'd had room in it for both herself and me.

I ran my hand across the rich leather of the saddle skirt. And then I thought: Of course I won't go back. It was long gone, the city of my childhood.

Up in the barn, I scouted around, found a small equipment room that seemed like the attic of a dead grandmother: all dust and cobwebs and weak light filtering through dirty panes. But there, on labeled wooden holders, were six bridles, and I made some guesses about Allie and about the horses by what each horse wore for a bit and by the various accouterments: martingales, breastplates, the like. I hung my saddle on an empty rack and traced my finger in the heavy dust on the back of one of the school saddles. For a minute or two, I considered spending the morning cleaning: the room needed serious work and all the tack needed conditioning.

But then I thought: To hell with it.

I found a sponge, a bucket, then at random picked a bridle and a breastplate off the wall: Sheila's. I wiped both down, dug up a brush and hoof pick, and went out to the pasture in search of a horse.

And so I began. Each day, I worked with each of the five schoolies. They were a lively but tractable lot. At first I tried each on the longe line, clipping the long white web rein to the horse's bit, then standing on foot, and putting them through their paces around me in a circle. I saw that Galen, a small sturdy bay, never took his left lead at the canter and that Sheila was clearly a retired broodmare who was pretty certain she knew more than I did. Occasionally, she planted her hooves, gave me a fierce offended look, and then, after she'd forced me to give the whip a little pop in the air behind her, moved off with a flat indignant stride. I thought she was sweet and feisty, and I admired her sense of what was right and what was not, and thought, if I lived that long, it would be nice to be just like her when I grew old.

After a few days, I began to ride them in the ring, one right after the other. I tried all their paces, their turns, their circles, their figures of eight, their serpentines. Lawrence was a purply-red Appaloosa, who, true to his breeding, poked out his nose and, when he wasn't trotting along in a world all his own, utterly oblivious to my legs and voice, tried to please in his own vague sort of way. Prima was probably the best of the lot, with long smooth gaits and a pretty, burnished neck and shoulder. She was the most spirited of the group, and it was my guess that all the girls aspired to ride her. I could imagine the mare in the ring at a small show, plump and gleaming, ears pricked, and, if not winning, then at least bringing home a ribbon or two.

As I rode, I made up long lists of questions

to ask Pierce. Where should I buy supplies? He was out of staples, like saddle soap and Koppertox. Would he like me to houseclean the barn? There were six nice airy box stalls down one side of it and a variety of rooms on the other. To me, it seemed wise to turn them out, scrub, dust, rearrange, and streamline— grooming stuff, tack and equipment all together. I could at least leave the place in good shape for the summer. Meanwhile, I significantly increased the rations of hay and grain; every horse on the place looked far too thin. Once in a while I felt a twinge of guilt: I really should tell him to start looking for an instructor. Another week or two and I'd be gone.

At the end of each day, Pierce pulled in the drive, waved if he caught sight of me, then ducked inside the house. The first few days, I waited for him to come back out and make his way up to the barn to see how things were going. He didn't. Each night I saw that the light in what I assumed was his living room was doused at ten-fifteen, that the upstairs lights came on, then fifteen minutes later went out.

I found myself inventing stories about him. He was writing erotica, risking his teaching job if he got caught. He was cataloging his collection of antique something or others. Postcards? Coke bottles? I tried out and rejected others because they were too ordinary: He drank. He played solitaire. He watched television. It had to be something odd, something half sophisticated, half Pennsylvania farm boy. What I dreamed

9

up kept me amused, although every once in a while I told myself it was a silly game, but dangerous. I had so little contact with him, soon there would be no way to distinguish between fact and invention. Other times I told myself it hardly mattered; my stay here would be so brief. Still, I could not decide what to make of the fact that he had just hired me, a perfect stranger, to tend his horses and his farm and that he didn't seem to care what I did all day long.

Finally, on Friday afternoon, I went to the door and knocked. It was just before five, and the horses were in, waiting for grain, but I thought that I should catch him in case he was headed out for the evening.

He came to the door looking exhausted. He was still in school clothes—trousers dark navy this time—but his shirttails were out, his shoes off, one sock twisted on his foot. He was carrying a heavy text, with his finger wedged into it as a bookmark. I could only make out that it was about photography.

"Oh," he said dryly. "Payday."

Suddenly I was angry. "That's not why I'm here."

His mouth turned impish, but he said nothing.

"We should talk."

"I'd pay you not to," he said, raising his eyebrows, his voice rising too with irony. "I have to listen to it all day long."

"But what about the farm?" I said.

"You're doing fine," he said. "I'm not worried."

How would he know? Did he snoop around?

Then I checked myself. Can a man snoop on his own farm? I was just the help.

"I doubt I'll stay long," I announced.

Humor lit his eyes, then died away. "As if any of us are."

I had no idea what to say.

"Come in," he said. "I'll get your check."

I stepped into the mudroom, which was similar to nearly all the mudrooms I'd seen before. Bootjack, a neat line of boots: paddock boots, barn boots, wellies, riding boots. And assorted things hanging from hooks and pegs: sweatshirt, visor, brand-new longe line, a whip with a broken tip, a rain slicker, a scarf with pieces of hay sticking to it. Mostly they seemed like small things, and I assumed they had been Allie's.

Pierce left me there, and disappeared into a distant room. Vaguely I studied a framed poster near the door. It was an early morning shot, all mist and pale sun, soft silhouettes of grazing horses, silvery fence lines. It looked familiar. Must be one of the posters so common in the tack catalogs. I frowned, then realized it was a well-angled and well-timed shot of the barn pasture on this very farm.

I heard the thudding of sock feet.

"This is beautiful," I said. "Who took it?"

"Easy tricks." He handed me a check. It was folded in half the long way, face down, as if he were slipping me a bribe. "I hope that's right," he said.

I opened it. It was written on his personal account: "Pierce Kreitzer."

I offered it back to him. "You either have to take out taxes or give me cash."

He nodded at it. "But that's what we agreed."

"I can wait," I said. "If you need a few days."

"Staying that long anyway," he cracked.

I ignored him. "I just need you to pay me on the farm account and take out taxes. When you get a chance."

"Farm account?" he said. "There's nothing in it."

"What about—?"

What about everything? Hay, grain, farrier?

"Credit," he said. "It's a small town."

I narrowed my eyes. My last job ended when the sheriff showed up one morning with a notice of foreclosure. It had been a posh hunter-jumper place, and I'd had a wonderful job as a manager. So wonderful I'd been there three and a half years. But, we learned that morning, the place had been in the red for years, and when the owner had had a major failure in wheat futures, he had taken a vacation to Belize, a country which had no extradition to the United States.

Had Pierce hired me just to make it look as if he were trying to make a go of things?

Before I could find a way to ask, he was closing the door. "All this was Allie's," he said. "Just do your best with it." He looked pale and ill.

That evening, I considered leaving. Pierce was just too odd, the situation too uncertain. I'd as yet to empty the truck; I could just give notice and go. Most of what I owned was still packed in boxes, each precisely labeled: bedclothes, kitchen stuff, books, mementos, winter clothes, spring clothes, summer clothes, formal show clothes. So far, I'd carried in one box of clothes and a few household things.

But I did nothing. The spring was soft and lovely, the chores were light, the horses simple to ride. I'd be careful, I'd pay close attention. I could leave at any time.

After the weekend, I began riding the horses outside the ring. One by one, I rode them along the county roads, and along the fence lines in the pastures. After Pierce pulled out to go to school, it was just me and the horses.

In Ohio, there'd been little peace. I worked with the head trainer, the head instructor, the business manager, and a variable staff of assistants, grooms, and stable hands. There were nearly fifty horses, and except for Mondays, there was always something going on: lessons, clinics, shows, horses coming in for training, people coming to try horses to buy, plus our boarders grooming and riding their own horses. I was on my feet, walking, talking, working, managing, from 6 A.M. to 6 P.M., often later.

Here life seemed full of simple luxuries. I did my own chores: I fed, I mucked, I groomed, and didn't have to worry about whether the work was getting done on time, never mind done well by the grooming and stable staff. There were no tiffs, no squalls, no rich owners to soothe or cajole, no one to dun for their back board bill. I felt as if I were camping out. In Ohio, I'd had all the amenities: two arenas, raked every other day; hot and cold running water; heat lamps in the grooming stalls; skylights; heat and carpets in the offices and tack rooms. Here life was elemental: cold water in one pressure hydrant, an outdoor ring in desperate need of repair, horses that had not seen clippers in God knew how long, and gates that had to be wrestled open, wrestled shut.

But, as long as I ignored Pierce, it made a nice vacation. I rode along the back roads, thinking not of the coming show schedule or getting bids on new jumps, or how to scare up the van space to get a long roster of horses to Florida for the winter shows. I kicked my feet out of the stirrups and swung my legs. I hummed. I admired the farms, and nodded to folks, wondering if it would be worthwhile to canvass the neighborhood and ask permission to ride through woodlots or along the edge of fields. I wished I could find some horse-crazy kid to show me all the secret trails in this part of the county.

More than once, I found myself thinking of Aunt Vee. Once, the memory was so strong I could almost sense her sitting behind me in the saddle. Of course, no one was there. I knew that. No one to lean back against, no one to whisper pointers and advice, no one to plant kisses on my cheek.

14

chapter two

Late one morning, to speed things up, I was riding Lawrence and leading Prima along beside me. The horses had all been going well enough, and I'd decided to spend the afternoon shuffling things around in the barn. If Pierce was going to be so damn aloof, I thought, I'd just go ahead and do what I thought best.

But then, as I was coming back up the drive, I heard the rattle of the Toyota.

I glanced at my watch: eleven forty-five.

I guided the horses off to the side and halted.

Pierce pulled up alongside me, rolled down the window. He looked tired and out of sorts.

"What's that called?" he said.

"Ponying," I said. "Getting them fit for lessons."

"Well, don't do it," he snapped. "Allie never did. She stayed in the ring."

I shifted in my saddle, kept my face still.

After you live on your ninth or tenth farm, the world simplifies: The tractor driver is the tractor driver, the accountant is the accountant, the head groom is the head groom. As long as they are good at driving tractors, figuring accounts, or tending horses, you no longer bother yourself about who they are in some other life, or how they are related to one another.

I gave Pierce a closer look. "What brings you home?"

"They let me out."

"They let you out?" I echoed.

"They do sometimes. I'm not well."

Again there was the shadow of an ironic grin, and I couldn't tell if he were serious or had just hooked out of school.

Prima flipped her nose in impatience. I leaned across and stroked her neck.

"Do you need anything?" I said.

Pierce leaned a little further out the window, studied the horses I had with me. "You're riding the wrong one."

"They all need work," I said neutrally.

I patted Lawrence's shoulder, looked at Prima. She was straining against her lead and nearly crossing her eyes in an effort to reach the grass down at her feet. A greedy mare, and an easy keeper, too. Soon I'd only have to wave a grain bucket under her nose to keep her in condition.

"You start Twister yet?" Pierce wanted to know.

"A little."

"You need to be getting on him. Soon, Natalie."

I nodded again, shrugged.

He put the car in gear and eased away from me. "I must be out of my mind," he said.

Well, I had been starting Twister. "To start" means one thing in one place and something entirely different somewhere else. Worse, whoever Allie was, I had no idea what she'd done so far with the black.

So I took my time. Each morning, I cross-tied Twister in the aisle. I curried his back, I brushed his head, his legs, his crest, I handled his feet. He carried himself like a veteran. So, I thought, he's used to grooming.

But the first time I put a saddle on his back, he arched his spine, pinned his ears back, and stamped one hind hoof. I stroked his neck. He danced a little, then licked his lips and sighed. And what did that mean? That it had been a while since he'd last worn a saddle? Or that this was his first time and that, after one quick snit, he'd decided to be sensible?

In the barn, I was gradually converting a cubbyhole into an office. I'd shoved a small desk underneath the dusty wall phone and found a chair so that I could sit and write lists for the grain store, lists of chores, lists of questions I would ask Pierce if we ever got around to talking to one another. At first, I explained everything I put on paper: *Need Koppertox—for thrushy hooves.*

Need fence repaired—to avoid nail slashes.

Need new halter—Galen's is tearing.

I made lists about the summer. *Who are the students?*

Do we need to advertise?

Ask Pierce!

Some days, since he never asked, I began noting what I did with my time.

Stripped bridles.

Clipped bridle paths.

Inspected girths.

And so I began writing about Twister.

What's this horse done? I wailed in the notebook.

17

Has he been backed?
Ask Pierce!
I never did.

Instead, I unpacked another box from my truck. Since I was getting no direction, I dug out the bit I would have used had the black horse been mine: a nice fat snaffle covered with black rubber. The horse was already four; I saw no reason to hurry.

The morning I approached him with the bridle, he hesitated, then opened his mouth.

In time, I took him into the ring and worked him on the longe line. He seemed to know some of the commands: *Walk on! Ho! Easy!* When I asked him to trot, though, he seemed to think it over for a few strides, and then, given the opportunity, would veer into the center of the circle as if to hide his face in my chest. Once I had the stupid idea that trotting made him want to cry. Perhaps I'd been alone on the farm too long, and I made a mental note to get into town in the evenings, or at least to go down to the house and force a talk with Pierce.

Almost every morning, I worked with Twister and soon he was moving steadily through his paces. He walked, he trotted, he halted, and in his own galumphing way, he cantered. Although I kept the circle large to make it easier for him, at times I felt a little cruel. You could see how much work it was for him, especially when his bad hock was on the inside of the circle.

Still, I thought the horse was better off with me than with someone else. If I could get him to go quietly at the walk and at the trot, then maybe he would at least make a good beginner lesson horse. The one good thing about him was that he was large, and every barn needs at least one big horse for the riders who are tall, or for some other reason cumbersome.

The day came when the horse seemed bored. He had mastered all his lessons at this stage, and the only sensible next step was to get on him.

There are as many ways of mounting a young horse for the first time as there are people crazy enough to do it. I had my own preferences, but I was alone here, so I would have to give up my usual method of having someone hold the horse on a line while I climbed into the saddle. It's harder for a horse to go berserk with a human being hanging on to its head.

But with Twister I had no choice. And in a way, it was as if the horse led me on. I'd been longeing him. I'd stood next to him and thumped on the saddle. I'd pulled on his stirrup leathers, leaned first on one iron or the other. He had the same reaction each time. His head went up, he stamped one hind hoof, then settled himself and stood quietly. And then one day in the ring I put my foot in the stirrup and hopped up and down from the ground. His head went up, his hoof stamped. I hopped up and down some more. I pounded on the saddle. The other horses were grazing in the far pasture. As much as I loved being outdoors in the spring weather and not

19

cooped up in some indoor arena with a pretentious hush in the air and lanolin worked into the tanbark, I suddenly wished I had this horse in a quiet spot. On the other hand, the gate was latched, the electric fence was turned off, and even the breeze had fallen away. I had no choice but to take those three quick bounces and get on.

There is nothing quite like the moment when a human first crawls onto a horse's back. If you're the horse, you suffer the bewilderment of having a creature hoist itself up behind your shoulders where you can no longer see it, where its legs cling to your sides and its bulk fouls up your balance. Yet it is almost as bewildering for the rider. What do you do? You need a secure seat, and yet scrambling for the stirrups and tightening up in the saddle can cause the very explosion you are trying to keep safe from. My own tendency was to just get on, lean forward on snug knees and otherwise stay loose. I also tended to talk a lot in order to let the horse know that I have made a transition from what can be seen—human with hay net, human with water bucket, human in middle of longeing circle— to what can only be felt and heard.

The problem is that you never know how the horse is going to take it. It can stand and breathe like a locomotive then suddenly blow up, its hooves slashing at the sky and your back and neck snapping with every buck. Some horses will stagger sideways. Some will bolt.

One horse I started ran in reverse until he rammed his butt into a fence that was unfortunately lined with electric fencing. Then he shot forward, with his head down between his knees. Sometimes a horse is so overwhelmed, it is quiet and obedient the first few times it is ridden. Then it seems to realize that this riding business isn't going to let up and it raises holy hell.

When I first mounted Twister, he did something no horse I'd started had ever done before.

Nothing.

He stood with his stockinged legs as neatly square as the legs of a table. He swayed a little at my weight coming up over his left side, but once I pinned my knees into the saddle, he did not fling his head or stamp his hoof. He simply stood. His breathing didn't pick up, and as far as I could tell his heart rate didn't go up either.

I stroked his neck, and for some reason I didn't speak. After a while, I found myself sitting with my chin tucked and my head bowed, and suddenly I knew what the horse was doing.

He was thinking.

Jesus Christ, I whispered.

I put the reins in one hand and rubbed my eyes: Tonight, I told myself, I will go to town and have a beer. I will sign up for the rec program at the high school. I will play volleyball at the park. I have been moving from place to place for twenty years, and I know how to do these things when I arrive somewhere new.

Meanwhile, the horse stood, hooves planted, neck arched. He seemed to be waiting, patient as the day is long.

"So," I said aloud. "You're taking this well."

I swear something I could not see wrapped around my knees. It had the airy warmth of the wool sheet I sometimes draped over my legs when I rode in bitter weather.

I sat. I stroked his neck. I chattered like an idiot: I told him that he was smart, that he was clever and terrific. I told him not to worry—I'd work him harder in the days to come.

What wafted back to me was sorrow and disappointment.

For a while longer, I stayed on his back. I closed my eyes, calmed myself. I lay my open palm under his mane on the warmest part of his neck. Then, in time, I broke free, kicked my feet from the stirrups, and vaulted off as nimbly as if I were eleven years old again.

That evening, after making notes in the notebook in the office—"Backed Twister" being my only notation of what had happened—I fled into town with my checkbook and a gym bag and signed up for the rec program. I scanned a bulletin board and got myself into a round robin volleyball scheme and began playing three nights a week. I found it odd to be back in a high school—the pep posters, the stern notices on bulletin boards, the nasty smell of disinfectant over moldy socks in the locker room. But I enjoyed the women in the league, enjoyed being new in town and not knowing who or what they talked about when we showered and changed after our games. Sometimes they asked me about my life. I was vague. I trained horses. I traveled the country. No, I didn't miss having a permanent home.

The days passed. I rode the horses, did the chores, worked with Twister. When I had the time, I played a little tennis, a little basketball, a little volleyball. I found a tack shop out in the countryside where I could buy *The Chronicle of the Horse*. Faithfully, I read the ads and starred job notices that looked promising. But I ended each day on Twister's back, and somehow I did not quite get to the phone to make my calls. Late on Sunday afternoons, I sat in the bakery and passed the time reading newspapers filled with local items that made little sense to me.

Shipville was a town of 12,000. There was one school system, where Pierce worked, some small manufacturing, a tiny Christian college on the far side of town, and of course the farms. Seventeen churches of varying faiths and stripes dotted the street corners and punctuated Sunday mornings with their bells and calls to worship. Women at volleyball invited me to their services and their fellowship suppers. Since I had no children, they assured me, going to church was how I would get to know people.

All my instincts drove me away. I didn't want

to get to know people. I would be gone so soon, it wouldn't be worth the trouble. I said the chores consumed my mornings, and as I began to think about it, I realized I knew few churchgoers in the horse world. You were a thousand times more likely to have a Monday morning off than a Sunday. With Pierce, of course, as long as the horses were fed and cared for, I came and went as I pleased. I could have had the free time easily. Still, I was not interested. The last time I'd set foot inside a church had been to attend my father's funeral. And he'd been dead for twenty years.

One morning, as I was raking the bedding in the last stall, the phone rang. It was a woman wanting to know about riding lessons. We had not advertised, but the woman said she'd heard that Pierce had hired a new teacher.

"That must be you," she said.

"Ah. Um. Well," I said. "Not exactly."

"Oh?"

"But I can talk to you about lessons."

Frantically, I looked at the calendar. The teaching was to start in just over a week.

"I'm sure it costs more than last year," she remarked.

"Remind me what it was," I said. Why had Pierce not discussed this with me?

She named a figure.

"That's right," I said, pretending to remember. And I told her that this year they'd be two dollars more an hour.

And then, after a brief discussion, I signed

her daughter up for 9 A.M. on the very first day of lessons, then hung up in a panic. What in hell was I still doing here?

All that day and all the next, the phone rang. I could hear it when I was leading horses back toward the barn. Sometimes I'd be tacking up a horse, and it would ring, loud and metallic, and I would ignore it. Sometimes I would no sooner hang it up than it would ring again.

Word was out that there was a new teacher. I smiled ruefully. In a town this size, there was no need to advertise. All the girls—and they all seemed to be girls—had either ridden there in summers past or knew someone who had.

When they called, the mothers often referred to Allie. She liked the girls there a half hour early, but they could be picked up when-ever. Was that still all right? I hesitated, then said I guessed so. Did I require helmets, too? Yes. Paddock boots? Yes. Several mothers asked about Pony Club and 4-H. Would I help their children qualify? Had Allie? Heavens no. I knew what she was like. Well, in fact, no I didn't. Well, she had been sweet. Good with the girls. Although perhaps not strict enough. This seemed an important matter to one mother after another. Was I strict? Oh, you bet, I said. You bet I'm strict.

After about ten of these conversations, with some reference to poor Pierce or to poor Allie, it became obvious that everyone thought I knew a whole lot more than I did about Pierce, Allie, and Allie's death. And, since I'd now been on the farm nearly a month, I felt foolish asking.

25

Finally one woman, the mother of a girl named Miriam, mentioned how hard it had been for her daughter when Allie died.

Vaguely I said that I was sorry, but all the while I was wondering if she might answer my questions: How had Allie died? How good had she been at her work? And, if she felt like telling me, what had she been to Pierce? Wife? Live-in girl-friend?

"What I'm concerned about," said Miriam's mother, "is whether it will be too difficult for Miriam to ride again." There was a pause, then: "Allie thought my daughter might have talent."

Oh God. I'd never considered the mothers would ask for favors. I picked up a pencil and made a note: "No special treatment."

"Natalie," said Miriam's mother. "May I ask you a question? It's somewhat personal."

I rolled my eyes. Underscored *no*.

There was silence.

"Sure," I said finally, eager to get off the phone and on with the chores.

"Did you experience death at an early age?"

The question stunned me. My throat tightened and my jaw turned to iron.

"Yes," I said after a while, barely audible. I cleared my throat, said yes again, this time too loud.

"Oh good," Miriam's mother said. "Then you'll know what to do."

I held the phone at arm's length and stared at it. I had never held with the popular belief that pain and suffering made you a better person.

"The thing is," Miriam's mother went on, "it wasn't just Allie. Miriam lost her best friend, also to cancer, two weeks later. Both in early January. What an awful Christmas. Miriam moped the entire time."

Lucky brat, I thought. Fair warning. Vee had not bothered with such niceties.

All that week, I spent the days riding horses, doing chores, answering the phone, and signing kids up for riding lessons. Each day, the determination to leave boiled up in me. I packed some boxes, carried them out to the truck. As each day ended and I was waiting for Pierce to come home from school so I could give my notice, I would ride the Twister horse. The big black gelding glowed with concentration, and I felt lifted up, not just on his back but on the force field of his thoughts. Soon my breathing kept time with his, my heart rate fell to the cadence of his hoofbeats. And each time, as we were finishing, I found myself stroking his neck, planning his next session, giving myself one more day.

Which was how, the next Saturday morning, I found myself standing in the middle of the riding ring. I wasn't even through the first lesson of the day, and I was already vowing to quit.

Maybe before the hour was out.

I'd never taught before. Although I'd thought

I had. But pinch-hitting is not teaching. Giving pointers is not teaching. Moving ground rails, changing the shape of an oxer, offering an opinion when you happened to have one: these things are not teaching.

All around me there was chaos. Girls for the next class leaned on the ring and called to the girls who were riding. The girls on the horses shambled all around the ring, some of them unable to turn or stop, others fuming because I would not let them do much for fear they'd kill the beginners. What had possessed me to stay?

And that morning I'd gotten off to such a good start. All five horses had been ready by eight-thirty: groomed, saddled, bridled, halters over bridles. On my clipboard was a list of which girls I expected at which times. The barn was clean, quiet, orderly. And then the girls started showing up. They thrust money at me, they ran down the aisle of the barn, they climbed up into the loft. The younger ones needed help with the chin straps on their helmets, or they walked down the aisle with the buckles flapping on their paddock boots. Because I had not assigned mounts ahead of time, the girls squabbled over who would ride which horse. One girl threw a tantrum because I put her on Archimedes when she wanted to ride Lawrence. Her face turned red, she gulped for air, and she stood muttering under her breath. Another girl, who had been holding Prima's bridle, suddenly dropped the reins, then bolted for the safety of the tack-room doorway. Through her sobs, she told me she was afraid of big horses.

Finally I got all five girls and all five horses out to the ring. I stood them in a line and interviewed each girl. Which horses had she ridden? Could she mount? Walk? Trot? Canter? I made notes, traded horses around, and by the end of the hour, although the lesson had been far from orderly, I had seen a little of what each girl could do. I wrapped up with the horses in the center of the ring, standing around me in a half circle, and I led the girls through a few of the drills that had turned me into a rider.

And so the whole day went, hour after hour. I thought to send someone to the barn for a bucket of water for the horses. I began having the girls mount and dismount in the shade of the maples that grew along the south side of the ring. I made a policy about carrots and other treats: they were collected in a bucket and I would add them to the horses' evening feed. I had no interest in working with horses who'd learned to bite because of hand-feeding. I took the crumpled fives and tens thrust at me, even checks written, I noticed, to DreamWeb Farm. I was surprised by that— it was the first time I'd heard the name of the farm. But then I forgot to note who had given me money and who hadn't.

By the end of the day, my feet hurt, my throat was raw, and the sound of my own voice enough to make me want to scream. I rubbed the horses lightly, promised them a better grooming in the morning, fed them, and turned them out. Then I headed up to my cubby over the garage.

The ceiling, open to the peak, sloped almost all the way down to the floors; at some point it had been finished with planks of knotty pine. It was like living in a wooden tent, some days cozy, some days claustrophobic. There were windows at both ends, one over the miniature kitchen sink and counter; I'd wrestled the little bed underneath the other so I could fall asleep looking out over the pasture. There were a few cupboards, a small bathroom, and a giant bureau. It was an old curio, a flea market special, and I rather liked it: an enormous mirror with the snaky vines carved into the wood, drawers that squealed when dragged open, legs with carved feet. It was chipped and gouged, of course, or it wouldn't be up here, but it had a kind of presence and somehow, here in eastern Pennsylvania, in such an old worn lush state, it seemed exactly right.

I pulled open a drawer, dug out clean clothes, looked at my filthy face in the mirror, then decided I would shower first. After that I opened a can of soup, ate a few bites, opened a beer, and headed back outdoors.

I'd not so much as laid a hand on Twister all that long day. Once in a while, during the lessons, he'd let out a long sorrowful whinny from his stall in the empty barn. Now I at least meant to have a look at him.

I made it all the way out to the pasture. I

leaned on the rail. Yes, the black horse was there. Through my general haze, that made me feel better, that strong odd horse cropping grass in the fading light. I watched him a while longer, wished he would come near the fence, but then, too tired to wait for him, I poured my beer out on the ground and went to bed.

Sunday was a little better. There were fewer girls for lessons, and before I let them near the horses, I asked them all my questions, took notes, and even remembered to write down who paid and who did not. I was done by one, and thanked God the good folk of this small town still went to church.

That afternoon, I worked on Twister. By way of saying goodbye, I gave him a full grooming. I not only brushed and curried, but I got out the clippers, too. I let him listen to their quiet hum, then pressed them, vibrating, against his neck and rump. He lifted his head, eyed me, snorted, danced a little. Then, one by one, he let me clip his fetlocks. I cleaned the clippers, let him rest, then clipped his bridle path and the edges of his ears. And then, because it was warm and because I had time, I found a bucket and shampoo. I scrubbed his legs so that his stockings turned pink-white, then shampooed his tail, too: sudsing, scrubbing, rinsing, the heavy strands of it gritty on my palms and fingers, the whole thing gleaming blue-black when I finished.

For feeds that night, I made hot bran mashes. The steam rose in my face and the bran caked around my fingernails. I chopped in the apples and the carrots and a few sugar cubes brought by the girls, then sat in the doorway of the barn, listening to the horses bang their feed tubs against the heavy plank walls, working their tongues into the creases of their buckets, chasing down the crumbs of their well-earned reward. I closed my eyes, leaned against the doorjamb, and thought I could be in nearly any barn I'd ever worked, except for the lovely fact that I was not one of a team of stable workers, nor the manager, the assistant trainer, the head groom. I was alone with six clean horses enjoying their food, then heading out to pasture for a soft early summer's night.

I sat a few moments longer, then when the horses were through eating, I turned them out. The schoolies trotted out, shook their heads, pawed, circled, then got down and rolled. I counted their flips that by tradition told their worth: fifty bucks for each half roll, one hundred for each complete side-to-side to maneuver. There was such satisfaction in the way they did it, and also in the way they rose and shook, as if, there, that's it for humans. The black got down and rolled too, coating himself and his freshly washed tail in dust.

I shook my head and smiled. Horses, I thought, and as always felt not just grateful but somehow honored to spend my days in their presence.

Then I went down to tell Pierce I was leaving in the morning.

It was early, not quite seven, but the living-room light was already lit. I rapped on the mud-room door.

In time, Pierce let me in. He looked drowsy and remote. By habit, I took a discreet sniff. Not marijuana anyway—the bad habit of too many grooms and stable hands. Pierce saw the envelope of lesson money, and the hand-made ledger I'd concocted, and instead of taking it from me, said, "Come on in."

Two doors led off the mudroom. One I guessed went to the kitchen. Pierce opened the other door. Music poured out at us.

I gasped.

Pierce lifted his chin, getting a better view of me through his thickish lenses.

"Not your taste, eh? Tchaikovsky."

As if I didn't know. My father had owned a music store. He bought, sold, and repaired instruments, and, when he got the chance, played his bass. My mother had died when I was an infant, and I had grown up in the midst of musicians. My father's jazz and session friends wandered in and out, played ditties for me on one instrument and another, and, as a joke, taught me and my older sister Lucy to call our father Potts—his nickname out in the clubs. Lucy acquired the family talent, quitting high school with our father's blessing to study piano in Philadelphia, but I had not. Except for the ever-present background to our days, music left me so entirely indifferent that I'd been elated in junior high school to discover the Romantics. Of course, Lucy taunted me: Tchaikovsky, she said, was like the measles. You got it once, it made you sick, and then you were immune for life. Even Potts had laughed.

Pierce stepped over to the stereo and turned it off. "So how'd it go?" he said, taking the money and the ledger from me and plopping them on a shelf.

"That's the *Pathétique*," I said, stunned.

Pierce stilled.

"In B minor," I recited in a haze. "The Sixth Symphony. So called." Even I knew that composers wrote their symphonies not by number but by key.

"Sit," Pierce said. "I'll get you something."

I backed toward the door. "I don't want anything."

But he turned away and disappeared into the kitchen. I perched on the arm of a worn stuffed chair and watched the silenced stereo as if I could still hear the adagio. The Symphony of Suffering.

When he came back, he brought me a plastic bottle of diet cola and a glass of ice. I loathe diet cola, but I poured it into the glass and sipped.

He sat across from me, on the edge of a dark plaid couch, hunched forward with his hands clasped between his knees.

"So," he said hopefully. "You know music."

I shook my head. "Only that," I said.

Immediately I thought: That's a lie.

34

He gave me that odd ephemeral grin. "Good," he said. "I don't want to talk about it, either."

I drank, nodded.

"Everything go okay this weekend?"

"Oh," I said, still taken aback. "Fine. Busy."

I didn't say *I quit.*

I didn't say *I can't do this.*

I didn't say *My truck is packed.*

"Allie loved it." He cocked his chin. "Looking at you reminds me how tired she'd be. Come down here all wound up but exhausted. And that was before she got sick."

I nodded. "The horses need tomorrow off."

"When school gets out," he said, "I'll get started. Paint the ring. Fix some fences. Fred Weirbachen comes and carts away the manure pile. And we can talk about which order to harrow the fields. That stuff."

"I won't be here," I said. "I'm leaving."

Pierce smiled. "What do you need? More money? More time off?"

"I can't take the teaching," I said, half truth, half lie. I couldn't take not under-standing, either: Why did he stay on a place he cared nothing about? Why didn't he tell me things? The usual problem on horse farms was that people cared enormously about things that hardly mattered and that owners bossed the help around as if the help didn't have an ounce of brains or two minutes' experience around horses.

"Ask a few of the older kids to come early and help," Pierce said. "They can groom.

35

Help with the mounting and the dismounting. That's what Allie always did. It'll make your life easier."

"I can't," I said.

He waved me off. "Try," he said. "Teaching's good for you." That odd smile again. "At least that's what everyone tells me."

Then he stood and went to the stereo. "We're coming up to my favorite part," he said, hitting a button. The Tchaikovsky roared back to life.

In the morning, I brought the schoolies in, fed them, and turned them right back out into their pasture. Twister I kept in.

I cross-tied him near the front of the barn so I could keep an eye on the driveway. I was expecting no one, but I was desperate for privacy and I did not wish to be surprised.

The big black horse stood quietly and sensibly. He accepted, even leaned a little into, the heavy circles of the currycomb, the endless brushing and the polishing. I picked out his tail so that it hung full and thick and free of twists, brushed the roots of his mane. With a little work, his four white stockings gleamed pure white.

I was still deciding. I could load the rest of what I owned into the truck, leave a note, and go. Or I could start thinking about next weekend: what to do with all those girls and all those long hours. Or I could really torture myself and take a drive to Bethlehem.

Then it came to me that I had not picked

Miriam, the girl with the dead school friend, out of the crowd. I tried to remember which one she might have been, then finally decided that if I couldn't tell, then she had probably been all right. Each of us bears tragedy in our own way. Why would she foist hers off on me?

I polished Twister's shoulders and his flanks, and in time I began to listen for the black horse's thoughts. But he seemed only to be, to breathe, to exist: a huge warm gleaming presence. And soon that's all I was doing too: being, breathing.

Half hypnotized, I put a saddle and a bridle on him and walked him out to the ring. Without much thought, I snugged up his girth, pulled down the stirrups, and got on.

He swayed a little, the way young horses do, then at my signal walked around the ring. I could feel him concentrating fiercely, carrying both himself and me with deliberate grace. We made loopy serpentines. We turned. We circled. We stopped, walked on again. My legs and seat felt heavy but sure: I hardly moved them and he picked up my signals. After a while, we stopped for good, and I sat there on his back in the weak June sun and stroked his neck. I would gladly have closed my eyes and slept.

The black horse sighed, and shifted his hocks.

chapter three

And so I stayed a while longer.

I scoured my notes, called all the mothers and rearranged the lessons. I made a chart for each group, as if that would impose order on the chaos of the weekend, hoping that I could see to it that sooner or later each girl had a chance to ride each horse. Even with a chart, I couldn't seem to get to know them, although gradually I learned to tell them apart—easier to do, however, when they were in the saddle than on foot. Sally had scoliosis, Margo had lovely hands, Phyllis turned her toes out, Brittany turned hers in. Miriam was one of the tall skinny ones. Whiny and somewhat self-centered. But beautiful legs and an almost natural seat. Saturdays at ten.

The second Saturday, by sheer dumb luck, I chose two of the same helpers that Allie had: Helen and Scooter. And soon the rumor went around that Allie had left instructions for the next teacher. The idea made me marvel: that the girls felt she regarded them so highly she would leave directions concerning them after her death. I could barely tolerate their presence two days a week—and I was alive and well. If I knew I was dying, I couldn't imagine I would give them a second thought.

Monday morning, just before noon, I had a call from Miriam's mother. I jammed the phone between my chin and collarbone, stretched the twisting phone cord out through the office doorway into the aisle, and continued stripping tack off Prima, whom I'd just been riding.

Miriam's mother began in a way that should have put me on guard, asking how I was settling in, and how the lessons were going, and did I think I was going to enjoy my summer teaching?

Jesus Christ, I thought, I don't get paid enough for this.

How did I think Miriam was doing?

Oh, fine, I said airily, having quickly decided that few of the girls had the talent or drive to amount to much. I assumed serious kids had horses of their own, which they kept at training barns focused on competition. Or they rode catch as I had done.

Was Miriam settling in? Working hard?

Oh, sure, I said.

Then she moved in. Why, then, had I not asked Miriam to be a helper? She was old enough. And, she reminded me, Allie had thought she had talent. Allie had invited her to be a helper.

Something new came into her voice. Concern? Worry? I had no idea if it was genuine.

Was something the matter? she asked. Was it wrong for Miriam to ride?

I shook my head, remembered all the calls the instructor and trainer in Ohio had fielded from mothers, and how smug I had been because I dealt with more normal people: grain dealers, hay growers, farriers, carpenters.

I didn't know, I said.

So was there or wasn't there a problem if Miriam were a helper?

Fine, I said, bewildered and annoyed. What was one more pair of hands around the barn? I was sure Miriam could brush a horse and sweep the aisle with the best of them.

When school got out, we switched the lessons to weekday mornings, eight to noon. Some girls rode more than once a week, and some seemed to spend their whole morning at the barn. Once Helen summoned me from the ring to break up a fistfight between two eight-year-olds in the tack room; I shook them like kittens by the collars of their tee-shirts. Sometimes in the evenings, I would go up into the loft and discover elaborate forts built of hay bales. Over and over I explained that the horses ate that hay, that I did not wish to have the girls' dirty feet all over it, or have the delicate leaves and stems knocked out of the bales. Sometimes when the older girls were finished riding, they sat on the cool clean-swept concrete of the barn floor, stretched their legs before them, and talked about life—as if they knew a thing about it. When I could, I put them all to work: picking up stalls, washing brushes, sweeping cobwebs, scrubbing buckets, wiping down equipment.

Miriam, Helen, and Scooter were faithful in their tasks, getting kids on horses, leading exercises, running along beside beginners as they trotted. Helen was blond with a round face and saintly smile. Scooter was thin and dark with a waiflike haircut and a quick wit. Miriam was tall and leggy, and she drove me crazy. Her feelings were easily hurt, if I asked, say, Helen to help with something she wished to do. She was good with the kids, though, cheering them on, demanding one more round of exercises, making sure they held their reins just so. But then, at the slightest cause, she might burst into tears and storm back to the barn. Scooter's lips would twitch and Helen would roll her eyes. In twenty minutes Miriam might reappear, composed, ready to work again. Frankly, as often as I could, I sent her on errands and kept Helen or Scooter with me. And often I made her run next to the beginners, thinking that if I could just plain wear her out, she would be too damn tired to throw a tantrum.

We settled into a routine, and in time, I began entertaining the girls with stories. A pause under the trees between lessons, a walk out to the field, a breather during class, and I was offering up my set pieces: the time I'd knocked a horse show judge clean off her feet; the size of the jumps in Virginia hunt country; an orphan foal I'd raised by hand; the manure spreader I'd repaired by dousing the feeder chain with Coke. But I noticed there were stories I did not tell, stories I'd told elsewhere, but not here. All the participants were dead: Jack Detweiler, Vee, Bill Painter. But here their souls hung too close to the ground.

When I thought about it, I sometimes worried that I was giving short shrift to my students.

My students. What an odd idea.

My barn: I was accustomed to that. Even *my staff, my horses, my owner.*

The girls came whenever it was not outright pouring rain. They rode and they puttered in the barn. Heaven alone knew what exactly they did to the leather when they cleaned it or if they understood why the horses were brushed or if they knew those bales in the loft were composed of timothy and alfalfa, or that Pierce, despite my questions, had as yet to arrange buying a winter's supply of first cutting.

There was no ferocity, no urgent transaction between them and me. Was that right?

My formal education had taken place in a tiny round paddock on a horse that wore a saddle and a bridle but no stirrups and no reins. Vee was on crutches then, and somehow she balanced on them in the middle of the ring, deftly handling the longe rein, the whip, the horse, and me. And, while she was kind sometimes, and encouraging, she was fiercely determined and nothing if not thorough.

She made me walk. She made me trot. She made me ride with my arms out to my sides, up over my head, folded behind my back. On her command, I swung my lower legs, I rode standing up on the strength of my gripped knees. I called out each time a certain hoof hit the ground, I counted, I rode with my eyes closed. I graduated to riding with a cup of water in each hand. I took my jacket off at the walk and trot, I folded it, draped it over my arm, put it back on, and zipped it up.

Other girls came to this same farm for lessons in classes with instructors. Sometimes I could see them over in the big ring and often I wondered if I would ever get to ride the way they did: holding my reins, my feet in the shiny stirrups, trotting over ground rails, playing relay games.

Jack Detweiler, who owned the farm, sometimes leaned on the paddock rails and watched my lessons. He wore puttees like the Great War soldiers in my history book, sucked on Mary Janes, and analyzed my progress as if I weren't there. He debated with Vee over whether my small size was a minus or a plus. He twisted his tweed cap back and forth across his forehead, and wished my legs were longer. He prescribed new exercises for me as if he were a doctor. I learned not to mind, learned to like the way they talked about the level of my chin as if nothing mattered more.

Sometimes I have been told that I am gifted: in the saddle or on foot around horses. But I have never thought so. What I have are skills, and in the beginning they were thrust on me, bestowed. Three sessions every week I did everything Vee and Mr. Detweiler told me, absorbed what they would have me absorb. Things were forced on me, withheld from me. Was I grateful? Mystified, more like. I loved the horses, and my afternoons with Vee all to myself, but left to my own devices I would have wished for less work, less drill, far less fanaticism, and

43

when I thought about it now, I knew I was much too cautious to inflict such teaching on anyone.

Another puzzle of those first few weeks of the summer was that Pierce, who had promised all sorts of things when school got out, seemed to disappear into the small white house with its fading green shutters. Once in a while, when the grass grew ankle deep, he roused himself and mowed the little swath of lawn and the edges of the lane. Other than that, as far as I could tell, he was doing nothing: He had promised to find some barrels and cut some new rails for jumps. Grudgingly he had even said he would get permission for me to ride with the most advanced girls across the lands of neighboring farms.

Every other evening, I walked down to see him. I knocked and, as he had instructed, let myself in. Actually, I stamped my boots in the mudroom, although only dust kicked up from the soles and creases. Sometimes he would call to me to come in.

He was often in the living room, sometimes in the basement, where he said he had a darkroom. No matter how beautiful the evening, he remained indoors. I had given up inventing a secret life for him. Frankly, I found him so dull and disappointing as to be irksome. He read technical books or stared at contact sheets through a magnifying glass. He played bridge with the computer. He watched the Phillies, faithful to the long slow ritual of the game played out on his grainy

44

screen. He said he developed pictures, although of what I couldn't imagine: He never went anywhere to take them. And of course, all the while, he listened to music.

Which was why I stamped my feet in the mudroom. It was too private somehow, to come in on a man listening to Brahms or Shostakovich, and I did not wish to talk music with him. Music meant my father, music meant, in a way, Lucy. Music was over. I did not even turn on a radio in the barn except to listen to the news and interview programs that came out of Philadelphia.

Once he doused the stereo or gave up his game, I came in and sat on the edge of the chair. He always looked the same: jeans, bare feet or torn canvas sneakers, denim shirt, hair shiny but uncombed. He seemed quiet, composed, dull. Teacups accumulated on the windowsill by his elbow, as if they kept count of something. The day's intake, the hours endured.

At first, I excused him. After all, school had just gotten out. Perhaps he was tired. Perhaps he needed a vacation. But June turned into July and still he sat there. Whenever I arrived with the ledger and the little wad of bills and checks, he hoisted himself off the couch and automatically brought me a diet soda. One day I realized it was not only way too late to tell him I loathed the stuff, but that at some point, he must have started buying it for me.

Each time I saw him, I talked about matters on the farm. I offered to go over the ledger, tried to interest him in the grain bills and the endless question of where he planned to buy hay for the winter. If he wanted local first cutting, he should already have bespoken it.

Each time he listened to me like a man in a bus station waiting to hear his bus called. It was as if all of this were temporary: the horses, the farm, the summer. What humor there had been, had vanished from his eyes. I didn't know if I should slap him or feel sorry for him.

One day, I found myself asking him if he minded if the girls brought their lunches. He perked up a little.

I admit it seemed a funny thing for me to do, but in the early afternoons, I thought we could bathe the horses, or clip fetlocks, or brush and trim manes and tails. If I gave them some of my time, they could learn some new skills.

"Do it," he said. "Allie always did."

I told him it would only be a day or two a week.

Of course, he said. Perhaps he would come up and visit us. Maybe he would take some pictures.

I shrugged. Anything to get him out of the house.

And then he asked the question I always dreaded: "How's Twister?"

I knew I should be telling Pierce exactly what time of the day I would be working the horse so he could come up and watch. Not only would it get him out of his house, but it was his horse. I knew, although I had never seen him ride, that out of courtesy I should offer him the chance to sit on the horse's back. I knew I should be keeping detailed notes on the horse's progress, recording the little breakthroughs that mark the training of any horse, especially one that has just begun work under saddle.

But I did not.

I could have ridden him in the afternoons when the girls were still here eating their lunches under the maples. They could have watched how I worked with the horse, and I could have shared with them the secrets of slow, patient training. Afterward, they could have bathed him, fussed over his mane, brushed his long white stockings.

But I did not.

I waited until every last one of them was gone, waited until Pierce was sprawled out on his couch watching the ball game or moping along to some heartbreaker symphony. And then I rode the Twister horse all by myself in the haze of soft, hot summer evenings.

I have never been this way about a horse. Never.

As a child, of course, I assumed I loved Vee's huge gray hunter Hadley, but that's because he was Vee's and he was the only horse I ever rode. After her death, I was so mad I never wanted to see another horse again, and it did not occur to Potts that he should make me keep on riding. I remember hearing that Potts sold Hadley to Jack Detweiler and that

Jack Detweiler was using him for lessons, and that made me mad, too, in a different way, until I learned not to be mad at all, not about that, not about anything.

When I was sixteen, Lucy, promoting herself to head of the family, told me that Potts might not get well, and told me, too, that I had to find a job. She claimed not to care what kind of job, so long as it kept me off the streets of Bethlehem. I knew she was lying, so, to spite her, I went out to Painter's Hack and Sale Barn, and I got a job as a stable hand.

Bill Painter was straight out of a bad Western. He rented hot horses, he rented poky horses, he rented horses that were not quite sound, even horses we'd already agreed to sell to someone else. How he loved to deal and trade. I sat on nearly everything that passed through, sometimes showing horses to buyers or riding in sandlot competitions to get horses out in public. I grew attached to nothing, but I sure learned how to size up horses—legs, brains, eyes, hooves, heart girth, age. I learned how teeth were doctored, I learned that a waterlogged horse was just as good as tranquilized, that a dull horse livened up if you put ginger paste underneath its tail. And I took satisfaction in the seediness of it all, knowing it was not what Lucy'd had in mind. Potts stuck up for me, all the way to the end.

It took a year for Potts to die, and during that time, I'd moved on to a more respectable farm, and the night he passed away I was crouched on my heels in the corner of a broodmare stall, watching a vet trying to foal out a breech presentation. The mare died sometime before daybreak, torn and septic beyond saving. Lucy was not able to reach me by phone, so it was not until noontime, stunned and exhausted from the long night and the death of the mare and foal, that I learned my father was gone, too.

In the last month of Potts's life, he sent me to see Mac Vorhees, our attorney. If I wished, Mac said, there would be money for college. I sat there in my jeans and paddock boots and told him I wasn't interested. He fingered a silvering sideburn, crossed his legs in his elegant wool trousers, looked up at the signed photograph of FDR that hung above his desk. I stared through the casement windows at the weeping mulberry in the formal garden where Potts had brought me visiting as a little girl. Mac and Potts had been friends for years, and although it must have half killed Mac to say this, he suggested I could certainly afford to buy a horse. He looked at me sadly: after all, his client had no mother, an older sister she could barely stand, and a dying father. But I bought only a truck and promised that, no matter what, I would always keep him informed of my whereabouts. And I had been smart. All those years I had never bought a horse, because at the end of a long day of barn work and schooling, I had no wish to ride another, even one I could call my own.

But now, every evening, after I had fed all the other horses and, two at a time, had walked them out to the pasture so they could

49

graze and loaf, I stood Twister in the aisle. I curried his fine black coat. I brushed and polished him, and the barn slowly filled with his presence. Yes, he was built downhill. Yes, my back hurt while I rode him, because his hocks were so uneven. But he was a big, calm, sensible horse, and he gave off something I had never before felt. As I worked around him, I felt his focus, his deep, clear-eyed attention. When I whistled the horses in for their morning grain, it was his gaze I sensed. Whenever chores took me up and down the aisle, dragging the hose or wheeling a wheelbarrow, he seemed to watch me with grave interest. Never had a horse been so aware of me. Never had I been so aware of a horse.

At the beginning, though, he gave me a good scare every time I rode him. Put plainly, I could hear him think. It was as if some channel had opened by mistake between us.

It is often said that the work of a young horse is to go out and see the world, and by early July I began to ride him outside the confines of the ring. And although Pierce and I had clashed on nothing yet, I rehearsed the speech I would give him if he objected to my hacking the black horse everywhere I could find to go.

One evening, we were riding in a back hill pasture. It was standing empty, waiting for Pierce to replace two rotted fence posts. We climbed a long sloping hill, then paused near the top. The evening light was soft, the shadows slowly darkening, and the black horse stood relaxed but attentive. Idly I ran my fingers through his mane and looked out at a broad valley. I could see church steeples, a school, farm ponds, patterns of roads and lanes, barns, silos, small groupings of houses. Whole lives are lived down there, I thought with some amazement. There was a picture-book quality in the air that night, the illusion that time hesitated here.

I stood a while longer, stroking Twister's neck, then we moved off along a thicket of trees. Grasses swished around his fetlocks, and his hooves rang hollow on the earth. He carried his neck and ears just so, and I could tell he was enjoying himself, that the world seemed somehow different out here, with me on his back, but otherwise alone in the dusk.

A wave of sadness wafted back at me, and I had the weird sense that this had been his natal field, that he had run these fence lines that first summer, trying out his new legs, then dozing, flat as a bath mat, at his mother's feet. For the first time, it came to me to wonder if one of the mares in the barn might be his dam. I'd never thought to ask.

Gone, the horse seemed to say. His hooves echoed on the hard Pennsylvania clay. Gone, gone, gone.

All at once, something exploded from the thicket. I startled in the saddle and snatched at the reins. Twister wheeled, and I thought: Now we'll have the fireworks, out here where there is no confinement.

And then the horse stood absolutely still.

51

His neck and haunches were rigid. He quivered and stared into the shadows. A form leaped between some trees and was gone.

Ah, a deer.

I began to laugh then, and touched him with my legs, and he moved off at a walk with a little bounce in his stride, not because he was going to blow up, but because he was out here with me and had just seen a deer and it had been beautiful and exciting. In a fit of sheer recklessness, I shifted my weight and let him canter along the fence line. He was hot and blowing when he got back into the barn, and I walked him up and down the lane until the first stars were out and he was cool as he cropped grass at the end of the lead rope.

After that, I worked him in the ring every third or fourth day. All the other days, I took him out. We hacked along what dirt roads we could find. I gave up waiting for Pierce, and got permission from Mr. Weirbachen and some other neighbors to ride the fringes of their fields. We climbed up along the power line, building up his wind and strength; we wove back and forth through apple orchards, bending this way and that through branches hung heavy with swelling apple sets.

Surprisingly, the horse did not distract me from my teaching. If anything, I laughed more. I had more patience with the girls, disliked them a little less. Our conversations had more freedom, more silliness. One morning while we were getting ready for the lessons, I asked about the name of the farm: DreamWeb. Whose idea had that been? Certainly not Pierce, I said, making a joke.

Helen and Scooter laughed.

Each of us was in a separate stall, brushing a horse, and our voices were carrying back and forth through the partitions.

"What's he like at school?" I said. I wanted to ask if he was a self-centered jerk, but thought better of it. More than one barn was wired with microphones, so that everything that was said could be heard in some other location. I knew that wasn't true here, but I didn't want to lose the habit of saying nothing in a barn I wouldn't say to an owner's face.

"Oh, he's okay," Helen said.

"He seems so miserable."

Scooter snickered. "There's a joke at school about him."

"Don't you dare!" Miriam said. "Don't you even say it."

I slipped out of Archimedes' stall, glanced up and down the aisle to see that we were alone. This would not be the best time for Pierce to make his first visit to us.

"Miriam's right," I said. "You'd better not."

I heard her sniffling. "You'd be sad, too, if your sister died," she said.

Then I heard Prima's stall door slam open and slam shut and, from her footsteps, knew that Miriam was flouncing down the aisle. I counted, heard the tack-room door slam shut, and guessed she was in there sniveling where I would have to deal with her before we could get the saddles and bridles for the horses.

Helen and Scooter were silent, then in a low voice Helen asked Sheila to move over and Scooter gave Galen's neck a noisy pat.

I wondered what they were thinking.

Then it struck me.

"Okay," I said. "I confess. I didn't know. Allie was Pierce's sister?"

"Yes," Helen said, coming out of her stall, halting near me and staring at the tack-room door.

"I'll go," I said. "But I didn't know that."

"Some people say it's unnatural," Scooter said.

"What?" I said, not knowing if I should even ask.

"The way he's, you know."

I could see her looking for the right word.

"Mourning," Helen said.

Scooter made a face at her. "She might as well know. It was all around town. Supposedly he killed her. And now he's feeling guilty."

I stared.

"I thought she had cancer."

"She did," Helen said. "At the end, he maybe did it. They got a warrant and searched the house."

"Oh," I said. "He helped her to die. Good for him."

Often I wished we had been able to cut the last few weeks off Potts's life. I hated the way Vee died, but I hated the way Potts went, too.

Helen and Scooter looked surprised.

"My father died of cancer," I said. "No one should suffer like that."

I patted Helen's shoulder. "Heavy stuff for so early in the morning."

She shrugged. "Innocent until proven guilty. My father's a lawyer."

Scooter stood staring at the tack-room door, hands on hips. "Medusa's guarding the saddles."

"I'll go," I told her, sighing.

Just as I reached the door, it swung open. Miriam stood in the doorway, sniffing and wiping her eyes. "You don't even care."

"Miriam," I said. "I do care."

"Allie's dead," she said. "And so is Jules." And then she swung herself up the ladder into the loft. I heard the rustling of grasses, then more sobbing.

I motioned to Helen and Scooter, who rushed into the tack room for equipment. The first girls would be here any minute.

Then I stood at the foot of the ladder. "Miriam," I said quietly. "Do you want me to come up?"

"No!"

Smart choice, I thought. I felt like shaking her. As if she were the only person who'd ever lost a loved one.

"All right," I said. "We're going to tack up and go on out to the ring. Let me know if you need me."

Scooter came out with a saddle over one arm and a bridle over the other shoulder. She stuck a finger in her mouth, miming making herself vomit.

I shook my head, smiled.

With Miriam over our heads, sulking, we got the horses ready in record time.

All that day I found myself thinking: his sister. Allie was his sister. Somehow that changed everything, but I couldn't quite figure how.

If it were true that he had helped her die, then good for him. But I had trouble imagining it: Did he have that kind of gumption? Had it been horrifying?

Mostly, I confess, I simply found Pierce all the more annoying. Why I felt this way because he had lost not his wife but his sister, I had no idea. Perhaps because I had been so wrong in my guesses and I felt tricked or stupid. Perhaps because I had never married and so was willing to allow any amount of grief over a lost spouse. Perhaps because Lucy had died a few years ago and because her death had been less tragic than it had been confounding and somehow inevitable.

At any rate, I thought it was high time Pierce got around to doing some of the work he'd promised on the farm. Shovel manure until his shoulders ached. Hammer nails. Cut brush. Sweat a little. That fixed most things.

Each time I had to go down to the house, bringing the lesson money, I debated taking a deep breath and either telling him to get off his butt or at least asking him some good hard questions. I would grill him about the upcoming fall, about the hay for winter, even about Allie. After all, it was just a month until the girls and he would be heading back to school. Perhaps I thought that since I was one of the few people he was likely to see in the interim, it was up to me to roust him out of his own living room.

But then I would swing open the mud-room door, stamp the dust from my boots, step into the living room, and hear the music or see the set of his face over a contact sheet or watch him playing cards with a pentium processor for an opponent. And I was mute.

Well, next time, I would tell myself, handing over the money, drinking my ridiculous diet Coke, and fleeing for the barn. Guiltily, I knew I had something he did not: Every evening I rode the bright black horse. Every evening his thoughts beamed back at me. Every evening I received the beneficence of his full attention.

One night it came to me while I was riding that I should ask the black horse directly about Pierce and Allie, and I had no sooner had the thought than a terrible wave of sorrow came back at me. Twister's hooves dragged. Then all at once, I was blanked out of his thoughts. Sitting there in the silence, high on the back of a horse whose thoughts had turned from me, I knew loss.

For the next few days, I kept him in the ring. It was still hot, but it was the time of the year when one whole aisle of the grocery store was lined with pens and notebooks for back-to-school. I bought a new one for the barn, vowed to write more than a few cryptic notes in it, and decided to get on with Twister's formal schooling.

The last weekend before their vacation ended, the girls came out to the farm for a picnic. They did it every summer, and began to plan it without me. Whose mother would make what? Who would bring the rolls, the salads, the hamburger patties? Even Pierce seemed to buck up, wheeling a grill out of the shed and dusting it off, laying in a supply of charcoal and lighter fluid. The horses were invited also, and the girls spent hours that morning braiding flowers into their manes and tails and tying ribbons to their halters. Twister was braided with red rosettes. They did it every summer, and for one quick moment I marveled at the way some things Allie had set in motion continued after her death. Then the horses were led down to the lawn. The girls let them drink from soda cans and fed them brownies and potato chips, and I made some jokes about being up half the night, nursing horses with bellyaches, but everyone just laughed.

Pierce was everywhere, cameras around his neck, snapping pictures.

"I'm glad to see you do that," I told him quietly.

He gestured at the girls, shrugged. "Willing subjects. They like it."

I looked at the happy chaos on the lawn.

"They do, don't they?"

At the very end, as they did each year, they crowded together so he could take their picture, but it turned out he had no more film.

chapter four

On the first morning of the school year, Pierce headed out at exactly five minutes after seven. I watched him from the barn door, trying to gauge whether getting back to work would do him good. Would it remind him that winter was coming, that the farm was not ready? But all I could see were his dark teaching clothes, his briefcase, and his longish hair freshly cut. He walked briskly to his car, and I took that as a good sign, until it came to me that perhaps he was only running late.

The morning horse chores seemed to take forever. The barn was slow and quiet, and I was surprised to find I missed the girls. I rode the school horses one by one, adhering to Pierce's rule about ponying even in his absence, and now I worked Twister during the afternoon instead of the evening.

If anyone had stood by the ring and watched, what I did with the black horse would have seemed absolutely standard. We worked on turns, circles, and straight lines, on walking, halting, trotting, standing still. In time we added the canter to our daily repertoire. No more hacks on a long loose rein: it was all serpentines, figures of eight, strong trots, working trots, canter right, canter left.

What one could not see was what happened between the horse and me. I can only say I have never ridden a horse who tried so hard. After that dark night when I had asked him about Allie, the horse seemed to turn more serious. His concentration bloomed around us like a rosy cloud in a Bible picture. If I so much as thought about it, and if it were remotely possible, he did it. He lengthened his strides at the trot and at the canter. He collected himself in the corners. Never had the geometries of an arena seemed so beautiful to me: the connected twenty-meter circles, the quarter lines and the diagonals, the measurement of his spine curving out just so from the boards, left and right, renvers, travers. If I encouraged him, he picked up his stiff hock just as high as the limber one. He was so physically difficult to ride that I did not know if he would ever be a good school horse. But somehow I convinced myself that, with a mind like his, all was possible: He could overcome his faults, he could beat his bad conformation. And I let myself imagine what it might be like to start him over fences when he turned five, imagined him in competition some years hence.

The days and nights grew cooler. Gradually, I lugged the last of my boxes up the narrow stairs to my cubby and unpacked them: turtlenecks, sweaters, gloves to wear early in the morning. I even groped through a box of mementos, found what I was looking for, and sheepishly slipped down to the pasture.

I'd filched this old Hohner from my father's workroom. It was dented in such a way it couldn't be sold, and when I was first on the road doing horses, missing Potts, I had learned to play it, picking out scales and themes from the classics as if I could bring him back. Once, by mistake, I'd taken a job at a summer camp where, in the evenings, I fled to the paddock to escape the mindless chanting of the color war. Down in the main camp, screams of "Kill blue!" alternated with "Kill white!" Up at the barn, I perched on the edge of the water trough and slaughtered Haydn, Mozart, and various Moravian hymns.

Here when I put the mouth organ to my lips, I could only manage a few faltering scales. But horses are neither snobs nor critics, and, just as the camp horses had once done, Twister and the five schoolies, like boats into the wind, turned toward me. Fascinated, they flicked their ears, inching toward me as they grazed. Gradually, the stars came out, and I played until my face was numb.

The next night it seemed silly and I gave it up.

In time, I went back to the high school and signed up for the rec program. But soon I missed one volleyball game, then another and another. It was just as pleasant to spend the day's end grooming the black horse a second time. Some evenings I slipped up onto his bare warm back and sat a while. In the few short hours since I had ridden him, I missed the ferocity of his thoughts, his unswerving attention, his consciousness beaming back at me. Riding him was like being carried on the sweet back of the universe. To myself, I joked that Twister had the mind of God.

• • •

On weekends, my riding students came back.
There were not quite so many of them, only
the more determined ones or the more lonely
ones, but once again I had to cram all their
lessons into Saturdays and Sundays. It was
not the same. The girls seemed changed by
their first few weeks in their new grades.
Their cliques and bonds seemed stronger
and meanspirited, and often they came, took
their lesson, then rushed off to some other
activity. Two of my helpers quit riding altogether. Helen became a cheerleader and
Scooter played flute in the high school band.
Both had rehearsals every Saturday morning,
football games every Saturday afternoon.

Miriam took over.

Somehow she conned her mother into
bringing her to the barn so early the horses
were barely finished eating. She shadowed me
up and down the aisle, in and out of the
office and the tack room. I would no sooner
grab a hoof pick than she would be cleaning
and checking feet. I curried, she curried. I
flicked a brush at a horse's tail, she brushed
a horse's tail. If I asked her to do something
else, she looked as if I had just bestowed
some honor on her, or, if she felt the task was
too menial, as if she had been rebuked.

Nothing means that much, I wanted to say
to her. Give it up.

But I said nothing. The teaching days were
long enough without hoping to give Miriam
much more than a sense of usefulness. I did
not have it in me to try to change her outlook

on life. Who was I, anyway, to presume to such a task?

By the end of a Saturday or a Sunday, I was desperately glad to see the last car pull down the driveway and turn toward town. Impossible to believe I had missed the girls at all during the week. Each weekend, although it was my intention to let the black horse rest, I slipped onto his back in the evening and rode him around the farm.

We had our first killing frost at the end of September, and before the week was out, Sheila, the old broodmare, had a mild case of colic. She did not eat, and stood curling her lip and frowning with puzzlement at her sides.

I called Dr. Mason.

I'd met him only briefly back in June, when he had charged through the barn, drawing blood for Coggins tests and vaccinating against rabies.

This time, he came into the barn with his square black bag in hand and his stethoscope draped around his neck. He had brown hair, a full mustache, and dark brown eyes. His pale blue coverall had a stain across the chest and frayed cuffs, and one barn boot was mended with a little patch of duct tape.

We went down to Sheila's stall, and he stood in the doorway, watched the mare for a few moments, then frowned at me.

"This it?" he said.

Sheila curled her lip and made a half circle in the stall.

63

"I don't know your preference, but most vets like to be called in early."

He smiled then, slung the stethoscope from his neck. "And in daylight, even." His voice was soft and cadenced. Certainly he was from somewhere south of Pennsylvania; he did not torture his vowels with the native nasal twang.

Stepping into the stall, he held out his palm for the mare. He was thin, dapper despite the duct tape on his boot, and his carriage and gestures were elegant and precise.

I stepped into the stall, caught the mare by the halter, snapped a lead rope to the ring under her chin.

Sighing quietly, Mason put the stethoscope to his ears.

"The thing is," I said.

He held the earpieces away from his ears and, looking down at the bedding, heard me out.

"I don't know much about her health," I said. "And I have almost no idea how old she is. Over twenty, judging by her teeth."

He ran a hand along her swayed back. "And this," he said.

He listened to her gut, carefully and at length. Again, I noticed his hands, elegant and gentle, moving the stethoscope and listening as if this old broodmare had his full attention, mattered every bit as much as a pricier piece of livestock.

I was grateful he was not one of those country vets who calculate a horse's worth in terms of what it would bring per pound at killers' auctions and then measure every treatment in pure dollar value.

When he was finished listening, he patted the mare's rump, went out to the truck.

"Horses look good," he said when he came back. "You do exceptional work."

I shrugged. "Small place."

He motioned for me to hold her head up, and as he ran the tube through her nostril and down her esophagus, discreetly sniffing the end to make sure he wasn't about to pump mineral oil into her lungs by mistake, he said, "I never thought you'd stay."

"I'm not."

"Too bad." He worked the handle on the pump. "You obviously know what you're doing."

I smiled, moved around to the far side of the mare. I did sometimes feel as if I were undercover, hiding ninety percent of what I knew in this small quiet place. Lately I had begun to worry that the longer I stayed, the more of my higher skills I was losing through lack of use.

When he was finished, he clanged the apparatus on the side of the bucket. Sheila's eyes widened. He patted her mane. "Old fool."

Sheila turned her muzzle toward his sleeve, rolled her eyes at some medicine smell, then stepped away.

He banged the pump again, letting the remainder of the oil drip into the bottom of the bucket. "I am so damn tired of horses," he said, eyeing me and smiling.

"Horses?" I said, guessing he was trying to

get a rise out of me. "It's people I can't stand."

He laughed then, dragged a finger through one corner of his mustache. "Like the ones who think a thousand-pound animal with a steel shoe on each hoof is a pet?"

We laughed.

Then he dug a syringe and a bottle out of his bag. "Allie was good. But my Lord, she filled Pierce's head with ideas." He drew serum into the barrel of the syringe, tapped the throat of it with a fingernail. "He doesn't have a clue," he said, sinking the needle into Sheila's neck. "Someone needs to get after that boy."

Colic can pass fairly quickly, a mere inconvenience to the person delegated to keep watch, or it can turn fatal. Mason left me with the standard instruction to check on her through the night, told me how to reach him if things turned worse, and took off.

By bedtime, the mare was better, picking at her hay, and although I checked on her twice during the night, she was fine by morning.

Two days later, though, the temperature shot up into the nineties. I kept the horses in the barn because it was cooler. They were already growing winter coats, and soon they were sweating through their furry underlayers. I hovered around the barn, taking one horse and then another outside and sponging it with water to help keep it cool. At noon, Sheila's knees buckled, and she lay quivering on her chest.

I gave her a quick look, then ran for the phone.

Dr. Mason's service told me he was out on an emergency.

"I have a horse down," I told the woman.

"And you are?"

"Natalie Baxter. Working for Pierce Kreitzer."

"Well, Natalie." She paused in a way that told me she was taking notes. "There's livestock down all over the county."

"Let me read you symptoms," I said, then realized I was talking to an answering service as if I were on the phone with a New Bolton specialist. "Oh," I said sheepishly. "You don't triage."

There was silence, and I knew I'd just offended her. The same poor woman was probably also answering the phone for an exterminator, a house appraiser, and a social worker.

She began to read from a prepared message: "Dr. Mason's best advice is to keep an eye on the animal's temperature. Offer water but don't force it. Bathing can help. Start rectal or pulse-point cooling if you know how. He also adds that if the animal is in severe distress, it might be just as wise to work with your healthy stock and try to prevent collapse."

I listened with my teeth gritted.

"I can do that," I said, trying to sound cooperative. Then I let my voice drop and a tone of pleading came into it: "Any idea when he'll arrive?"

"Dr. Mason synchronizes his own farm calls. I'll phone this out to him. But I am not in a position to make promises."

This, too, I knew, was a rehearsed speech, dictated by Mason.

I waited.

"Probably not until this evening."

"This evening?"

"Ma'am," the woman said, "there's livestock down all over the county."

And now I missed having a staff.

Sheila had managed to stagger to her feet. She was standing with her head down, her tail wrung off to one side. Diarrhea poured out of her. I freshened the water in her bucket, poured another bucket of water over her neck. Then I bolted down the aisle for my thermometer, and up into the cubby for ice.

By the time I came back, she was on her knees again. She drew in a long awful breath, groaned, then rolled down onto her side. Sweat ran into my eyes. I packed the ice in towels, laid them under her jaw and behind her ears, and with a track wrap tied the ice in place. I pulled the thermometer out: too high. Breaking toward 106.

I ran for the hose, hooked it up, then cursed the simple amenities of the barn. Rectal cooling was simply a matter of gently running cool water from a hose into a horse's rectum. The tissues are thin and full of blood vessels, so the water running over them cools the bloodstream. It was a trick that had saved more than one horse's life. But the water blasted out of the hydrant, and in the end I had to put two cricks in the hose to slow it down.

One way you can tell a horse needs rectal cooling is that it doesn't put up a fuss. Sheila lay there, a large white half-dead carcass, and the water ran inside her, and back out into the stall. I was making one hell of a mess, but there was no choice.

I gave her twenty minutes, then shut the water off and went for a wheelbarrow of shavings to toss in on top of the water. The ice was melting around her throat and ears. I replaced it, gave her a pat, and knew all I could do was wait.

I went to see to the others.

Most of them were standing quietly. Lawrence's ears were drooping in a way I didn't like, and nearly all of them were standing with a slack hip or neck. One at a time, I led them outside and soaked them with the hose. Then I pinched a tiny fold on each horse's neck, and counted how long it took to flatten out. All, except Lawrence, were pretty fast. One serious case and one mild one.

I spent the afternoon hosing Sheila, then the others. Twister and Archimedes held up the best. Twister found a little breeze in his stall and stood in it, seeming not to give in to the heat but to accept it. He was the youngest of the lot, and, despite his funny legs, perhaps the most robust.

Sometimes as I watched the water pouring onto the skin of one horse and then another, I wondered what Pierce had for a well. That was the kind of thing I should have known. Whatever it was, I prayed it wouldn't run dry. I thought about going down to the house and letting myself into the kitchen for a bucket of ice, but I decided things were going along well enough without that.

At four-thirty, I heard the Toyota coming up the drive. I went and stood in the doorway to the barn, and waved my arms over my head, as if I were stranded on an island trying to flag down a passing aircraft.

Pierce gave me a sketchy wave, then went inside.

I went down the aisle, meaning to give each horse one quick look before running down to the house to let him know what was happening. I heard a groan, and saw Lawrence sway, then go down on his knees and chest.

I ran for the hose, and started him, too, on rectal cooling. By now I was soaked and filthy, and as I knelt there in the stall, stroking his flank, I tried to will Pierce to come up to the barn.

He did not.

Lawrence took well to the treatment. Before fifteen minutes were up, he lifted his head, swung around, and looked first at me, then at the long black hose snaking into the stall. He gave his head a little shake, and moved his legs as if to get up. I pulled the hose away, and he rolled himself up onto his chest. Feeling better, he lay there and seemed to compose himself.

I was just flinging shavings around the stall when Mason's truck roared up the drive.

"How many?" he said, charging into the barn. In one hand he had his meds box. Cra-

70

dled on the other arm were plastic pouches of electrolytes.

"Two," I said. "Sheila's worst."

She was flat on her side, but more alert than she had been earlier. At the sight of Mason, she pricked her ears and lifted her head.

"Gallant," he muttered.

"I want to be like her when I grow up," I said.

He gave me a look. "Help me with this line."

I held the bag and Mason lay a needle into her jugular and we began running electrolytes. He crouched beside her, pinching her skin, dragging down an eyelid with his thumb, pressing a fingertip against her gum and timing how long it took the fingerprint to pink back up.

"Is this the low point? Or was she worse?"

"Worse," I said. "Much worse."

"Credit's yours then," he said. "You saved her."

I shook my head. "Long-term?"

"No idea. We've lost a few today. The young, the old, the infirm."

Suddenly I found myself looking at his shirt. Pale green with a dark blue stripe, it had a vee neck and no collar. The sleeves were rolled up past his elbows into soft floppy cuffs.

"I'm too tired," he said. "But you go ahead and laugh." He rocked back on his heels. "Four A.M. and a cow fell through a rotted barn floor. Then a colic, then this heat. This used to be my nightshirt." He wiped his face on his filthy sleeve, and glanced at his watch. "We've even seen a dairy cow or two abort today."

71

"So much for the dapper Dr. Mason," I teased. "Don't you have any help? Someone to bring you a shirt?"

"Obviously not," he snapped.

I was sorry I had spoken.

When the whole bag had dripped in, he gave the mare a pat and stood for a moment with his hands on the small of his back.

"Can we do anything for you here? Pierce must have a shirt. Can we find you some food?"

"Just show me the next patient. I have nine more farm calls after this."

I led him down to Lawrence's stall. He glanced inside.

"Where's Pierce?"

"Home from school," I said.

"I'll start this line," he said.

Again, we did the drill, and while the fluids ran into the Appaloosa's vein, Mason strode out of the stall, went down the aisle and into the office. I heard him dial the phone.

At first I assumed he was calling his service, then I realized he'd slammed down the phone and that now it was ringing. When it stopped, Mason snatched it up.

"Pierce?" he said. "Mason here."

There was a pause.

"Where am I? In your own goddamn barn. We need you up here."

Another pause.

"Now."

Then he hung up and came back into the stall. "That boy," he said. "My Lord."

In time we heard Pierce's footsteps, hesitating along the aisle. As far as I knew, it was the first time since the morning of my interview that he'd been in the barn.

"Down here," Mason called.

Pierce stood back from the stall door. "What's going on?"

Mason, crouched next to the horse, propped his elbows on his knees.

"What's going on is that it reached ninety-eight degrees today. Every goddamn piece of livestock in this county is wearing at least half a winter coat. There've been deaths, Pierce."

Pierce stood with his hands in his pockets and his head down.

"Natalie here saved two of your horses. I just thought you should know that."

Pierce's head came up, and he gave me a look that was half angry, half amazed. His eyes were suddenly quick and bright.

"You owe her," Mason said.

Pierce looked away.

"Here's how you'll pay her back."

I crouched beside the horse.

"She may or may not have guessed this, but she's going to be up all night. I'm leaving her with two syringes full of anticonvulsive medication. Either one of these could seize before the night is out and if they do, she has about sixty seconds to get a needle in. If she gets them through tonight and if the weather breaks, they'll survive."

I closed my eyes. I'd done this kind of duty more than once before, but not alone and not after a day as hot and draining as this.

"So here's the deal," Mason said. "Natalie

73

will do feeds." He turned to me briefly, ordering mashes and half rations. "Then she's going to shower and change into clean clothes. While she does that, you're going to babysit. And then you're going into town and getting her something to eat. Something substantial." He gave me a wicked grin. "Any requests?"

I shook my head.

He eyed me shrewdly. "Then I'll prescribe a small steak, a large salad, some dessert, and something to drink. A beer?"

I shrugged.

"And a thermos of coffee for the night. And then, in the morning, she gets the whole day off. She'll do feeds and she'll call in with a progress report. You'll do the rest." He stood. "Okay?" he asked. "Okay."

"I have school," Pierce said finally. "They'll worry."

"Or," Mason said, "we can just put these two down right here and now. Especially Sheila. Ever seen a horse die of convulsions? Shall I wait while you call a neighbor for a backhoe?"

Pierce stepped backward. His face was white. Mason, I thought, was getting a little carried away.

"No," Pierce said, looking as if he might faint. "We're not putting horses down."

"I don't want that, either," I said. "I'll stay up."

Mason snapped his box shut, gave each of the horses a final look. "Then cook your help some dinner and call in sick tomorrow," he

74

told Pierce. "It's your farm, chumpers, but Natalie's been doing all the work. Someone has to be good to her or she'll leave us." He punched Pierce lightly on the shoulder. His voice dropped and slowed, briefly took on a richer, more southern tone. "Do I have to tell you everything?"

chapter five

I mixed the mashes, fed the horses, and turned the healthy four out to pasture. From a distance, I saw Pierce making his way up toward the barn, carrying a tray with a cloth over it. I watched for a moment. It seemed odd that he would have a tray and cloth and that he would think to use them, but then I remembered Allie and supposed he'd had some practice.

He turned the office desk into a table. There was a bottle of cold beer, some steamed broccoli, and a small steak garnished with mushrooms. He'd even thought to bring pepper, salt, and steak sauce. I had a cloth napkin, too, and a matching fork and steak knife.

"You're good at this," I said.

He pulled up another chair, turned it around, sat on it backward, and leaned his arms along the back.

I cut into the steak. It was tender, the inside a perfect pink. I put a piece on my fork, then glanced up.

"What about you?" I said.

"Later."

I pushed the meat around. "But if you have things to do," I said. I knew full well that he didn't, but I couldn't bear to have him sit and watch me eat.

"I'll wait," he said. "Take the tray back. And I didn't bring dessert yet."

I decided I might as well get on with it, and put the piece of meat into my mouth.

"It's fabulous," I said after a while. The steak was the best I'd had in a long, long while, and the broccoli was steamed perfectly—neither hard nor mushy, which was how mine usually turned out. "You really know how to cook."

"Where there's food there's hope," he quipped.

I puzzled.

"Kreitzer's German," he said. He seemed to take inventory of what was left on my plate. "Is it true what Mason said?"

I frowned.

"You saved the horses?"

I shook my head. "I was just here. Did what needed doing."

He looked down at his hands then up at me. "I never thought something could happen to them."

Horses were probably among the most delicate of livestock. They had evolved to run free, not to live indoors in box stalls. In nearly every way, their bodies fought domestication. Their stomachs were so small they could die from breaking into grain rooms, and they were susceptible to everything: bad hay, digestive

76

problems, various weird viruses and respiratory syndromes, to say nothing of what happened when their legs went bad.

I finished eating.

"Dessert?" he said. "I don't have anything, but I'd be happy to go into town and then come back and make something. You could have it later, break up your night. That's what Mason said."

I gave him a funny look. He sounded so sincere, so young. The edge, the mysterious humor were gone.

"That you needed dessert."

"Does Mason always order you around like this?"

"When Allie died, Mason thought I should sell the horses. So did everybody else." He shrugged. "But we kept them while she was sick—she liked to watch them out the windows. And now I just can't get rid of them." He looked away. "So yes, I do what Mason says because I know zilch about it."

But she never could have meant for him to keep the horses afterward. Surely she knew he was a complete incompetent.

"Well," I said. "I should check on the patients." I got up and tidied the tray. "You're a fabulous cook," I said again.

Pierce got up then, too.

It was nearing eight, and the evening was already dark.

"You'll be all right? I could come up and check on you."

I thought. "Never mind."

"Even if you just need company." He gathered up the tray. "I'm good at that. I always sat with Allie." His odd grin was back and his eyes glinted. "I'm an old hand at the bedside. Although maybe not the bedsides of horses."

As it happened, there was an empty stall between Lawrence's and Sheila's, and I set up a little camp in there. I found a wool horse sheet and settled in. A flashlight and the needles with their full syringes lay next to me in a small clean bucket. To stay awake, I got up every now and again, and paced the barn. I cleaned each of my saddles, wondering if I would ever ride a horse again over a four-foot jump, or sit on the back of a horse schooled to the higher levels of dressage. Later, I sat in the office and reread all the notes I had written since I'd arrived. The entries had steadily fallen off, as if I'd realized no one but me would ever read them. Sometimes I stood at the end of the barn, and watched the light burning in the mudroom. A front blew through, and I listened to the breeze and watched the sky darken as the haze moved off to the east. It seemed clear to me that I would never return to Bethlehem and that it was long past time for me to move on.

By four-thirty, Sheila and Lawrence were sleeping well and soundly. Their skin was taut again, and I knew they were out of danger. It's an odd feeling to be a 130-pound human who, with the prick of a fine-gauge needle, hopes to save the life of a creature so large, so vulnerable, and so complex. I huddled in the stall, wrapped the wool sheet around myself, and fell asleep. A quick nap, then I would get up, do chores, and go properly to bed up in my cubby.

What woke me was the sound of the grain-room door. Pierce had actually come up to start the chores.

Awkwardly, we fed and hayed and watered. It may have been his barn, but I had rearranged it; we were constantly in one another's way, then wasted time deferring to one another. Together we turned the healthy four right back out to pasture. I gave Sheila and Lawrence small rations of grain while Pierce threw hay down from the loft. Gratefully, I slipped into the office and called Mason's service and left a message that we'd had an uneventful night and that all was well. The two stalls still needed to be cleaned and the aisle needed to be swept.

"Can you do it?" I asked Pierce. "I'm heading up to bed."

He hesitated, and I found myself looking at my watch. He still had time to get to school.

"Or I can just do this later," I said. "After I get some sleep."

He stood with his hands in the pockets of his jacket, abashed and ill at ease. "I called in sick."

I stopped in the barn doorway.

"Then it's all yours," I said. "It would really help if you stripped Sheila's stall and filled it with fresh bedding."

"But are you tired?"

"Fine," I snapped. "Leave it. I'll get to it later."

I turned away.

"No, no," he called after me. "I thought that maybe I could buy you breakfast."

I yawned, stretched. What I felt was not so much tired as depleted. And I knew it might be wiser to stay awake all day, and then get to bed earlier than usual. Besides, now that I had his attention, we could settle some matters on the farm.

"Okay," I said.

I decided I would shower first, and I hoped that Pierce, in the meanwhile, would get busy in the barn. Instead, when I came back down from my cubby, he had showered, too, and was sitting quietly on the back step of the house. He was wearing jeans and a gray sweater that picked up the blue in his eyes.

"I was thinking," he said. "It might be better if we took your truck."

I cocked my head.

"Well, I took a sick day. Not a personal day. And people know my car."

I shrugged. The truck was long empty of all my stuff. I brushed the paper coffee cups off the seat, put the gym bag I hadn't used in quite some time in the cargo well.

At the bottom of the lane, I said, "Which way?"

Pierce pointed right and we headed into

town. But as we drove along Main Street toward the bakery, he chickened out. "Let's go somewhere else," he said.

I smiled. "Someone will see you."

He gave me a sheepish smile.

"So," I said. "You don't play hooky often."

He pointed south. "It would make them worry."

I pondered that, put the truck in gear; we drove out into the countryside.

"How hungry are you?"

The truck was warm and I was happy to be on the road, and, although dopey from my lack of sleep, preoccupied by the strangeness of the moment.

"Not very," I said.

I half felt as if someone might stop us at any moment and whisk him back to the high school. I kept thinking how young he seemed this morning.

Pierce said very little, merely pointing one way or another when we reached an intersection. Soon we were off in a maze of dirt roads, and I felt a wave of relief. At this rate, we wouldn't by accident end up in Bethlehem.

We passed a private amusement park, with a lozenge-shaped lake. It had been drained of water and a giant blue fiberglass whale lay in the center of the expanse of mud and sand. I could see the owners were building a new dock.

We drove past high narrow Pennsylvania farmhouses, past churches with red doors, through orchards of apple and peach trees, with workers busy at the picking. The roads had names like Durham Forge and Gallows Hill, Applebachsville and Sheimertown Hill. Some of the fields were harrowed for the winter, the silos no doubt full; horses and cattle grazed in the pastures and drank from farm ponds, strong again after the searing heat.

After a while, Pierce asked me if I minded pulling over. He pointed to a turnout beneath a row of willows. Their whip branches with their yellowing leaves tapped the hood and roof of the truck.

Pierce sat and looked out the window. I turned off the ignition. He gave me a startled look, then looked away again.

A stone wall, neatly pointed, ran along the road. Behind it stood ranks of gravestones, some old and splitting, some polished and new. Beyond the graveyard, on a flattened knoll, stood a church.

After a while, he popped open the door latch. "I'm getting out," he said. "Just for a minute."

I sat in the cab and watched him go. His collar was up around his neck, his shoulders hunched. From the back I could see the slight wayward lift of the cowlick. He walked quickly—not a man strolling, but a man with a destination. I looked away then, because it suddenly occurred to me he might be headed to the hedge or out under the trees to relieve himself.

For a long while, I sat looking out through the curtain of the willow whips. I had no idea where we were: on an unnamed road near an unnamed village somewhere in eastern Pennsylvania. And now I wished we had veered closer to my home territory. Sitting here, just far enough away so the country churches were just that much different, I felt bereft. I looked over at the church, with its scrolling dark red trim, and I tried to think of the austere graves of my father and mother. They were buried along a walk in Nisky Hill cemetery, just across the river from the mills. And I thought of Vee quiet now in her own grave, lying still under every ilk of sky.

I got out of the truck.

In the distance, I saw Pierce standing with his hands in his pockets, looking up, apparently at the tree spreading over the graves. I circled among the stones, gradually drawing nearer, and stopped some ten feet away.

He turned and beckoned.

I hesitated.

"It's okay," he said. He seemed calm, almost happy, and when I moved alongside him, he put his arm through mine.

It felt cumbersome and odd, standing there with our elbows linked. Soon my shoulder began to feel wrenched. If I weren't so damn tired, I thought, I wouldn't put up with this for a minute.

The center gravestone, large and somewhat ornate, read "Kreitzer." Around it were smaller stones, and I read the names and dates, the one-line epitaphs, and as if unraveling a mystery, tried to guess who was what to whom. Two of them had died on the same day, some six years earlier.

Pierce caught my look, then nodded at the stones.

"Car accident," he said.

With his free hand, he nudged his glasses, smoothed the hair on the back of his head. As he moved, my shoulder wrenched a little more.

"And they were—?"

He nodded, as if confirming something to himself. "Parents," he said, and lifted his chin.

"Allie was twenty. On leave from Penn State. Away at riding school in Virginia. We bought the farm so she could run it and have a home. She was that devastated. We could just about afford it. But it kept her from falling apart."

And there were two newer stones, a little way to Pierce's right. I cocked my head, read them both, stared, then forced myself to focus on just one.

It was Allie's. Alexandra Ruth. I did the math. She'd been twenty-six.

A chill ran down my neck.

"And she died of...?"

"Cancer," Pierce said. "Adenocarcinoma."

He pronounced the word like a secret password.

"It was very fast. She was already dying before we even knew she was sick."

I shuddered.

Because I was standing arm in arm with the man who may have helped to kill her? But hadn't I approved? Or was it the eeriness of standing at the grave of someone whose horse I now was riding? Suddenly I calculated: How old had Vee been when she died? Forty? Forty-one?

"Hard to believe," Pierce said. He tugged his arm free of mine and stepped away. "I'm here. And they're there. Wherever that is." He took off his glasses and scrubbed them on his shirt, staring up as he did so at the tree. "Every time I come here," he said, "I expect something. No idea what, though."

He lay his hand on my shoulder and tried to turn me away.

I wrenched free and stood staring down at the other brand-new stone.

"I'm sorry," I said. "But I have to ask."

I pointed.

It read "Pierce Boehm." I could guess that Boehm was his mother's maiden name. There was a birth date and a space for the date of death.

"Doesn't it bother you?"

He gestured to the plot. "There was only one spot left. I wanted dibs." Then he looked at me and laughed. "I got a bargain. Two for one on purchase, carving, and setting. It means nothing. That's the truth."

I shuddered.

He put his arm across my shoulders.

"Here's what matters," he said gently. "Allie and I had a deal. I didn't keep up my whole end of it." His face contorted briefly. "But I did promise to find someone to start Twister."

The Saturday after the heat, I could use Lawrence and Sheila for only a short time, and only for the lightest of lessons. Sheila, I worried, had aged dramatically. She seemed slower to respond, duller, as if she had lost some of her sass, had yielded her opinions.

I told all the girls about the horses being ill, because I thought they should know such things could happen and because I wanted them to understand why the horses were doing so little work.

They responded in all the ways I thought they might. They dripped with sympathy and sentiment. They confused the heat prostration with their own ailments, everything from stomachaches to ear infections. One older girl asked about the biology of it. How was dehydration related to osmosis? Only Miriam surprised me.

She came early that morning, and her eyes grew dark while she listened. She stroked the horses extra long as if to prove to herself that they still lived. Then, as we were working on the grooming and the tacking up, she stopped me in the aisle. Her eyes were bright and full of awe. "You made them live."

And nothing I could say about simply learning skills and using them could change her mind. I had saved the lives of horses and now she watched me in a new way.

chapter six

We had fine weather that fall. When it rained, the storms were brief and the footing remained manageable. The temperatures fell gradually. I rode in turtlenecks and sweaters, and with the first hint of colors in the trees, and the Michaelmas daisies blooming all around, I fell into the habit of selecting a different horse each day and taking it out galloping.

Granted, the schoolies found this baffling. Archimedes' gallop was only an increment faster than his sleepy school-ring canter. Galen and Lawrence, although amazed, seemed to enjoy it. Even Sheila, feeling better, gave a little squeal and let herself rip for about three strides. Prima was the one who reveled in it, shooting out her head, roaring up the hill in the back pasture, and bucking every other stride. Galloping made her so wild and gay, I walked her on a long loose rein and later galloped her again. I thought it was good for her soul.

And I galloped Twister, too. He was stronger than he had been, but even when let out, with me crouching over his neck, there was something so self-contained in the way he carried himself that, a day or two after his first gallop, I decided he was ready for cavaletti.

Cavaletti are a marvelous Italian invention. The simple ones are rails laid on the ground, spaced careful distances one from another. The level of training of the horse, the pace, and the commands of the rider all determine what the horse does as he passes over them: extend, collect, or simply trot with more flexion and precision.

Four feet is the normal distance for a

normal horse, but Twister's stride was short because of his conformation. I spaced them shy of that, and a few times each schooling session trotted him through. He pricked his ears with concentration, and I could feel the hard work of his left hind leg, lifting and flexing, feel the correctness in the spring of his back. That was all I wanted: gradual greater strength and an awareness of where he was putting his feet.

He learned quickly, and as the days passed I moved the cavaletti from one spot to another in the ring and inch by inch moved the rails apart to lengthen his stride. And each day, once he'd done his exercises over the rails, I either worked him in the ring or took him out for a hack.

I spent as much time as I could riding the horses. I could have worked on the fences, or done some painting or other work around the barn, but I felt that was up to Pierce. Besides, I was getting restless; my hours in the saddle were all that made life bearable. I was definitely jittery, and although it was long past time for me to leave, one thing kept me at DreamWeb Farm: I could not give up the black horse.

And God alone knew what would become of Twister if left in Pierce's care. Since the heat prostration and our ride to the cemetery, he and I were more relaxed with one another. Once in a while I went down to the house and sat for an hour to watch the news with him. His presence did not seem quite so weighty, and something nearly like hope sometimes came into his face. But that hardly meant he was to be trusted with a horse as marvelous as the black.

One evening, after showering and changing, I was puttering in my cubby. The place seemed cluttered, so I got out the boxes I had carefully slit and flattened, found my roll of packing tape, and, drawer by drawer, put things away: certain clothes in the spring boxes, others in the summer box. Gradually I had unpacked books and lined them up on the shelf over the bed. There was something pleasant about their progression: the latest technical newsletters on one end; in the middle, the books of theory and technique written over the last one hundred years; on the other end, translations from the ancient Greeks. There was even the first equitation book given to me by Vee.

I sat on the bed and browsed through it, looking at the familiar drawings by Sam Savitt, smiling over the last chapter. How often I had sprawled on my bed, memorizing the etiquette of fox hunting, as if, at any moment, I might receive a last-minute invitation to ride to hounds across the lands of Upper Bucks and I would have no chance to study up on where I belonged in the field, or how to handle my horse, or what the traditional calls meant as they wafted back to me from the huntsmen.

I let the book fall shut on my lap. I'd ridden to hounds here and there and there'd been little of the elegance and fluidity I'd imagined as a girl: it was rough and crazy and half out of control. I'd even cubbed wearing a golf jacket, rather than tweed, and in the winter I'd sometimes bundled up far beyond the point of old tradition.

Letting the book lie on my bed, I got out my jackknife and sliced through the tape on my mementos box. Without much thought, I took the things out one at a time. I held them in my hands, laid them around me on the bed or placed them on my bureau. I felt neither sentimental nor analytical, merely at ease: these things were mine, and my hands and eyes needed to take them in again.

A pale blue bone china cup, with a circle of silver at its lip: Grandmother Baxter's wedding china. Often, over the years, I had thought I would unpack it and drink my morning coffee from it, a touch of eccentric elegance. I smiled. There had been so much china in our apartment: a full set from each of two grandmothers, a third set from a great-grandmother, and another from our mother. Potts often said he could hardly wait for us to marry—Vee, Lucy, me—so he could give us each a set.

There was a tree ornament, a book of Moravian customs that had belonged to Potts, a history of Bethlehem published in a special edition when I was in about the sixth grade. Even a Dennis the Menace comic book in which Dennis visits Central Moravian Church for Christmas Eve and roasts a marshmallow over his beeswax taper.

There was a yearbook from high school, and

briefly I flipped open to a picture of my best friend: Alec McGonigle. A hundred tales wanted to tell themselves over in my memory.

Toward the bottom were packets of letters and photographs. Some were family shots: me on Hadley, a shot taken by Vee; snaps of my parents before my birth; Lucy's wedding day; a bridal portrait of my mother. I laid them aside. Somewhere also was a prophetic picture of me riding determinedly away from the camera on a tricycle, trying to make my escape. I wore little red cowgirl boots, and a miniature ten-gallon hat hung down my back. Moments later, I fell off the bike and chipped a tooth.

Although I had not examined them for years, all of these were so familiar that all I had to do was hold them in my hands.

I hefted a packet of letters—letters Vee had received from Harris, the man she had meant to marry. I had only ever read four or five of them from start to finish, although I had peeked at most of them. What had come off the page was sheer love and sheer torture. I put them aside. Not tonight.

Next I lifted out a box of jewelry. The scattered pieces belonged to our mother, to Vee, and to our grandmother. I had played with some of these as a child, and saw the rest on Vee or, more rarely, on my sister. I opened the clasp, wondered if I could tell what was whose, then snapped the clasp shut again without looking.

At the bottom of the box, wrapped in corduroy, lay a pistol.

I unwrapped it.

It was a small piece, delicate. I traced the etchings on the grip, the entwined violets and daisies, the letters: VB and HS. Harris, a gunsmith, had engraved it himself. I lay it across my hand, let my wrist test the balance. It was a small, sweet thing: Harris' engagement gift to Vee.

The riding lessons gradually wound down. According to Pierce, they would finish for good before Thanksgiving, earlier if we lost the footing. I still rode the schoolies in order to keep them legged up, but my serious time and work went into Twister. I raised his cavaletti a few inches from the ground and coaxed him to lift his feet that much more. He seemed to talk to himself as he bounced through them, and there was such strength in his muscles, such focus in his thoughts, that I decided that, one way or another, it would be me who started him over jumps. There was no way I could give the horse up.

One choice was to stay on the farm. Another was to buy him from Pierce, pay a little board, then go find a real job, and have him shipped to me. The days passed, the mornings grew slowly colder, and I came to think of Twister as my own.

But what does it mean to say a horse belongs to us? Until I met Twister, I thought I could pretty well recite the common variations:

He's mine. And here's the bill of sale to prove it.

He's mine. And the more others covet him, the more I will value him myself.

He's mine. And I will interpret every flicker of his eyelid and stomp of hoof and thus invent for him a personality.

He's mine. And no one else can tell me what to do with him. I can dose him with vitamins, massage his legs, buy him the best of saddle pads. Likewise I will feel free to neglect his hooves, blister his legs, leave his blankets on when he's too hot, leave them off when he shivers.

But Twister was mine, I believed, because he worked his heart out for me, and because I felt stronger, clearer, quieter whenever I so much as laid a hand on him. He'd grown in these past months, taken on a presence I had not created. With a little burnishing and strengthening, he had emerged with all his fine powers of execution and concentration. True, his hocks weren't terrific, but more than one great horse had overcome a handicap. Privately, I thought he might be something of a miracle.

I worked around the barn, thinking of little else. I didn't know how Pierce would take my offer, or when I would feel ready to make it, but in the outside world every horse was for sale, and based on what I could guess about Pierce's finances I could make him a tempting offer. I thought about Allie, about pitching the fact that I could bring this horse to full potential. He and I had clicked. I had no specific plans for him, other than a gradual move into competition. And I indulged in a childhood fantasy: appearing in competition on a horse no one knows, then turning in such a fine and polished performance I couldn't help but win.

Of course, it wouldn't be like that. I only wanted to give Twister every chance, and, more than anything, I wanted to keep him in my life.

When I thought about these things in his presence, he pressed his face into my chest, and I rubbed my thumbs along the insides of his ears until he sighed with contentment.

The temperatures warmed a little, then dropped. Again I had weather colic in the barn: Thank God it was not horses down on their knees and losing fluids. Instead it was Prima, biting at her sides, and Sheila once again, curling her lip and refusing to eat or drink.

Mason came that afternoon, and when I asked him why I was having such a colic run, he patted my arm. "It's everyone this year. You handle it better than most."

Pierce happened to arrive while Mason's truck was still parked at the barn, and he came straight up before going into the house.

"Everything all right?" he said.

"No," Mason said. "More colic." He gave me a wicked grin. "Put your order in for dinner."

"Sure," Pierce said. "I'll cook." He looked scared. "How, ah, well, how serious is it?"

"Oh, they'll live," Mason said. "What with Natalie and her nursing. Frankly, I'm thinking of stealing her from you."

He stood for a while, though, looking over Sheila. After a few moments, he pried open her mouth and examined her teeth. He let her lips slide shut and clucked.

"What?" Pierce said. "Steal Natalie for what?"

I looked down. Mason was only bantering.

"She's getting on," Mason said. "This is her third colic."

Pierce turned white and gave me a frantic look.

Mason looked away, hiding his amusement.

"She could go for years," I said.

Pierce breathed.

"Then again," I said quietly. "Winter's coming."

"Take it as it comes," Mason said, serious again. "But she's aging. Let's all keep that in mind."

"I could go start dinner," Pierce offered in a rush.

I shrugged. "It won't be like the last time."

Mason and I watched him flee the barn.

"You don't have to keep doing that," I said, amused and annoyed.

"It's good for him. He should have sold this place when Allie died."

I put the mare back in her stall.

Mason gathered his equipment. "Call me," he said. "Weren't you the one who said I needed an assistant?"

I puzzled over that while I did chores, then decided he couldn't be serious. Even if he was, nursing was a secondary part of my work. Soon I would get busy researching jobs out of *The Chronicle*, buy Twister, and move on. Before I'd finished sweeping the aisle, the phone rang in the barn. It was Pierce. He had a stew on the stove. Whenever I was ready.

Again I ate supper from a tray. This time he had a tray, too, and we ate together in the living room, watching the news.

The food was good, and Pierce, pleased to hear it, offered more. Then we both went back to half watching the news and half making conversation. During the commercial breaks, we talked about the horses, Pierce wanting to know if I'd be up all night.

I told him no. I'd set the alarm for every two, three hours and go check on them. We'd caught it early enough that Mason's medications should keep them quiet.

He cleared his throat.

"But don't you have to walk them? Allie walked a horse once, all night long. Up and down the drive, hour after hour. She said if it got down it would die."

I put more stew in my mouth and thought.

That was, of course, how we treated colic in the old days. But now we knew what mattered most was simply keeping the horse on its feet. If it lay down and rolled from the pain, yes, it could die of a twisted gut. Recently there had even been some question about the harm of making a sick horse walk to the point of exhaustion. So now it was medication first, then just a lot of vigilance. But what did you say to a man whose dead sister's method had not been quite right?

All of a sudden the news resumed, and on the screen were the mills in Bethlehem.

I stared.

The story said that the mills were closing for good. The last few hundred workers, who were keeping open one small final rolling mill, would be receiving pink slips within the year.

I knew in a general way that Beth Steel had been gradually losing business. For one reason or another, I had avoided the place for twenty years, but now I felt as if someone had just announced that an entire continent, specifically the one of my birth, was about to vanish.

The story went on to say that the steel had today made public its plan to raze the entire Bethlehem plant. The center of Bethlehem would have several hundred empty acres.

"That's like saying you'll tear down all of...All of...anything. All of Shipville. Half of Harrisburg."

I put down my spoon.

"You're interested in the steel?" Pierce said. "We have some kids at school tracking Bethlehem in the media." His voice slipped into a kind practiced classroom enthusiasm. "It's a fascinating urban dilemma. What other city will ever get to rebuild the land lying at its heart?"

"It wasn't the heart," I said, stupefied.

It was what? It was walking hand in hand with

my father across the Minsi Trail bridge, the mills sprawling east and west below us along the river, the stacks rising high above our heads. It was listening to him predict that the hearths of Bethlehem would never darken. It was memorizing for school the number of miles of railroad tracks inside the Bethlehem plant, the lists of famous bridges, famous buildings raised with steel made in my own city. It was the rumor of another death, in the coke works, on the open hearth, in a mishap with a crane, skittering across our playgrounds. It was the traffic of the city ebbing and flowing in rhythm with the shifts, our income at the store rising with steel bonuses, falling during strikes. It was telling the rank of the family in the car in front of you in traffic by the color of the helmet resting above their back seat, and knowing, by the hours your friends ate their meals, whether their fathers were on salary or shift.

A whole world was about to lose its foundation. My world.

The news moved on to other stories. I stared at the screen.

chapter seven

Every day while I rode Twister, I thought about Bethlehem.

Pierce thought I should go back and see it. He even offered to come with me. He could take some pictures. There were bound to be some great shots.

As much as I thought the trip would do him good, I said no, thanks. I couldn't bear the thought of my hometown examined under anyone's lens.

Still I found myself wishing I had someone there to call. Over the years, I had sometimes sent my new addresses to John Casey, Lucy's husband, and every once in a while he had written me a letter. Baxter's Music, of course, had been sold years ago, and John Casey now managed a music store out at a mall. In one of his letters, he had recounted some of the changes in downtown. All I could remember was something about a Viennese bakery and the shocking news that the Moravian Bookstore now sold gourmet foods. In addition to books, I presumed, but one never knew.

And to think that Bethlehem had once been like no place but itself.

I did think about calling Alec. The razing of the mills seemed crisis enough.

Sometimes, as a kind of test, I let myself remember when he was a freshman at Lehigh, that miserable year before he transferred down to Penn, where he stayed until he was a doctor. It was the same awful time my father was dying and Lucy had banished me to the farm. But I often came back into the city, to Lehigh University up on the South Side to see Alec. Weekend after weekend, we walked around the campus, wisecracking about the teams of freshmen surveying the layout of the place, as they had for the past one hundred years in the introductory engineering courses. We watched cheap films in

Packard lab, went drinking down on Fourth Street with fake IDs, even sat in the top of the old stadium, looking down into the bowl of the city, down at the strings of bright street-lights. That spring, we had mixed ourselves up beyond repair. Lonely and confused, we had exhausted ourselves on his dormitory bed, then in the early hours of the morning, with no idea of what to say, we held tight to one another and watched the stacks burn off up and down the river.

What I found myself remembering most, though, was the shooting.

One morning, I went into Shipville, and for old time's sake, I bought some shells and a simple gun-cleaning kit. At lunch, I spread a towel on my bed and, for the first time, dismantled Vee's .22. I swabbed and oiled and polished, and in the middle of the afternoon, I carried the gun and the shells far out into the back pasture. It was a long walk, and I hiked here and there, looking for a place to shoot. I found a ravine that suited, but when I looked around I saw nothing to shoot at.

No target.

I remembered Alec and his dogged insistence on a formal target.

Still, I got my stance, raised the pistol with both hands. How this came back to me: the pistol sight rising with my inhalation, falling with my exhalation; the stark touch of the trigger.

So, I thought. I will find a target.

• • •

One rainy afternoon, on the way back from Agway, I stopped at the Shipville Library. At the desk, I asked for the Bethlehem phone book. I was stunned by the heft of it, four times the thickness of the book of my childhood. I carried it to a table, and browsed through it, thinking of and then looking up one business and then another from Broad and Main streets. The Boyd Theater and the Moravian Bookstore had survived. A jeweler remained, too: Seifert's Silver. And of course the Hotel Bethlehem.

In the yellow pages, I looked for Alec. No listing. None in the white pages, either.

I paused for a moment, discomfited. Where could he be? And then I reassured myself: certainly it couldn't be all that hard to track down a doctor. What would I say anyway?

Can you believe they're tearing down the mills?

Can you forgive me?

John Casey, of course, was in the book, although no longer living at his and Lucy's old address.

Just to be certain, I looked up the offices of Potts's attorneys. And there they were, same address out on Center Street. Vorhees, Hirsch, and Maxfield.

I gave the book back, then noticed a pile of maps. On impulse, I found one of the area, and with rain dripping outside the windows, I spread it out. I could not entirely retrace the ride Pierce and I had taken to the cemetery, but there, easier than I could imagine, was the road back to Bethlehem.

Out of restlessness, and the lack of much to do on a rainy fall day, I headed off onto a back street of town. I would detour around, drive forever, think a little, and sooner or later find my way back to the farm.

Two blocks along a side street, I saw a hunting and fishing store. I pulled the truck to the curb, went in and bought a dozen targets.

In memory of Vee, and in honor of the long Pennsylvania autumn, I began concocting a little plan. I decided to see the back roads of Bucks County again. That would be easier than going into Bethlehem, more private, too.

At first I thought I would simply drive there. Skirt Bethlehem, find my way to 412, and work my way east to the river roads. I'd see if I could scout out Jack Detweiler's lovely old farm with its stone bank barn and then wander the back roads from there.

Each day, however, I found a reason not to go, until finally I realized this enterprise would be more fun if I took Twister with me. I could load him in the trailer, find a nice pullout, tack him up, and ride him through the marvelous lanes and byways I remembered.

Still I hesitated. Days passed, and I considered the ins and outs.

It was a stroke of genius.

It was completely reckless. For all I knew every last dirt road had long ago been paved.

I had the horrible image of driving hither and yon with a horse dragging along behind me looking for a farm I cannot find.

Finally I thought of Twister. I suspected shipping might be extra hard on him because of his legs. And then I realized it was entirely possible he had never before ridden in a trailer.

In the end, I went on a long ride in the truck, scouting out a fifteen-mile circuit that began and ended right here on Pierce's farm. On a bright clear morning, I did the chores, filled a water bottle, saddled Twister, and headed out. We were only three miles from home when the air turned colder. Soon I began to shiver, but I would not turn back.

Twister was delighted. He pranced. He snorted. He was utterly gay. He spooked at things out of sheer silliness. Several times, I huddled over his neck and let him gallop. I could practically feel him grinning. His thoughts streamed back at me: the sheer joy of galloping on packed dirt, the trees whipping past, the simple pleasure of being a strong black blur across the landscape.

I stroked his neck, knotted my fingers in his mane, wiped the wind tears from my eyes. You're mine, I thought.

Beneath me, Twister lifted his back and strode home as if he owned the whole damn county.

By the time we got back to the barn, my hands were numb and the temperature had dropped a good fifteen degrees. Although I was half frozen, I rubbed Twister down, massaged his legs with liniment. He lipped my hair. I leaned against his neck, grinned, and giddily decided to go scout the roads of Bucks County. Riding high on Twister's back, it would be nothing but a pleasure to return.

That night, I kept the horses in, and twice I set the alarm and checked them all for weather colic. There were no signs of it at midnight or at three, but at six, when I walked into the barn, only five horses greeted me over their stall doors. Twister did not.

I paused a moment in the aisle, and bowed my head and listened for him—*felt* for him—over the din of his hungry stablemates. And there it was, his presence, slow and calm.

So I wasn't all that worried. He wasn't fine, or he wouldn't be lying down, but I was sure he had a perfectly good reason for not getting to his feet. He was a dignified horse, and sometimes I caught myself forgetting that he was, not older, but younger than all the rest.

The stall door slid back easily, and he simply lay there in the middle of his stall. He was propped on his chest, his legs folded beneath him like a lamb. His ears were up, his eyes bright; he watched me closely.

I watched him in return. The other horses seemed about to tear the barn down, frantic for their hay and grain, but I stood in Twister's doorway and looked into his eyes. I waited for him to swing his head and nip at his unhappy belly. He did not. He simply stared back at me, then lowered his head and neck.

Well, that's okay, I thought. A horse will often flatten out as it gathers itself to get up, then swing its head and neck like a counterweight.

But his head did not lift. He was settling in for a rest.

I slipped into the stall, crouched beside him, stroked his neck, then leaned my ear to his gut. Things were rumbling along just fine in there. I held my breath, watched him a moment longer, then went out to feed the others. I tossed them hay, checked their water buckets, rattled grain into their feed tubs.

The black did not rise. When I went down the aisle with an armload of hay, he rolled back onto his chest, lifted his head and watched. I debated. Should I leave the hay where he could reach it? Or put it in the corner where it belonged and force him to his feet?

I offered the hay just out of his reach, then tossed it in the corner. He glanced at it, then back at me. His nostrils fluttered. Finally, he twisted his neck, flung his head, and gathered his hind legs beneath him. He had some trouble straightening his forelegs, and when he got up at last, he lurched forward a half step then stood quietly on three legs. His right foreleg pointed out at a slight angle. The toe of his hoof just barely rested on the ground.

I thought that I would vomit.

After a moment, he seemed to resign himself to being up, and clumsily made his way over to his hay.

I crouched next to him, running my hands

down the pointing leg, testing for heat. I leaned my face into his neck, I bit a hole on the inside of my cheek, I combed my fingers through his mane.

The other horses, finished with their grain and almost finished with their hay, were growing restless. It was time to muck the stalls, to groom, to ride, to get on with the day.

But I could not leave Twister, could not let this moment end because the next moment would come rushing in behind it. The horse was calm, matter-of-fact. Bemused almost, at my reaction. Wiping my eyes, I went to the grain room and measured grain. I brought him what one brings any horse that cannot work: less than half a measure.

Mason arrived early that afternoon. All the other horses had been turned out and the barn was quiet. Golden October light lay in a diagonal patch across the concrete floor and created a still pocket of warm air. I led Twister from his stall. Mason shoved his hands into the pockets of his coverall and watched. He shook his head as the horse made its way stiffly toward him.

Twister lifted his head and stood quietly. His right toe was turned out as if he were a dancer.

Mason moved around him, studying his legs, running his hand down the length of his shoulder blades, stroking his neck.

"This was Allie's horse, wasn't it?" he said.

I stiffened.

Mason looked away, fingered one corner of his mustache. "Let me go back out to the truck."

While he was gone, I stood under Twister's neck and leaned against him. All morning, I'd been feeling dizzy and disoriented.

Then we began the testing, wedging up first one hoof and then another, pressing on the wall of each with the testers, looking for pain. At one point, Twister's right knee buckled and he lurched forward.

Mason straightened, let the hoof testers hang loosely at his side.

"I guess you know what that means," he said.

He was looking out through the barn door at the sagging fences, shaking his head.

"No," I said. "Tell me."

Mason inhaled loudly, as if bored or annoyed.

"No heat, no pain but in the hoof. And it's what? Opposite that hock?"

He slung Twister's tail off to the side, glanced at his back legs, and let it fall free again.

"He's awfully young," he said. "I could never imagine what Allie saw in him. What with those hocks."

"Pierce said start him," I snapped. "So I started him."

"Yes," Mason said. "Pierce." He looked down at the testers, opening and closing them.

"You're not to blame," he said. "He's got lousy conformation. I'm sure you didn't ask for much."

Ask, I thought, and felt sick with guilt.

Mason sighed. "You know what the choices are. You've been around."

"No," I said. "I don't know. I mean yes, I've been around." I rubbed my eyes on the back of my wrist. "But he's—"

Mason watched me. His dark brown eyes seemed unrelenting.

"You don't understand," I said after a while. "This horse—"

I wanted to say: *He's mine.*

I wanted to say: *He has the mind of God.*

I saw that Mason was now deliberately looking away from me. "I can't explain," I said at last, on the verge of sobbing. "But I've never ridden another horse like him."

Mason banged the hoof testers open and shut. "I'm surprised you could ride him at all," he said. Then he gave me a pitying smile. "You're beginning to sound like Allie. Wouldn't listen to me about these legs. Said this horse was one of a kind."

I scowled at his tone.

"Smarten up, Nate."

I recoiled. My father had called me that, rarely anyone else.

"You're so damn grounded. That's why you're good." He touched my arm and sighed. "This is not a favorite part of my job."

"I'm not saying he's a pet," I snapped.

"I didn't say you did," he told me. "But Allie. My Lord, even at the end, she was saying she'd beat the cancer." He shook his head with distaste. "And I can't say Pierce didn't believe her. Or believed something. You're smarter than that," he said. "A lot smarter than that."

• • •

That night, I crouched in the corner of Twister's stall. I had as yet to tell Pierce about Twister, and I thought I had at least a few more days. I dug my elbows into my knees, massaged my jaws, my temples, and again and again went over the options.

We could medicate him every day for the rest of his life, reshape his feet with radical trimming and corrective shoes, and limit both his freedom and his work. He would never hack along the roads again. He would not be turned out to graze except when the ground was soft. The footing in the ring would have to be changed. Pierce would have to be willing to pay all of those bills, and I confess I thought that, because of Allie, I might be able to get him to pay for anything. Still, there was no telling how long the horse would hold up. He would eventually break down again. Or the medication would begin to destroy his liver.

Or Pierce and I could come to terms, and even if I never rode him again, I could take the horse with me when I left. I might never sit on his back again, but I could keep his presence in my life. Once I had thought of the world as empty, had thought it suited me. Now the idea terrified me.

The third choice I could barely bring myself to think about.

For three days, I agonized over telling Pierce. I had no idea what I would say, and I felt stupefied by my own blindness. How could I have missed what was happening to his legs? Each day I vowed I would not go to bed until I had spoken. But each evening, I avoided the house and went to bed without so much as having written in the barn journal.

Finally, on Saturday, Miriam asked why Twister was lying down in his stall.

I found myself looking at her. She had all the long bones and gawkiness that might one day turn her into a first-class rider. I didn't know. Like Vee, I thought bitterly, I never stuck around long enough to watch a young rider grow up.

"He's lame," I said.

Her face clouded.

"No use," I said. "What he has is degenerative. He'll never heal."

"Why not?" she demanded.

I led her into the office and on a sheet of paper drew a horse's foreleg from the inside: the lovely net of tendons, the intricate puzzle pieces of the bones. And underneath, a tiny fulcrum for the foot, I sketched in the navicular bone. In Twister's case, the little bone was diseased—pitted, inflamed, cracking, all its rough edges fraying the deepest tendon.

Miriam drew a loose hank of hair from behind her ear, began to chew it, and watched ferociously.

I told her that the damage could be slowed, but not reversed.

"I'm sorry," I said. Riding was a sport that included some hard truths.

I hesitated, then pulled the hair from her

110

mouth, put it back behind her ear. "I can handle the rest of the chores," I said quietly. "Would you like to groom him?"

"Can we just go look at it?"

I shook my head. "Nothing to see. It's all inside the hoof."

Her jaw began to tremble. "Will he die?" she asked at last.

"Not this morning," I snapped.

She whirled away then, and ducked into Prima's stall. I stood in the aisle, furious but guilty, then went after her.

"Miriam, these things happen. Come on," I said. "We have a hundred lessons to give. I need your help. I'm sorry."

She draped herself dramatically around Prima's neck and refused to look at me.

Fine, I thought. It takes more than long bones to make a rider.

As the first students appeared in the doorway of the barn, and asked in whispers what was wrong with Miriam, it came to me that, by the end of the day, every girl on the place would hear about Twister. I would have to talk to Pierce.

"What's navicular?" he said Sunday night.

He took the lesson money and stuffed it into an envelope lying on the bookshelf next to his chair. I could see that it still contained the lesson money from the week before and perhaps the week before that.

I found myself wondering again if someday

the feed store would stop delivering our grain or the farrier would refuse to come because Pierce was not paying the bills.

"Shall I deposit that?" I said.

"No. I'll get to it. You could sit."

I picked at a dirty spot on my riding breeches, then glanced at the books and school papers piled on the couch.

"Come on out to the kitchen," he said.

I had never been deeper into the house than the mudroom and the living room, and I hesitated on the kitchen threshold. A bulletin board just inside the door was strewn with photographs of a small fine-boned woman. She had hair as pale as Pierce's, and she rode with a deep, confident seat. There were pictures of her riding over fences, pictures of her next to, or still on top of, horses with prize ribbons fluttering from their bridles. One, of course, was Prima, who looked quite the star in her show braids and glistening chestnut coat. I moved a little closer, and saw a picture of her with her arms wrapped around the neck of a black foal with a crooked blaze and four white stockings. She was grinning just as if she'd won the lottery.

Pierce was at the stove, and before I realized it he was bringing me a bowl of soup.

"Sit," he said.

I stared at the bowl.

"Beef and lentil," he said. "I've gotten back to cooking. I was hoping you'd come down."

I sat, picked up the spoon, tried the soup. "It's good," I lied. I couldn't even taste it.

Pierce settled across from me, and I found

112

myself wishing he would take off his glasses so I could read the expression in his eyes without the twisted lens between us. He looked tired, but I wasn't even sure that was true.

"Aren't you going to eat?" I said.

"I'll watch." He glanced up at the clock. "My mealtimes are erratic."

He was so thin I wondered if he ate at all.

"So," he said. "Navicular." He jiggled a tea bag in a mug of hot water.

"What do you want to know?"

"Actually I don't." He dumped the tea bag in the trash behind him.

"It's degenerative," I said. "But for a while, maybe a long while, it's possible to treat it—" Then I stopped. "Oh."

He sat looking down into his tea.

I had another spoonful of soup.

"It's been ten months," he said. "Almost eleven. All along I've thought I might just as well be miserable. You know, suffer. Really suffer and then it would be over."

I kept putting soup in my mouth and swallowing it.

"Stupid horse," he said finally.

"He's lame," I said, setting down my spoon with a little bang. "Not stupid."

I pushed the bowl away, folded my arms on the edge of the table. We sat in silence, and I felt graceless and intrusive, felt more alone, more devastated sitting in this kitchen than if I had been sleeping alone in my cold truck parked somewhere along a highway.

"Well," I said, pushing back my chair as soon as it seemed remotely polite. "I should go."

113

"Don't," Pierce said. "Please."

I was already on my feet. I sat back down.

He looked up at me, then away. I still could not read his eyes.

"There's no rush," he said. "All you have to do is feed by seven."

I must have stared.

"Allie told me to find someone to start Twister."

I shuffled my feet under the table, held my breath. I'd heard all this before.

He studied the tea in his mug. "I think you should keep your promises to the dying. Even if they are half out of their gourd on drugs." He turned his mug this way and that, then stilled his hands. "Part of it I couldn't do." His face turned hard. "Didn't do. And now this."

I sat absolutely still in my chair.

He gave me a long, bitter look. "Obviously you're used to this," he said. "Dead horse, live horse—it's all the same to you." He wrenched his glasses off and wiped angrily at his eyes.

I would have liked to slap him. I would have liked to lay my head on the table and weep, to wail, to shriek, to ask how I could be used to something I found unendurable. I stood and jammed my hands into my pockets.

"What shall we do?" I managed to say, my voice soft with rage. I moved to the back door, paused with my hand on the doorknob.

Pierce stared out the darkened window.

"About the horse," I said quietly.

"You decide," he said, seeming no more interested than if we were talking about a stray cat.

● ● ●

I left Pierce sitting in his kitchen, and went up to the barn. For a while I simply stood outside and listened. I thought I heard some ordinary restlessness from Sheila; I'd left her in to keep Twister company through the long night. Oddly, despite her age, she seemed Twister's only true contemporary.

I went down the aisle and slipped into the office, closed the door, then turned on the light. Of course the horses knew I was there, but I didn't want to stir them up.

I sat for a long time at the desk, convincing myself that Alec was still back home somewhere. I imagined him in a sprawling mock colonial out near Black River Road. Then thought: No, he had more taste, and imagined him in one of the stately homes on Church Street. In one of John Casey's letters, he'd said houses in the historic district were now on the market for only about half a day. The realtors had waiting lists of buyers and held mini auctions over the phone. Then I thought: No, too pretentious for Alec. Maybe he'd rehabbed a place in Allentown.

I picked up the phone and called Bethlehem information. He wasn't in the book, but perhaps the number was unlisted and the operator would say so.

"We're sorry," said the tape. "We have no such listing."

I hung up, tried Allentown.
Same tape.
Then Easton.
Same tape.
Sorry, sorry, sorry.

115

Did it matter? I wasn't getting in touch with him tonight. For a moment, I considered calling John Casey, but I just snapped off the lights and went out into the darkened barn. I slipped into Twister's stall, wrapped my arms around his neck, pressed my face into the satin coat, and took long deep breaths as if I could inhale him into my soul.

Up in the cubby, I poured a drink and, for a little while, gave some thought to keeping watch through my window as the moon rose and set in the autumn sky. I could supervise the constellations as they wheeled through their ten-hour shift. But I was tired, and suddenly I felt too wise for the melodrama born of staying up all night, too drained for the pacing, for the heroism that comes of keeping watch into the wee hours of the morning.

Tonight, I found it all sickeningly suspect.

chapter eight

In the morning, I felt rested, although full of my night's dreams. I dressed, poured coffee, kicked my way into my boots, and, once inside the barn, flicked on the radio and set about feeding horses.

All of them were happy to see me. Even Twister craned his neck over the door of his stall, and for one brief moment, I let myself think that he was better, that I would be back in his saddle before noon, that I would feel his thoughts wrap around me. My chest grew tight, then loosened up again, and looking at the black horse, calmly eating his grain, I knew what I would do.

After feeds, I neither rushed nor hurried. It was Monday, the schoolies' day off, and Pierce would be late coming home because on Mondays he coached his debating team. I had plenty of time.

One by one, I led Galen, Prima, Lawrence, and Archimedes out to the pasture. Sheila and Twister I kept in. Then I mucked the barn, taking an odd pleasure in the pull of the wheelbarrow handles on the muscles of my arms, enjoying the smell of fresh bedding as I flung it around each stall.

As I worked in Sheila's stall, the mare seemed half puzzled, half perturbed that she was not out grazing, and that she was forfeiting her daytime status as dowager of the herd.

Twister, though, moved toward me each time I stepped into his stall. Strangely, although he'd always been a big horse, his height now surprised me; it was as if he had grown taller since I'd last stood next to him. He pressed his forehead to my chest, and, smiling like a fool, I rubbed his ears and smoothed his forelock. It embarrassed me that Sheila stood in the next stall, although, with what I had planned, I would have to get used to her.

When the stalls were done, I went into the office and made two calls. At the feed supply, they said yes, of course, no problem, seemed almost puzzled that I had called ahead. To Mr. Weirbachen, I admit, I had to do some begging and some lying, but finally he gave in and said, yes, okay, someone would meet me if I promised everything would be ready.

Even then, I did not rush. In fact, I could not rush, did not want to break the solemn but oddly celebratory spell the black horse cast on me. If he read minds, if he cast his thoughts toward me, then I thought that he was glad.

I put some tools into the truck and drove into town. At the feed supply, my materials were waiting. A lanky boy loaded them without question, I signed Pierce's name to the invoice, then headed back to the farm.

At the drive, I did not turn in, but followed the perimeter of the farm and turned up to the abandoned gate under the power lines. It was a metal livestock gate, and the loop of wire that held it shut had badly rusted. I broke the wire with my hammer, propped the gate open for Mr. Weirbachen, then drove up into the field.

This was Pierce's back pasture, the field where I believed Twister had spent his first summer and which Pierce had been allowing to stand idle. From here I had looked down across the low flat valley, had sat on Twister's back in summer twilight, had heard his thoughts come back to me about the deer exploding from the thicket.

I was already at work when I heard the pop-pop of the Weirbachen tractor. I had pried the rotted posts from the ground and, together with the broken boards, I stacked them in the back of the truck. Turning, I watched the tractor work its way up the hill. Then I waved my arms over my head.

It turned out that Mr. Weirbachen did not send one of the farmhands, but came himself. He backed the tractor around, drilled new holes, and, without my asking, stayed to help me set the posts and get the replacement rails cut to length and hammered into place. He worked with a quickness that might have seemed like irritation, except that his work was also careful and precise and that he stopped every now and again to ask me about Pierce and to inspect the view down out of the pasture. He took a minute and admired the rich green of his alfalfa fields, then pointed out his other land and sketched out his plans for rotating his grain crops for the coming year. He commented on the worth of Pierce's land. "Ach," he said. "If only."

"If only it were tended."

Mr. Weirbachen eyed me shrewdly, went back to work.

"I used to have a friend," I said. "Up in Schoharie County."

Mr. Weirbachen nodded.

"He used to tell me that all he ever wanted was to own one little piece of land." I paused for effect. "And all the land around it."

"Ach," said Mr. Weirbachen, his face twisted with a smile. "Thou shalt not covet."

When we were finished, he hoisted up the posthole digger until it rode behind the tractor like the tail of a scorpion. Then he hitched up the knees of his heavy farmer's jeans, with their triple-sewn seams, and swung up into the seat. He paused then, rammed the tractor into gear, and, before driving off down the hill, lifted an age-stained hand and wished me luck.

Puzzled, I watched him go. Then I remembered that I hadn't exactly told him the truth about the repairs to the fence line.

Back at the barn, I pulled my truck up to the horse trailer parked next to Pierce's garage. It had not been used since my arrival; I had gone nowhere. I backed the truck toward the hitch, and was about to line it up precisely, when I decided to look the trailer over first. There was no use for all the fuss if the trailer were out of commission.

The back doors opened easily, and one quick look told me things were fine. The rubber floor mats had been swept clean and scrubbed. The clips on the tail guards worked freely, the tie ropes were in place. Allie had been a good housekeeper. All I would have to do was fill the hay nets.

I went forward through the hatch, and was about to open the escape door when I saw a carryall lying on the equipment shelf. I hesitated, thinking first that I would take it into the barn and leave it in the equipment room. Then, realizing it might be a travel kit of some kind—various first-aid remedies, maybe some flares and flashlights and a can of WD-40—I zipped it open.

For a moment I just stared down into the bag.

On the top lay three horse-show ribbons: one red, one pink, one white. There was also a prize list, dated nearly a year ago. I opened the little flyer, and I saw neat check marks next to half a dozen classes—probably the classes she had entered. I looked carefully through the pages a second time, then at the backs of the ribbons, but she had not noted which horse she had been riding or which classes she had won the ribbons in.

I stood there in the trailer, thrown open for the first time since she'd wheeled back up this driveway hot and sweaty and at least a little bit victorious, and I thought how much, in just one year, was already gone and forgotten.

Then it occurred to me that she might not even have been the rider. Perhaps she had just been coaching one of her students. No, I thought, because a student would have taken the ribbons home, or hung them in the barn.

I poked a little deeper into the bag.

A wrinkled riding shirt lay in a ball, and there was a silk choker tie, and beneath that some granola bars wrapped in foil, a water bottle, and some vegetable artifacts that must have been carrots for the horse. I was about to stuff all these back into the bag and pack the ribbons, too, when I saw the name tag on the tie: Allie Kreitzer.

I lifted out the shirt, folded it gently, put

it back into the bag. Except for this, I thought, she'd tidied up before her death.

Sheila loaded easily, following a bucket of grain up the ramp. Once in the trailer, she took more steps than seemed necessary, as if testing the hollow-sounding floor. When she was settled, I clipped the tail guard behind her, tied her head, and she began pulling hay from the net and eating.

Twister, on the other hand, was less certain. As I suspected, he'd never before been on a trailer. I led him up to the ramp, let him have a good look, and waved the grain bucket just out of his reach. For the first time in my life, I knew that if a horse that I was loading decided not to get on, I would take no sterner measures. I would not call for help, I would not use a longe line to pressure him from behind. I looked at my watch, looked up at the sky, and decided I would give him an hour. Then we would turn back to the barn. I pressed my face into his neck and thought: It's your call.

Ten minutes later I gave up. What was the point? I unloaded Sheila and slipped a bridle onto her head. Then in the thin light of the afternoon, I wriggled up onto her back, caught hold of Twister's lead rope, and led him away from the barn. We were down the drive and out of sight of the house long before Pierce could catch us.

• • •

I knew it was wrong, but I didn't tell Pierce. If he cared so little that he didn't even notice that two of his own horses were no longer standing in the barn, well, then I didn't care, either. On Saturday, no doubt, the girls would force the issue. They would ask where Sheila was, and some little girl would be disappointed not to ride the sweet gray mare while she learned to do the posting trot.

But that still gave me time. Each morning I fed and grained the other four. I turned them out, mucked the stalls, then got into my truck and drove around the back of the farm with two buckets of grain balanced on the seat beside me.

Sheila seemed to miss the barn and her herd, and at the sound of my truck working its way up the bottom of the power line, she would whinny and come trotting toward the gate. Twister would always pause, standing watchful where he was—up along the tree line, down along the brook, grazing along the incline of the pasture. Then he would gather himself and come toward me, too, his head rising high and sharp each time his right fore touched the earth.

What grain I brought them was a mere token; the field was in fine shape and they were not working. They hardly needed sweet feed. But I needed to check on them, needed to see them coming toward me, needed to see Twister in possession of this field, bright-eyed, relaxed. I got a brush and hoof pick from the truck, checked their feet, kept up their coats. I always worked on Sheila first, then let her wander off so I could tend to Twister alone.

I was giving him time, I told myself.

A rest.

A chance to be just a horse.

A reward for all he had given me.

I brushed his coat until it shone blue-black, combed the burrs from his mane and tail, and I knew that I was lying.

Each morning and each evening, I went out to the pasture. I brushed, I sweet-talked, I visited. I tried to memorize the horse. I tried to imagine the sky empty of his silhouette. I practiced remembering the way warmth fell down around me when I stood under his neck. Once I even cried. The horse seemed calm and just a little distant. I told myself he didn't know.

Late Friday night, before I went to bed, I loaded grain in the truck for the next morning. My plan was to get up extra early and visit the horses in their pasture before I went to the barn to feed and to get ready for the first lesson at nine. At some point I would explain to the girls where Sheila and Twister were and that evening I would tell Pierce.

But the air turned bitter during the night. The frost was thick, my hands were cold, and I had had to rush back up to my apartment and dig through a box looking for a hat and gloves. As I headed out to the pasture, I was not worried about the horses: their coats were turning woolly. But I did worry about the ground: would it freeze before I was ready?

As I turned the truck up onto the power line, I touched the brakes with surprise. The horses were already down at the gate. I wondered why. Then I saw someone leaning toward them over the fence, offering them handfuls of treats. I inched the truck up the lane, parked it, took the grain buckets from the seat beside me, and got out. I was preparing my speech about the dangers of hand-feeding horses, especially strange horses that belonged to someone else. I figured it was a hunter scouting for game or a casual day hiker, but as I drew close to the fence, the figure turned and lifted a hand in greeting.

It was Pierce.

I slipped on the frozen grass, and the grain buckets banged together. Both horses began whickering, and Sheila bobbed her head and pawed. Ignoring Pierce, I stepped forward, ducked under the fence, and gave the buckets to the horses.

What's he going to do? I thought. Fire me?

I stood back from the horses while they ate and stared down at Twister's leg. It was still turned out, the weight resting lightly on the toe. While Sheila kept her head in her bucket, Twister ate as casually as ever, filling his mouth with grain, then raising his head while he chewed. I thought I could hear him wondering.

"I'm waiting for Fred," Pierce said finally.

I turned.

Pierce pulled a hand from his pocket. "I saw him down at the store," he said. "Yesterday morning. Getting gas."

I stared down at the ground and, through my heavy barn coat, felt his hand wrap around my arm.

"Mr. Weirbachen?" I said.

"We're going to scout a spot," he said. "Fred and I."

I stood absolutely still. His hand fell away.

"I've left you with too much," he said.

Before me, the black horse finished his grain. He moved off a pace or two, eyeing us as he grazed. My eyes filled with tears and suddenly his shape grew loose, his coat luminous.

Not yet, I thought. I'm not ready. It's not time.

Dully, I pointed up the hill. "Up there," I whispered. Then I moved forward, turned my back on Pierce, and pressed my face to the horse's woolly neck. His skin was warm, his heartbeat resonant and strong. Beneath my feet, the ground seemed iron hard.

In time I heard another truck, and Mr. Weirbachen's grumbling German accent.

"Ach, it's best," I heard him say.

Then it was quiet. I pulled my face away from the horse, and looked at my watch.

"When?" I said.

Pierce looked up the hill.

"I'm trying to help," he said sadly. "Mason called me, too," he admitted. "And chewed me out."

"Early," Mr. Weirbachen said. "Before church."

126

I could not look at either of them, but slipped past them under the gate and headed back to the barn to get ready for the lessons.

I fed the horses quickly, feeling guilty that only four of them had to do all of the day's work. When Miriam arrived, I could barely stand to look at her. I set her to brushing horses and went outside and pretended to arrange the equipment in the ring.

When the first car drew up, we were still getting the saddles on. When I glanced up to say hello, wondering how I would ever make it through the day, I dropped a girth and martingale in surprise. The three girls standing in the doorway were in costume.

One of them was wearing a long cape and a hat with pointed brim and a ridiculous plume. Another was wrapped in what looked like a winding sheet. The third was dressed as a cowboy. All three of them were shivering.

"Good Lord," I said, staring at them.

They giggled. Another car drew up, and two more girls got out in costumes. Even Miriam whipped an opera mask out of her coat pocket.

"Didn't you know?" she said. "We always do this."

"Trick or treat," said the girl in the cape. She blew her plume up out of her eyes and laughed. "And this year for once it's right on Halloween."

I had nothing for them in the way of treats, and I certainly was not in costume, but I did give up on the idea of lessons altogether.

How could anyone work on canter leads with a dress down to her ankles? Instead, they played tag, ran relays, rode with slips of paper under their knees, balanced cups of water while they walked and trotted. I taught them some monkeyshines, too, showed them how to click their heels over their horses' rumps and how to do skin-the-cats off the side of the saddle. I led them through all the games I had watched with such jealousy when Aunt Vee was indoctrinating me, but it was her exercises and her monkeyshines that the girls enjoyed the most. Even the older girls thought it was the best Halloween they'd ever had, and as the day wore on, I actually found myself laughing, rather hollowly at first, then later with more warmth. As I cleaned up the barn after the lessons, and got the horses ready to turn out, I found myself thinking of Allie, found that I was grateful to her for the saving grace of this tradition.

It was almost dark by the time I got out to the back pasture with the horses' grain. They greeted me eagerly. Sheila pawed, bobbed, and ate, then moved down toward the brook. Twister ate in his usual slower way. I leaned back against the fence and watched him. I did not throw my arms around his neck, or even warm my cold hands under his mane. It was as if I were enjoying the perverse luxury of having the chance to touch him and choosing not to, rehearsing for what it would be like tomorrow night when I would no longer have this presence in my life.

It turned full dark while I stood there. I pulled my collar up around my neck, and kicked my heels against the ground to warm my feet. The black horse grazed nearby, a little above me on the hill, and as the stars brightened above us, he made a horse-shaped hole in the night.

chapter nine

The next morning, the air was even colder. I pulled on extra socks and took my hat and heavy gloves the first time I left my apartment. My mind seemed numb, as if it had received some blow, and as I rushed up to the barn, I tried to remember if I had slept.

The little barn seemed half empty. The four remaining horses whinnied wildly for their hay and grain, sounding as if they had been locked in their stalls for days without food or water. Up in the loft, I counted the remaining bales, then threw hay down into the stalls. The horses quieted, and from downstairs all I could hear was the tearing of the dried grasses and the occasional ring of a hoof blow against a stall wall. I looked around the loft again, tried to guess when we would actually run out of hay, then climbed back down the ladder. I grained the horses, and they quieted completely. Then I filled two buckets with grain, grabbed two halters and two lead ropes, flipped off the overhead lights, and rushed out to my truck. I cursed myself for not just coming out and asking what they meant by early. Surely they had set a time, to get Mason and Fred Weirbachen there together.

Out in the back field, I fed the horses their grain and watched Twister eat in that casual way of his. I hate feeding horses by hand; it teaches them to bite. But I pulled carrots from my coat pocket and fed him those as well. As soon as she caught a whiff of them, Sheila shouldered in, and I hand-fed her, too. No telling how much longer she had left, either. Then I brushed the burrs from Twister's forelock and tail, whisked the dirt from his coat. I stood under his neck and tried to feel his thoughts shower down around me.

After a while, my feet grew cold, and it came to me to walk the horses down to the brook. Twister followed willingly through the trees and, for a few minutes, I leaned against his shoulder and watched the brook meander past. It seemed impossible that, within the hour, within minutes maybe, this presence next to me would be gone.

Without thinking, I lined Twister up next to a fallen log. Pulling the lead rope like a rein along his neck, I climbed up onto the log, and slipped my leg across his back. He stood there quietly among the trees, and I lay along his neck, basking in his body heat and imagining galloping up along the pasture slope. All at once, I put my leg into him. His head went up, we broke free of the trees, and judging from the happy bounce in his hindquarters, I knew it was entirely possible I would fall off. I turned up the hill, away from the gate. No one would know. He leaped into the canter, surging and jerking with every stride. I vaulted off even before I managed to get him to slow down.

Okay, I thought. So now he's tried to canter on three legs. For me. Because I asked. No other reason.

And then, leaning against him, I wept.

I had been trying to avoid one last thing about this horse: he thought so hard about me, I had not thought enough about him. I had barely asked and he had given and he had given and I had been so happy and so thrilled that I had never had the wisdom to stop him. Would he have had navicular without the way I had ridden him? Yes. But not now. Not this soon.

The bleat of a car horn cut the morning. Then someone called hallo and I could hear the sound of Sheila's hoofbeats heading toward the fence. A piece of heavy equipment popped-popped in the distance. Horses, they say, cannot imagine such a thing as the future. I closed my eyes and quieted my mind so that I might listen to Twister's. Maybe it was true: in this moment the big black horse seemed only content and calm.

I walked him far enough up the hill so that they could see us at the gate. Then I gave one big slow wave and turned the horse away.

The engine grew louder and closer, and soon, without looking back, I knew that it had come through the gate and was working up toward the top of the hill.

I led the black horse here and there, felt him loose and confident beside me on the lead. Sometimes he stopped, threw up his head, and studied the backhoe scuttering back and forth at the top of the hill. I chewed the inside of my lip and patted his neck. I didn't know how long it would take to dig, and in time I turned and walked back toward the gate. We cut down through the trees, out of sight of Mason and, I realized, Pierce, leaning on the fence. I pulled the horse to a halt and wrapped my arms around him.

I love this horse, I thought, and although I had not been allowed to choose the time, I vowed that I would hold him for the needles, vowed that I would talk to him and stroke him until he could no longer hear or feel. I prayed there would be no freak convulsions, no drug rebound, no horrors.

And then my mind turned numb and we came up out of the trees and walked over to the fence.

We chatted about the weather, of all things, and about how Sheila was doing since her illnesses. We looked up the hill at the backhoe. Pierce wondered if Mr. Weirbachen would make it to mass. Mason said he thought it was a saint's day for the German Catholics. Then the engine cut, and we fell silent.

Mason sighed, then nodded at me. I turned to walk the horse up the hill.

"No," Mason said. "I'll take him."

My hand tightened on the lead. I held my hand beneath Twister's nose. He wriggled his lip in my open palm.

"No," I said. "I will. He trusts me. I can talk him through it."

Mason switched his bag to his other hand. "Natalie," he said. "I'm going to bolt him."

I drew back.

"It's faster," he said. "Injections make the human feel better, but I've always believed they're harder on the animal."

He reached out for the lead.

I handed it to him.

All along I had been praying for a quiet death. And now Mason was going to shoot a spring-loaded bolt into Twister's brain and he would go as quickly as if he had been shot. All that would be missing was the rifle's loud report.

I pulled my arms into my chest and looked down at my feet.

I heard Pierce say my name, but I did not look up. Once I glanced behind me, and saw Mason with my horse's lead in one hand and a small black case in the other. Twister freely walked beside him, swinging his tail left and right. He was curious about the fuss, turning his head this way and that, taking it all in. Gamely, he worked his way up the hill. From the rear, I could see his legs hitching sharply with every step.

I let Pierce give me a leg up onto Sheila, and with my face set I turned down the lane and rode toward home. I listened to the steady clip-clop of her hooves along the edge of the macadam, and I thought I would know the exact moment the black horse went out of this world. But Sheila's whinnies tore the air and rattled me on her back. Each time she called out, I stroked her neck and tried to shush her. I was still listening with my heart for Twister's death when Pierce drove slowly past. He was bringing my truck back to the barn. Then Mason came up behind me, too.

He pulled his jeep to a halt, leaned across the seat.

"You okay?" he called through the passenger window.

I bowed my head and stared at the long curly waves of Sheila's yellow-white mane.

"You women and your horses," I heard him say. Then he cut the engine on the jeep, got out, and leaned his elbows on the roof.

"I don't know if I should tell you this," he said.

I sat with my head bowed. "Did something happen?" I said finally.

"No," Mason said. "That's just it. I asked him to walk up to the grave. He walked up to the grave. I asked him to stand. He stood. I asked him to hold still, he held still."

I made a fist in Sheila's mane, turned my face away, blinking hard.

Mason squinted down the road, drummed his fingers. "Maybe you were right. Maybe there was something about him." He slapped his open palm on the roof of the car.

Sheila snorted and stepped to one side.

"Cows," he said. "Cows I understand. Give me cows."

I glanced up. I was finding it difficult to breathe.

He smiled sadly, shrugged, gave me a little salute. "I don't know what to say." He got back into the jeep, started up the engine, then leaned again to the open window. "But I did tell Pierce to get his tail to the barn and give you a hand with the chores. And don't you go sneaking out of town."

Sheila and I clip-clopped up the driveway. It was seven forty-five. My plan was to ride past the barn and out to the paddock. I would simply take her halter off, and turn her out with the others. I let my legs dangle, and checked inside myself for some sense of cataclysm.

In front of the barn, I sat a while on Sheila's back. She was so old and swayed, I felt as if I were riding my own grandmother. From there I could see the paddock out back was still empty. I shook my head. Pierce didn't even know enough to turn the horses out before cleaning up the barn. I swung my leg and slipped off Sheila's back.

She whinnied to her herd.

One of them whinnied back.

I stamped my feet as we went in the barn, and Sheila's shoes rang on the floor.

How stupid I was. Pierce was nowhere in

sight, the horses were still in their stalls. All we do is put a horse down and once again he's beyond coping.

Suddenly I wished I'd thought to take a lock of Twister's mane.

And then I thought: It doesn't matter. Nothing matters. I'll clean up. And then I'll go.

Pierce was in the office, sitting at the little desk I'd cleared. His back was toward me, his face half turned away.

I stood in the doorway with Sheila's lead in one hand. I realized he had all my papers spread out on the desk before him.

How dare you, I thought. Then I kicked my boot toe on the threshold, cleared my throat.

He did not turn around.

"That's it for me," I said.

He waved at me over his shoulder.

"Go," I thought he said.

Then his voice came crisp and clear: "Mrs. Heilman? This is Pierce Kreitzer. Calling from the farm."

Jesus Christ, I thought. The lessons. In another hour the first of the girls would be arriving.

"Yes," he said wearily. "It *is* cold today. That's not why, but we're canceling all of today's lessons."

I stood transfixed.

"Next week?" he said.

For the first time, he swiveled all the way around and looked at me. He raised his eyebrows, put one hand over the mouthpiece. "Next week?"

I shook my head. "No. It's over."

He frowned.

"Mrs. Heilman," he said back into the phone. "Natalie and I will need to discuss that."

Pierce continued calling, and I led the schoolies out to the pasture. For a moment, I stood and looked at them. They were nothing without Twister.

Out in front of the barn, I heard a car pull up, a door slam.

Miriam.

I slipped along the outside of the barn and went up to my cubby.

Packing was a simple matter. The books slid easily into their carton. I dumped the drawers into one box, the bathroom things into another, kitchen things into a third. Finally, I began packing what lay on top of the bureau.

Gently, I wrapped Grandmother Baxter's teacup, which I still had not used for my coffee. I put the harmonica and the jewelry box in with Vee's letters and the photographs.

Then I can't help myself. I stand before the gnarled bureau, study my empty face in the graying glass. What next? I stand a long while. Not a single clear thought comes to mind.

I take the pistol into my hand. Heft it in my palm. Spin the cylinder. Load a few shells, spin the cylinder again. Then I lift the barrel to my temple, settle the black hole of the muzzle this way and that in the soft portal of my skull.

I wait.

Watch.

Notice that my head tilts left, away from the muzzle.

Notice that my eyes are flat.

Notice that my wrist is cumbersome and angled.

My finger jerks the trigger.

The gun flies up, discharges into the ceiling.

My wrist flaps. I should know better. Jerk the trigger, lose your aim. Stunned, I drop the pistol at my feet.

The room reeks of gunpowder.

I look into the mirror. Now there is something in my eyes: unmitigated terror. I stare into them. Then I look down at the gun, watch my toe sidle toward it.

Down below, I hear a door. I freeze.

Then a voice: "Natalie! Natalie? We heard a noise, and Pierce sent me to check."

I scramble for the gun, shove it into an empty bureau drawer, rush to open a window. My hands are icy, trembling. I cannot feel my face.

"I'll be down in a minute," I call.

Miriam, I think.

Miriam would have found me.

Part Two

chapter ten

I am in the eighth grade, sitting in Mrs. Boscawen's English class, reciting with my classmates a list of spellings, derivations, and definitions. Mrs. Boscawen is an old woman with an old method: she unscrolls new material from a long roll, reads it aloud to us, then makes us recite, beating time with her pointer. She tells us we are ignorami because we are no longer required to study Latin. With these recitations every Thursday, she intends to make up for the stupidity, the cheapness, the small-mindedness of the school board who voted Latin down to an elective.

She turns a page. Her face is caked with old lady makeup, her hair is bottle-black, and her gigantic hips are draped in a dull black skirt. Sometimes she tells us with what is supposed to be a smile that she knows we hate her, but that she doesn't care because we will be able to recite these lessons until we die.

Actually, she is one of my favorite teachers because she is so easy to send up. Alec, who sits in front of me, cannot even look at me until we are halfway down the hall after class. She is so old we are pretty certain she was an eyewitness to the stabbing of Julius Caesar.

—Et tu, Mrs. Boscawen?

We laugh until we snort.

Today our list is based on words with dual meanings. With my classmates, I half listen, and then, without paying much attention to the actual words, I repeat:

—Temple. T-*e*-m-*p*-l-e. Temple. From the Latin *templum,* or sanctuary. Also from the Latin *tempora* or *tempus,* portals of the skull.

Mrs. Boscawen smacks the podium. My classmates give an exaggerated jump. A snicker erupts somewhere off to my left. But my hand flies up to...my temple. The class fades away. I prod my finger, hold it still, close my eyes. So that was how Vee did it.

chapter eleven

The night of Twister's death, I lay on Pierce's couch. I had as yet to take off my barn clothes. I propped my booted feet on the arm of the couch and stared past them at the weekend news, then at some National Geographic special, the point of which seemed to be that the ancient Maya were far more bloodthirsty than had been thought previously. Were they? Bloodthirsty? Weren't they?

Pierce sat across from me in the armchair. He seemed wary but kind, and once it crossed my mind to wonder if Mason had given him directions about my care and feeding.

When the special ended, Pierce rose, went over to a set of shelves crammed with books, videos, and scrapbooks. Odd wood and wax figurines danced along the edges of the shelves: angels, medicine dolls, gargoyles, saints.

His finger ran along the backs of the videos. "Like to watch one? These were Allie's, mostly."

I shrugged. I wanted to ask about the figurines. Did she believe in those?

But I was afraid that he might say yes and that something nasty might rise from the bottom of my numb black soul. Nothing saves us, I might say. Didn't she know that?

Didn't I know that?

Pierce popped in a cassette and Fred Astaire went through his fabulous paces. Elegant, expressive, light.

Afterward, I said, "Is he still alive?"

Pierce doubted it, rewound the tape. "Another? There are plenty. Some world championships, too. Dressage, I think."

I shivered, sat up, looked for a blanket or an afghan.

"Cold?"

I rubbed my hands on my arms.

Pierce went to a closet beneath the stairs. I followed him.

"Quilt?" he said. "Wool blanket? My mother made the quilt."

"Blanket."

He freed it from a jam-packed shelf, shook it out, put it in my arms.

"Anything else?" he said with mocking grandeur. "Pillow? Heating pad?"

I stilled. Pointed.

"Well," I said dryly. "That's quite something."

In the corner of the closet stood a shotgun, muzzle up.

Pierce's eyes glinted.

"Something for everyone."

Back on the couch, I wrapped myself tight in the heavy blanket. Pierce made herb tea, spiked with a tiny bit of liquor I could just barely taste but not quite identify. I thought about asking what it was, but didn't. Somewhere during the late news, I fell asleep.

When I woke, the television was off, but a small table lamp remained lit. I lay still. Tried to conjure a sense of safety, tried to imagine taking off my boots, jeans, and bra and sleeping more comfortably. Instead, I tiptoed over to the closet, eased open the door. Looked, blinked, looked once more.

No shotgun.

I padded over to the window, stared up at the small light always left burning in the barn, and tried to imagine heading back up to the cubby.

I had pulled that trigger inches from my head. Now the pistol lay, loaded and rattling, in the empty bureau drawer.

Back on the couch, I lay flat, legs neat, arms folded across my chest. Then I reached down, pulled the blanket over my face, and held very still, breathing the warm flat air of my own lungs and, as I had done after Vee's death, tried to imagine how it felt to be dead.

And there in the stuffiness of my own breathing, I had the first new thought I'd had in years about her death: Vee had tended to the details.

• • •

By daybreak, I had been awake an hour. I moved to the armchair and huddled there under my blanket staring out the window. Outdoors it looked clear. Cold. Overhead, I finally heard Pierce.

He came down in corduroys, a shirt, an old sweater. His shoulders were fine and square, and his hair fell back from his face.

"I can call in sick," he said quietly.

And say what? Yesterday we put down the best horse that ever lived and breathed?

"You don't have to."

In the kitchen, he brewed coffee, pulled muffins from the freezer, offered me a plastic cup of yogurt. I was impressed by his efficiency and preparation. If someone suddenly had breakfast with me, we'd have to flip a coin over the leftover soup from the night before or split what remained of the Rice Krispies and pray that there was milk.

Then it turned out that the muffins were homemade. When I said something, Pierce's only response was to ask if I'd like him to do feeds.

"You must be dead."

"I'm not," I said. "I slept. I've been fed. You go on to school."

"Come back down to the house," he said. "Watch some videos. Read. There are beds upstairs. A bathtub. Help yourself. Call me at school if you want."

145

· · ·

Up in the barn, I hardly knew what to do. Water, hay, grain: I recited the horseman's adage. I filled buckets, threw hay, measured grain. Like an ancient sailor, I navigated with care, as if the floor of the world might give way.

The horses ate. I turned them out, passing Twister's stall on each trip. As I came back with the last halter in my hand, I stopped in his doorway.

All my years of efficiency lay before me. How automatically I'd flung the clean shavings into the corners, stripped away every bit of soiled bedding, raked the floor and powdered it with lime. And so it would stand, airing out, the clay floor drying completely, until some other horse came along to take his place.

Not likely.

I draped the halter willy-nilly onto a hook, and without sweeping the aisle, snapped off the lights and fled back down to the house.

I wandered blankly, back and forth, living room to kitchen, out to the mudroom and back again. I examined the photographs on the walls. More than competent. Downright stunning. I fingered Allie's books: *The Complete Training of Horse and Rider, Life After Death, The Bible, The Native American Spirit Guide, You Can Beat Cancer, When Bad Things Happen to Good People, The Pony Club Manual, Lameness in Horses, Goddess Power.* There were some medical books, too, and psychology and literature and some well-worn paperbacks. I scanned the videos. Mostly dressage. A John Lyons tape or two. A tape of the last Olympic three-day trials. I didn't touch the scrapbooks. In their midst was the program guide to the National Horse Show the last year it had been at the Garden. I paused. That was the last year I had been there, too. On Pierce's desk stood his computer: blank, of course. I scanned the linens and supplies in the closet: sheets, towels, trays, heating pad, lamb's-wool bed pad, blood pressure cuff. The door next to it was locked. Basement? Darkroom? I stood in front of the mirror in the hallway, jammed my hands in my pockets, watched myself breathe, wondered what I looked like with my eyes closed. In the kitchen, I opened cupboards. Not much food, but very serious cooking equipment: yogurt maker, rice cooker, well-sharpened knives, ceramic cookware. The freezer was well stocked, the pantry, too. Legumes, herbs, several kinds of rice, spices I couldn't identify, a small stock of wine. He seemed too thin to me, but obviously, should the occasion arise, he was well prepared to eat.

By the time Pierce came home, I was back on the couch, trying to read a history of bits and bitting. Pierce dropped his briefcase at the foot of the stairs, loosened his tie, kicked off his shoes.

"You didn't call."

I shook my head.

"Give me a few minutes," he said. "Then I'll do feeds."

"The horses are out."

"So?" he said. "I'll bring them in."

"The barn's a mess."

"You should see it when I take care of it. I had to clean up before you came for your interview."

He went upstairs, came back down. I had my eyes closed, listened to him leave the house, and then, almost too soon, come back again.

"Everything okay?"

He hung his jacket on a peg. Kicked off his boots.

"I really should go up."

"They're my horses."

He came into the living room.

"Any requests for dinner?"

I forced a smile. "I should go back to the cubby."

"Dinner first. It's better to cook for two."

"You weren't kidding about being German," I said, three nights later. I was staring down at a dinner plate deep in dumplings and gravy.

He nodded, patted his mouth with his napkin. The table was spread with a dark green cloth. The napkins were substantial.

I nudged my plate.

"The dumplings give me away?" He laughed.

"No," I said. "You believe food fixes things."

I poked a dumpling with my fork. What were those book titles? *Fifty Foods to Cure Your Cancer? Classic Comfort Foods?*

He smiled, almost shy. "I like to cook when someone else is here."

I pushed my plate away for good. "I'm sorry."

He immediately rose and took my plate. "Too much?" He picked up his own plate, too.

"Wait," I said. "Don't let me stop you."

He scraped both plates into the compost bucket.

"But aren't you hungry?" I said.

He hit the switch on the coffeepot, then reached into the cupboard for cups.

"But what's Pierce?" I said.

He gave me a puzzled look.

"If Kreitzer is German, what's Pierce?"

"English. Do you still want this black? You haven't eaten."

"Black is fine."

"Dessert?"

I made a face.

"Angel food," he said. "Store-bought, but good."

We each had a piece. The sweet vanilla dissolved on my tongue.

And then he began to explain that the food they ate while they were growing up had veered back and forth between English and Dutch.

"Dutch?"

"German."

"But you said Dutch."

Dutch, he explained, was how the English said Deutsche—which meant German.

"Okay," I said, half confused.

He grinned. "And when the Dutch—the Germans—said English, they didn't mean English as in London and the queen. They meant not German."

I shook my head. "I'm lost."

We sat and ate our nothing cake instead of our dinners and vaguely I listened to him explain the food. They ate English on Christmas and Thanksgiving and certain days of the week: roast red meat or roast poultry, vegetables, potato, maybe salad, maybe not, dinner rolls, maybe a soup, maybe not.

I could see he loved to talk about this.

"And what was Dutch?"

Dutch was simple: seven sweets and seven sours. No ups, no extras. A meal was planned the way one might balance an account. His mother joked about it, but the meal always came out right. His father joked about it, too, but always counted before they blessed the meal: the relishes, the sour vegetables and marinated meats had to balance out the candied potatoes, sweet pickles, breads, desserts.

"And what did you eat growing up?"

Cheese-shop cheese, bakery bread, greengrocer fruits and vegetables. Eggs. Canned soups. Hot milk and crackers. The occasional roast bird. Bachelor-father pot roasts.

I left my cake unfinished.

The next afternoon he called from school. How was my appetite?

Not good.

How about a clear soup and a fresh loaf of bread?

Fine.

Over the weekend, he stir-fried shrimp.

I picked at it.

The next night he broiled steaks.

One night it was tapioca pudding, stirred in a double boiler.

Then a small roast.
Sandwiches the next night.
Eggs Benedict.
Poached eggs.
Allie had eaten eggs easily, willingly. I rather liked them, too.
Broccoli quiche.
Mushroom quiche.
Eggdrop soup.
Tomato quiche.
Omelettes.
Eggs in hell.
Two and a half weeks passed. I fed horses, ate, stared out windows, wandered, fed horses, ate, made small talk, tried to read, slept—always on the couch and always with the lights on.

chapter twelve

One day I climbed into my truck. Put the key in the ignition, turned it. Again. Stomped on the gas, turned the key some more. Finally it caught. I sat there, looking through the frosted windshield, running the engine. After a while, I put my foot on the clutch and worked through the shift pattern: first, second, third, fourth, reverse.

I ought to drive it but did not. Where to? But when it occurred to me the tires could get out of round, I put it into reverse, backed it down the lane, along the house, then drove up to the barn, circled, stopped.

That same night, I thought about going up

to the cubby and digging through my photographs in search of what I knew did not exist: one of me on Hadley with Vee behind me in the saddle. I recalled the way she pinned her hair back, her twill jodhpurs and green jacket. What did her face look like? Strict, impish, relaxed, protective? Or mine? What I could see in my mind's eye was the erectness of our spines, the correct angle of elbow, knee, and ankle, me her smaller, parallel image.

I fed the horses, topped off water buckets, threw hay, and told myself that in the morning I would do a better job: empty and scrub buckets, sweep the aisle, houseclean the stalls. Pierce said nothing about the state of things, and when I did not cash my check, he took it to the bank himself, deposited it in my account.

Back at the house, while Pierce cooked dinner, I paced from one room to another. Again and again, I came back to the photos on the bulletin board, studied the images of Allie riding, Allie winning, Allie smiling, as if I might somehow see my own memories in them.

We sat down to chili and briefly it distracted me. "This is wonderful," I said.

"Secret ingredient."

I went back to the pictures. "Did you take all of these?"

He looked disappointed. "You don't want to know about the chili?"

I glanced down at my bowl. "It's good," I said. "Really. But I don't cook."

"Cinnamon."

"In chili? I can't even taste it."

He gave me an odd grin. "Allie couldn't taste what was in her food, either. Not that it helped."

I frowned.

He nodded at the bulletin board, changed the subject: "You must have pictures, too."

"Packed. But I've been admiring the ones in the living room."

He turned a little pink.

"Your work is beautiful."

He said nothing.

"It is your work?"

No response.

"The one by the stairs is my favorite."

It was not of a horse, nor Allie, nor the farm. Rather it was of a man on a city street. Perhaps poor, perhaps not. Flapping overcoat, mysterious bundle pinned beneath his elbow. Mysterious look on his face: secretive, defiant, glad. Pierce had caught him at a brisk walk. Behind him the city was reflected in rank on rank of windows.

"That one won a prize," he finally admitted. "Someone had it enlarged for me and framed."

"And you're doing what? Teaching media arts? Whatever that is."

He made a face. "And speech."

I laughed. "You hardly speak."

"I can if I have to."

"But why?"

He finished his chili, carried our bowls to the sink. "Wine? A little late, but—"

He poured two glasses, sat across from me, reached up, stretched, folded his arms behind his head.

"I came back for Allie," he said finally.

"Because she was sick."

He shook his head, tasted his wine. "Before that. When our parents were killed. Allie fell apart. So I came back, we settled all the money and the insurance and we bought this place. I was freelancing and convinced myself this was as good a home base as any." He shook his head, an old man looking back: "It's one thing to live on the cheap in a walk-up." He flung out an arm. "But this place? Horses, land, sister, mortgage, doctors—"

Outside it was dark. Pierce rose, turned off the brightest of the kitchen lights. The small bulb under the stove hood cast a mild glow and deep shadows around the kitchen.

"And then she got sick."

He closed his eyes. When he opened them, he looked blank.

"You're very generous," I said, regretting I'd once thought him such a jerk.

He shrugged. "I got something, too. I got to know my sister. How many people get to say that? We had a deal—I got some terrific shots."

Of what? Cancer? Then I thought: Could be. If he's the real thing.

I tried to drink some wine, but choked on the fumes. I'd known as much of my sister as I'd been able to bear. How she'd monopolized Potts's attention. If only she would do her work, he'd say. If only she would do her work. And the piano did seem to steady her. Or at least distance her, which was all I wished for: Lucy downstairs for long hours in a practice room, Lucy on the train to Philadelphia, Lucy up late going over scores with Potts. I recalled a recital, her first in Philadelphia: the auditorium not quite full, promising pianists being a dime a dozen. The lights fall, the spotlight waits. A tall slender girl steps into it. She wears dark blue, with sequins. I grab Potts's hand. He crushes my fingers. Polite applause. She plays Chopin. Stormy applause. A solitary bravo. Potts kisses my cheek. Lucy bows, again, again, again, too far away, too glittery to be kin.

Tears welled in my eyes. I coughed.

Pierce made as if to rise.

I waved him off. "But you could leave now," I sputtered. "Sell up and go. Get back to your real work."

He shook his head, then stared out into the dark.

"Forgive me," I said. "You don't need my advice."

He looked at me, his face full of pain and anger. "I do my work," he said bitterly. "The best of it has no market. What's left is third rate. There's little in between."

I wiped my eyes. What did I know?

"You win," I said. "God knows I'm safe from the hazards of talent."

Pierce stared.

"My sister was quite gifted. My father was thrilled that I was not."

"But you're good."

I held up a hand: "Good, skilled, serious, hardworking. No gift. But you—"

"I'm fine."

"But think of it," I said. "The timing's perfect. You won't get much selling horses at this season, but you'd save a fortune on hay and grain all winter."

He shook his head.

"That's what costs," I insisted.

"What would I have left?"

"Maybe you have to give something up. Maybe everything."

I touched the lip of my glass. "Maybe I should tell you about my sister."

My words stunned me, but suddenly I wished to make the effort, if not for my sake then for Pierce's. I looked across at him, watched him top off the wineglasses, watched him settle in, eager and relieved to hear someone else's story.

I tried. I really did, but I could bring myself to tell only parts of it: About the piano and her wildness, about marrying poor besotted John Casey for the wrong reasons. About watching Potts weigh the risks of encouraging her gifts and at the same time taking great care to guide John Casey on what should have been a safer, more secure path. But I could not tell about my father falling ill or her taking a leave from the conservatory to nurse him or the way she began taking medication as if she were ill, too. By the time Potts died she was on sedatives, then more and more drugs as time wore on. Illness or medication kept her from her work when work might have eased whatever ailed her. And I could not tell about her death, either, although I somehow wished to warn him. She had died of an overdose, either deliberate or accidental, during a change of medication.

The doctor had said that such deaths were not uncommon; there were rebound effects, dislocation. Mac Vorhees, in a letter, had speculated that the meds change had been poorly supervised.

As if it had ever been possible to supervise Lucy.

We cleared up the kitchen, watched a news program, then turned it off so Pierce could correct some papers. I pointed my face down in the pages of Allie's copy of Podhasky, although I could not quite read it.

After an hour or two, Pierce took a break and asked if I would like to see some other photos. Sure, I said, thinking he meant serious work, but instead he pulled some albums from Allie's shelves.

It was fun to look at the school horses when they had been under her care, and I recognized some shots of kids I had taught over the summer. Another album was skimpier: pictures taken at the riding school she had attended in Virginia. Then I opened the third. On the first page was an enlarged picture of Twister as a foal: all knees and hocks and wispy baby coat. I closed the album, handed it back.

"Sorry," he said. "I should have checked."

"I could try another."

He regarded the shelves. "They just get worse. One is full of pictures I took for Allie after she was housebound—everything I could think of she might miss." He laughed. "Even the manure pile."

He turned quiet for a moment. "I wish you could have met her."

I said nothing.

He reached for another album, tapped its spine, then let his hand fall. "And this one," he said. "Kills me. They're pictures she took, some from the windows, what she could see. I have a lot of lenses, so there are some good shots. Then stuff around the house. You can see her going—less and less range. You look at those pictures and it's like dying yourself."

"Then don't look," I said.

Pierce nudged the backs of the albums into a neat line on the shelf. "She might have made a good photographer. Although I think you have to love your subject somehow. Not like it, necessarily. Let it govern your breathing."

He glanced over his shoulder and apologized. "Shop talk. You got me started."

I drew my feet up under me, prepared to listen, wondering if it would be a kindness to say again that he didn't necessarily belong here.

Pierce stood, leaned against the bookcase, studied his prize-winning photo. "It's not for nothing they call it taking pictures. *Take*."

I nodded at the man in the photo. "He should be honored."

Pierce eyed me. Then, out of the blue, he said, "Thanksgiving's coming. What would you like to do about it?"

"Ignore it."

"Really?"

His voice was dry, as if what I had suggested

were a sheer impossibility. But we hermits in the horse world have the luxury of ignoring all the holidays we like: horses eat, drink, and dirty stalls every day of the year.

"I hate Thanksgiving," I snapped.

I felt a little stunned. This surge, this bitter angry surge.

"I can't imagine skipping it," he said. "That's so—"

"Suit yourself," I muttered. "Make a turkey. That's right, isn't it? Turkey?"

Pierce pressed for a reason, a story to explain my sudden mood, but I shook my head, got up, went out to the kitchen, helped myself to more wine. No more stories, I told myself. I wasn't good at sharing them.

The last Thanksgiving, Vee does not come to dinner. She never does. Because she is unmarried and has no family of her own, she works every holiday.

—But I'm your family, I remind her at every opportunity.

—No children, they mean.

—But I'm a child.

—Nate, says Potts.

But John Casey does come that last year. He is Potts's shop assistant and, without asking permission, Lucy has invited him. Potts hesitates, wondering what mischief Lucy might be up to, then says all right, we can hardly disinvite him. And anyway, we all like John Casey, a pale blond boy from Maine, with fine hair and huge hands and feet and a huge forehead. He is studying music at Moravian College, although Potts is worried that John Casey, unlike Lucy, doesn't have what it takes. He's already an organist but in a little church of no musical consequence, and Potts encourages him every day: to teach, to learn to run a business, to repair instruments. Potts decides the invitation is logical and kind, and tells me holidays should be shared with the lonely.

I think it is exotic. Lucy gets the crazy idea of setting each of our places with a different kind of china. We use scads of silver and I find the meal quite thrilling although John Casey spills his water, drops the gravy boat.

Afterward all four of us wash dishes, then John Casey and Lucy sit in the kitchen drinking coffee while Potts and I curl up on the couch. Sleet pats at the windows. Potts reads, pulls an afghan over me, taps sleepy rhythms on my arm. I press my ear to his chest.

In time, Lucy walks John Casey downstairs to say good night.

I doze.

Potts says:

—I'll have to talk to that sister of yours.

I murmur.

He says that all the time.

When Lucy pierced her ears with a darning needle and bleached her hair white with peroxide. Or when she got caught clinging to the back platform of a slow-moving freight crossing Third Street. Or taught dirty words to the junior choir instead of the doxology.

I fall asleep.

The phone rings. Potts lifts me off him, goes to the top of the stairs, calls for Lucy, then picks up the telephone. I snuggle deeper under the afghan and when Potts returns he has to wake me.

—That was Vee.

I rustle.

—Nate, he says. She's hurt. She broke her leg.

—She's at work, I murmur.

Vee is a nurse at St. Luke's.

—There was an emergency on another floor and she ran for the stairs and slipped. The floors were wet because of everybody's boots. All the visitors for Thanksgiving.

Weeks pass. I fret for Vee, make cards for Potts to take to her. Then one day he tells me to get my coat and we walk the four blocks from our apartment to our garage.

Potts backs our old gray coupe out into the alley. A silver plume rises from the tailpipe. My father nods and I walk the doors shut, then climb back into the car.

We swing out of the alley, turn onto New, then down Church past the old pale stone Moravian buildings: Bell House, Gemein House, Brethren's House. A single white candle burns in each window.

The seat scratches the backs of my legs. I pull my kilt down as far as it will go. On stretches of cobblestone, I sing out a note and the bumpy street turns my voice vibrato.

—You're flat, Potts says, and smiles.

On the south side, streamers of lights are slung across the streets. Gold and silver garlands line the windows of the stores. There are fewer wreaths than on the north side, and more of the new aluminum Christmas trees hung with blue satin balls. Spanish carols blare from a grocery store, and I know not to stare at the people on the sidewalk: the old ladies with their thick square ankles and their babushkas, the young men in their tight trousers, the Lehigh boys in their white button-downs and brown jackets.

Outside St. Luke's I am left waiting in the car. When Potts finally comes back, he huffs, his glasses fog, he pats his chest.

—Where's Vee?

He points, then starts the car, and we drive around a circle, pull up under a roof, and there is Vee, sitting in a wheelchair with her cast sticking out before her. A blanket covers her lap.

On the way home, it begins to snow. Light pellets of it tick against the windshield.

Vee admires the Christmas lights, and says it is wonderful to be out. She thanks my father for inviting her, and when she says she is glad to hear she will be sleeping in the box room because then no one will be put out of their room, I turn and lean over the back seat.

—You'll be between me and Lucy, I announce.

I watch her riding sideways, her back against the door, her cast lying the length of the seat. In the waning light, I see that her hair

has grown long and shapeless. Each time th[e]
car turns or stops, her long thin hands grip
each other hard, and her waist takes up the
motion, just as if she is in the saddle.

On Christmas morning, Vee sits enthroned on
the couch in a heavy green robe. A Christmas
ball dances from each earring
    I open Vee's gift to me: a note promising a
riding jacket and new jodhpurs.
    —Too much, says Potts. Jodhpurs, maybe,
but she doesn't need a jacket.
    —Yes, she does, says Vee. Riding is an ele-
gant sport.
    I look up at her, queenly, lively, despite her
heavy cast and pale skin. Her simple presence
brings us gifts: hilarity, graciousness, light.
    —Don't spoil my girls, warns Potts. He
pats my arm. I lean toward him and let him
kiss my temple.
    Lucy opens Vee's gift to her, then holds it
up: a cunning transistor radio in a leather case.
The smallest I have ever seen.
    Irritated, she hands it to me.
    —I don't want it, she announces.
    Vee watches her calmly.
    —But I thought music was your life.
    —Not on the radio, Lucy sniffs.
    It's true. We get only news and weather
over the radio. Our music is on scores or on
recordings. Or, more usually, live.
    Anger and understanding war in Potts's
eyes.
    —Lucy, he says, his voice full of warning.

163

I snap on the radio.

Potts nods toward the stereo. Haydn plays.

I turn the volume low, hold the radio up to my ear.

Disgustedly Lucy whisks through the empty wrapping papers.

I see that she is on the edge of a storm and I can't help myself, and begin giggling with fear. She explodes.

She is not so much my sister as she is a force of nature. She is like the lightning in the fine glass tubes at the Franklin Institute, or the heavy gold pendulum, powered by something as mysterious and elemental as the rotation of the earth.

Lucy stalks out of the room and the apartment falls silent. The bathroom door slams.

Potts looks at his watch.

—Church in ninety minutes, he says, as if we'll be lucky to get into the bathroom to get ready.

I am just about to ask if anyone would like to try my new game, when Potts says:

—Maybe that was it. Her last stunt.

He gets up, apologizes to Vee.

Every time he says that, I wonder what he plans to do with her. Give her away? Send her to the conservatory and tell her not to come home again? But I watch him leave the room and I know that he is going to reason with her. I've overheard this same conversation a hundred times.

He will tell her why he must be strict with her. Or that being talented is no excuse for

bad behavior. Sometimes he says he's so
that she has lost her mother or he plea
with her to understand that he is doing th
best he can.

I am only eleven, but it does not escape my
notice that he never says any of these things
to me.

Vee pats the couch, and I perch on the
edge of the cushion.

—I hope he lets me have the jacket, I
whisper.

—What's going on?

I shrug.

—It's just Lucy.

chapter thirteen

I got ready for Thanksgiving by calling
Miriam's mother. Immediately she asked if
it were true, as Miriam had said, that I had
stopped teaching because a horse had died?
Her voice seemed full of questions, innu-
endo: Could someone care that much about
a horse? And still be considered sane?

Clearly, although she allowed Miriam to ride,
encouraged her even, she didn't begin to
comprehend this horse stuff.

"He didn't die," I said. "He was put down.
It's—" I chose my words. "It's something
you have to get used to. In the horse world."

I made my proposal to her concerning
Miriam. What I had in mind was Thanks-

...ng morning. It was too cold for regular ...sons, but I thought Miriam would enjoy one ...st ride. I lied: as a thank-you, I said.

What I really wanted was to force myself back up onto a horse, and I didn't think I could do it alone. What's more, I felt terrible that, under other circumstances, Miriam would have found me with half my head blown off.

Miriam's mother hesitated. Not on Thanksgiving. Then she decided that the house would be so hectic that one child less couldn't possibly make a difference.

For the next few days, I forced myself to spend more time in the barn. I curried and brushed the horses. I clipped their bridle paths so their heads would look neat but I left the hair growing in their ears for warmth. I made a note to call the blacksmith to pull shoes for the winter, then trimmed their fetlocks so that when bad weather came they would not get balls of ice in their feathers or cracks down their heels.

I did not ride. I dusted off all the tack. I combed manes and tails. I leaned against Galen, wrapped my arms around Sheila's neck. She seemed to have more sag in her back these days, more old-lady cowishness in her hocks, but if she died these were just the harbingers—not the things that would actually do her in.

Sometimes I wandered up and down the aisle like a visitor. Often I touched things, as if they might somehow rouse me: the satin stems of hay, the cold metal of the hosepipe, the light dimples of a pigskin saddle. And I would pause, feeling with my heart. The barn was

empty of the big black horse, but the wo
was not. Somehow I had expected the univer
to explode, had expected a sundering th
very moment the stainless-steel bolt sprang
through Twister's brain. But I leaned in the
doorway of his bare stall and sensed not just
sorrow but the black horse, too. I would wait
until his presence left me, and when it did,
I would know what to do.

Miriam arrived at ten Thanksgiving morning.
She stamped her feet in the cold, and Lawrence
looked over his stall door and whinnied. She
took a shoe box from under her arm, thrust
it at me, then went immediately for a grooming
kit. I lifted the box lid, folded back the tissue
paper, and peeked inside.

"They're beautiful," I said, and with a
gentle finger touched the precise and intricate folds of origami flowers: a lily, a rose, something resembling a daisy.

Miriam blushed. "My mom said you would
like them."

"Did you make them?"

She nodded. "They're for your table. I
make them every year for place cards."

"Come on," I said, and led her into the office.

Pierce had made us a thermos of hot chocolate. I poured two cups, handed one to her,
then admired the flowers again. That Miriam
had made them for me was both touching and
surprising.

I leaned on the edge of the desk, and
sketched my plan. The horses needed exer-

e, but it was so cold and they had been anding around for so long doing nothing, ny of them might be silly and excited. We would start in the ring to give them a chance to settle down, and then if they were sensible we'd go out for a hack. If we stayed warm enough, we could each ride two horses, Miriam the calm sedate ones, me the ones more capable of high jinks.

Miriam stood listening, smiling. She seemed taller, more adult, and I told myself she was easier to like alone. Again, I fingered a paper flower. Her hair was drawn back into a pony-tail, and she stood with her chin tucked into the puffy collar of her down jacket. Nervously she joked about how big her thighs looked because she was wearing long under-wear beneath her breeches.

"Will you be warm enough?"

I had dug out my insulated paddock boots, heavy leather chaps, and thermal gloves.

"I think I'm wearing ten pairs of socks," she said.

I said nothing. If that were true, her feet would freeze, crammed into her boots.

We emptied our cups and went out to groom. I asked who she would like to ride: Galen or Archimedes? Sheila was finished for the year as far as I was concerned, I wasn't sure of Lawrence in the cold, and Prima would probably be too wild for her.

"But Prima's my baby," she said.

I shook my head. Then I thought, this is her day, too.

"I don't know," I said. "Horses change in cold weather."

I saw the look of disappointment on her face, and relented. "You can groom her if you like. We'll start there."

We cross-tied Galen and Prima in the aisle, and soon I noticed Miriam's grooming was keeping exact pace with mine. I picked hooves; she picked hooves. I curried Galen's shoulder for just so long; she curried Prima's. And so I eyed my watch and led her through a classic thirty-minute grooming: hooves, body, legs, head, face, ears, mane, tail. Besides, it would warm her up. I remembered one old boss who'd insisted that we groom in shirtsleeves even in twenty-degree weather: if you were doing your job, you'd be plenty warm.

As we worked, I discussed the ins and outs of working Prima. The first thing the mare would need was a longeing in the ring to get the bucks out.

Miriam nodded.

"You wouldn't get to do that." No way was I letting her hold a longe line for the first time on a cold morning with a rowdy horse.

"Honest," I said. "Why don't you ride Galen and I'll start out on Lawrence?"

Maybe it would be good for me to have my first ride since Twister on a horse so thoroughly absentminded.

"But I'd like to see it."

I glanced up sharply.

"Longeing," Miriam said. "I've read about it."

I crept around Galen's shoulder, spied on her, busily brushing out a dull spot on Prima's flank.

"Where?"

"I get books from the library. I forget which one."

"I didn't know that."

"I read in study hall," she said, switching her brush to the other hand. "Or before I go to bed."

I sighed, then said, "Okay. I'll longe Prima and you'll watch. It's something that should be done and someday—" I hesitated. "Someday you'll need to learn how."

And so I put up Galen, and sent Miriam for Prima's saddle. The mare snorted at the jingle of the girth buckles and tap-danced sideways. I stood patting the mare's neck, but otherwise let Miriam struggle through it. I showed her how to figure-eight the stirrup leathers through the irons so the stirrups wouldn't come free while Prima longed, then we buckled boots around the mare's ankles to protect her if she happened to kick herself. I let Miriam slip on the bridle, but when she was finished, I took the reins myself, and handed the longe whip and tape to Miriam. The whip slipped from her hand and Prima spun in a circle and flung up her hooves.

"Careful," I said.

Miriam's eyes were huge. "Sorry."

We went into the ring. The mare posed, then gave an earsplitting whinny, as if she had suddenly found herself alone on the tundra. Someone in the barn whinnied back.

I did up the reins, and told Miriam that although there were plenty of ways to longe, I preferred the simplest: a direct rein attached to the inside of the bit. Then I sent her to close the gate and stand outside the ring.

"But I want to help."

"Outside," I said. "Stand somewhere I don't have to worry about you. This horse hasn't worked in weeks. It's cold and she's alone."

She scowled, the old Miriam again, then flounced a few steps away. Suddenly she became her more grown-up self once more and walked, hands jammed in her pockets and head up, to stand outside the ring.

I started the mare to the left: rein in my left hand, whip in my right.

"Watch," I called.

I asked the mare to walk.

She arched her neck and eyed me.

"Walk," I said again. I lifted the whip behind her, a gentle motion as if I were conducting an orchestra.

The mare exploded in a long series of sunfish bucks. Miriam stepped back from the rail. I bent my knees and guided the bucking horse in a circle.

"All right," I called. "All right."

Eventually Prima gave up corkscrewing, came down to a high winging trot. Again I asked her to walk. She stretched her neck, blew a little.

"Goose," I said. "Now walk."

She tried. She would walk a few strides, convince herself she had seen or heard something, then shy or buck or break into a trot.

171

"Notice this," I called to Miriam. "I keep her moving forward at all times. When she stops is when she gets into trouble. That's rule one: go forward at all times."

For people, too. Or so I had always thought.

Eventually, Prima settled down. Her paces were longer, more regular, less high and wild, and I had the chance to explain to Miriam that Prima was responding to what she heard in my voice and what she saw of me and my whip from the corner of her eye. I tensed my voice; Prima's back hunched. I got in front of her eye; she whirled and stood looking at me. I lowered my voice and my hand; she settled down.

Finally I let the mare walk. She was blowing a little; great plumes of dragon steam came from her nostrils and caught in the morning light. Her old ballerina attitude had come back into her stride, and she reached down and stretched her back.

"She's gorgeous," Miriam called.

I studied the mare. She had a head I didn't quite like, and she got by more on attitude than on skill or grace. Still, the slanting November sun picked up the red-gold highlights in her coat. To me, she was just another okay horse, but I knew that, to Miriam, Prima was a golden mare.

I halted the mare, took a breath, and against my better judgment, gave Miriam her choices:

We could put Prima up and ride two of the others.

Or...she could try to longe the horse herself.

Or...she could sit in the saddle and do exercises while I longed the mare.

Miriam waited. Her longing reached me all the way inside the ring. I looked back at the mare. She seemed quiet, more or less.

"Or," I said, "you can get on and ride her around the ring."

Vee, I thought, would never have given me a choice.

Miriam was already slipping between the rails of the paddock and coming toward me.

"Quietly," I said. "Remember the performance you've been watching."

I coiled up the longe line and stood by. Knowing I was watching like a hawk, Miriam was precise in everything she did: she checked the girth, measured the stirrup leathers against her arm, held the reins. She settled her toe in the stirrup, bounced, swung up. The mare immediately stepped forward.

"Ah, ah, ah," I said.

Miriam gave me a guilty look.

I grinned. "We'll let it go this time. Everything else was picture perfect."

Miriam beamed, fiddled with her reins, wiggled her feet.

I took off a glove, stroked Prima's neck, felt the tension in her muscles. I gestured around the ring. "We'll use just this half. Walk a little, then trot. No canter. I want to see almost constant figures."

Miriam looked blank.

"Circles, serpentines, turns, figures of eight. Keep her busy."

I was beginning to regret having let things

get this far. What was this sudden urge to make Miriam happy?

She patted Prima's neck. "She'll take care of me."

I wanted to tell her not to count on it.

She rode away, and I could see the mare was mostly quiet. She shied twice, but Miriam recovered easily each time, and although I studied her face as she rode close to me, what I saw were pride and excitement—no particular fear.

Quietly, I called directions to her—a little more inside rein, heels down, deep breaths. Always I kept her near me, and kept on talking. Both girl and horse were steadied by my voice. What fears I had I kept well buried. Miriam had no need to know how nervous this was making me. And for the zillionth time I wondered about fear. Did it keep us safe? Make us vigilant about dangers? Or did fear itself trigger disasters that might otherwise not take place?

Meanwhile, Miriam kept the mare at a steady trot. She made some halfway decent figures of eight. Her shoulders were light and square, her legs long and correct, and she kept Prima looking in the direction she was traveling. Seen from a distance, they made a nice silhouette. I hated to see young riders grow attached to particular horses. You learned to ride well by sitting on all the odds and sods, the flakes, the plugs, the clumsy and the gifted. But Miriam and the horse were actually quite suited to one another.

In a while, I spoke less and paced more. I

rammed my hands into my pockets. Finally, I looked at my watch and called for Miriam to walk and after a few minutes more called her toward me.

She halted proudly.

"That's it," I said.

I didn't want the mare to get sweaty under her woolly coat.

"But we just went in a circle." A whine crept into her voice.

"Miriam," I said gently. "This is what people do when they school. Not always, but sometimes. So give the mare a pat, let's see a nice dismount, and we can get on two more."

I thought we'd pressed our luck long enough and, I admit, I was anxious for my turn.

I stroked the mare's chest.

Miriam threw the reins down, dug her fists into the mare's withers. I saw that she was going to do a full military dismount: swing both legs high over the mare's rump, click her heels, land feet together, knees bent, facing forward. It wasn't necessarily the choice I would have made on a day like today, but when you're young, it's a fun and flashy way to get off a horse. After about thirty, it's a little hard on the knees and feet.

Absently, I reached forward to hold the reins. Then, just as Miriam's legs were in full swing, a little gust of wind kicked up. The mare stepped sideways, and Miriam's heel whacked her in the delicate hollow just in front of her hip. The horse squealed, her head shot down, and even with me hanging on to the reins, her back hooves flashed up. Miriam shot over the mare's right shoulder, hit the ground, rolled flat.

There is always a terrible moment when a rider hits the ground—a silence, a stillness, a waiting. Is there breathing? Motion? Sound? Life?

Without thought, I snatched the mare's reins, led her clear of the girl lying on the frozen ground. The mare pranced, spun, snorted, posed.

The two of us stood watching, and in an instant Miriam was struggling to stand.

"If it hurts," I called. "Don't get up. Just sit."

She was cross-legged now, rocking forward, head down, moaning. Her left arm clung to her right.

I stepped a little closer.

"Miriam," I said quietly. "Can you look at me?"

She looked up, blinked, looked down again.

"Can you tell me if anything hurts?"

Besides your arm, I thought, but I didn't say it. I had to know if she could register it.

"I can get up."

I was grateful to hear her speak, and before I could stop her, she managed to stand. She dropped her arm, squinted, grabbed her arm again. Making a face down at her feet, she took a wobbly step toward me. Then she reached for the stirrup. "I'm getting back on. You have to get back on."

Inside, I felt a shearing. The low register was the dead deliberate calm that overcame me in catastrophes: always able to dial the number for the ambulance, always able to pick up the fire extinguisher, to give orders to grooms, to fill the hypodermic. But now there was a high, horrifying counterpoint: I was alone out here with an injured kid and it was all because I had been dumb enough to try to make her happy.

"Not so fast," I said, and asked her if she knew where she was.

"With you."

I asked her the day of the week.

Nothing.

I held up a finger and asked her to follow it.

She looked irritably at the ground. "It's too bright."

"Miriam," I said, my voice level. "Prima has to go back to the barn."

"I want to get on." Her voice was downright cranky.

"I'm sorry."

I ran the mare's stirrups up, left the longeing equipment where it lay outside the ring, and headed for the barn. Miriam scuffled along to my left. I longed to reach out and take her by the arm—but I knew better than to touch someone who'd just fallen off a horse.

In the barn, I hustled Prima into her stall, snatched off her bridle and saddle, dumped them in the tack room. I was just eyeing the barn phone, when Miriam said, "I fell off, didn't I?"

Thank God.

I nodded. "First time?"

She didn't know.

In the house, Pierce was putting up a second thermos of hot chocolate and frosting a plate of hot cross buns.

"I was just coming up," he said.

I touched Miriam's shoulder. "She's hurt," I said. "She could use an ice bag and I need to use the phone."

Miriam's mother was amazingly matter-of-fact. Her dinner preparations were at a good stage to leave. About the injury, all she said was: "We discussed that this could happen."

I turned my back on Miriam, walked the phone across the kitchen, lowered my voice. "I'd like to call an ambulance."

The idea of driving a hurt kid alone to the hospital gave me the willies. I well remembered one of my own trips to the hospital after I'd fallen and had been caught in the horse's hooves. I was in the back of the ambulance, we passed over a railroad crossing, my broken ribs suddenly grated and I could no longer breathe. There was something to be said for having a team of paramedics hovering over you, oxygen and expertise at the ready.

Miriam's mother thought that was a bit much. She asked exactly what I thought was wrong, and when she heard that it was probably a broken wrist and a concussion, she insisted I simply drive her to the hospital and she would meet us there.

We made our way to the truck: ice bag, thermos, Miriam walking a little better, though clearly her arm was hurting. I helped her up, went around to my side, buckled her shoulder belt, then mine, and suddenly wished I'd thought to back the truck around before she got into it.

Miriam was still keeping her eyes down, but she was shooting glances at me and around the truck.

"Did you see the table?" she said out of the blue.

I held my breath. Table?

"Candles and everything."

I began to laugh. She was talking about Pierce's kitchen.

"Are you his girlfriend?"

I snorted.

"We have a big speech due."

I was driving gently, long easy stops, quiet and slow on the curves, vigilant about the mirrors, snatching looks at Miriam.

"I'm sorry. What?"

Mr. Kreitzer had assigned it because he hates holidays.

"He says there's worse to come for Christmas."

"I thought he liked holidays."

"Are you his girlfriend? I think he likes you."

I hoped it was wise to keep her talking. "And do you think I like him?"

Miriam looked at the ice bag, then asked which was the best horse I had ever ridden.

I glanced at her. Her disjointedness was making me nervous. Her lips weren't blue, but her skin was plenty pale.

I sucked in air. "All horses are great in their own way," I said, talking low and quiet. "Take Sheila, for instance. She's a great horse because—"

"Oh, Sheila. She's for little kids."

The conversation veered to an uncle Miriam especially liked who would be coming to Thanksgiving dinner, then she wondered if her mother would keep a plate warm for her.

"She's meeting us at the hospital. I'm afraid you all might be having dinner late."

Then she told me I was lucky.

"Lucky?"

"You ride every day."

I smiled at the irony.

"Today was my best riding lesson," she offered all at once. "Ever."

"How?"

"I rode Prima."

"Do you remember what happened?"

They would want to know this at the hospital, and I admit I was curious.

She sat frowning down at her feet, then was off again: Why didn't I have a horse of my own? Had I ever fallen off? How long did it take to learn everything there was to know about horses?

"I don't know everything."

"More than Allie."

"Miriam," I said gently. "No one knows everything."

I wasn't sure this was exactly the time to start talking about dead riding teachers.

"My mother says I've learned more from

you than Allie. She hopes you'll be here next year, too."

I kept my eyes pinned on those neat blue hospital signs.

We got there before Miriam's mother. It was a low-flung brick building that looked something like an elementary school with an ambulance ramp. I parked as close as possible to the door, and we made our way: Miriam looking down and holding ice on her arm, me carrying her helmet in case anyone wanted to have a look at it.

The woman at the desk had blunt-cut graying hair, round tortoiseshell glasses, and startling mauve fingernails. Her nametag read Hattie Mims. She handed me a clipboard and offered Miriam a wheelchair.

Miriam refused. "I fell off a horse," she muttered, as if this were an explanation.

"Horses and house cats," the woman quipped. "The two most dangerous domestic animals. Fall off 'em. Fall over 'em."

Miriam rolled her eyes, then squinted with pain.

We sat, and I interviewed Miriam: date of birth, address, nature of accident, allergies to medications. Then we waited, since her mother had the insurance numbers and would have to sign for treatment.

"Tell me how you learned to ride," she said.

‧ ‧ ‧

On my eleventh birthday, my aunt Vee picks me up in her rattletrap roadster. It is black, glossy where it still holds wax. The hood is sculpted, the leather seats so low you feel as if your bottom is dragging inches above the street. We cross the Hill-to-Hill Bridge, weave through South Bethlehem, then up Wyandotte. The car is so old it has a double clutch, which means nothing to me, except that, high on the sharp shoulder of South Mountain, Vee does something fancy with her feet and seems to balance the car on its pedals. She is proud of this clutch business and, while we hover there at the light, she reminds me not to be a priss when I grow up.

At the farm, she turns abruptly serious. She brings her big gray horse in from the pasture, brushes him, cleans his feet, saddles and bridles him. She talks the whole time—the name of this, the term for that, the correct adjustment of this strap and that buckle. I pet Hadley's shoulder, cradle friendly barn cats in my arms, watch the pigeons on the rafters in the loft. She leads Hadley out to a ring, gets on, maneuvers him to a mounting block so I can climb on in front of her. We ride twice around the sandy track of the white-railed ring, and then out onto the dirt roads of Bucks County.

This is my first ride, ever, and it is not what I expected. I'd not expected the sheer height and breadth of Hadley. What is he? Sixteen hands? Is this where my love of giant horses begins? The feel of all that bulk and strength beneath me? The fact that it is harder to lose your balance, harder to fall off a big horse than a small one?

That first day I expect we will run and gallop, but Vee informs me that horses do not run and that I am far from ready for a gallop. I also expected that I would have a horse of my own to ride, but high on Hadley's back I am grateful to have Vee, slim and erect, behind me in the saddle.

By the time we reach the end of the farm lane, I fall in love with Hadley's rolling walk. The rest of the ride fills me with impressions: the corn high and thick and green in the fields along the lanes, the extra-sharp prick of Hadley's ears as we enter the dark mouth of a covered bridge, the hollow dance step of his hooves on the heavy wooden planking, the stuffy shadows all around us. Afterward, the sun cuts crisply through the leaves of trees, and the shade seems deep and pleated. We ride the edges of fields of yellow grain. Farm dogs fling themselves at Hadley's hooves. We give wide berth to a herd of white-faced cattle, napping ankle deep in a streambed. From the cool dark porch of an old stone house, a woman calls hello. Vee halloos back, nudges me to wave.

It is not all sightseeing on horseback. I must keep my eyes up, my chin level with Hadley's ears. My heels are down and my toes forward even though I have no stirrups.

At the end of the ride, Vee pries me off Hadley's back. I am not sore. I simply see no reason to set foot again on solid earth. Ever.

Later, when Vee's leg is broken, she simply announces over dinner one night that it is time for me to learn to ride. "Properly," she says. My father objects—she can't drive us out to the farm, and he doesn't have time to chauffeur us—but she beats him to the punch. She has researched a pair of bus routes that will get us out to the farm and back. I am to have three lessons a week, and despite my father's doubts— why can't we wait until Vee is better? or until school gets out?—Vee is adamant. And so I learn to charge home from school, change my clothes in three minutes flat, and meet Vee on the correct street corner, where she has already made her way because she is so slow on her crutches.

Miriam interrupted. "My feet are cold."

I looked down at her boots.

"You said you had ten pairs of socks. You can't cram your feet like that. You need winter riding boots."

"It's bright in here," she said, and I saw that she was squinting down at my feet.

I lifted a boot and waggled it.

"Tell my mom that I want boots like yours."

And then we heard footsteps and a voice. Miriam's mother.

She sat on the other side of Miriam and patted her right knee. "This the arm, sweetie?"

She was wearing corduroys, a leather coat, driving gloves. She had Miriam's dark hair and oval face and delicate chin. She seemed tired, but patient, amused somehow. She was probably close to my age, and it occurred to me

184

that women differ more from one another at forty than they do at twenty.

"I never thought I'd be here for you," she said.

She caught my look. "Miriam has three brothers and they're here all the time: soccer, baseball, falling off garage roofs."

I handed her the clipboard. "You need to finish this so she can go in."

Miriam's mother filled in the remainder of the form and Miriam began chattering: She had ridden Prima. I had worked her on the longe first.

"And then she threw you?"

I held my breath.

"She didn't throw me," Miriam said haughtily. "I fell off."

Good girl. A real rider never blames the horse.

"So can we buy her?"

Miriam's mother looked at me.

I couldn't help grinning at her pluck.

"Where would you keep her?"

"Our neighbors have a barn."

I smiled. This wasn't concussion; this was horse fever. I'd once figured I could keep a horse in our rental garage. I'd planned to walk him down Broad Street, across Main, and then ride him in the little park along Monocacy Creek.

Miriam's mother signed the form, sighed. "We've talked about a horse. But I don't know. She seems to want one."

I shook my head. "This wasn't my idea."

Miriam was now laying her hurt arm on her

185

lap, shielding her eyes from the overhead lights.

I stood, took the clipboard over and got Miriam checked in.

The emergency room was fairly quiet. A man doubled over with possible appendicitis, a woman with a sprained ankle. No heart attacks, no hunting accidents, no car wrecks.

I asked the woman at the desk if she would like me to leave the helmet with her or send it in with Miriam.

"Whatever for?" she said. "She won't be riding in here."

I tried to smile.

"So the doctor can see it?"

"I'm sure it's her head he's more interested in. She can always buy a new helmet." She smiled at me as if idiocy were common in emergency rooms.

I went back to Miriam and her mother. Miriam was now whining that she thought she was going to throw up and her mother was asking when she'd eaten last and saying that it might be the excitement.

Your daughter's just landed on her head, I wanted to say. Not bad, but you never knew.

"When can I come out again?" Miriam asked. She squinted at her arm.

"You should wait to be invited," her mother said.

I looked at Miriam's arm.

"As soon as you feel well enough. You don't have to ride, you could just visit. Depending."

"Tomorrow?" Miriam said.

Her mother smiled. "You haven't been listening to the radio. There's a storm coming. Rain." She frowned. "Or ice."

"Tomorrow?" Miriam said again, then threw up on the floor.

A nurse was already on her way out.

"Oh, dear," she said, and called for someone with a mop. "You fell off a horse?"

Miriam vomited again.

The nurse grabbed a basin and led them away. Miriam's mother turned, gave me a wave, said she'd call. Miriam turned then too, forcing herself to look up. "Pat Prima for me," she called. "Tell her you won't let me get back on." Then she vomited again.

I stood feeling helpless and extraneous. Then I perched on the edge of a chair. There were falls off horses and then there were falls off horses. In the grand scheme of things, this was a mere tumble, but wouldn't they want to know how she hit? Whether she'd been unconscious? If she were telling them what really happened or some garbled version of her own?

I wrung my hands, and felt a little queasy myself. Ten minutes passed. Twenty, thirty, forty. Finally I went over to the desk and, feeling neurotic and compulsive, asked if anyone would want to talk to me for the details on the accident. After all, I was the only one who could say for certain what had happened.

The woman gave me what was supposed to be a sympathetic smile.

"We have a neurologist on call, dear. I'm sure she'll sort it out."

I sat a while longer. It was now midafternoon. Still no Miriam. Finally I went back to the desk, left my name and the phone number, and then, feeling more anxious with every mile, headed back to the farm.

I stopped at the kitchen, told Pierce that Miriam was still at the emergency department. He poured me a cup of coffee, which I drank, and then, in desperate need of something to do, made my way to the barn. Pierce said he would let me know as soon as there was news.

Up in the barn, I first went to Prima's stall and took off her ankle boots. I was glad to see she hadn't broken out into a sweat beneath them. Then I went up to the ring, picked up the longe whip and the tape, closed the gate so that it would not hang open and sag on its hinges. Back inside, I topped off water buckets. Wheeled the wheelbarrow down the aisle and tidied stalls. Swept. It was still too early to feed, so finally I went into the tack room and decided to clean bridles.

Without thought, I took Twister's bridle off its hook, and once I saw I had it, I could not put it back. Matter-of-factly, I took the whole thing apart and made a sloppy pile of its various straps: cheekpieces, cavesson, rein stops, reins, crownpiece, browband. I remembered the first time I had done this when I was a kid, how nervous it had made me, and then I thought: And now I can put bridles back together in my sleep.

"It's just a skill," I said aloud, and felt profoundly aware of how alone I was. If

Miriam had been here, I could have quizzed her on the styles of reins, the kinds of nose-bands, the difference between a runner loop and a keeper.

Piece by piece I scrubbed the leathers with castile soap, scoured residue from the folds of the leather, then toweled the pieces dry. Then, making as big a production as possible, I gathered every cleaning supply in the barn:

Glycerin for leather already in good shape.

Lexol to add fat and thus suppleness to the leather.

Neat's-foot oil to do the same and darken the leather, too.

Saddler's dressing for the dried backs of nose-bands.

And, to finish Twister's bridle, a light coating of petroleum jelly before the leathers were sealed in a plastic bag so they would be clean and soft and free of mold when someone had a use for them again.

I worked the leathers, buffed them to a shine, coiled them gently.

Bridles, I thought, I know how to preserve.

I sat looking at all the leathers which might need my attention. I looked at my watch. Out in the aisle, the horses were getting restive. I heard a hoof strike the wall of a stall, heard someone squeal a retort. A feed bucket banged against the wall.

All right, I thought. All right.

I took my time over feeds, measured the grain with peculiar care, swept the aisle, shuffled papers into neat piles on the desk, walked the length of the place, and looked in every last grain bucket to make sure the horses had eaten.

It was absurd, and I knew it, but I was now more and more frightened for Miriam. What was taking so long? Maybe they had figured out how bad her head was. Maybe they had forgotten to call me. Maybe she had gotten worse. I remembered all the wrong stories now: The girl who'd flipped a horse and crushed her pelvis. The famous rider paralyzed. Freak accidents in which people had died: a horse slipping on the ice, a horse doing a cartwheel over a fence on a clear dry day, a horse running loose and trampling someone in the aisle of the barn; an acquaintance dying of a thrown blood clot hours after a hospital discharge.

I paced the tack room, then turned off the light, sat on a trunk, and watched the dusk thicken into dark.

My first fall comes in early May. Mr. Detweiler holds the line, Vee rests in a chair outside the paddock, and I am working at the canter, swooping in the saddle to the waltz beat of the gait. As ordered, I am circling my arms, front to back, and my seat digs into Hadley: *one*-two-three, *one*-two-three. The rhythm is simple, natural, and I think about it no more than a tree thinks about bending in a breeze.

And then I begin to giggle and, without even trying to save myself, I jiggle off to the side and hit the dirt.

—That's one! Mr. Detweiler calls.

Terrified, I scramble to my feet, shake my head. My hands tremble, and I dust off my jeans, check for what might be broken. Beneath my feet, the ground seems less trustworthy than before.

Mr. Detweiler leads Hadley over.

—Seven falls make the rider, he says, and he grabs my knee and legs me up so high I nearly shoot over the far side of the saddle.

I wriggle on Hadley's back, but the horse seems remote beneath me, as if my flying through the air like that has distanced me from him in a way I cannot fix.

We resume the canter. I struggle for the beat, find it, lose it, fear I will never ride in rhythm again.

When we stop for a breather, Vee says:

—She might as well hear the rest of it.

I stare.

—Seven falls, says Mr. Detweiler, make the rider. The next twenty-one are for the hell of it.

—You stop counting at one hundred, Vee adds under her breath.

For the rest of my lesson, I think:

Seven falls.

Twenty-one.

One hundred.

And I find myself wishing that I will never fall again and wishing just as hard that I will start falling and keep falling since that is what so inevitably lies before me.

No, Pierce said. No one had called. I would have heard the phone ring in the barn.

I'd gone down to the house, carrying the paper flowers.

"You're worried," he said.

I nodded. My eyes were wide, and I was doing my best not to imagine a plate in her skull, pins or screws in a shattered wrist.

"She didn't look that bad when she was down here."

I looked at my watch.

"Call the hospital if you're worried," he said. "Or call her house."

I thought.

"I'll call," he offered.

To my amazement, I let him. He looked up the number in the phone book, spoke to someone who said, No, there was no word from the hospital and they were getting worried, too.

Pierce looked at his watch and asked if I still wanted dinner. I could see preparations all around him.

I said I guessed so but that first I would take a shower and change my clothes.

"I'm going to change, too," he said.

I hesitated at the door, tried to make a joke: "Shall I wear my little black strapless number?"

He whirled toward me, grinning. "Do you have one?"

"What do you think?"

No, but I did have a pale gray cashmere turtleneck I'd found in a secondhand shop and a pair of gray wool trousers. I showered, dressed, and for a few minutes considered digging through my box for a piece of jewelry, as if I might find some lucky token to hasten Miriam home from the hospital.

But it's one thing to shower and throw on clothes, another entirely to rummage through a jewelry box studded with memories and half recollections, searching for the right ornament. Besides, I could almost hear the pistol rattling in its drawer. I shook out my hair, pulled on my barn coat, and hurried down the cubby stairs.

chapter fourteen

Outside the house, I stood a minute, my collar up around my ears. The living-room windows cast a butter-yellow glow, but I couldn't bring myself to go indoors. Up in the barn, the safety light was as comforting as a child's night light. I had also left a small light burning in the cubby: soon I would have to resume sleeping there. I stamped my feet, still well outside the mudroom door. One pale star shone in the east, soon to be snuffed out by the cloud bank slipping in from the west.

Closing my eyes, I felt for the black horse, felt for all the livestock on this farm—the beating of their hearts, their warm hay-scented breaths—and soon I was thinking about all the animals: the mice in the loft, the birds still roosting in the barn, the various squirrels, fox, deer, mink, inhabiting this bit of land; all those hearts beating in the dark, all those lungs taking in air, expelling it again.

The mudroom door burst open.

I leaped, thumped my fist against my chest.

"Come on in," said Pierce. "You've been standing out here forever."

"Admiring the night." I followed him in.

He was wearing a neat shirt, a tie, and a leather vest.

"You're dressed up," I said, and shrugged out of my barn coat, hung it on a peg.

"And you."

I smiled ruefully. "I do clean up once in a while."

He took me by the elbow, led me toward the living room. "That's what holidays are for."

"Good heavens," I said.

On the coffee table were a bowl of fruit, a cutting board with a small assortment of cheese, champagne flutes, and an ice bucket with a bottle.

I drew back. "Pierce," I said. "We can't—"

He blushed. "It's a holiday."

"But Miriam. Has she called?"

He paused, looked down, then up, with a trace of sheer mischief. "Maybe whiskey? While we wait?"

I sat on the couch, took a piece of cheese. "Any gin?"

"I'll see." He went out to the kitchen, calling back for me to look at the cases of the

CDs on the corner of the table. "Could you stand those?"

I picked them up. He had not listened to music, nor even mentioned it, since I'd been camping out on his couch. I read the labels of what he'd chosen and found myself laughing.

"Just how much gin do you have?"

He stepped out from the kitchen.

"None, in fact." He held up a bottle of table wine.

I shrugged, then nodded at the stereo. "Go ahead. Although my father will roll over in his grave."

Pierce flinched, looked at me a moment longer, then stepped over to the stereo and turned it on. The first disc was a best of Mozart—short sections of his best-known works, nothing in its entirety. The second was a so-called best of classics, with such chestnuts as the Hallelujah chorus and the cannon firing of the 1812 overture back to back, and the third was famous ballet waltzes.

A Mozart divertimento filled the room. Pierce turned the volume down and went back to the kitchen to pour wine. I sat thinking of Lucy, who pretty much thought it was blasphemy to listen to music and speak at the same time.

Pierce came back with two glasses of wine.

I took mine, hoisted it in a toast, and said, "There'll be hauntings tonight."

His face turned pale.

"A joke," I said. "My musicians."

He tasted his wine, and I sat chatting about whatever came to mind: that I had cleaned some bridles, that Miriam's mother had said the forecast was bad, that I thought—again—that Pierce had better order hay.

We both kept pausing, listening for the phone, as if we might somehow miss its loud wrangle in the kitchen.

"I meant to offer sooner," Pierce said after a stretch of quiet. "But if you have people to call—" He gestured toward the ceiling. "You'd be welcome to use the phone upstairs if you'd like some privacy."

I'd not had a phone installed in the cubby; I simply used the phone in the barn. I cut a piece of cheese.

"Really," I said. "There's hardly anyone."

Alec I had not been able to find. John Casey was a thought, but I guessed his life was about as flat as mine. Beyond that, there were no survivors.

"Did you call people?"

"I was cooking. I thought about it. Some friends."

"You should have."

"You're here."

"You should have."

We let the Mozart fill in the gap. A movement of a popular symphony. Forty? Forty-one? It surprised me that he owned these music-for-idiots CDs.

Then I remembered to tell him that Miriam was smitten with Prima and that, even after falling off, she wanted to know if the mare were for sale.

"I don't know if they're serious. Her mother's hard to read."

Pierce looked away. "Not tonight."

"It could be a help. Although now I'm sure she wouldn't want the horse until spring."

"Not tonight," Pierce said again.

"I found some ribbons in the trailer," I said. "A while ago. Did Allie take her to shows?"

"You could show her, too," Pierce said.

Oh, boy, I thought. Not tonight.

We were sitting quietly, the sale of the mare hanging in the air, when the phone rang.

I would have liked to run for it, snatch it from the wall, but Pierce merely set his glass down, rose, went out to the kitchen. The ringing stopped.

I was dying to follow him, listen in, then it occurred to me that it might be someone else, a friend perhaps, and clinging to my wine, I clamped one leg over the other as if to prove to myself that I was relaxed, and stayed put on the couch.

I looked around the room. I reached forward and examined the label on the champagne. I took a deep whiff of the roasting turkey. I closed my eyes and listened to Mozart, trying not to hear Pierce's voice going up and down in the kitchen.

When he finally came back into the room, with his mouth twisted into that odd grin, all he said was: "Now can we open the champagne?"

"She's okay?"

He smiled. "There was some trouble with the X rays and then with having them read.

That's what took so long. Her wrist is cracked, but it's not bad. She'll have the cast six or seven weeks."

"And her head?"

Please let them have been careful about her head.

"They're keeping her the night."

I let out a breath of relief. "For observation."

He nodded.

I remembered a roommate somewhere along the line who'd hit her head and had been told at an emergency room to set her alarm every two hours throughout the night, to get herself up, and check to see if her pupils were still the same size. We'd both thought it was mad, and I'd been the one to rouse her all night long—terrified each time that she would not wake.

"Thank God," I said.

Pierce lifted the champagne from the bucket.

"You worry too much," he said.

I laughed with relief, quaffed the rest of the wine in my glass. "It's new for me," I said. "I'm not good at it." Then I held the flutes while Pierce opened the champagne and poured.

Dinner was not turkey, after all, but Cornish game hens, served with an elaborate salad, Parker House rolls, and a lot more champagne. We ate in the kitchen, but Pierce had covered the table with a festive cloth, set it with good china, and had turned off all but the small light over the stove and lit a battalion of candles. Miriam's paper flowers cast elegant shadows among the candlesticks.

We made more small talk: What were the game hens stuffed with? How had he learned to cook? If you could read, he said, you could cook. What were his plans for the long weekend? None, really. I thanked him for the hot chocolate and sticky buns Miriam and I had enjoyed up in the barn. We discussed whether we would save dessert for later. Over and over I said how glad I was that Miriam was all right, and somewhere near the beginning of the second bottle of champagne, I offered a toast: to Miriam and a speedy recovery.

As we lifted our glasses, it came to me that if I were a good person, I would stay until she was able to ride again, and see to it that she got on a horse again and had a good safe first ride. I drank, and thought she might have to be willing to climb on a horse standing up to its knees in snow.

At one point—out of giddiness? inebriation?—I swayed a little in my chair in time to the ballet waltzes playing in the living room.

With that ironical gleam in his eye, Pierce pushed back his chair, came around to my side of the table, bowed low, then kissed the back of my hand. I drew back, then thought what the hell, Miriam was all right, I was happy for once, and I put my napkin down, walked into Pierce's arms, and we waltzed around the kitchen. Potts had taught me to dance in our living room—waltz, fox-trot, tango, polka— and in Pierce's arms I felt the fine sense of someone taller than me, holding me, hinting for me to turn this way, that way, keeping watch that I did not barge into something. I closed my eyes, leaned against him, gave myself up to the waltz. As it ended, I looked up, saw his eyes glittering—mischief, irony, tears? His arm tightened around my waist, and suddenly I shook him off, rushed to the bathroom, and doused my face with water.

We sat back at the table. Flustered, I held my glass out for more champagne. I would regret it tomorrow. Pierce filled his glass, too, then said he thought we should each say what we were thankful for.

I swallowed hard. "Shouldn't we have started with that?"

"I'd say anytime was appropriate."

In the candlelight, I now felt I couldn't read his face.

"Okay," I said. "You start."

What was it Miriam had asked? Was I his girlfriend? I suddenly felt as if the table between us were twenty feet wide.

"All right," he said. "I'm thankful for you. Mason's right. I owe you a lot." He lifted his glass, as if in a toast. "To a new field of vision."

I twisted the stem of my own glass, tapped the bowl of it, and watched a little flotilla of bubbles rise to the surface. I dismissed his words as empty gallantry.

"Your turn," he said.

I hid my hands in my napkin.

"I'm thankful that Miriam isn't hurt. Seriously, that is."

He shook his head, smiled. "Too easy."

I gestured. "I'm grateful for a roof over my head. Does that count?" I looked around. "Grateful for good food. You've been kind to let me turn into a leech."

"You're not a leech." He lifted his glass. "To bed and board?"

I kept dreaming that the couch was floating. Sometimes down a river. Sometimes on the ocean. Sometimes in a lagoon. Across a pond. Each time I woke, believing in the first moments that I was seasick, then waking into the realization that I'd had far too much champagne. Finally, I got up, slipped out to the kitchen. I lit the light over the stove, drank some water, stood for a long while looking at the pumpkin pie. We had not gotten around to cutting it at dinner—we were both a little drunk—and now it seemed too familiar to make the first cut. The fact that he would approve made me all the more reluctant. I refilled my glass, found an extra roll, sat at the table.

I nibbled and drank, let my stomach settle, and let my head get used to being in a vertical position. Maybe I would spend the rest of the night sitting up. I was less dizzy upright.

I found myself fingering the sharp creases of Miriam's flowers.

chapter fifteen

I meander into the shop after school, my book bag crammed with valentines and cellophane packets of cinnamon hearts. John Casey is at the front desk, checking invoices, and through a heavy window I see Lucy working at a piano. I say hello to Potts, watch his quick sure stroke as he matches up the edges of a double reed. The workroom smells of valve oil and cork grease. The bell rings on the shop door, and I consider running upstairs so I don't get stuck waiting on customers. But it is a delivery boy, not someone in need of cello strings. He has shaggy hair and carries a long white box tied with a voluptuous red ribbon.

—Is there a Miss Baxter?

—What is it? calls Potts.

—Flowers, says the boy.

John Casey glances at the box, looking worried.

—Then get your sister, Potts says, coming to the doorway of the workroom, wiping his hands on a rag.

I run for Lucy, rap on the door of the studio.

She refuses to stop playing.

I open the door.

—Lucy! Lucy! You have to come.

—Get out, she says, still playing. Where's Potts?

—It's flowers, I say. For you.

She breaks off. A devilish look flits across her face.

—Very well then, she says as if this is some burdensome duty she alone must carry out.

We go down the little corridor. Lucy lays the box on the counter.

—They're roses, aren't they?

John Casey looks terrified.

—Isn't that too much? Potts says.

Lucy smiles like a field hawk feasting on baby rabbit. She knows her manners, though, makes us suffer, reads the card first.

John Casey's face is scarlet.

—Oh! she cries, then stuffs the card back into the envelope. She scoops the box up into her arms, glad somehow.

—They're not for me, she says.

That night I prop myself just so in the chair next to Vee's bed. Tonight my homework is colonial history, and I am about to read to Vee about Lexington and Concord, but when I glance up she is smiling at the roses. Soon I am smiling at them, too.

—Natalie, she says, noticing me after a long while. Would you like some for your room?

I close my history book. It would be nearly magic to sleep with them next to my bed.

—We need a knife, she says. And a vase.

I launch out of my chair. My history book smears across the floor.

—Bring two! Vee calls after me.

In my room, I find the jackknife that I

have won off Alec in a secret game of mum-blety-peg. Potts would have made me return it if he'd known I'd had it, but at some point I know Alec will win it back. We are best friends; my lucky fifty-cent piece goes back and forth between us, too.

Carrying two small vases from the china closet, I pass Potts in the hallway.

—Homework okay? he says.

—Sure.

To my surprise, Vee takes all the flowers from the water and with the wet ends dripping onto the bedclothes she pares the stems. She uses the knife exactly the way Potts has expressly forbidden: with the blade toward the ball of her thumb. And while she trims and arranges, turning the roses this way and that, I watch with creepy fascination, waiting for the bright blood certain to come.

She pauses, holds a single rose up for inspection.

—White for sorrow and apology.

—They're red.

—For Valentine's, she says. Of course. The white ones come in July.

She snaps the knife shut, flips it to me, and I hide it in my pocket. She regards her diminished bouquet and the two smaller ones.

—Pick yours first, she tells me. Then deliver Lucy's before you go to bed.

I say my thank-yous and although I can barely take my eyes off the roses that will soon be mine, I force myself to read aloud. The farmers and shopkeepers are assembling, day dawns in Lexington, and someone is ordering: Don't shoot until you see the whites of their eyes.

Potts raps on the door.

—It's about that time, Nate.

Vee kisses my cheek, nods at the flowers.

I pick up the little vases.

Potts darkens.

—I thought she was exaggerating. Are those from—? He glances at me. All of them?

I hold up the rich red flowers in each hand.

—From Vee, I say. Lucy gets some, too.

Abruptly he kisses my forehead, swats my butt.

—To bed, he says.

Late that night, I am still awake. I smell my roses in the dark, reach out to touch them, wish I dared turn on the light to look at them some more. And so I am awake when Potts says:

—It has to stop.

And Vee says:

—He was stupid. That doesn't mean nothing's left.

—It has to stop, Potts says. I'm raising daughters. You know what Lucy's like.

—We write, Vee says. And twice a year he sends flowers.

—It has to stop, Potts says a third time. At least under my roof.

—I can leave.

I fling myself down and yank my quilt over my head. My bed frame squeals.

I hear Potts in my doorway.

—Nate? Nate?

205

In the morning, I flunk my history quiz: I am irritable and worried and I don't know anything about a bridge or a poem. I can't even name the victor.

That afternoon, when I come home from school, the roses have been taken from my room. Within days Vee returns to the hospital, and when she comes home again, her cast is fresh and white, her face is gray and thin, and she defies my father, insists on teaching me to ride.

The morning after Thanksgiving was dark and wet: rain and more rain. I ate breakfast standing at the sink before Pierce was up, then headed out to the barn with the full intention of spending the day nursing my hangover. Maybe I would curl up in the tack room and take a nap in a wool sheet, listening to the horses munching hay as I dozed off.

I fiddled with the radio in the office. Because of the fluky weather, the clearest station I could find was from Bethlehem. The call letters were unfamiliar, but I wasn't sure I could remember any stations from childhood, anyway. I turned the volume up so I could hear it in the aisle, began the chores, and before I had a chance to let the sound of the radio fade into the background, a forecast came over the air: heavy rains combined with dropping temperatures. Plus the possibility of heavy icing off and on for the next few days.

As I mucked the stalls, pausing now and again to wish I'd taken more aspirin, I made a mental list of things to check around the barn: grain, flashlight batteries, colic drenches, first-aid supplies. I wondered if I should fill extra buckets with water. Sometimes I stopped and wrote things down, and often I paused for a drink of water from the hose. It was bitter cold, but I knew enough physiology to know that part of my problem was dehydration. The rest of it was fatigue—I soon needed to start sleeping in a bed again. In horses, there is a sometimes fatal condition called double stress: a second injury, shock, or illness, on top of a first, pushing a horse's system past the limit of endurance. I told myself I felt like that: I was double-stressed.

Around eleven, Pierce wandered up to the barn. What time would I like lunch?

I wasn't hungry.

Well, what was I doing? He followed me around the barn. It was not what I would have wished. I asked him to fill some buckets in case the power went out. He didn't think it was necessary. I suggested he go to town and buy supplies. Maybe later. Finally, I sent him up into the loft and made him count the remaining bales of hay.

"Thirty-five," he called.

"Divide by six."

"Five and change," he called back, mystified.

"We feed six bales a day." I stood in the aisle, looking up at him and massaging my temples. "That means we have hay for five more days. That's it."

He came down the ladder, surprisingly at ease on the rungs, and went into the office. I heard the squeak of the old wooden chair, heard drawers opening and closing. As I passed, I glanced in. He was poring over my notes and records. I wanted to go in and snatch them from his hands.

"You could start by calling Fred," I said from the doorway.

He looked up, blank.

"For hay," I snapped, then moved off.

I was going down the aisle with the wheelbarrow when he stepped out of the office.

"Could you come in here, please?"

Outside, the first pellets of frozen rain rattled on the windows.

He sat at the desk, and I leaned nearby.

"I have some questions."

And he went through all the files, examining invoices and bills, jotting down figures, using the calculator. I watched him like an angry schoolgirl having her homework checked.

Finally he looked up and said, "Well, it's not too bad, is it? We're managing."

"Pierce," I said. "For Christ's sake, can't you get it through your head that you can't manage here?"

I glared at him, horrified by my tone, but damned if I would apologize.

"You know I'll leave someday," I said quietly.

He sat looking at me, hurt at first, then smiling a little down at the desk.

"I'll tell you everything I can before I go," I said by way of offering a truce. "Try to get you set up. If that's really what you want. But I still think—"

"You could ride and run the barn. I'll keep teaching." He rapped his knuckles on the pile of papers. "You could take horses in to train. You were doing so well on Twister."

"But what about your work?" I said. "Your real work? What about my real work, for that matter?"

"Shh!" he said. "Listen."

On the radio was a report about Bethlehem. While various groups were lobbying to save parts of the mills as a museum, the EPA had just announced it might consider a request to waive testing the site for chemicals before freeing the land for development.

"But that's crazy." I was all but shouting. "Everyone dies of cancer there, so as it is. If they don't get in there and clean it out, that filth will go on forever."

Pierce put his hand on my arm.

"Calm down," he said. "You don't live there. Maybe they don't know what to do with it."

I fumed, and shook him off. "That's no excuse."

"There's a spare room upstairs," he said. "You could move into that."

I stared.

"In the house. It wasn't Allie's. You'd be more comfortable."

I said nothing, felt the resolute set of my chin and the lowering of my brows that had accompanied my tantrums as a child.

He lifted his chin and studied me, then pushed back his chair and left.

"Wait!" I called, humiliated. "What about the hay?"

"You do it."

I sat with my feet on the desk and considered tearing up all the careful records I had left, getting in the truck and taking off. But that wouldn't feed the horses. And we had as yet to hear that Miriam was home safe.

Near the end of the afternoon, I relented and dialed Fred Weirbachen. I had not seen or spoken to him since Twister died. The phone rang and rang. I hated chasing him from his work.

Finally Mrs. Weirbachen answered. "Ja? Weirbachen."

"Mrs. Weirbachen," I said, speaking slowly. For some reason I assumed she was hard of hearing. "This is Natalie Baxter. I'm calling for Pierce Kreitzer."

"Ja."

I imagined her velvety wrinkles, the rigid lines of her steel-crimped curls, her denim work apron.

"The new woman."

"I am not the new woman," I said, slow and clear. "I work here. I'm calling about hay."

She clucked with disapproval. "Hay? It's Mister you need. And there's the storm."

"The storm," I said. "That's why I'm calling."

"Ach," she said. "Mister's out." And she hung up.

I put down the phone, dumbfounded. There was still five days' worth. Pierce would simply have to sort it out. The Weirbachens were his neighbors, not mine.

• • •

That evening, Pierce was in a funk. He had stayed down in the darkroom, he did not cook, then he sat morosely on the couch, staring at the television. At one point, he went down to the basement, came up with a gun-cleaning kit, then went upstairs and came down with the shotgun.

I sat shuddering.

"Obviously you don't care for this," he said gruffly.

I shrugged, tried to make a joke: "Only if you don't shoot somebody."

"A clean firearm is safer than a dirty one."

I struggled to sound casual: "I know that. I used to shoot."

He dismantled the shotgun, spreading the pieces on a sheaf of newspapers on the floor. His hands were quiet, deliberate, as if laying out a game of solitaire or setting a table.

"I like it. Every farmer needs a shotgun. It drove Allie crazy even to have it in the house."

"You're not a farmer."

He ignored me, laid out his equipment: oil, brush, rags.

"I have a pistol," I volunteered.

He eyed the parts lying at his feet, then palmed the bolt. "Too loud, I guess. Too messy." His eyes were bland, but something I could not name creased his face. He seemed full of anger and satisfaction all at once.

"What kind is it?"

I stared.

"You said you had a pistol."

"Twenty-two. A family piece."

"A toy."

Not if you point it at your head.

But I said nothing, merely watched him work, methodical and attentive, and saw that he was quieter somehow, more relaxed. When the pieces were all wiped down, he seemed to lose interest in the chore, and for a moment lay back on the couch, one hand dangling over the edge, his clean, dismantled shotgun at his feet.

After a while, eager to have the gun out of the living room, I said, "I can finish that."

And then I realized that he was asleep.

During the night, the temperatures dropped. The rain came down steadily and froze immediately, and in the morning I fell four times on the way to feed the horses. I decided to hide out in the barn for the day, or to go back to the cubby and make it comfy enough to sleep in. Perhaps I could lock the pistol in the glove compartment of the truck—if I could bring myself to touch it. Certainly I would not spend another night in the house.

The horses ate, and I mucked stalls. I had to use an ax to chip the ice from the back barn doors to roll them open far enough to wedge the wheelbarrow through. Then once the doors were open, I built a path of soiled bedding and manure so I could make it to the manure pile without breaking my neck. Each time I went outdoors I pulled on an oilskin and hood; each time I came back in, I took them off again.

It was a long laborious morning, but I didn't care. I had little else to do. When I finished the stalls, it was nearly noon, and I stood leaning in the barn doorway, staring down at the house. I stood for a long while, resting and thinking that I should have built a manure path to the house. I wondered where Pierce was. Reading? In the darkroom? I knew I would soon need something to eat, but I stood in the doorway with twenty-five yards of ice and rain between me and the house. I was tired of Pierce, but I felt sorry for him, too. He hadn't lost any more than I had, but I'd been toughened up early and now it came to me that maybe that wasn't such a bad thing.

I was thinking that maybe I would just skip lunch and sit in the office and make some phone calls when, in the distance, I heard a rumbling and popping. I cocked my head. It seemed to be growing closer and then, by God, I caught sight of old Fred Weirbachen wearing a slicker and a hat, with chains on all four of his tractor tires and all six of the wagon tires. A heavy canvas tarpaulin was tied down tight over a load of hay.

He drove straight up to the barn, and waited for me to shove the barn doors open all the way. They were frozen and I got the ax.

"Dunnerwetter," he kept saying, hacking at the thick rime. He was also coughing from time to time.

"You shouldn't have come today," I said, taking my turn with the ax.

"Missus said to."

I felt guilty. "We're nearly out," I said. "But we would have lasted a few more days."

Fred straightened, pointed angrily at the house. "This year did he think it wouldn't come? The winter?"

"I've been after him to call you."

We freed the doors, and Fred strode out into the rain, pulled the tractor and trailer straight into the barn, lining up the trailer with the loft, then jumping down and leaving the tractor running.

"She's diesel," he said.

I nodded. How odd it had been when diesel tractors first made their way onto horse farms—morning chores were ten times noisier because it was cheaper to keep them running, and they also had the odd effect of bringing the smell of city buses into horse stables.

"Now what?" I said, eyeing the pile of hay and the loft.

Fred coughed.

"Up."

I looked at the load, the distance to the loft. "Let's just stack it in the aisle," I said. "For now. Or at least let me go get Pierce."

Fred shook his head. "There's only one right way."

He produced two pairs of hay hooks from under the tractor seat. We peeled back the tarpaulin and worked out a system. Fred swung a bale up to the edge of the loft, I nailed it with my hooks, carried it to the back of the loft and stacked it.

Fred worked fast and hard, but seemed to use little energy. Within minutes I had to ask him to slow down, and soon I had to come down out of the loft for gloves.

"My hands," I said. "I'm sorry."

I pulled on thin leather riding gloves. Fred meanwhile was piling bales higher on the wagon, unloading it in careful layers to ease the work. I climbed back up into the loft. "Ready," I said. "Or do you want me to call Pierce? You shouldn't have to do this."

He sunk the hay hooks into a bale.

"Missus said to come today. She frets over you."

"Me?" I said. "I'm fine."

He looked down at the house, tasted the inside of his mouth, looked up at me with watery blue eyes. "You're a good worker."

I smiled, knowing he could have unloaded this entire trailer of hay already if it weren't for me slowing him down.

He swung the next bale up to the lip of the loft. I sank my hooks into it, but he paused before pulling his out.

"You come to us," he said. "Day or night. We have the spare room. Missus said to say."

He looked me straight in the eye, released his hooks. I carried the bale to the back of the loft and stacked it.

When he swung the next bale up, I said, "I'm probably leaving soon."

"Good," said Fred. "He should sell."

It took two hours, and when we finished I offered to take Fred to the house for coffee.

He waved me off. "Ach, no," he said. Then from the toolbox of the tractor he produced a loaf of homemade bread.

"How lovely," I said. "I haven't eaten lunch."

"You go down, then."

Instead, I offered to drive the tractor for him so he could keep out of the rain. He could drive my truck back.

"Ach no," he said. "You go and eat."

"I'll stay and sweep."

He gave me an approving nod, climbed back onto the tractor. The chains clanked on the floor, then he rounded the barn and headed down the drive. I stood in the doorway, waving at his back, half wishing I were going with him.

Then I closed the doors and swept, opening each stall door in turn and sweeping in a pile of the fresh leavings. When I was finished, I stood in the doorway, scowling at the house. I couldn't imagine how Pierce could have not come up to help.

Back in the office, I took a hunk of bread and ate, determined to stay in the barn long enough to do the evening chores. Then I would go down to the house, tell Pierce exactly what I thought: of his arrogance, his presumption, his laziness. And then I would spend the night in the cubby.

I fell and fell and fell going to the house. Pierce, it turned out, was surprised to hear Fred had come.

"In this weather?"

He'd been in the basement, running water into the spare water tank in case we needed it. Then he had spent the rest of the afternoon down there in the darkroom, printing contact sheets, and getting out the kerosene lamps, filling them and trimming wicks.

I spent the night on the couch again after all. It wasn't worth falling on the ice and breaking an arm.

Sunday Pierce cooked a huge breakfast. I hesitated in the doorway, then let him coax me into sitting. Halfway through, he asked if I were angry, and I no longer knew. The weather was bad, but at least there was hay. Maybe I was merely miserable. I had not ridden in weeks, and clearly I could not start now, and, although I had gone almost nowhere for the same amount of time, I was now irrationally restless to be caught on the farm because of the icy roads. What's more, we'd had only one brief additional call about Miriam: she was home, she was fine. Her mother's dismissiveness made me nervous. I admit I would have liked more frequent reports, as silly as that was, and I would have liked to speak with Miriam, but she had been asleep, and Miriam's mother had made it clear that she'd seen plenty of injured kids and that there was no need to make a fuss. That I wanted to make a fuss was of no matter.

"It's not your fault," I told Pierce grudgingly, and afterward I went to the barn and brushed all the horses. Then I spent the afternoon plucking hairs from the horses' tails and trying to remember how to weave them into a bracelet. I thought Miriam might like it as a get-well gift. I doubted her mother would appreciate the traditional sackful of manure from the horse you'd fallen off. But I sat in the office, grubbing over the hairs, twisting them this way and that, braiding and rebraiding, and all I made was a tattered mess that, in the end, I was too embarrassed to show anyone. When I picked up stalls that evening I threw it in the wheelbarrow and buried it in the manure pile.

Monday morning at six the phone rang. I was in the kitchen. I could hear Pierce in the shower. I picked it up. It was a woman from the junior high. The opening of school would be delayed two hours.

"I'll tell him," I said.

"You must be Natalie," said the woman on the other end.

"I work here," I said. "I'm the help."

"I'm glad." Her voice sounded either motherly or suggestive. I couldn't tell which and so, saying I was in a hurry to get on with the chores, I hung up.

Upstairs, the shower stopped, but I wrote a giant note, taped it to the coffeepot, and headed for the door.

I had my hand on the doorknob when the phone rang again and quickly stopped. I hesitated.

In a minute Pierce shouted down the stairs. "It's for you," he said. "It's Mason."

I told him about school.

"I'll go in anyway. I have work."

I asked him to be sure to check on Miriam and tell her I said hello.

In the kitchen, I picked up the phone, listened to what Mason had to say.

"Don't apologize," I said. "I'd love to."

I took the note off the coffeepot, crossed out my original message, wrote a new one. Then I grabbed extra socks, extra gloves, a down vest, and picked my way across the ice up to the barn and hurried through the chores.

chapter sixteen

I waited in the doorway to the barn. The chains on the Jeep tires jingled as Mason came up the drive. I inched toward the passenger door and got in.

"I didn't expect you to stand outside," he said.

I shrugged. "Cabin fever."

He backed the Jeep around, headed down the drive, and pointed to covered Styrofoam cups in the dash tray. "I didn't know how you took it," he said. "So one is black and one has cream and sugar. You pick."

"Which do you want?"

He shook his head. "We have a long day."

"Cream and sugar, then," I said.

He pointed to the cup nearest him, and I took it and wrapped my hands around it.

It was warm in the Jeep. I opened my jacket, pulled off my hat, and stretched my legs.

"This is great," I said. "It's like a little yacht."

Behind our seats were a tow chain, a pile of heavy wool blankets, an extra thermos or two. There were rubber boots, a spare coat, a giant box of rubber gloves and another of rubber sleeves, a heavy flashlight, the morning newspaper, a laptop, a clipboard, the phone on the dash, a tape deck with a tape jutting out. And, of course, the neat trunks of medicines and tools.

"Prepared for all contingencies," he quipped. "Although in the last few days I've been trying to remember why I ever left North Carolina."

"It does this there, too," I said. "As I recall."

I opened my coffee.

Mason checked his notes, and turned us here and there. He seemed brisk yet relaxed. I was feeling torn—glad to be leaving the farm but unnerved too.

"So why did you?" I said.

He glanced at me, fiddled with the dial for the heat.

"Leave North Carolina."

"Boring, really. I was tired of being a junior in the practice. My marriage ended." He frowned, smoothed a corner of his mustache. "Vets are never home. Especially when there's no reason to be. So I came up here, looked at this practice, liked the look of the land. I presumed I'd be best off solo."

I raised an eyebrow. "And are you?"

"I don't know anymore. Some days, yes. Some, no."

"So what's on for today? That you need help?" On the phone he'd said he could use an extra pair of hands and I'd asked if he was sure I could help. Horses I knew pretty well, but except for having to put up with the occasional flock of geese, which I loathed, or having to throw hay for someone's pet beef herd, I knew almost nothing about the variety of livestock Mason surely dealt with in a rural practice.

"I lied." He mimicked a heavy drawl. "Just wanted to lure you out."

Puzzled, I put the lid back on my coffee and saved it for later.

"Trust me," he said. "We'll find things for you to do."

Our first call was to check on a new litter of beagle puppies. The eight little brown-and-white sausages paddled over one another in a heap. When Mason had the mother stand so he could check her over, the puppies mewled. When it was their turn, he held each alone in the palm of his hand. They flopped there, tiny in the basket of his fingers. He offered a fingertip, examined their mouths, their bellies, and their bottoms. His face lit up as he returned the last one to the mother.

"He'll be the champ, I think."

The owner chuffed, looked pleased. He was a retired military man in his early sixties and that was one of three puppies he had selected to start as hunting stock. Later he would keep the best-started puppy and sell the other two.

Mason went over some directions, routine matters about feedings and what to expect when from the puppies and the mother.

The major offered him a puppy. First pick after his own three.

Mason shook his head. "They're fine pups," he said. "But one dog is it for me. It's an occupational hazard to take in animals."

After we left, I wondered if the call had been necessary. The mother was fine, the puppies were fine, and the owner had had no burning questions.

Mason held up a finger, shook it at the windshield, clearly mocking himself, and preached: "Neglect routine and tragedy ensues. That's one of my commandments."

He told me of a family who lost their epileptic Irish setter over the weekend. The animal was young, otherwise healthy, a favorite of the father's and particularly one of the girls, but they had run out of its medication and during one of the stormy nights, when the roads were solid ice, it had seized and died.

I nodded. The world of animals was full of stories, many of them sad. I asked if there were more commandments. "Nine, maybe?"

He laughed. "Never counted. They're all hokey. But I damn well believe them." He lay his fingertips on the dash, and as if playing a scale, counted them off: "Do what's right. Follow through. Don't give up. Ask for help. Remember you're neither God nor Mother Nature. Don't forget tincture of time."

I smiled. "I haven't heard that one in a long while. Tincture of time."

"It works. Sometimes all I do is speed things up."

"That's not true."

"Think about it."

"You save them, too."

222

He nodded, almost shy, definitely humble. He turned toward me, his eyes so dark and liquid brown I thought he must have been a retriever in some past life.

He straightened at the wheel. "And yours?"

"What?"

"Commandments."

I shrugged, tried to joke. "Water, hay, grain. In that order."

He nodded. "I go for that."

"Let's see. The horse takes the credit and the rider takes the blame."

He thought. "Okay."

"Head up, heels down."

Nod.

"Always look to your next fence."

I drank some coffee, made a face. "And, when in doubt, clear out. There's always a new place just over the next ridge."

Mason turned us into the driveway of a small farm, parked, and set the brake.

"That last one I take exception to. I admire much about you, Nate. Especially all those fine capabilities. But all this leaving seems like..." He hesitated, turned those brown eyes in my direction, glanced down at his clipboard, then back at me. "Laziness? Cowardice?"

I stormed out of the Jeep, slammed the door, and hissed at him over the roof: "And where the hell do you think I got those—" I spat his word back: "Capabilities? Not in a god-forsaken place like this."

He sighed, went around the back of the Jeep, and put together a small kit. I leaned against the fender, arms folded, angry and embarrassed. When he was ready, I let him go ahead without me, but within a few moments after he disappeared inside, I decided I might as well go in, too, and see what there was to see.

Inside the little two-stall barn stood a tall lanky gray gelding with a huge, blood-filled swelling on its chest. The owner rushed out from the house to greet us, explaining that the horse had fallen on the ice. Mason examined it, palpated gently, asked a few questions. I kept my gaze level, avoiding his eyes, but I soon gave up being mad in favor of watching him work. I'd seen this procedure before, and although it was relatively simple, Mason was so quiet and efficient, I felt as if I were watching a ballet. He shaved the area, disinfected it, opened it with a scalpel, drained it, washed it with antiseptic, administered antibiotics.

There was nothing for me to do but pat the horse's neck and make small talk with the owner. But afterward, Mason thanked me profusely.

"I didn't do a thing," I snapped, ready to resume our quarrel.

He removed his cap, wiped his brow with the back of his hand, resettled his cap. "You have no idea. The horse held still and you certainly made Helena less crazy. She can be so ditzy the horse goes nuts, too."

"So maybe what you need is a degree in psychology."

He looked out the window. We were passing through a patch of suburban houses dropped into what were once fields for crops. He started to laugh, then launched into the tale of the very first hematoma he'd lanced on his own. He'd made the slit too small, had angled it incorrectly, and blood had shot all over the owner's shirt and trousers.

I couldn't help but smile. It was so easy, in the presence of horses, to appear foolish or incompetent.

Our next stop was a mild colic. Then he dressed a surgical wound, checked on a persistent case of mastitis, examined a pair of sheep who had aborted within a few hours of one another. Between calls, Mason retold his worst moments:

The colicking horse he'd given too much sedative, so that when he tried to do the rectal exam the horse had pitched forward onto its face.

"You could have been hurt."

"I wasn't," he said. "But you're right—that's an easy dislocated shoulder."

Then there had been the treasured family pony he'd been called to euthanize. The whole family had gathered for the event: grown children, grandchildren. The grave was dug at the foot of a lush meadow. A decanter of sherry waited on a sideboard in the dining room. The pony was impeccably groomed, mane braided, tail brushed. It wore a show bridle with a silver nameplate. "The whole deal," Mason said. To make it go more smoothly, he'd tranquilized the pony, then positioned it just so next to the grave, and administered the barbiturate. But there'd been rebound—synergy, to be precise—and the pony threw up its head, broke its bridle, galloped fifty yards across the immaculate, cross-mown lawn, then pitched over dead somewhere between the boxwood and the heirloom roses.

"How awful," I said automatically. I'd heard such stories before.

Mason readjusted himself in his seat. "I'm sorry. That was thoughtless."

Then his face crinkled up and he roared. "But you should have seen me in my fresh white coat watching that pony come back to life and gallop off. Oh, Lord. The look on everyone's face. Then the gardener—" He thumped the heel of his hand on the steering wheel. "What he and I went through to get that creature into its grave."

Mason wiped the corner of his eye, and even I had to laugh. Then tears came to my eyes, too, and I looked out the window.

"When I came up here," Mason said after a while, "I thought I was done with all that. I thought all my big mistakes were behind me."

I thought he'd made one in the way he'd put Twister down.

Or I had, by letting him take the black from me the way he did.

But he was already telling the story of one of his brand-new Pennsylvania clients, a small-time breeder who'd decided to switch from natural cover to artificial insemination.

"I thought she should just call me when the mares were ready. But oh no, she wanted a lesson."

So they had had a teaching session—using an old vial of semen kept in an ordinary domestic freezer at entirely the wrong temperature and an elderly but well-built mare who'd never been able to conceive.

I picked up my cue. "She took?"

"Not a sign," he kept saying. "Not a single sign of heat. Dropped that baby in November. This was seven years ago, my first full winter here, and I have an out-of-season foal which I have goddamn bred all by myself."

"Do you like it?" I said suddenly.

"What?" he said. "Vet work?"

I shook my head. "No. Here."

He thought. "I do. I get tired of the cheapness and the thrift sometimes. But I like the variety. And I like the history. Lots of great field trips. I go and get back in a day."

"And the neighbors are good."

He turned those eyes on me, and I told him about Fred and Mrs. Weirbachen offering me a place to stay if I should need it and about Fred coming over during the storm to deliver hay.

"My Lord," Mason said, his voice full of disapproval. "If people would just stop coddling him. Let him go after hay. I'm sure you told him you were nearly out."

"A dozen times."

"Let him suffer, then. Experience some consequences."

"Before, you said that he should sell."

"He should. He doesn't know a damn thing about animals and he doesn't care."

"Fred Weirbachen thinks he should sell, too."

Mason laughed. "He's a shrewd old bird. He sees good acreage gone to waste."

"But why offer me a place to stay?"

Mason had no idea. "Perhaps it's just unseemly. Your being there."

"I'm just the help." I hesitated, wondering to what extent Mason would be willing to discuss Pierce. "He has been through a lot. Watching his sister die. It probably changed him."

"So?" Mason's voice was surprisingly hard. "Play the cards you're dealt. It's always best. You're a pair, actually. You run. He sulks."

"Thanks a lot," I said, angry again.

Our next call was to diagnose a lameness in a saddle horse. It, too, had fallen on the ice. Although I was barely speaking to him, Mason introduced me as his assistant, and asked for my impression. The swelling behind the cannon bone made it an easy call: bowed tendon. Like a very bad sprain, it would require months of care: whirlpools, massages, bandaging, restrained exercise by hand. But with effort and patience, they would have their horse back for light riding by spring or early summer.

We were quiet in the Jeep afterward, and in an effort to break the silence, I dredged up a tale of my own.

I had been asked to run a training clinic at a posh hotel. The riders brought their own horses and I worked with them in groups, two sessions a day with videotaping. In the evenings after dinner, I would critique the tapes for the riders. The day before the clinic started I was schooling one of the hotel's horses over jumps. The man came with the video equipment and asked if he could film me while I rode and check the light. I kept schooling, and we chatted back and forth so he could check the sound levels, too. As I talked, I rode into a corner, came out at a reasonable angle, and headed for a jump. But because I was paying more attention to the camera man than to the mare, she stopped cold and, in one of the classic falls, I flew over the fence without her.

The photographer got it all on tape, and he was so pleased with it that he saved the footage. And so, each night, as I sat down with my sore and tired riders, there I was again: coming at the fence, sailing over it alone. For five solid nights, I watched myself fly through the air and hit the ground.

Mason laughed. "And did you analyze it for them?"

I shrugged. "I dropped her. Served me right."

"Of course." Then he laughed again. "I have no idea what you're talking about."

"Out of sync? Not paying attention?"

Mason nodded.

"Pierce is like that," I said. "Have you ever seen his photographs?"

Mason hadn't.

"He's gifted," I said. "He's won awards. That's why I think he should sell the farm. So he can do what he was meant to."

Mason considered. "So then he should."

Suddenly I felt protective. "It's harder than

you think." And I faltered, debating the merits of trying to explain that when you had a gift, from what I had seen of Lucy, it was terrifying to pursue it, to gamble all, but if you did not, you ran the risk of poisoning your soul.

"I think he might be like my sister," I began, turning in my seat, and watching his reaction with some care. "She—"

The phone buzzed.

Mason signaled with his index finger for me to wait, picked up the phone, listened, spoke briefly, then hung up, whipped the Jeep into a driveway, and backed around.

"Goddamnit," he said.

"What's up?"

He drove in silence, hunching forward over the steering wheel.

"At best? Exposure. Shock."

"In what?"

He shook his head and drove a little faster.

We pulled in the lane of a ramshackle farm: house in need of paint, collapsing porch, tractor shed, rambling barn with board and barbed-wire fences.

"Replacement heifers," he said. "Veal calves sometimes. Odds and ends."

We drove right up to the barn, and both of us popped open our doors.

He shook his head at me. "You're staying here."

I held up my hands. "I can carry stuff."

"Nate."

"Then why'd you bring me?"

His eyes seemed liquid. "Not now."

"At least let me feel useful."

He was reaching into the back, but stopped, straightened, looked at me, then did not speak.

I went to the back of the Jeep, touched his elbow. "It's better if I can do something."

The calves lay bleating in a stall filled with bedding that could have been a whole lot cleaner. The barn was on the dark side. Mason shined a flashlight. The calves were doe-eyed jerseys, beautiful champagne blondes with black-brown eyes and haunting faces.

Mason moved the flashlight from face to face. "Son of a bitch."

I stooped and felt an ear: not just ice cold but stiff. The calf cried. I touched a leg: frosty cold. Two of the calves lay with their eyes rolled up. Already dead.

Mason crouched beside me, looking, touching, shaking his head.

We heard footsteps behind us, then a woman's voice: "I thought they were in the hutches. I thought he'd put them in."

"Where were they?" Mason said.

"The back pen."

Mason clucked.

"Nate," he said. "Come on."

I followed him down the aisle, away from the woman in the baggy jeans and buffalo plaid coat and woolen watch cap. Out at the truck, I stood by, ready to carry things. Mason opened my door. "Get in."

"But I can help."

There were nine calves. Surely there was something I could do.

"She shouldn't have brought them in." He wouldn't look at me.

231

I sat on the seat, swiveled around, and watched him draw out a black case.

"But I can help." I stared stupidly.

"Just shut your door and wait. Or turn on the engine and keep it warm."

He came around and stood in my open door. "If they were mine, I'd just bang them on the head with a baby sledge. Or slit their throats."

I pictured the huddle of calves. "Are they—?"

"Frozen. The old man drinks sometimes. Then he sobers up and turns into God's best citizen. He'll weep for days over this. It would make you sick."

"But can't you do anything?"

What was I picturing? Blankets? Warm baths? Heat lamps?

I stared at the black case.

"You'll make it easier for me if you stay here." He paused. "I'm going to bolt them."

Afterward, we crept down the lane from the barn and drove in silence. It was almost noon, but the day was dusky and the sun weak. Far between farms we stopped along the road.

"I brought lunch," Mason said. "You never know where you'll be."

I shook my head.

He paused, then reached behind his seat for a small cooler. He pulled out a sandwich and handed half to me. "Eat this," he said. "Doctor's orders."

I felt a little numb and my mouth was dry. I choked down the sandwich. He split an apple, and I ate half of that, too, staring straight ahead out the window.

"Oh, what the hell," he said finally, nodded at the glove compartment. "Ther a bottle in there somewhere."

And, way in the back, under the registration, extra socks, flashlight batteries, a box of Band-Aids, a container of juice, and a solitary glove was a small bottle of bourbon.

I passed it to him. He twisted off the cap, said, "Don't be shocked," then took a sip, and a second, and offered the bottle to me.

I shook my head. I was not a bourbon drinker. "Smells too much like sweet feed."

He took a third swallow. "Well, it is grain, after all." Then he capped the bottle and handed it back.

"Three maybe four times a year, I pull off and have a drink." He laid his hand on my arm. "And never in front of a client."

His eyes were large and sad, and I said nothing.

He wrapped his arm around my shoulder, pressed his cold cheek against mine. "I thought I could give you a good day. I thought you needed one. And now I've made things worse."

He broke away, started the Jeep.

"It's not your fault," I said. "I'm just not sure there's anything for me here."

He shook his head. "Is it so different from anywhere else?"

"It's not exactly horse country, is it?"

He rumpled his lip, thought a while, then spoke: "No. But we could use your expertise."

"I don't know," I said quietly. "I don't belong here."

And all the while I kept thinking: Coward.

233

ay is the farthest you've gone from the place
ere Twister lived and died, and you're
ragging about leaving.

He shrugged, looked not so much defeated
as thoroughly sad.

"I'd finish rounds with you," I said, "but only
if I got to do something."

He sighed, put the Jeep in gear. "And you
think Pierce is the one who has the gift."

One afternoon, Mr. Detweiler studies me
from under the brim of his tweed cap, then
pulls a laced snaffle rein from the pocket of
his coat.

—We've given you a gift, he says. One
almost no one gets. Not from the start.

I wait. I have no idea what it is.

—We've made your seat entirely indepen-
dent of your hands.

I puzzle.

He attaches the rein to the bit, then shows
me how to weave the laced leather between
fingers, how to lay my thumbs just so.

—These talk to the horse, he tells me.
Nothing else. Just talk.

He smiles, tugs the rein, again, again.

My hands give and give and give.

In memory, the very next week, I tear in
through the store, land a kiss on Potts's
cheek, and whirl away.

—Wait, he says, and holds out a change
purse.

—She says you know the buses.

I roll my eyes. How tired I am of having recite the number of each bus, the sequenc of the stops.

—I didn't know either, he says. She's gone back to the hospital.

He puts his arms around me. I smell cork grease.

—You have about seven minutes, Nate. She'll understand if you don't want to go alone.

I tear up the stairs.

—Your aunt can be very hard to love, he calls after me.

I make it on time to the corner, say hello to Mr. Stanis, who drives the first bus, and hello to Mr. Koerner, who drives the second. At the Eagle Hotel in Orchard Creek, I get off the bus and start walking up the hill. I march along, convince myself that I am intrepid, but when I reach the farm and step into the end of the cool sweet barn with the breeze wafting through, so gentle and yet so full as if it can lift the whole place a few inches from its foundations and magically float it above the earth, I burst into tears.

I rush down the aisle into Hadley's stall. In the corner by the hayrack, I crouch and press my eyes against the knees of my twill jodhpurs. Hadley snuffles over; I lay a hand on his warm muzzle and sob even harder.

After a while, the stall door rumbles on its rollers. I wipe my eyes on the backs of my hands. Mr. Detweiler pinches the brim of his cap, slides it left, then right, then back to center.

235

-I came to ride, I say finally.

—That's usually best.

I look up at his face, at his mild eyes, and I know he knows about Vee.

—Tack up, he tells me. And go on out to the large ring.

I keep dropping the curry, dropping the brush. I want to believe Hadley knows I am upset, but the big horse is his usual self: warm and somehow present and absent all at once.

I get my tack on without trouble, lead Hadley out, and mount with care and with precision. Then I hardly know what to do with myself. I walk and trot, try to make my turns and circles using only my eyes and the bottoms of my hip bones, and long after I am tired and bored, Mr. Detweiler comes down to the ring, opens the gate, waves me out. I kick my feet free of the stirrups, glad to dismount, go home, and wait for Vee to come home, too.

—Not yet, he says. Go on out to the meadow. At a walk. To the far end and back.

I snatch at my reins.

—Natalie.

I loosen my grip.

He nods toward the meadow, shifts his Mary Jane from one cheek to the other.

—A new horizon, he says. It's for the best.

And, because I am accustomed to, I obey, even though I find it terrifying to ride outside alone. Hadley picks his way down the hill, and I stare at the banks and ditches, the big log jumps, the giant coops. Will Hadley take it into his head and jump them, all of own wild free will, with me clinging to his nec I wish Vee were behind me in the saddle an I am pretty certain I will never shake my sorrows and my fears.

We make it to the far end of the meadow. I turn, see the barn in the distance, hear the cool rustling of the woods, ride through the growing shadows. Then I ride out into the open and pass obliquely between a ditch and a post-and-rail. Hadley stretches his neck, sighs to be out in the sun again. I ride past another obstacle, then another. Hadley walks on, long and loose. I stroke his neck, speak to him kindly, and as we head for home, I slip my feet from the stirrups, let my legs hang free, and I feel almost quiet, almost happy.

chapter seventeen

For the next two weeks, I milled around. I half wished Mason would call again, was half relieved that he did not. I didn't call him, either. What would I say? It's not your fault the world is sad? I counted the weeks until Miriam might have her cast removed. Her progress reports were good, although her mother thought there was no point yet in her coming out to the farm for a visit. Perhaps over the winter break. When she mentioned she would like some ideas for Miriam's Christmas gifts, I spent hours marking up a catalog for her. I dragged myself off to the tack shop, bought books for Miriam, and talked the owner ⸺o letting me sit and take notes out of the ⸺st half dozen *Chronicles*. I wrote a clean, careful copy of my résumé, then balked over using Pierce's computer for fear that I would screw it up and I had no wish to ask for help. Perhaps I could find someone in town to do it for me. I did make some phone calls to horse people I'd once known or worked for. They all said the same thing: Call back after the holidays, maybe there'd be something then, wonderful to hear from me. I had always left people and places behind me the way a ship sheds its own wake, and I was baffled by their evident warmth and pleasure in hearing my voice again on the phone.

Between times, I took good care of the horses. I did not ride because of the footing, but I mucked and groomed and raked and swept and polished. Once I slid up onto Sheila's bare back and sat on her in the crossties.

I wondered how I looked, a lone woman nearing forty sitting on an old white mare in the aisle of an isolated horse barn. But I liked her warmth beneath me, tried to recall the exact words of the Arab proverb about the wind that blows back through a horse's ears, and I wondered: What does it mean that one species should ride upon another's back? I leaned forward, pressed my cheek against Sheila's neck. Then, in a weird fit of impishness, I decided to see if I could still stand and balance on a horse's rump.

As it turned out, I could.

What odd trick was this?

I stood on her rump, my feet turned just so, chin level, hands out. Then I began to laugh, and jumped down. I was a little rusty on the dismount—I stumbled forward and banged my elbow against a wall.

Was I crazy? If the mare had spooked, as she had every right to, I could have cracked my skull, broken a bone, gotten stepped on.

For the rest of the day, I wandered around the house with ice on my elbow. Out of sheer nosiness, I decided to look into Pierce's darkroom. The door was locked. I shrugged, turned away, and examined Allie's knick-knacks.

Ridiculous.

Then I checked myself. Maybe so. But then normal people don't hear horses thinking, either, and I had certainly heard the black.

I took down some of the books, and opened them here and there, as if, like the old Moravians seeking guidance from their Bibles, I could open to a passage that was not random, but chosen for me by God to guide my path.

Instead, I found the books were marked. In time, I came to realize that Allie had made neat brackets around passages she especially liked and that Pierce had left his own trail by way of bent-down corners and back talk in the margins.

Allie had apparently liked biographies, stories, and poems. She had bracketed so much of T. S. Eliot's *Four Quartets* in an old college textbook, she might as well not have bothered.

Pierce's reading was more often medical and

psychological, which I found somehow surprising: the stages of cell changes marked up in a medical book, what must have been Allie's medications tracked in the margins of a physician's desk reference, lay books on the progression and types of the disease. Then there were the books on active death, passive death, bereavement, decision making. What the kids said may have been true: there was a considerable trail of notes alongside passages about watchers, nurses, and what one writer called death angels. Next to a section on making the decision between an active and a passive death, he had written: "Either way, it comes."

After a while, I gave up, put all the books away. I felt sad, overwhelmed, but more than anything I felt stuck. In the old days, I could have simply packed my stuff, headed south, visited farms, knocked on doors. But now I wandered from room to room, from house to barn and back again. I told myself I was staying until I'd seen Miriam safely back into the saddle, but the truth was that I still could not imagine straying from the place where the black horse lived and died.

One afternoon Pierce called to say he would not be home until late. Ten or eleven at the earliest. An old photographer friend was in Harrisburg and Pierce was meeting him for dinner. He asked how my day had gone. All I could say was that it had.

"Did you ride?"

"The footing's bad. You know that."

Silence.

Then he said, "Listen. Why don't you come into town and meet me. You'd like this guy. We'll all three have dinner."

I told him no.

"But I'm following your advice. Rick's a photo editor now." He named a relatively well-known magazine. "We're going to talk about assignments." His voice dropped. "Sure you won't come?"

I told him no again. I'd only keep them from the task at hand. "Good luck, though. You're doing the right thing."

"You really won't? Don't you think you should get off the farm more?"

And just exactly who had spent the whole damn summer on the couch?

After I hung up, I walked the barn aisle. There was little to do, yet Pierce's call had rattled me. What if his friend came up not with assignments but with a job? Would that catapult both of us out of here at last?

I examined the horses, let myself wonder what would become of them. Then, automatically, I reassured myself: I had treated the horses well, kept their manners up to scratch, tried to keep them happy but willing, too. The well-behaved horse with the pleasant attitude nearly always meets the best treatment at the hands of its next owner. It did no good to worry about their fate.

I stood at the end of the aisle, looked out

at the frozen pasture, the dark gray afternoon, and suddenly I was rooting for Pierce's friend; it would be the best thing in the world to have this decision made for me. The Carolinas, I thought, had lovely horse weather this time of year. I decided to get on with my packing.

Up in the cubby, I was brisk, relieved. I filled boxes, taped them shut, stacked them neatly by the door. I put Grandmother Baxter's china back into its wrappings, gave the harmonica a few toots, wiped it on my jeans, and packed it, too. Carefully, I tucked the yearbook and the loose photos in just so. I owned little; I took good care of what I had. I picked up the packet of Harris' letters to Vee, tapped their edges into alignment, looked for a place in the box.

Then, idly, I stood hefting them, pressed them a moment against my cheek. These had been Vee's. I had only ever read four or five of them from start to finish, although I had peeked at parts of most of them.

Without thought, I sat on the bed, tugged the letters from their cord, shuffled them out around me. I glanced out the window: still light. I checked my watch: too early for evening feeds. Then I sorted the letters into order by their postmarks, and slipped the first one from its envelope.

It was dated in July, some seven or eight years before my birth. "I am a coward, Vee. I think you always knew that. Late Saturday night I married Elaine. Easy Elaine. When there is really only you. H."

I'd read this one before, had always meant to read them all, one by one, in order. I never had. Somehow I was saving it—the full sweep of the letters, the story, if there was one. Equally I was avoiding it. After all, I knew some of what happened and had filled in the rest. He'd fled Bethlehem with a woman he'd just barely met at the Elks Club while Vee was already in the bride's dressing room at the old Moravian chapel, in her shoes and slip. For some reason, I'd always imagined, on the face of it, that she'd had no immediate reaction to the news.

Vee was quick, cheery, philosophical. A rainy day was a chance to wear your bright red rain boots—that sort of thing. And, by the time I knew her, she'd had a way of being surprised by nothing.

I ran my hand across the letters, as if cards for a fortune-telling game, then picked up the next one, but could not bring myself to read it. I knew, from the times I'd peeked at the letters before, that they were full of news of Elaine's ailments and Harris' gunsmith business, responses to Vee's comments about her work, passages of sentiment that in some letters was a comfortable affection and in others close to torment.

I closed my eyes, selected a letter. By sheer dumb luck, it was one I'd read before. In it, Harris included a long description of a picnic they'd taken at Lost Cave in Hellertown. Now I could only skim it: How cold she'd been down in the caves, how corny the guide had been with his jokes, but how taken he'd been with the mystery of it all.

I, too, had felt the same thing in those caves on school trips: the slippery limestone beneath my feet, gripping the railing, peering down into the green white water of the Lost River, bitter cold, rushing, no one knowing where it came from nor where it went, all attempts at dropping dyes and tracers into the water having failed completely.

Harris' letter went on: about earlier years in Hellertown when the young people had slipped into the caves late at night, before they were owned by anyone in particular, and had danced all night long in the more spectacular rooms, the light of their kerosene lanterns glittering off the stalagmites.

Poor Harris. "Wouldn't you care to dance again? Can't we even meet?" And he answers his own question: "I know. I should be glad to have you write."

I folded the letter. Always I'd admired Vee's gumption, her backbone in refusing to see him again. How firm she must have been, how strong. Now a small doubt gnawed at me.

I searched for the letter I'd read most often: the last, dated during the time she lived with us, days before she died. I could just about recite it: "My fifth letter to you with no answer. All these years, Vee. Elaine is not well. July first is coming. White for apology we said. Tell me what to do. Are you ill? Do these letters even reach you?"

A mystery. Someone had opened the letter.

And she hadn't been unable to answer. Had Potts broken the correspondence? It was difficult to imagine him keeping five whole letters from her. But then again, why had she not responded?

I glanced up. The sky was darkening. Time for feeds, time to settle the barn for the night. I shuffled the letters into a neat pile, left them on the bureau, and headed down the stairs, grateful as ever for the demands of barn work.

Afterward, by habit, I went down to the house. I turned on lamps, peeked in the refrigerator, then the freezer. I considered making coffee or pouring wine. I paced, and finally admitted that in the six or seven weeks since Twister's death I'd grown used to having company in the evenings.

Finally, I put on my coat and went to the Schwartz Hotel. Famous in the area for its odd specials of pizza, white birch beer, and wet-bottom shoo-fly pie, it was busy every night of the week. That would do.

But, just inside the door, as I stood looking for a small table that was not taken, I felt overwhelmed by the crush of families, by the giddiness of teens on early school-night dates or adolescents traveling in small packs, even the solemnity of older couples, dining at the tables covered with red-and-white-plaid tablecloths. I was too edgy to sit. Had I lost my ability to be alone, and if not happy, at least oblivious?

I stepped over to the take-out window, and as I stood waiting, I caught sight of Mason in the far corner of the dining room. He sat, focusing on his meal, a small beer near his plate. For a while, I watched him, unable to approach, unable to do something as simple as ask if I might share his table. When they finally called my number I took the pizza and fled back to the farm in confusion.

In Pierce's living room I could not concentrate on the news, could not focus on what had happened in the world that day. There was no news of Bethlehem.

In a fit of irritation, I slapped the pizza box shut, pulled on my coat, and headed up to the cubby.

Now it was unnerving going up the stairs, and more than once I stopped on the wooden treads, and found myself listening for footsteps following my own.

I snapped on the lights and found things as I had left them. Gently, I tied the letters in their cord, wrapped them in a cloth, made a place for them in the box. I took one last look at my assembled souvenirs and was reaching for the packing tape when I remembered the gun.

Cautiously I circled toward the bureau drawer, then moved away. Again I circled toward it, and when I finally pulled it open, I studied the little pistol lying with its muzzle toward the door, but could not bring myself to touch it. It reminded me of a rat hiding under a water trough. You don't want it under there, but if you scare it out with the handle of the broom, it might run in any direction and you don't want that, either.

I closed the drawer, found some cleanser and a sponge, scrubbed the little bathroom, then the kitchen sink and counters.

Again I opened the drawer.

Still there.

Still loaded.

I can just leave it, I thought. But the idea was just as frightening, just as paralyzing as the fact that I might pick it up and, out of idleness, bewilderment, point it at my head again.

—Nate, my father says. I'm not sure I'm up to church.

I give him a stricken look. He has promised—*promised*—to drive me and Vee out to the farm. He has not yet seen me ride and I am hoping to show off for him, although after yesterday I see it is in vain. Even at the canter, waist light, back regal, I will never be as beautiful as Lucy in her wedding dress, baby's breath caught up in her hair.

The phone rings. It is the Hotel Bethlehem asking if we would like to come get the wedding gifts or if they should send them.

—Send them, says Potts.

Downstairs we wait by the front door. I trace the letters on the glass: *Baxter's Music.*

—Fingerprints, says Potts.

I take my hand away.

—Are you mad?

—Tired, he says. The day after is a letdown.

The doorman and two helpers come up the sidewalk carrying armloads of gifts in white and silver paper. It takes Potts and me three trips to get them upstairs. We pile them on the sideboard, and one by one I examine them.

—Look, I say. Here's one from Vee. And one more. I wonder what she gave them.

—Something marvelous and strange.

Potts wanders off, then returns. I am counting the packages.

—You've made me wonder, too, he says.

—Call, I say. She'll tell us.

—She's packing.

The plan is that, after their honeymoon, Lucy and John Casey will move into Vee's apartment and Vee will move in with us. I think it is the deal of the century: get rid of my sister, lay permanent claim to my aunt.

A funny look crosses Potts's face. He pulls his tiny silver clasp knife from his trouser pocket, hooks the blade under the tape.

—But that belongs to Lucy!

—Not yet it doesn't. I'll wrap it up again.

I stare.

—Then go downstairs or in your room. Or walk yourself to church. You're old enough.

I stalk down the hall to my room. In truth, I am dying of curiosity, too, and for a while, I stand just inside the door, straining to hear. Nothing. In time, I wander around, miffed at Potts, and I pick things up and put them down. I dig through my bureau and my closet, in search of I have no idea what.

I find all kinds of things: a book report I'd

never bothered to hand in, a black patent-leather doll shoe, a whistle I'd won at a fair, horse chestnuts in their spiky shells from the commons at church, even the small transistor radio Vee gave to Lucy for Christmas. I lie on my bed and, filled with a mysterious sorrow, turn it on.

I keep the volume low, hold the radio to my ear. The music is tinny, but I listen to it determinedly, as if to prove Vee's gifts are as good as anybody's.

After a while, I flick the station dial. The problem with the radio is that nothing of great interest ever comes over it. From the kids at school, I know the stations where the Beatles play, but I cannot tell the difference between John's voice and Paul's, and I have no particular wish to do so. We have their sheet music in the store, under "Contemporary," and I think the words are stupid.

Gloomily I listen to a girl sing a gunky song about her boyfriend. Then I am thinking about Lucy. To my surprise, I miss her.

Suddenly an eerie beeping interrupts the music. An announcer follows, trumpeting something about a shooting death on Winding Hill. One person dead. No further details at this time.

I snap the radio off, lie silent on the bed. After a while, I slink down the hall.

Potts is sitting at the table. Just sitting, holding something in his hands and staring at it. His hands move, reveal a silver bowl. He sets it down, fingers the inside lip of it, shoves his glasses up, and whispers:

—How could she? Her bride's gift.

—Can I see it? I blurt from the doorway.

He jams the bowl back into the tissue paper.

—I thought you were in your room.

—Someone was shot on Winding Hill.

He turns sharply.

I wish I had never turned on the stupid radio, wish I'd stayed in my room. I slide backward on my sock feet.

The phone rings.

We both jump.

I turn and bolt down the hall, shut my door. When he comes to find me, I am hunkered on my bed. My knees are tight to my chest and I am gnawing on one kneecap.

He stands in the doorway and tells me I am right.

Vee is dead.

I feel a brief surge of joy. It serves him right. He was mean to Vee and now she is dead.

But in the next instant I am terrified. I lie back on my pillows. Pain rumbles in my bones.

—I have to make some calls, he says. His voice is shocked and hollow.

He turns away, then as he closes the door, adds, as if telling the air rather than me:

—She shot herself in the temple.

I huddled on the cubby bed, pictured myself finding a broom and sweeping. I did not. I stared at the ceiling, spotted the hole. I tried to see myself, calm and strong, rising to my feet, wrapping the pistol in its old corduroy cloth. But I could not. I could not bear to touch it, could not bear the weight of it. Maybe I could lift the whole drawer out of the bureau and dump the pistol in an open packing box. For a long while I stared at the gaping drawer, and knew that, whatever course I chose, I would first need to empty the chambers.

In the end, I closed the drawer with my elbow, turned off the lights, and headed back to the house.

Still no Pierce. I found myself wishing he would hurry home, or that someone would call or would turn up.

I tried to read. Couldn't. Tried to watch television. Couldn't. Tried to choose a video.

Warily, I scanned Pierce's music. Finally I put something on the disc player, cued it up, then more for protection than warmth, went to the closet for a second blanket. There in the corner stood the shotgun.

I studied it. Did it ever save us to look into the eye of the barrel? Or should we always look away? I slammed the door, as if the force of it were somehow magic.

On the couch, I could not make myself at home. Half a dozen times, I got to my feet, turned the music up, then turned it down, wrong to have to strain to hear it, wrong to have to wince.

In time, staring out the dark window, I was able to hold still. Brahms filled the air.

⬤ ⬤ ⬤

—Nate.

He stoops, presses his cheek to my forehead.

—That's enough.

My face flares with rage.

—But it's not *fair*.

He folds his arms, bows his head.

I wait. Forever.

—You go to church, he says.

I look away.

—It's not right to feel sorry for yourself. What if she's in heaven?

—I loved her more than you did, I say meanly. More than anyone.

He weeps. His body heaves. He says:

—It's not right to cry so much.

Two weeks later, a silhouette slips into my room.

—Don't, he says. I heard you.

I press my wet face into the rough cables of his sweater.

We rock.

—She lived her life, he murmurs. Let's not begrudge her that.

I stiffen in his arms.

But I do. I do begrudge her that. I begrudge her everything.

I hoisted myself to my feet, started the Brahms again, loud this time. I doused the living-room lights, then stretched facedown on the floor, let the music build. And wept.

For Vee, of course. Whose one true love had fled, afraid of fullness. "I'm a coward," he had written, but even so he'd been brave enough to write to her, brave enough to read her letters.

And then somehow I was weeping for my father.

Near the end, he lived his whole life in his chair. Lips blue, fingers swollen, ankles swollen, slippers tight. On the stereo: all of Beethoven, all of Tchaikovsky. Hour after hour, day after day. All of Shostakovich, all of Brahms, all of... His face rumpled. Smoothed. Stilled. He cried: sorrow, fatigue, joy, apology, farewell all overflowing at the end.

I began to sob, loud messy racking sobs. Hideous. The floor was hard, unyielding. The carpet burned my face. The Brahms roared. How I missed them: Vee, Potts, even Lucy and John Casey. My ribs ached, my throat turned to iron. I sensed a fatal void, a chasm at my feet.

I sobbed until I thought my ribs would break, and then I stopped, took my hands from my face, and screamed a black bloodcurdling scream. Stopped. Breathed. And then, because I could, because I had something to learn, screamed again.

Eventually, I went back to plain old crying. I lay there, wiping my face, snuffling, and gradually it came to me that, although I hurt like hell, my heart was still beating, my lungs were still breathing in, breathing out. I saw Twister again, calm and dignified, climb the hill beside Mason toward his grave, and I wished

I'd stayed with him through the end. In time, I turned over onto my back, flung my arm across my eyes, and lay there dozing. It came to me out of my fog that, without a willingness to suffer, we keep nothing in our lives.

The Brahms was almost over when I thought I heard someone call my name. The sheer terror in the voice jolted me awake—that and being shaken by the shoulders.

It was Pierce.

I roused myself, squinted in the lamplight.

"Are you all right?"

"I'm fine," I said, still mostly asleep. "What's wrong?"

"I came in and I saw you and I thought— I thought—"

"I fell asleep. I was listening to music and I fell asleep."

More like into a coma.

"For heaven's sake, the *Requiem*?"

I covered my face again.

He lifted my hands away. "Come on. Up."

"The floor is fine."

"Get up," he said again. "You're scaring me. You didn't take anything, did you?"

He rocked back on his heels.

I have never seen a face do what his did next: it shifted, softened, hardened, settled this way, that way. I read his whole history: fear, sorrow, rage, appraisal, gratitude, martyrdom, loneliness.

I touched his cheek.

"Actually," I said. "You're scaring me."

"I'm glad," he said. "Someone should."

He took me by the wrist, helped me up.

"Come upstairs," he said. "I can't have you living down here anymore."

I gathered my blanket. Pierce took my arm again, and at the top of the stairs, grateful that he did not let go, I followed him down the hall.

chapter eighteen

It wasn't a room for seductions: bed without headboard, bedside table, bureau, chair, a pile of clothes tossed tidily in one corner. By the half-light slanting in from the hall, I could see the walls were bare. On the bed were a couple of thin pillows and a heavy, old-fashioned knotted quilt. I sat on the edge, undressed, then dove underneath the covers.

"It's freezing," I said. Even I was more of a hedonist; in cold weather I always slept between flannel sheets and under a fluffy comforter.

Pierce stood in the doorway, looking down at me. Then he smiled, came into the room, turned his back, stripped, slipped in beside me.

Because of the light, he could see my face, but I saw his profile more than his features or expressions. I didn't care. I snaked my arms around his neck, wound my legs through his.

He kissed with his jaw stiff, his muscles tight. I took his face in my hands. "No, like this."

As if I were fixing the angle of some kid's ankle during a riding lesson, I loosened his jaw and taught him a more languorous kiss.

"Whew," he said after a while. "I never pictured it like this."

I ran my thumb down the soft groove in his neck. "It means nothing. It's all in the joint."

In time his hand dropped to my breast, measured its weighted contour. Of their own will, my breathing deepened, my back arched.

"And this means nothing, either?" He touched the nipple, smiled. "It's all in the what? The tissue?"

Blackness blossomed behind my eyes. Pierce lay hard against my thigh, his hand moved on my breast, and all I could think of was how Alec had reveled in the entire magic of sex. Look, he'd say. Or can you feel that?

After a while, Pierce rolled toward the far side of the bed, dug in the drawer of the bedside table. The perfect junior high school teacher, following the advice of the school nurse.

I closed my eyes. Alec had dealt with matters of birth control with such a cool scientific head that I sometimes teased that he would include his efforts on his applications for medical school.

And then I was weeping.

Pierce froze, propped on one elbow. "Natalie," he whispered. "What's wrong?"

I turned on my stomach, buried my face in a pillow. Gently he covered my leg with his, spread his hand between my shoulder blades.

In time I quieted, but I kept my face hidden. I felt truly mortified.

"What is it?" he said.

I shrugged. Took comfort in the small movement of my skin against his, tried to imagine a dignified way out of this.

"It's Twister, isn't it?"

I lay utterly still.

"You know I'd like you to stay. I'd like you to run the farm."

I shook my head, focused on my breathing.

"Is it Christmas?" he said after a while.

And then I began to laugh. I rolled over, flung up my arms. "You and your frigging holidays." I looked at his astonished face and laughed some more. "I'm sorry," I said, wiping my eyes and running my foot down his leg. "I'm hurting your feelings."

He smiled then, shrugged. His legs mixed themselves up with mine. I moved closer, pressed my face into his neck, and suddenly, lying in a now warm bed, with all of a dark Pennsylvania night outside the window, with the earth bound up in ice, I found myself aching for all the light and hope I recalled of full-blown Christmases.

"Well," I said, "we'd have to have a tree."

His hand moved on my hip.

"And cookies."

I conjured the paper-thin Moravian Christmas wafers.

"And beeswax candles. And we'd have to listen to Handel."

Pierce began to laugh. His arm tightened around my shoulders.

"So you've given it some thought."

"Not until right this minute."

But now I felt that I could reach down to some place inside myself I had not touched in a long while. I could drive to Bethlehem, window-shop, get us a Herrnhut star with its twenty-six geometric points; we could piece it together and hang it in a doorway. We could put candles in the windows, too, cut some greens.

This time when I kissed him, I think I meant it. I liked the light in his eyes, the wry disbelieving grin, the way our breathing soon kept time.

Afterward, I cried again. Not hard, no sobs, just tears leaking down cheeks: mysterious leftovers from the thousand times I had not cried. Pierce traced the line of my eyebrow. "Don't you want to talk about it?"

I shook my head. It would be the work of a lifetime to get caught up on my weeping, a silly task I had no intention of carrying out.

Instead, I told him about barn traditions: making sweet balls of grain and molasses for Christmas treats, hanging greens and tokens on each stall door. "There's a legend, too," I said sleepily, "that horses speak at midnight on Christmas Eve. And anyone who hears them dies before dawn on Christmas Day."

"Beware the barn," Pierce whispered, joking.

After that we lay quietly. Once in a while one of us would shift, and there was a brief moment of pleasure in the sensation, a comforting reminder that we were not alone, that for this brief moment we were more or less satisfied and content. After a long time, I turned, pressed my back into his chest, lay looking sleepily out the window at the night.

Just as I was dozing off I heard him whisper. "Natalie. Natalie? Are you awake?"

"Mmmm." I didn't want to be.

"Can I tell you something?"

"Mmmm."

"I'll get up," he said.

And I felt the cold behind me as he pulled away and lifted the covers.

Digging deeper into the bed, I pulled my knees up. Then I cocked an ear and listened to him, going down the hall to another room, opening a door, coming back. I rolled over to watch his return, a tall lank figure in the dark. I flung the covers back for him, but he came around my side of the bed and perched on the edge. I could see he held something like a box.

"You must be freezing." I moved over, as if to let him crawl in on my side.

"I wanted you to know why I was so frightened."

"Frightened?"

"Earlier. When I came in and found you."

"Can't you come to bed?"

"Hold out your hand."

I pulled my hand out from under the blanket, palm open in the dark. I felt his fingertips, then a plastic cylinder with a metal cap.

"Know what that is?"

I closed my fingers around it, held very still. Then I nodded toward the box. "Do you have them all there?"

He bent down, kissed my forehead.

"Yes."

I sat up, lifted the box away from him, opened the lid, felt inside. One missing. The one in my hand. I replaced it, then leaned down, shoved the box under the bed.

"Should I get rid of these?"

He sat round-shouldered, then lifted me toward him.

"I couldn't do what she asked," he said. His voice was hoarse. "In the end she went ahead without me."

"But I thought—"

Then I stopped. Probably this was no time for gruesome details. But hadn't she disliked the shotgun?

"I'll get rid of them," I said. "I can do that much."

I would give them to Mason, or to Fred Weirbachen. I would go and throw them in a river, hand them over to the police. And tomorrow, after he left for school, I would have a look at the shotgun and see if I could find a piece to take out of it. I would get rid of that, too.

"You're freezing," I said, and after a few moments, he got up, went around to his side of the bed.

After a long while I heard him say, "There's more I'd like to tell you."

I breathed slow and deep, pretended I did not hear.

"Sleep well, then," he whispered, and soon fell asleep himself.

Once in a while during the night, I reached under the bed, felt the metal lace that reinforced the corner of the box. And I would lie very still and look out at the stars, and try to make myself believe that I could see the hilltop where Twister lay. As the night wore on, it came to me that I had as much here as I had anywhere.

In the morning when I woke, Pierce was already in the shower. I lay listening to the water, curling my toes, flexing my feet, enjoying lying late in a warm bed. The shower turned off. There was quiet, then the sound of a razor, and in time a hair dryer.

Perhaps I could make the barn a little bigger, add a few stalls. Take on lay-ups and leg-ups. Start young stock. Maybe buy a first-class broodmare or two. I'd always wanted to do that. I would do no teaching—no riding lessons—but I could take on working pupils, or an apprentice or two. I had the skills, I could build the reputation. I smiled. Mason could refer his loony clients to me.

I admit I felt a little odd—shameless somehow, transparent– loafing in Pierce's bed, scheming, but I was bathed in sleepy, early morning optimism, and instead of getting up to start the chores, I lay there thinking: What is love, anyway?

A pistol?

A woman standing in her slip in a bride's dressing room, hearing that her groom has eloped?

As long as we were kind to one another, what could it matter? For starters, I would get rid of the shells and disable the shotgun.

Soon Pierce was back, shaved, showered, towel around his waist. He came over to the bed, bent to kiss my breast. In surprise, I pulled the blankets tight.

"Such modesty," he quipped, and kissed my cheek. "After last night."

My toes curled. The tide turned deep in my gut. What on earth had I been thinking?

He sat on the edge of the bed, kissed my neck. Gently, I pushed him away.

"You're right. I'd never make it to school." He grinned, ironic yet somehow sweet. Then he stood and began to dress.

I lay there, horrified, embarrassed, and listened to him head downstairs and rustle around the kitchen. I knew I should get up, but now I wanted to wait until he was gone, as if being alone to rise and wash and dress would help me think. I looked out the window. Outside, the footing was still slick, the ground unrideable. I would need to find a way to occupy myself. And then I erased all the sketches I had made: there would be no serious training on these grounds without an indoor arena. Not in this climate. And I knew what arenas cost.

Pierce did not come up to say goodbye. He stood at the bottom of the stairs, called up to me to enjoy the day, to call him at school if I felt inclined. He'd see me tonight, he called, his voice full of gaiety and impishness.

Ruefully I wondered how much he would give away today: a different light in his eye, his gestures freer, his jokes faster and funnier, a little more forgiving toward his students.

Then I rolled out of bed, headed toward the bathroom, showered. I would feed the horses, clean the barn, ditch the shells, see to the shotgun, go somewhere, anywhere for a while, and try to clear my head.

As I was coming back into the bedroom, I saw the top bureau drawer was open half an inch. I was about to close it when I noticed a tag of clothing sticking out. Without thought, I opened the drawer, tucked in what turned out to be the toe of a sock, and was about to shut it again when I saw that underneath the socks was a stack of photographs. I pulled them out.

I had to stare at the top one a long while. And then it registered: it was a beautiful shot, taken from this very window with a telephoto lens.

Of me, riding Twister in the ring.

I stared at it a while, then lay it on the bed, looked at the next one.

Me again, riding Twister in the ring. I compared it with the first. Same day.

The third was of a different day: me on foot with Twister on the longe.

Faster and faster, I flipped through the pictures: me, me, me.

Teaching various girls in the ring.

Working with Miriam on Thanksgiving day.

I raked my eyes through the shots, to see if there was a picture of her falling off. None.

Me pushing a wheelbarrow.

Sweeping the aisle.

Standing in the doorway, staring down at

the house, spookily almost straight into the camera.

I squinted. When had that been? When the horses were ill?

There were close-ups of my face, endless pictures of me with Twister. There must have been fifty of them, printed individually, and on the bottom of the pile were contact sheets, rows and rows of prints: Fred Weirbachen and me unloading hay in the ice storm, me on the same day, chipping ice with an ax, me a few days later waiting for Mason, getting into Mason's Jeep.

I stood, terrified and bewildered. Should I take them? Burn them? Put them back? I thought of Pierce's face in the dark last night, his voice, his grin, the shells under the bed.

For one long last minute, I looked at the picture of me and Twister on the top of the pile. Then I snatched it, shoved the others back into the drawer, slammed it shut, threw on my clothes. And bolted.

Part Three

chapter nineteen

It was Mason who found me.

I had dashed up to the barn, and fed and watered the horses, but had left them standing in half-soiled stalls. Then I had blasted away from the farm. All I had with me was what I kept in the truck: a blanket, a hat, some gloves, my driver's license, a little cash, a credit card. I had not taken time to scrape the frost from the windshield, and three miles from the farm, I put the truck in a ditch.

My only consolation was that I had been heading in the direction opposite from Pierce's school. I wasn't hurt, but the truck was tilted sideways. I huddled in the blanket and, over and over, counted to one hundred, struggling for control of my breathing and my mind. I could barely see, and my hands were not so much trembling as jerking about in my lap like dying fish.

I gave myself instructions:

I will pull myself together.

I will get out of the truck.

I will walk to Fred Weirbachen's.

But then I would think that Fred was Pierce's neighbor and not mine, and that Fred would be sure to mention it to Pierce, and then I would wonder why they had offered me a room, and I would recall the pictures, calculate the falsehoods, and panic again.

I closed my eyes, I breathed, I counted. And began again:

I will pull myself together.

I will get out of the truck.

I will flag down another driver.

A car passed.

My heart roared, and I sat crooked but motionless in the truck cab.

No one I recognized.

I went back to counting.

In time, I thought I heard someone pull in behind me. This is it, I thought. I needed to appear calm, embarrassed perhaps, but not scared out of my mind. I needed simply to ask for help, to say nothing about Pierce or the pictures or the shotgun shells. I looked in the rearview mirror but it only reflected the sky, and before I could aim it elsewhere, I heard a voice calling, "Nate! Nate! Is that you?"

Mason.

I closed my eyes, willed myself not to begin twitching again, then struggled with the door. It was too heavy to lift.

"Can you roll down the window?"

I hadn't thought of that. It groaned a little but it opened.

"Are you hurt?"

I shook my head.

"Then let's get you out of there."

I hung on to the steering wheel, leaned down, unlocked the glove box and got my wallet. I caught sight of the photo of me and Twister and swept it under the seat. Then I let him help me out.

He walked me to the Jeep. My hand was so weak, I couldn't open the door latch.

"Wait right there," he said. He made me take

a deep breath, hold it, and count to ten. "That hurt?"

I shook my head.

He asked me to make fists, move my arms and feet. He held up a finger, asked me to focus on it, moved it this way and that. He asked what day of the week it was.

"I'm fine," I said. "I also know my name and where I am. Want to check the color of my gums, too?"

Trying to make a joke, I pushed up my lip with my forefinger. Instead he pulled my free hand toward him and took my pulse.

"I'm even up to date on my rabies."

He held on to my hand.

"You're in shock, Nate."

I rolled my eyes. "No one plans to drive into a ditch."

I looked back at the truck. It was really buried. I rolled my shoulders. "All that hurts is from the seat belt. Can we go?"

I used both hands, opened the door, and got in.

Mason watched me, then got in on his side.

It was then that I noticed his clothes: tweed cap, corduroys, boots without duct tape, a wool turtleneck, and clean parka.

"Where are you going?"

"Field trip. I'm off until ten tonight. Then I said I'd take the late calls."

The area vets worked out a rotation so they covered one another's calls when someone needed time off.

He eyed my truck. "I have tow chains in the back."

I shook my head, reached over, lifted the phone from its holster on the dash, handed it to him.

"Call a tow truck."

He nodded, thought, called his service and asked them to send someone. He put his hand over the receiver. "And take it where? Back to the farm? Or should we just sit and wait?"

I panicked.

Stay with me, I begged inside.

"Well, you want to get going." I tried to sound utterly casual.

He put his hand on my arm. "You could come with me. Then I could keep an eye on you."

I shrugged, relieved.

"So they can take it to Pierce's?"

I shook my head wildly. "Have them take it back to the garage."

He looked puzzled.

"The front end probably needs aligning. After this."

He spoke into the phone, eyeing me all the while.

After he hung up, he asked if I had everything I needed. Was there anything else we should get out of the truck? Would I like to stop at the farm first?

I checked myself over. "Coat. Gloves. Wallet. Money. Nope, I'm fine."

Mason started the Jeep.

For a while, we had little to say. I watched the scenery and listened to the radio forecasting

especially bitter weather for the next fiv
ten days.

"Shouldn't you be home?" I said finall.
"Tending the flocks or whatever?"

He smiled.

"It's a rare day off. Don't wreck it."

I nodded and fell quiet. Everything I could
think of seemed unspeakable. I'm scared out
of my mind. You wouldn't believe what I found.
Or I could pose a hypothetical question about
a hypothetical friend with a shotgun. But what
right had I to ruin Mason's day? He looked so
cheerful, so presentable, so at ease, except for
his worries about me: Was I warm enough? Too
warm? Thirsty? Was I sure I wasn't hurt?

We wound our way through the countryside.
Soon he began to talk. It turned out he had
had a second major back in college—American history—and he spent what spare time
he had visiting a wide variety of sites in the
region: Gettysburg, Harpers Ferry, Washington Crossing, Lancaster, Ephrata, Inde-
pendence Square. He loved Blue Ball, and the
pies, and the Amish auction at New Hol-
land, the pretzel factory at Lititz.

I smiled ruefully.

"I've been to half those places."

He was delighted.

We got onto the highway.

"But I can't conjure how," he said. "I wouldn't
have picked you out as a history buff."

I smiled. "Guess."

He asked about college.

"Never went."

He thought.

Family vacations?"

"Never took one. We had a store."

And I took a little time out and told him about Baxter's Music—the practice rooms, the customers, the beautiful gleam of new instruments, the smells, the apartment upstairs.

He pointed to a highway sign. "There we are. Forty-two miles." He checked his watch. "We'll at least have time for a good long walk around the North Side."

I braced myself against the dash.

"Bethlehem?" I said. "We're going to Bethlehem?"

The new highway was unsettling. It was too wide, too white, too fast. It changed the texture of the Lehigh Valley, erased it. We got off at the exit in Hellertown. At the foot of the ramp were convenience stores, signs for McDonald's. All I really recalled of Hellertown was that back in the unspeakable dark ages of my father's boyhood before World War II there had been an airstrip where Potts had watched stunt flyers. He had ridden the trolleys there, down the clattering cobblestone streets with a crowd of friends who had names like Scout and Moxie and Hamilton.

I pointed north toward Bethlehem, then realized the interchange for the highway had erased the old airpark altogether.

We passed the Champion spark plug factory on the left and the old coke works on the right, and I told Mason that, each year, people on

certain streets in Hellertown had had to repa——
the north sides of their houses because t——
chemicals drifting toward them on the prevailing
breeze blistered the paint right off the clapboards.
Rumor had it that the surface of the pool at the
Steel Club was skimmed of black particulate
each morning before the children of middle
management came for swim classes.

We passed a place that specialized in
Portuguese food and billiards, and across
from it a large yard crammed with gazing
balls and plaster statues. Today among the
clutter stood a statue of Christ painted in
flamboyant colors.

Then came Saucon Park, with its deep
circle slide, which I had ridden down on
sheets of waxed paper, and its push-go-round,
which I'd run beside with Vee flinging myself
onto it while she stood back and cheered me
on. We had leaned over the stone parapets along
the brook, cheering on the swans like race-
horses as they charged for the bits of bread
we threw.

Near the bend in 412, a neatly painted
sign hung from a high mesh fence: "Local 2259
Vote for Lasko and Naccarro." I pointed off
to the right. Somewhere in that direction
was a drive-in theater, and a place in the
Lehigh River where people often drowned. Now
a sign directed passersby to "The Center for
Positive Change Hypnosis."

And then I gasped.

Mason hit the brakes.

"No, no, go on," I told him.

Surely it had been this way before I left. They

built the basic oxygen furnace before finished high school. I remembered all the hoopla: that it was the largest in the world, that such and such number of Statues of Liberty would fit inside it, that it made heat in a fraction of the time of the old open hearths. Once the BOF was up and running, four lanes of cars had poured in and out of the gates of the parking lots as the shifts changed.

Now the lots were empty. Chain-link fences closed them off and "No Parking" signs hung everywhere. Leafless sycamores with their peeling, raw-looking trunks lined the streets.

At the top of Daley Avenue, we hit the red light.

Mason bent over the steering wheel, studied an old brick building. "What is that?"

"Machine shop. Number One, I think, but maybe not."

Once upon a time the Beth Steel machine shops had been the largest in the world.

When the light changed he asked me the direction.

I hesitated. To the right, Daley Avenue angled down to the Minsi Trail bridge. I pointed straight ahead onto Fourth Street. I wanted to see what was left of the part of town where I had gone to escape.

At the first light, I made the mistake of telling Mason the trick of pinning his speed exactly on the limit and so we paraded steadily through one green light after another, and I barely had time to see it all: the Orthodox cemetery, the furniture store with garish crushed-velvet sofas in the window, the corner groceries and cubbyhole drinking clubs, even the Philly steak place.

Mason tapped the brakes. "Do I detect a longing to stop somewhere?"

I shook my head, looking hard now for Smugglers'. It was to Smugs' that the Lehigh boys, and white kids like us, went in search of relatively safe adventure. Drugs were bought and sold, money won and lost. Everything in the place was painted black, and near the pool table hung a series of posters of sexual positions guaranteed to ruin at least one joint before either partner achieved any level of satisfaction. The place reeked of stale beer and stale smoke, and the only food they served came out of cellophane wrappers. And we had loved it there, had gone for the show, I guessed, or to fool ourselves that we were street-smart and adventuresome.

"You hungry?" I asked Mason.

"More or less."

I rattled off some options: Greek diners, a pizza place at the Five Points, a new Thai restaurant we'd just passed, and of course a whole range of Italian places. "You won't get food like this in Shipville."

And then I knew just the place.

We parked the Jeep near a social welfare office, locked it up, and dodged across the street. The front of Packer's had changed so much that I hung back. The heavy old front door had been replaced by one with airy stained-glass windows. In fact, the whole front of the building was covered with broad expanses of glass—to make it safer, I supposed, more inviting.

Mason pointed with his chin. "Who's Packer?"

"Lehigh's founder," I announced, and went on in.

Inside, wood still paneled the walls and on the ceiling was the same dark maroon plaid wallpaper. Even the Tiffany lights and overhead fans looked familiar. The bar and the old university scenes behind it still ran the length of the right-hand wall. I led Mason over to the lines of high-backed wooden booths and was deeply disappointed: each booth table was lit by a small bright white lamp, the tables were covered with crisp white cloths, and there was hardly anybody there.

I paused. In the old days, at lunch, the place had filled with businesspeople and with reporters from the *Globe-Times* next door, and between three and four, the steelworkers had swarmed in. In the evenings, there were professors from up the hill, two men who owned an antiquarian bookstore, roofers, contractors, and idle young people who had long, earnest talks about getting out of the valley—Alec and I among them with our fake IDs.

"Where is everybody?" I whispered to Mason. "Maybe we should sit at the bar."

"You pick."

I hesitated, then led us to a booth, one that had been a favorite, halfway down the far wall.

The seats and backs were the original wood, still hard and narrow and still carved with dates and initials. I hadn't been the carving type, but now I wished I had left behind some hieroglyphic.

Mason slid in across from me.

"Check this out," I said. I pressed a small white button on the wall. There was no sound, but a waiter appeared magically at the table.

Mason looked surprised.

"Isn't that great?"

The only better service I'd ever had in a bar was a farmers' place in western New York State where you simply held your empty glass up over your head until someone came along and filled it.

For old times' sake, I ordered a Rolling Rock and a cheeseburger.

"What do you want?" I asked Mason. "It's either that or chili."

"Isn't there a menu?"

The waiter recited a variety of items: fried mozzarella cheese, buffalo wings, curry, salad plates.

"Yuppie food," I said, and laughed. "Only the burgers and chili are authentic."

"She wins," said Mason. "I'll have a burger. And a Rolling Rock."

The waiter turned away, and I kept looking everywhere. At the false Tudor woodwork above the wainscoting, at the bas-relief of Asa Packer, at the grainy photographs of Lehigh teams from years gone by. About twenty times, I must have said, "I can't believe I'm here." And I found I did not approve of the rawness or the excessive size of the recent carvings in the booth or of the baseball caps hung over the bar. Somehow I doubted Packer's was shut down anymore by the liquor board because someone in the kitchen had been caught in the fine old tradition of numbers running.

The Rolling Rocks came, and I examined mine: small green bottle, white horse's head. I held it up and read: "From the glass-lined tanks of Old Latrobe."

Mason sat shaking his head. "You can get this stuff in Shipville."

"Yes, but why would you?" I turned the bottle, pointed to what was printed beneath the number: *33*. "Know what that means?" But then I couldn't remember, either, only recalled a silly bet about it at the bar one night, and someone writing a letter, and even an answer coming back—but not what it said.

The burgers came, on china no less, with pickles and a garnish. In the old days they had been served on tiny paper plates, which were promptly soaked with grease.

I bit into mine, chewed, swallowed, then said, "Old Bethlehem tradition."

Mason nodded wryly. "Apparently they leave all sorts of things out of the history books."

I would gladly have whiled away the afternoon at Packer's: pinball, beer, dominoes, reading the *Globe*, chatting up the people at the bar—the laborers, the drunks, the businessmen. But soon it began to dawn on me that without the *Globe* and without the steel, there would be no ebb and flow of customers.

As we paid the tab, I asked the waiter if it was always this quiet.

"Lehigh's on vacation. We mostly do dinner trade now."

Outside, I kept saying, "The dinner trade. At Packer's?" I supposed they frowned on seven-hour domino tournaments these days.

Mason stood looking one way and another. "Where to?" he said finally.

"Let's walk," I said, but I was so thoroughly transfixed with possibilities I hardly knew which way to go. Finally we cut down to Third Street and walked past the old steel headquarters, which I remembered touring on a school trip. I had been impressed by the doormen in their uniforms and by the Beth Steel I-beam insignia on the heavy glass doors. Then we turned up the mountain. I told story after story, about Alec, about the cobblestones on Wyandotte when I was a kid, about the star on South Mountain, about the engineering students surveying the Lehigh campus every spring. We passed through the stone pillars of the old campus and wandered up toward the old Linderman Library. Now I wished we had the car so we could drive up to the lookout. I told Mason about bushwhacking through the woods on South Mountain with Alec and running into a military patrol armed with heavy weapons—once there had been defense contracting at the Research Center.

We walked down another way, through street after street of row homes, some gentrified, some not. Mason studied the various roof pitches and crenellations, and I explained that different ethnic groups tended work in different parts of the mills and that ow your house fronted the street indicated our wealth: a door leading down one step directly onto the sidewalk, a small stoop, then the roofed and railed porches of the row homes, and finally the gracious lawns of the bigwigs. But there were surprising back-yards, hidden Edens filled with birdbaths, lus-cious grape arbors, apricot trees, flower gardens.

Mason asked about Millionaires' Row, where the steel barons had built their man-sions.

I pointed. "We can drive past. Colonel Drake was born here, too," I volunteered. "And Stephen Vincent Benét. H.D. is buried in Nisky Hill. *Oh give me burning blue.*" I quoted from some grade school recitation list.

Mason smiled. "Yes, I hear Washington slept here, too."

It was beginning to get dark. He glanced at his watch.

"It's beautiful at night," I said. "At Christmas, the whole city is full of lights."

"Like Paris? Let's get coffee."

He took my arm, steered me into a diner. He seemed a little tired, but rested and cheerful, too. The coffee came and slabs of pie that obviously had not been baked on the premises. We had a few bites each and didn't bother to finish.

I leaned forward and whispered. "It's a scandal. Bad pie in Pennsylvania."

He patted my arm and reached for his wallet.

I volunteered to get it.

He waved me off. "Payment for the tou He covered the check. "I've learned mo about you in five hours than in—how long?

"Months," I said. "But you haven't seen anything yet. If we drive across the Minsi Trail bridge you can see the mills. And there's the whole North Side."

"Nate," he said gently. "Just how long is it since you've been back?"

"Years." I looked down at the table. "Lucy was still alive."

She had been married to John Casey and they had been living in our old apartment, trying to keep Baxter's going, which turned out to be almost impossible without Potts, who had known every musician in the city and had been so magical with repairs. Friendship, skill, and loyalty had kept the place afloat.

"You didn't go to the funeral?"

I had been on the road in Florida, playing nursemaid to a whole barnful of horses on the winter circuit. Someone in Bethlehem—John Casey or the minister or the attorney—had called the farm and someone there, in a hurry or in a fit of exhaustion, had misread the travel schedule and given the phone number for the next week's show grounds. Someone there had simply held the message for me. By the time I received it, the funeral was six days past.

I burrowed deep into my barn coat, and when we left the diner, I walked close enough to Mason so that our shoulders brushed. "Let's drive across the bridge," I said finally. "That was really home. You'll love the North Side. That's what you came to see."

Mason sighed, shook his head. "Another time. I need to be getting back."

"But you have until ten."

"Nate," he said. "It's nearly six."

"Just one quick drive-through."

He stepped away from me, put a few feet between us. "I thought we were seeing what you wanted to see." His voice had an edge.

I stopped dead on the sidewalk and stared at him.

"Another time," he said, turning back and gesturing for me to walk with him. "I mean that. It's what I came to see. The Moravian buildings. And I've heard they're tearing down the mills."

"Well, I'm not leaving," I heard myself say.

He stopped and waited for me, shook his head. "Don't you have to get back? Where will you stay?"

"Hotel Bethlehem. That's historic," I snapped.

"Yes," he said dryly. "I've read about it."

"Stay with me," I begged. "Just another hour or two."

"I have calls at ten."

He hooked his arm through mine, tried to get me moving again. I planted my feet.

"At least you could drive me over there."

"I don't believe in encouraging bad behavior."

"I'm not some damn animal in your practice."

He dropped my arm, stepped up to the curb, then began looking from one street to the next.

I pointed. "The car is that way. Take 412 south back to the highway."

"I hope you're planning to call Pierce," he said.

I took a deep breath, recalled the photos. Well, hadn't I encouraged him to resume taking pictures? I began to shake. But not of me, I thought. Not of me.

"Couldn't you call him for me? Tell him to feed the horses?"

He grimaced. "You want me to call one of my clients and tell him to feed his horses? Should I give notice for you, too?"

I could tell he was disgusted.

"Just do it," I pleaded, and began to cry. "Please. And don't tell him where I am."

"Nate, what's going on?"

I squeezed his arm, then strode away, cuffing at my tears, fearing that I might break down and tell him what I barely understood myself. I paused once and called over my shoulder, "I'll be in touch."

"I hate this in you," he called back.

I caught the words, but was too far away or too muffled in my coat to catch the tone.

The tree burned bright on the Hill-to-Hill Bridge, but it was a scarier walk than I recalled. The bridge was newly paved, but in the dark the railings seemed much too low. Down below, where Lucy had caught the trains to Philadelphia, Union Station was black—if in fact it hadn't been torn down. The wind was sharp and I hunched down into my coat and felt terrified and alone, afraid to stay here on my own, equally afraid to go back. I told myself I would hide out and think for a day or two, try to come to some understanding, and for a little while I thought about staying somewhere else so even Mason wouldn't know where to find me.

But as I reached the tree, and looked up its great height with its twinkling lights, then turned the corner, I had the sense I'd had as a child that this leg of the bridge led me home. To the left was the Hotel Bethlehem, its sign changed by tradition to shine only the word "Bethlehem" into the night sky during the Christmas season. Up ahead rose the stately west facade of Central Church. The pale green belfry had been lit for the night, and there on the left were the winding red sandstone stairs I had climbed each Sunday morning with my father.

I admit I walked up Main Street first, eyeing the hotel marquee and the golden cloud of light trapped beneath it. I had my credit card in my wallet and, because I almost never used it, the company faithfully upped the limit. The logic of that evaded me, but because I hadn't gotten around to changing my address, I hadn't received a statement in some time, so I wasn't sure the card was valid.

There was only one way to find out.

I sauntered in. A creaky doorman held the heavy glass door for me, and as I made my way across the lobby, I half expected to glance back through time into a private dining room and see my sister Lucy's wedding party going on

284

once again—all of us alive, oblivious to the next dark turn our lives would take.

At the desk, the clerk wore a black bow tie, a white tuxedo shirt, and the traditional dark green Hotel Bethlehem monkey jacket, but he wore his bright red hair in a high, elaborate crew cut.

He grinned, warm, utterly undignified, and asked if I had a reservation.

My face was red, my hair windblown, my eyes tearing. I was wearing jeans, a turtleneck, paddock boots, my barn coat, and trying to look unflustered.

"No," I said. "I don't."

He drummed his fingers on the marble counter and asked if I was alone.

"Yes."

Then he shot his cuffs like a gambler, tapped away at the computer, and after a few moments gestured broadly.

"See?" He flashed the grin again. "No problem." He named a price.

I couldn't believe how low it was. I wondered if I should ask for a view of Main Street, but instead handed over the credit card and wished the Moravians had a few saints to pray to. The card went through, and the clerk handed it back, then pulled a large key on a large brass tag from the cubbyholes behind the desk. With a great flourish, he banged the bell.

"I have no luggage," I said, abashed.

The clerk lifted a dramatic eyebrow.

"At the moment."

He banged the bell again. "The valet will park for you."

Ah," I said. "No car."

A bellboy materialized at my elbow. Same bow tie, same white shirt, same green jacket, black trousers, and remarkable fuchsia high-tops.

"You take care of our Miss Baxter," the desk clerk ordered. Then he leaned toward me across the desk, tapped himself on the chest. "You need anything, you call down and ask for Marko."

The bellboy walked me to the elevator.

"Is he for real?" I asked under my breath.

"Oh, he's all right. He's a drama major."

When we reached my floor, and the elevator doors opened, I paused before stepping out onto the carpet with the inlaid monogram of the Hotel Bethlehem. The furniture and draperies seemed worn.

A sudden fear shot through me. "They're not going to tear this place down, are they?"

I remembered with a jolt that on this very spot had stood the first house ever built in Bethlehem, and that it had been torn down to make way for the Eagle Hotel, which in turn had been torn down in the twenties to make way for the Hotel Bethlehem.

"Worse," the bellboy said. "They're turning it into condos."

"Condos?" I said. "Condos?"

"There's information in the lobby."

He walked me down the hall, waited while I unlocked the door, stepped in, and turned on a light. "We'll call you when your luggage arrives."

"It might be a while."

When he left, I skirted the bed, fumbled with the draw cord on the drapes, and looked out. If I pressed my left cheek to the glass and looked hard to the right, I could see the belfry on Central Moravian Church. I didn't know if I belonged here, but for now there was no other place I wished to be.

chapter twenty

In the morning, I had coffee and a roll in the coffee shop, and while I ate, I decided one pair of jeans, one turtleneck, and one barn coat would last only so long, even at the ageing Hotel Bethlehem. I signed the breakfast check, stopped at the front desk, arranged for my room for a few more nights. A young woman took care of me. She was very sweet and competent, and wore the traditional hotel jacket, but I could not take my eyes off her inch-long nails, painted with mauve and purple flowers and set with tiny rhinestones. I turned away for a moment to keep from staring. On my right stood an easel displaying floor plans for the new condos.

"It's hard to believe," I said, focusing once again on her nails.

She leaned toward me, propped her elbows on the marble countertop. "I just hate the way everything is changing," she whispered.

I shook my head, smiled at her despair. She was perhaps all of twenty-two.

At the front door, an elderly doorman had

taken up his post. He wore a dark green overcoat, shoes polished to brilliant black, and a dark green cap, and he looked far too old to be holding doors for anyone.

"Good morning, Miss Baxter," he said, drawing the door open and holding it just so.

I tried to look polite, appreciative, and nonchalant all at once, and I wondered what it would be like to spend your whole day being not only attentive but nice, and I thought the simple pleasure of shoveling manure still had something to be said for it.

Out on Main Street, I turned left. There across the street was the Moravian Bookstore, larger than before. A jewelry and gift store, a Viennese bakery, a cafe, a bagel place, and a half dozen gift shops lined the streets. One store sold goods from the Southwest; another sold Irish imports. On my side of the street I passed the office for the Allentown newspaper—Bethlehem no longer had a paper of its own—and a store selling crystal and cut glass. Of course, Woolworth's was gone, as was the drugstore Lucy had so faithfully supported with her purchases of cosmetics.

I browsed through a boutique, and there among the sachets and the seventy-dollar scarves, I found nothing to wear. I left, figuring there was still Orr's. Up ahead I could see the signature blue-and-white awnings. I had bought almost nothing there as a teenager, preferring instead the Silver Nut for my jeans and bracelets and the stores in Allentown for everything else. I smiled ruefully. Now that I was older I might actually find a thing or two at Orr's.

But the big picture windows were blank and the store was dark.

No Orr's.

I stood looking in at a display set up by some civic group and suddenly recalling the hot dog shop that had taken up the front corner window. Then slowly I began focusing on what was reflected in the glass. The whole opposite block of Broad Street was gone. Baxter's with it.

Well, I had known that, hadn't I?

I turned, stood under the awning with my hands in my pockets and my collar up around my neck as if I were waiting for a bus in bad weather. The sun was pale and a blade of wind blew along near my feet. I stared across the street. John Casey had written that the building had been sold, and surely I'd been told that the whole corner had been turned into a parking lot.

Still, I stared. A directional sign pointed to the Bethlehem visitor center, and just below the street sign for Main was another that read "Moravian Mile." Cars from other states jammed the parking lots on the corner. I looked up the block and tried to measure the distance to our front door, then looked up into the thin gray air and tried to place our old apartment. I blinked and blinked, like a person operating a jammed slide projector, not quite able to bring up the desired image.

Finally I crossed Main and walked up the opposite side of Broad. Glass doors now sealed off the opening of the arcade and a "For Rent" sign hung from a door handle. Lane's

Women's Fashions, however, was still in business, still displaying "foundation garments" and clothes I was not nearly old enough to wear. The restaurants all were new—Italian, Greek, seafood—and none seemed to have a liquor license. Guth's Leather was still going strong, with its beautiful upscale pocketbooks, as well as the Boyd Theater, and Linderman Shoes, selling shoes I might actually wear.

I looked down at my feet. I had on relatively new black paddock boots. Just about the only thing I didn't need was shoes.

Discouraged, I walked down New. There was the old Bethlehem Club, a shoemaker, a used-book store, and a frothy milliner shop where you could order a custom-made hat. I stood looking in the window foolishly hoping to see someone I knew.

I cut down Market. The old public library, with its broad porch and columns, was now the Moravian Academy middle school. How we city kids had kept our distance from the preps in their maroon blazers and gray skirts and trousers. Alec's father had wanted him to go there, but his mother, rebelling against the culture of executive steel wives, had insisted he be publicly educated. Apparently his hanging around with a shopkeeper's daughter would make him more egalitarian. Today, of course, the buildings were all dark. The preps were out on one of those long vacations the rest of us had so resented.

On Main I hung a left, and deciding to put off going into the Moravian Bookstore, sauntered halfway across the Hill-to-Hill

Bridge. But when I realized I wasn't going to have any better luck shopping on the South Side, I turned around and went in to have a look.

With blinders on, I could pretend it was the same old place. That is to say, the two rooms where they kept the books was still jammed with titles, with an emphasis on languages, local books, and works by and about the Moravians. I tried to browse but could settle on nothing.

I slipped through a sort of greenhouse to a deli, ordered some soup and coffee, and ate, although I found the experience every bit as odd as eating in a library. On my way out, I had a look at the gourmet this-and-thats, at the hand-sewn table linens, the beeswax candles, stained-glass Moravian stars, even handsome Moravian Bookstore tee shirts. The place was fairly crowded, and I had the urge to stand on a stool and ask for a show of hands: "Who here is really from Bethlehem?"

But what had I expected? Moravian garb? Liberty High jackets? Beth Steel baseball caps?

Outside, I crossed the street to the hotel. At the desk, I asked about shopping. I needed clothes, not souvenirs.

The young woman with the remarkable fingernails recommended Hamilton Street in Allentown or one of the malls.

I asked about a bus schedule.

She gave me an odd look.

As a kid, I'd ridden buses everywhere, not just out to the farm, but all over the Lehigh Valley: to Allentown to roam around, even to

Easton (two transfers) to a Chinese place where Alec and I had liked the egg rolls.

I went up to my room, spent an hour calling car rental places, then caught the hotel shuttle to the airport.

It was your basic rental: blue, small, clean, a radio. And it made me smile to drive it. I was so used to trucks and jeeps that the little front-wheel sedan felt like a toy.

I signed the papers, drove it twice around the airport, then blundered out onto the highway in search of a mall.

Before I found my exit, I saw a highway sign that said eighty-three miles to Harrisburg and felt a twinge of fear. Pierce and the farm were not so far away.

It turned out there were two malls across the street from one another. I pulled into the nearer one, parked, and once inside, paused near the directory. Wasn't John Casey last heard from managing a music store in a mall?

I walked along the mall itself, and felt what I felt every time I set foot inside one of these places: all geography had been erased. Elsewhere, I didn't care about this, but now I hated it. I wanted to be in Bethlehem, not in Marketing U.S.A.

And so I hurried from store to store. Very quickly I found a pair of black corduroys. On a whim, because they fit and because they were on sale, I bought a pair of black velvet jeans. Garb for the Hotel Bethlehem. Soon I added a black mohair sweater, then another black sweater of lamb's wool. I'd have to move again before they sent me another credit card bill.

I passed a music store, feeling tense. What if I saw John Casey? I didn't, of course, and felt relieved. The next music store, I paused in front and looked for him, did not see him, and felt sad and disappointed.

In Sears I bought socks, underwear, and two more turtlenecks, and in a boutique I bought a black wool overcoat.

My last stop was a bookstore. I knew it was dumb to shop here, but the Moravian Bookstore might be closed before I got back. And besides, I was ambivalent about the way they had changed. I found the local books, and selected a history of Bethlehem, a volume of stories about the Moravians and their customs, and a guidebook to the Lehigh Valley.

And then I headed for my car—dragging with me all the luggage that I would have. I smiled. Did they call the bell captain for big-time shoppers? And as I drove back to Bethlehem, getting turned around twice on highway exits, I wondered why it was that some people automatically took care of themselves and why others forced the rest of the world to dance attendance.

One day after school, I bang through the store. John Casey is at the counter, his face stiff. In the workroom, Potts picks up the bell of a disassembled cornet, buffs it with a jeweler's cloth, puts it down, picks it up, buffs it some more.

—How was school? he says.

I tell him, but he studies the cornet, runs his hand up through his hair so that it is standing up in waves around his head. Lucy and I call him Albert Einstein.

The front door opens, the bell rings, and Potts startles.

—They're here, John Casey calls.

And then he steps into the workroom with two policemen just behind him.

Potts turns, holds out an arm.

—Your sister didn't come home last night, he says.

I go lean against him, stare at the police.

One pulls out some notes, goes over what he knows: that she hasn't been heard from since the day before, that Potts has called everywhere he can think of.

—And she's never done this before?

He has a double chin and his fingers are thick on the pen he fishes out of his pocket.

Potts says no, she's never been out all night.

I give a little yelp.

John Casey shifts from foot to foot, gives me a look.

Does he know, too? Or am I the only one?

Potts rubs my shoulder, kisses my temple.

—This is my youngest, he says. My tame one.

All that evening, Potts and John Casey sit, stand, pace, look down into the street.

—She's not an easy girl, Potts says at one point.

John Casey blushes.

I stare into a schoolbook. In time, Potts s me to bed, and I drift in and out of sleep, lis to the clock, the phone, to John Casey and Po talking. In the morning, I am sent to school.

On the playground I lean against the brick wall. Dopey little kids twist themselves into knots on the heavy wooden swings, then swing free in wide surging circles. Alec finds me and says he's sorry about my sister and I punch him in the stomach. The monitor sends me to the principal, who knows about my sister, so he sends me to the library.

After lunch, they keep me in the class-room. Vacantly, I do my math, take a quiz. When it is my turn to report a current event, I announce that my sister is now officially a missing person. Then I am sobbing and gulping, standing beside my desk the way we have been taught, not sitting down again until I have received permission.

Mrs. Sook leads me from the room. The prin-cipal calls my father, and all agree I might just as well go home.

I walk fast and keep my head down, and at the front door, I do not look up but turn and go straight upstairs. In my room, I tear off my school clothes and pull on my heavy socks, my jodhpurs, and a jersey. Vee is in the hospital again, but Mr. Detweiler is expecting me.

There is a rap on my door.

I sit on my bed, a boot in one hand.

—Keep out! I say. I'm changing.

—Natalie, Potts calls. I'm coming in.

door opens and he is breathing a little
. One cuff of his cardigan is pushed up
is elbow. The other is loose around his wrist.
is tie is crooked.

I ram my foot into my boot.

—You're not going to the barn, he says.

I pick up my other boot, fling it across the
room.

—I'll run away, I threaten.

That evening I spread my schoolbooks on the
kitchen table. Potts and John Casey barely
speak, but the phone rings and rings. I gri-
mace at every interruption until finally, still
in my riding clothes, I stomp down the hall,
sprawl on my bed, and fall hard asleep.

Around four, I slip out of bed. Potts is
dozing slack-jawed on the couch. John Casey
stands at the window. For the first time, I realize
how very tall he is, how huge his hands are.
He takes me by the arm, walks me back to my
room, throws back the covers, and motions
for me to get in. I do. He pulls the comforter
up to my neck, arranges it just so, then, to my
surprise, lies down beside me on top of the
quilt, balanced on the edge of the narrow
bed.

I wriggle over to give him room.

He lies with his knees drawn up and his feet
propped on the bed rail. The whites of his eyes
glow blue in the early light, and something
quiet fills the air around him and all at once
I feel sorry I ever thought he was doofy and
then I am sobbing because Lucy might be dead.

When I wake, he is gone. I realize I hav[e]
sleeping in my boots and that I have t[o]
hole in my sheet. Then I see that it is n[...]
o'clock.

Gloomily I swing off the bed, bend down,
and unbuckle the ankle strap on one boot and
then the other. Vaguely I hear something fall
and crash below me.

Then Potts calls up the stairs and I am
running down the hall, my unbuckled boots
clattering on the floor.

At the top of the stairs I grab the rail and
stop. There below me is my sister. She looks
up, smiles. Light catches in her hair. My
heart fills with something I cannot name,
and I think: She is back and now I will not have
to tell what I know. And I think this, too: She
is back and now I will not have to find my own
courage to run away.

chapter twenty-one

For two days I hid in my hotel room. I lay on
the bed. I napped. I paced. I told myself it was
ridiculous. I read one of the books and wept
over Moravian Christmas customs: the hand-
carved figurines brought from Bohemia, the
legend of the trombone choir scaring off a party
of raiding Indians, the titles of chorales
played on Christmas Eve. I read the history
book, too, got an absurd lump in my throat
reading again the story of the naming of
Bethlehem and knowing I was sprawled on a

...ed five stories up on the exact same spot. ...d forgotten how the Moravians had ...ected among several different tracts of ...ennsylvania wilderness for their new set-...lement: they had put their decision to the lot, the adults praying for God's guidance, a small child reaching a small hand into a box for a marker.

Potts attends Central faithfully, but never enters the church's brotherly agreement. Lucy is baptized, but because of my mother's illness and death so soon after my birth, I am not. In turn, Lucy and I each attend catechetical classes. Lucy confirms, but I do not. I am not able to write the letter in which I am required to declare my faith. I am fourteen. The Moravians do not allow confirmation until you are old enough to be deliberate. In fact, as part of my religious education, I have been required to visit other houses of worship. I have sat silent with the women in the synagogue, have recited the grim litany of the Episcopalians and the flat litany of the Lutherans. I have stood for an hour and a half through a haunting service at the Greek Orthodox cathedral.

But Vee has shot herself in the temple. I have one dead aunt, one dead mother, a miserable married older sister. And no faith. Reverend Nussbaum questions me with great gentleness, offers to speak to my father. I thank him, say I think my father will understand.

—Come back, he says. You're always come.

Then he takes my hand, and, in that old tr. of ministers, does not let go.

That Palm Sunday I attend church. I will not miss the traditional singing of the Hosanna, several hundred born Moravians falling out into four-part harmony for the hymn that opens Passion Week. I watch my classmates in their robes, the boys in black, the girls in white and wearing white lace *haubbes* in their hair, tied with the white silk ribbon of the sacrament. I sit there on the heavy velvet bolster and I regret that I will not have the benediction said over my head, feel that I need it more than the others.

Potts sits next to me, glancing at me once or twice, touching my hand during the long ceremony of confirmation. At one point, I close my eyes, make a wish, pull the hymnal off the rack before me. I am in luck. The hymnal is an old one, and pasted on the inside cover is a piece of heavy paper. On it is printed "A Prayer to Be Read in Times of War or Attack." I read it twice.

Sometimes I stood looking out my window. If I pressed my left cheek to the glass and looked south along Main, I could see the Central belfry through the stark lace of bare tree branches. Beyond it a flying buttress shored up the thick stone wall of the old chapel. There was the roof of the Moravian Bookstore—slate, with copper trim—and beyond it, at the head

church green, the lightning rods and
slate roof of the Christian Education
building.

I told myself I could walk up there, join the
people on the busy walks of the green, heading
to see the putz. We would wait forever in the
auditorium, then be led to the downstairs room,
cool, shadowy, the air heavy with the smells
of fir and moss. The folding chairs would be
chilly, the risers hollow under booted feet. In
time, the room would darken, then the darkness would somehow deepen and the curtain
would swing back.

As a child I sit taller and taller in my chair,
settle my eyes here—no, there—trying to
guess where the first tiny light will appear. And
then the opening scene illuminates: carved figures and tiny buildings, a landscape of rocks
and moss, a painted sky. A tape plays, and on
it the president of Moravian College reads the
Christmas story, and all the while, keeping perfect time, the light of one scene vanishes,
darkness intervenes, then the next scene illuminates: startling, dramatic, chiaroscuro.
Each year real water ripples in a stream, the
Wise Men on their camels cast long shadows
against a desert sunset, invisibly suspended
angels visit astonished shepherds, Herod
threatens in his palace, hot little stars burn
in a pitch-black night, and a frightened Joseph
steals through the wilderness with his wife and
baby. When it is over, the whole putz is
lighted, scene by scene, and we file along in
front of it. Even fully lit, it is magic. I am proud
to know that by tradition carved wild animals

hide among the scenes, although only
in all my years of putz-going do I spot the
ther crouching in the shadows near the Ch.
child's stable.

I could do that. See the putz again.

Or I could walk through the old burial
ground and try to connect the legends to
the legends of the stones. The last of the
Mohicans. The first Moravian child born in
this country. The famous painters, the composers of well-loved hymns, the victims of epi-
demics. The travelers, the soldiers, the
Revolutionary War surgeons buried in
Strangers' Row.

Or I could walk across the bridges, go back
to Packer's. Probably if I were to ask, someone
would let me sit quietly in the back of Central Church. Surely it was already decorated
for Christmas: the greens, the enormous star
overhead, the painted manger scene behind
the pulpit.

Or I could walk the length of Wall Street,
Market Street, Church Street, and admire the
old houses.

Instead, I paced. I thought about the car
parked down in the garage, costing money. I
thought about me, parked up here, costing
money. I read the guidebook, considered a drive
to Nazareth or Ephrata. Or over to Easton to
see the restorations.

The hotel maids dictated my schedule.
When they showed up in the morning, I went
down to the coffee shop and ate a little breakfast. In the evening, when they came to turn
down the bed, I headed for the pub and had

wine and supper. I slept a lot, too, as if
ly being here were enough, as if I had
aped or were waiting like a fugitive slave
n the Underground Railroad for the patterned
knock and for some brave soul to set my feet
in a safe direction.

Late one night, I pushed back the drapes,
looked down at the busy cafe across the
street. To the left, a neon sign for a bank, whose
name I didn't know, lighted up the night,
but to the right, at the foot of Church Street,
the belfry glowed. I felt comforted; I was
back, I was home. I spread my hand against
the cold pane, took it away, looked up the street.
Once when we were kids, Alec's older brother
told us that we celebrate our birthdays but that,
each year, without knowing, we get up, go about
our lives, and later go to bed on the very day
that is the secret anniversary of our death. Vee
was already dead and I began to wonder: Is
this the last time I will wear these shoes?
The last time I will shoot a basketball? Run
across this playground?

I traced a pattern on the cold pane of the
window.

Lucy and John Casey get engaged.

Vee and Potts and Lucy argue: her age, her
honesty, the rightness of it, even the meaning
of love. Then Lucy runs away and within days
of her return, Potts sends her and John Casey
to the church to make some plans.

They come home with the exact same date
as Vee's failed wedding.

An act of devilment? Innocence?

Potts asks them to change it.

Lucy refuses.

Potts calls the church, finds that the old chapel is reserved for long months ahead, relents.

—But Vee wouldn't want that, I say.

He touches my shoulder.

—Just now, I'm far more worried about your sister.

What little battles. What huge consequences.

I stared down into the street and remembered a lamp store that had been somewhere across the way. How I had loved to walk past it at night: the clouds of light from the chandeliers and pole lamps and table lamps and desk lamps drifting out across the dark sidewalk. I looked down into the dark windows of the gift shop that had replaced it and I knew I would never come back to Bethlehem again. After a while, I found myself looking up again at Central's belfry bathed in soft white light, and I decided that, this one last time, I would stay for Christmas, but only if I could scrounge a ticket for vigils on Christmas Eve.

"No," Marko said. He was sorry. Even he couldn't get me a ticket.

There was no charge, I knew, but seating tickets were required for each of Central's services on Christmas Eve.

"How about Children's Lovefeast?"

A noisy charming service, it was an early afternoon lovefeast of children's hymns and rich sweet sugar cookies and chocolate milk served in ice-cold mugs.

Marko tapped the open book before him. He frowned, lifted an eyebrow, gestured dismissively. "Impossible."

I suspected he was impersonating a concierge in a bad movie and thought that at any moment he might slip into a French accent.

"I attended there as a child," I said. Then added what I'd deliberately planned not to say: "I grew up on Broad Street. My father owned Baxter's Music."

Marko rubbed an invisible pencil-thin mustache. "If you're a member, then."

I said that I was not.

He suggested I attend services elsewhere. "Bethlehem is a city of churches," he said grandly. Or, he suggested, I could walk over to the church itself and plead my case in person.

I dawdled over my coffee and then, gathering myself up, stepped out under the marquee. The air was a little warmer, softer. By habit, I looked at the sky and thought a storm would come. A more reasonable person would turn on the television in her room and listen for a forecast.

I crossed at the walk, passed through the cast-iron fence, and after a moment's hesitation, walked the length of the church to the next set of doors. The handle on the double wood-paneled doors was a hand, cast in bronze, holding a scroll. I took a little breath and went in. I found myself in a foyer, stairs with a railing and white posts curving gracefully up to my left. To my right a pair of doors closed off the front of the sanctuary. Despite heavy carpets, the floor creaked under my feet.

When I was a very little girl—kindergarten or first grade—Potts sent me here for piano lessons with one of the choir directors. I practiced daily in one of the studios down in the store, and although, in theory, no one could hear me, Lucy mocked my playing. I had fingers like bananas. I was tone-deaf. The mannequins at Orr's had more talent. And I believed her. Every Thursday I walked to my lesson in the CE building, sat beside Mr. Heidt on the piano bench, and, at each mistake, cringed and hunched my shoulders. Then one Thursday, because the CE building was closed for renovation, he led me up to the organ loft of Central's sanctuary. The bench was so tall he had to lift me onto it. In front of me lay a waterfall of keyboards and what seemed like a thousand stops. One touch of a key and the whole back of the church came to life: the entire wall of organ pipes breathed and sighed. I played eight whole bars that lesson, and although Mr. Heidt stopped the organ down as far as he could, I would not touch it again. Later that week he and my father agreed that my lessons could wait until the building was finished, but by then Mr. Heidt had moved on to another church and I had no wish to play again.

I felt oddly fearful entering the office, but the woman at the desk was friendly enough. Fresh flowers stood in a vase, a familiar old engraving of the church some decades earlier hung on a wall, and in a corner on the floor were boxes of leaflets for a service.

The woman asked if she could help.

305

"I'm here for the impossible," I said.

She smiled and shook her head. "Tickets went out to members weeks ago."

"I just thought I'd ask."

The church had started issuing tickets so that members could be guaranteed seats at their own services without having to wait in line, trying to beat out perfect strangers for the right to worship in their own way and their own place on Christmas Eve.

"I've just come back to Bethlehem," I said. "I attended here as a child."

She folded her arms, leaned forward on the edge of her desk. "Are you a member?"

Her voice was friendly, but suddenly I understood Ben Franklin, who sometimes loathed the Germans in general for their industry and the Moravians in particular because, in the early days, Bethlehem was a closed cooperative community: If you were a Moravian and a contributing member, you were in. If not, you were out.

"My mother was," I said. "My sister. My whole family was buried from here. I even attended catechetical classes. Did you know Reverend Nussbaum?"

She smiled. "Yes. He officiated at my wedding."

I felt a leap of warmth.

A door opened across the room, and a tall, white-haired woman came in wearing a dark green dress.

"Reverend Willis, this is—"

"Natalie Baxter."

"She was hoping for a ticket for Christmas Eve."

Reverend Willis shook her head. She seemed kind, too, but busy with other matters. For a wild moment I considered offering to be tested. I knew the theology, the lore, the history. I trusted my recollections, and I'd been reading. I just hadn't been able to trust that I had faith, and I hadn't been able to lie about it, either.

"I'm so sorry," said the secretary.

"You understand," said Reverend Willis.

I strode around the block: up Main to Market, out to New, down along Church and back. And all the while I cursed the Moravians and my attachment to them. But that had been the crux of it, hadn't it? I loved Central, holding my father's hand, the peace that fell on us during services, the music pouring down on us, and the light sifting upward across the ceiling. But perhaps even at fourteen I had been able to sense that it is one thing to believe in God, and entirely another to love the trappings and the traditions of a sect.

Still, as if making a case for my admission to services on Christmas Eve, I silently rattled off all the odd things I knew: Which well-loved minister had been called all his life by the name of the butler he'd played in a college theater production. A silly but bitter argument over whether lovefeast buns could have raisins in them or not and how Potts had joked that we might be witnessing the next schism. Even the little old ladies from the Widows' House sitting near the front where they could listen to the service amplified through headsets and how, if they didn't care for the sermon, they took off the earphones, folded their white-gloved hands, and glared at the pulpit.

What is it, I thought, that makes one belong? And then I had an idea.

I wasn't in the mood to go back to my room, so I walked around the block again and went to the library. Inside the lobby I remembered the same old wall sculpture of wire and geometric shapes, and I figured I could certainly find a phone book.

But as I slipped back toward the reference section, I glanced into a side room where a young man was sitting at a bank of computers. On the door a sign announced a day-long workshop on the Internet.

"Come on in," he said. He had a ragged haircut, three gold hoops in his right earlobe, and a Moravian Academy sweater. Leaning toward me, he whispered with mock criminality, "Whatever you want in the library, there's more of it on the Net."

I shook my head. "All I need is a phone number."

He immediately began tapping keys.

"What's the name?"

I stepped closer and peered over his shoulder. "Is this for anywhere?"

His face looked pained, and I felt old and hickish.

I sat. "I'm a horse trainer. I've never seen all this before."

He bobbed his head. "This is cake. Who do you want to find?"

I thought: I'm not trying to find anyone. I just need a phone number.

Then I heard myself say, "McGonigle. Alec."

Swiftly, he typed it in, even spelling McGonigle correctly, then gestured at the screen. "Do you have any other information?"

"Well," I said. "I'm pretty sure he's a doctor. And the middle initial is a B."

He added those, and when I said I didn't know what state, he punched a button.

And there he was: Alec B. McGonigle, MD. Philadelphia. Complete with street address and phone number.

I couldn't take my eyes off the screen. "Do you have a pencil?"

The young man made a face, tapped a few keys. The printer rattled and soon, in my hand, was Alec's address and phone.

I stood, kept staring at it.

"Don't you want to see anything else? There's the whole rest of the Net."

I shook my head, backed out of the room, thanked him again and again.

Stunned, I headed back to the hotel. I kept looking at the printout, folding it up, trying out one safe place or another to keep it. Back in my room, I put it aside long enough to look up the law firm that handled Potts's affairs. Once a year, I got a statement from them, which I barely read. They monitored the residue of the estate, but since the money came from the deaths of my father and my sister I wanted as little to do with it as possible.

I dialed the number.

"Vorhees, Hirsch, and Maxfield," said the receptionist.

I introduced myself and before I had a chance to say I was calling to speak with Mr. Vorhees, the receptionist cut me off.

"Miss Baxter, we've been trying to reach you, but our letters have been returned."

Well, that must be true. I'd never bothered forwarding my Ohio mail because I hadn't planned to stay in Pennsylvania.

"Is something wrong?"

She wouldn't say. Instead, she asked if I could be reached by telephone that afternoon between one and two. Mr. Maxfield would call me then.

"Mr. Vorhees," I said.

"Ah," she said. "Mr. Maxfield will explain."

"Is he still alive?"

Yes, Mr. Vorhees was still living. She had one of those voices which serve to remind all callers that law offices are the last bastion of formality in America.

I told her I could be reached at the Hotel Bethlehem.

That changed everything. Would I be able to come to the office?

I said I would, although I wanted to know why. After all, even though they were inviting me, they would be certain to send me a bill.

"To discuss your estate."

I thought my estate was fine. I assured the receptionist that I trusted Mac Vorhees' discretion in my affairs. Then I smiled to hear myself adopting her mode of speech. I didn't say that, even though I didn't entirely trust her, I had preferred it when Lucy had been left in charge of the attorneys and the residue. I had been simply content to reinvest my quarterly portions and after Lucy died I'd left directions to reinvest her shares, too.

"I'd like to see Mr. Vorhees if that's possible."

There was silence. "He's very ill."

And then I realized how old he must be. I remembered his beautiful office in the corner of the building. Window seats ran under casement windows, and beyond the windows lay formal gardens with trellised roses and flowering crabs, magnolias, and mulberries. On Sunday afternoons Potts and I had sometimes visited Mr. Vorhees in his garden. One day when I was about five, I had asked Mr. Vorhees to marry me. Of course, he and Potts had laughed, but I'd thought Mr. Vorhees the perfect choice: he let me run without warning me not to fall, his maid brought cookies and drinks, and at the end of each visit, he produced a clip knife from a pocket and cut me a flower to take home.

And then I wondered: How old would Potts have been if he had lived? Seventy? Eighty?

Stunned, I agreed to see either Mr. Vorhees or Mr. Maxfield early Monday afternoon.

"Is that convenient?" the receptionist inquired. "It's Christmas Eve."

I assured her it was, and I was about to hang up when she thought to ask why I had called in the first place.

"Well," I said, sheepish and bewildered, "I was hoping for a ticket to vigils at Central Church."

"I'll make a note," she said, as officious as if she might also be in charge of ordering up the weather.

chapter twenty-two

Saturday morning, I settled with the desk clerk for a few more days, and then I decided I might as well go somewhere. I pulled the car up out of the hotel garage, drove along Main, hooked one turn and then another until I realized I was heading toward my first high school. It was the old brick building both Vee and Potts had attended, and when the second high school was built, a sprawling modern educational factory full of luxuries, Potts had mildly objected when Alec and I chose to be bused out there. Alec had opted to go because of the science labs. I opted to go because of Alec.

I wandered the city, doing no doubt what anyone does when they return after twenty years. I exclaimed to myself over what was new, rejoiced over what remained. As I came upon them, certain streets looked familiar, but I groped my way along, trying to recall how one street connected with another. Did Elizabeth connect with Highland? Where was Illick's Mill? Sometimes I felt a little jolt of triumph—the mere glimpse of a church on the same corner where I had last seen it was enough to bring this on. All the while I had the equal and conflicting sense that I knew exactly where I was and that I had never been here before in my life.

In time, I slipped through Freemansburg. Wasn't there a park here somewhere? A drive-in movie theater? I crossed the Lehigh canal and then the river and turned left toward Steel City. I had Alec's address and phone tucked safely in my wallet, but I had no idea if I would find what I was looking for.

As I drove, I recalled the wonderful names of roads: Applebutter, Wassergass, Hexenkopf, Tickle Belly. We had been forbidden to drive on Hexenkopf: Witch's Head Road was said to be hexed, and sometimes reports of sacrificed animals surfaced in the back pages of the *Globe-Times.*

Fear of the evil one was prevalent in the the immigrant populations in the Lehigh Valley, and although Potts was clear that we did not believe, he was also clear that when visiting my school friends I would respect their traditions without comment. In one home, a penny lay face up in every corner of every room. At yet another, in order to keep the circle of the house closed, we were required to always come back in whatever door we had just gone out. Even Alec's house, a brand-new sprawling ranch, had had chicken bones ground into the mortar of the foundation in order to ward off the hex. The very last time we drove on Hexenkopf Road was in the middle of a downpour after school. Outside the windows of Alec's shiny new VW Bug, the thunder roared and the rain came down. The headlights were watery in the gloom and the Tinkertoy windshield wipers barely cleared the glass. Inside, feeling very cheeky, we recited passages from *Macbeth*, which we were studying in school. Our recitation was badly garbled and punctuated with our laughter. Then an enormous tree came down, just feet behind us. Lightning split the sky, and suddenly we were reciting the age-old antidote to evil: "Angels in heaven, ministers of mercy, protect and defend us."

I turned and turned. Stopped, backed around, tried another road. And there I was: at the locked gate of Alec's gun club. I sat with the car running. The woods were bare, the sky the color of slate. On the gate hung a sign: "Members Only. Steel City Gun Club." Some wise guy had shot a hole in it. Ahead of me lay the long curving gravel lane.

A few weeks into the first year at our new school, Alec turns secretive and aloof. I tease him, harass him. I am only here because he is: I refuse to be neglected or abandoned. I dog his tracks, and finally he confesses: the new school has a rifle range built beneath its stage and he has joined the rifle team.

I rag him mercilessly. Is he going to shoot poor innocent deer? Wear a goofy orange cap? Doesn't he know what will become of him if he is drafted into Vietnam?

—They'll make you a sniper.

One day he grabs my arm, looks me in the eye, and demands whether I have ever, in my whole life, held a gun in my hands—much less shot it?

Well, no, in fact, I haven't.

—Dare, Nate?

And so that Wednesday, after last period, I creep down the dark concrete stairs, open the heavy metal door. Gunpowder instantly dries my nostrils. I am the only girl, but the coach silences the teasing and proceeds to fit me with a rifle and a sling. I lie on the mats, all the way at the end, and the coach's quiet voice explains that I do not need to learn to shoot, but only how to breathe and how to see, and to everyone's astonishment, by the time the late bus is announced, I am shooting solid 90s in prone.

It is difficult for me to understand why this so upsets the boys, and the next day the coach will tell me that I have two things in my favor: The first is the intelligence to listen to good coaching. The second is a gift.

I become addicted. My coach tells me that "shooting with the body and the breath" creates the same brain waves as prayer and meditation. At sixteen I only know I love to shoot. I love the strange quiet in the instant before the shot, the satisfaction of a clean hit, the power to pierce a target or some other object fifty paces off just by thinking about the trigger. I love what is for me the easy success of it, love the delicious irony that, within weeks, I am a better shot than Alec. When I am on the range, bored because I have fired my rounds while the boys are still fiddling with their scopes or ear protectors, I amuse myself by shooting the tacks off the corners of their targets.

That fall, I shoot anything I can get my hands on, and I shoot as much as possible. I am wild to shoot, desperate. I never miss a practice, come early, stay until the last possible minute. When another girl joins the team, I despise her: she spends the whole time giggling and she is a lousy shot. One weekend Alec and I visit a friend of his father, who lets us shoot his antique muzzleloader. The day is damp and half the time we can't get it to fire. The rest of the time we miss everything we aim at.

—They fought the Revolution with these things? we say.

—Keep your powder dry, we tell each other all afternoon, and laugh our heads off.

One day my coach brings in his .45 and puts it into my hands. It is far too much gun for me. Even two-handed, my eleven o'clock draw is so pronounced I fear I will shoot a hole up through the stage. I lack the strength to let it fall properly through the targets. Still I am ready to struggle with it, do what it takes to learn the piece, when Mr. Krowell lifts it away from me, making some remark on the virtue of humility.

And, one Friday after school, Alec brings me here. It's a surprise, he says. Wear warm clothes. But other than that he won't say. He'll bring everything we need. Between us, something has been changing. My school pal from grade five, my confidant, my sidekick, Alec is not my boyfriend, although, in

316

the weird logic of the heart, it would be disloyal to find another steady. Lately, though, we have been growing distant. Alec seems quieter, troubled somehow, not quite happy. People assume we are, if not lovers, then on the verge of becoming so. Certainly we touch each other: on the arm, the leg, the shoulder. Not the face, not the hand. Nor do we walk arm in arm. For some reason, as we drive through Freemansburg that afternoon and out onto the country roads, I get it into my head that we are going to find some back lane and teach one another how to kiss, maybe more.

Instead, we pull up at the gate of the Steel City Gun Club.

I sit, waiting for his lead. This is his excursion.

—Come on, he says, then hesitates. Unless you don't want to.

—Sure, I say. I want to.

Alec gets out, digs in the back seat, and takes out a case and two small boxes. He opens the case and puts into my hands a .22 target pistol. A simple, workmanlike piece. Nice balance.

He holds up the boxes.

—And for you, he says, more rounds than even you can stand to shoot.

Carefully, he places targets at several distances and, behind his back, I smile at his particularity. Then we take turns with the pistol, and long after Alec tires I shoot and shoot and shoot. I love the sharp report, the echo off the limestone walls, the solitude, the wildness in the air.

When the cases are empty, I am high and wild. But sheepish, too. Guiltily I offer to buy him some new ammo.

He packs the gun into its case, then looks at me and says:

—We're years underage.

When we get into the car, I lean toward him. He cocks an eyebrow, but before he has a chance to make a joke I snake my arms around his neck and kiss him.

For a moment, he freezes. I know Alec always needs time to think, but before I can pull away, offer my own joke to cover up, he is kissing me back. His hands are on my face, in my hair, on my neck, searching for the zipper of my jacket.

In time we break free.

—Uh-oh, he says, and laughs, a little shaky. He turns, kisses me some more, then makes a show of gasping for breath and starts the car. We drive away from the range, but without saying so we both know we are not ready to go home.

After a while, Alec gets the idea that we can go to a gunsmith's and look at pistols. He knows a guy, he says. Belongs to the gun club.

It is a little place, out in the sticks near an old run-down garage and a country lunch counter. I think it's fascinating, and soon I am peering into the glass cases, admiring the handles, noting the prices of one pistol after another. I can't help but imagine what it would be like to have my own pistol, to have

it in my power to pick and choose my quarr
afternoons without waiting for Alec.

At one point, I notice the man's name on
a business card. It doesn't register. I am too
busy wondering if I am too young to hold one
pistol or another, to have them brought out
from under lock and key and laid on the
same kind of velvet pad we have at the store.

The man watches me. He is large, round-
shouldered. His fingers are neat and blunt,
his gray hair wispy. As he moves back and forth
behind the counter, I hear his feet shuffle as
if he is indifferent or ill. But his eyes are full
of light and soon he begins to smile.

—Do you shoot, too? he says finally.

—Better than me, Alec says, half proud, half
rueful.

The man lays his hands on the edge of the
counter. I notice he has acquired the shopkeeper's habit of keeping his fingerprints off
the glass countertop.

—How much better? he jokes.

—A lot, I say, and we all laugh.

Then Alec remembers his manners:

—Harris, this is Natalie Baxter.

The man tilts his head. His smile is quiet
now, ironic.

—I see the resemblance, he says after a
moment. Now that I hear the name.

I frown.

—You're from the store, he says. Yes?

—Baxter's Music, Alec tells him.

Because his father is a muckety-muck at the
steel, Alec takes pleasure in the fact that my
father does something "real."

319

—I knew your father's sister, says the gunsmith.

—Vee? I say stupidly.

When Alec finally takes me home, my sister
asks how the afternoon went.

—Wonderful!

She smiles bitterly, rolls out dinner biscuits
with slight bangs of the rolling pin. John
Casey spends all day in the store and Lucy runs
things. Potts is tired all the time, but still he
insists that Lucy doesn't have to be in charge.
She could be downstairs, working at the
piano. She could resume her studies. Things,
he says, can run themselves.

—And how was Alec?

I shrug.

Lucy smiles, calculating. I know she thinks
Alec is a nice boy from a nice wealthy family,
and I know she hopes I have the brains to marry
him someday. I watch her lean into the dough,
chaos all around her, and I think that she of
all people might be one to warn against the
dangers of reckless marriage.

—Alec is my pal, I say. My best friend.

I touch my lips and wonder.

That evening I sit with Potts. I have done the
dishes, wiped the counters, but Lucy is still
banging around out there like a martyr. John
Casey has gone back down to the store. In a
low voice I tell Potts I met Harris Schlegel.

—He's a gunsmith, I announce.

320

—I knew that, my father says, sounding weary.

He leans back, closes his eyes. After a while, he tells me that Vee was always meeting unlikely people, and that she was already out of nursing school, already at the hospital, working one tough rotation after another, when she met Harris. What she liked was that Harris Schlegel knew how to have a good time.

I nod, but do not say that for an old man he still has a fabulous laugh.

—They drove for hours, Potts remarks.

Everywhere. On larks: all the way to Philly for roasted chestnuts or hot pretzels, out to Blue Ball for slabs of pie, into New York for New Year's Eve or rush opera tickets, down to Kintnersville to watch the netting of the shad.

—Two of a kind, he says. Only Vee was more so. She was so—So—

I try to tell him I know. I had seen it, too. He shakes his head.

—She wasn't half herself after Harris. Once I set up a date for her. She went, but afterward she chewed my ears off.

Of course, it was Harris who had taught her to shoot: pistol, rifle, shotgun, targets, skeet, the works. And when they finally got engaged, Harris gave her a pistol.

—And she used it, too, Potts says.

—Of course she did, I say, wondering if this might be a good time to mention that I would like a pistol, too. For my next birthday. Or for Christmas.

—I mean *used* it.
I puzzle.
—At the end.
Oh, my God, I think. So that's love.

Flakes of snow hit the windshield of the rental car. I got out and pulled my collar up around my neck. The weight of the wool overcoat was unfamiliar, and I felt like a horse in a new winter blanket. I walked the lane, and saw that little had changed: the open meadow, the picnic tables in a grove of trees, the pavilion for the shooters, and across the meadow the high walls of the limestone cliffs and the sandpit underneath the empty holders for the targets.

I slung my arm around the pillar of the pavilion and stood a long while before heading back to the car. The snow was coming down thick and fast. I turned on the windshield wipers, backed out into the road. For a little while, I thought of turning on the radio for the forecast. Instead I looked up at the sky, and figured it was snow, it was snowing hard, and it would obviously continue until it stopped. Not a day to go to Bucks County to see what had become of Detweiler's farm.

For a moment, I thought of Pierce, stab of relief that I had finally ordered had helped fill the loft before finding pictures. I shuddered. At least he fed the horses. Briefly I wondered if I should call him. I also wondered if the shoes were still under the bed and

322

truck had been repaired. I thought, too, of Miriam, reminded myself that I had a gift for her.

Near the center of the city, I pulled in at a pizza place. I would do well to conserve money. I went in, ordered coffee and the smallest pizza they had, wondering if I could smuggle the leftovers up to my room. I sat staring down into my coffee, trying to remember more shooting with Alec. Perhaps there had been none. Kissing and other things continued, but as near as I could recall, I walked away from rifles and from pistols at some point, had begun doing other things with my body and my breath.

Or was it later that I quit?

I left the pizza place, and noticed a florist across the street. I stood under the overhang and thought. There would be little to do that afternoon once I got back to the hotel. I corrected myself. A lot to do, really, but I was in the mood. It was like an opening with a horse, a readiness, and I couldn't guarantee when it would come again.

The woman behind the counter was wearing a smock and glasses on a chain. Again I had the eerie sense I could be anywhere: the coolers with the buckets of flowers, the wreaths and Christmas centerpieces.

I had the urge to go in and remind her: This is Bethlehem.

I wanted desperately to say: I grew up here. I left. And now I'm back.

But when she asked if she could help, I said I wanted roses. Red ones.

How many?

I counted on my fingers.

"Are they for a bouquet?" she asked. "A dozen is nice, but six or eight can work well, too."

"I'm laying them on graves."

She clucked. "That's a waste."

"I haven't been back in twenty years."

She clucked again, counted the roses, wrapped them in cellophane, and covered their heads with tissue paper.

chapter twenty-three

Normally I didn't mind driving in bad weather. I always owned a four-wheel-drive vehicle, used my head in snow and ice, and as a general rule, kept some distance between me and lunatics. But driving the toy rental back through the city was harrowing. Even with the defroster on full blast, I had to stop and dig the clotted snow and ice out from under the wipers. I made it up hills, the front end clambering, my shoulders hunched over the steering wheel. All around me, other cars skidded and fish-tailed. For years I'd made smart remarks about city cars, so maybe it served me right to have to drive one in the snow. As I inched along, I frantically tried to reconstruct the pattern of one-way streets in the center of Bethlehem. With the snow thick in the air, and the pale candles in the shadowy stone buildings, I wouldn't have been surprised to see Zinzendorf himself marching up Church Street, the hem of his black cape swirling about his calves, snow collecting in the deep brim of his hat.

I managed to stop at the foot of Church, took a right, shimmied up Main, prayed the car behind me would see my signal, then hooked a left into the dry, yellow-lit garage behind the hotel. Collecting my flowers, I went up through the lobby and headed toward my room. Then I stopped, thought, and went straight toward the front doors.

"Miss Baxter," said the ancient doorman.

He saw I was going outside in a heavy storm with an armload of flowers wrapped up like an infant and offered me an umbrella.

I accepted.

Out under the marquee, he shook it open, held it, and I took a minute pulling up my collar. The coat was big enough so that I could tuck the flowers inside it. Except for the fact that I was wearing corduroys and paddock boots, barely visible below the hem of the coat, I suddenly looked like one of the little old ladies on the South Side during my childhood.

I picked my way across Main, climbed the stairs at Central. The high cream-colored walls of the church rose above my head. As I passed the vestry doors, I wondered if churches still offered sanctuary to storm-tossed travelers, and for a brief moment I thought of turning back. The snow was up around my ankles and fell in heavy flakes around the perimeter of my umbrella.

I crossed Heckewelder Place, paused at the foot of the triangular green, and, for a moment, tilted back the umbrella and let the snow touch my face. Then I took the path past the Old Chapel and behind the Sisters' House.

Lucy is ready so early for her wedding, she decides that we should walk. The coupe, all decorated, stands at the curb in front of the store. Potts plucks a streamer from the fender and twirls it around his neck, then takes each of us by the arm. It is a late afternoon, a Saturday, a shopping day. The owners of other stores come to their front doors, wave, cross themselves, call out to us. Lucy has to go on tiptoe so the tiny points of her high heels won't catch in the spaces of the brick walks. I trip along in my flats, and our skirts stream around our legs in the hot, late-day breeze. The photographer walks with us, sometimes going on ahead and turning back to get a shot.

Potts looks at his watch. "For the next hour," he says, "I'm the luckiest man in the world."

We turn up onto the green, up the old stone stairs, take a few pictures near the herb garden. Lucy's hair is short and wispy, and she wears her crown of baby's breath with an odd sense of entitlement. She carries her bouquet the same way, proud but easy, as if she knows she and her flowers and her hair and her whole self are beautiful—and as if she knows they damn well ought to be.

We stroll up Heckewelder. Potts points to a place where a small building once housed the bodies of the dead before they were buried.

—Daddy, I say.

Then Lucy giggles, and I giggle, too, and knowing we are laughing at the same thing, she pulls all of us to a halt, reaches across Potts, and kisses me on the cheek.

Then she straightens, eyes the scene. People are arriving for the wedding, and because she has no intention of being cooped up in the bride's dressing room, we go the rest of the way up Heckewelder and wander in the old burial ground. I recite the famous graves to myself as we pass them, and in one of my rare reflections on my nonexistent mother, I think that maybe dying isn't scary if you get married first.

Finally Potts looks at his watch.

- -Well? he says, and kisses both of us.

We go down the hill then, under the umbrella of the ginkgo trees, and at the foot of the stairs of the Old Chapel, Lucy lifts her hems, runs up to the double doors, and without looking back, disappears into the bride's dressing room.

The snow fell all around me. My feet were damp, and for a little way, I picked up my pace. Then I checked the time, tilted the umbrella, and decided that, so long as the wind did not pick up, I had several hours before dark. I went down to Church Street. Snow stuck to the steel sculpture in the city center courtyard, and I remembered the bitter-cold night that Alec and I had sat near it, clutching candles and one another, listening to the long roster of names of the Vietnam war dead, read one by one into the city night. Alec had lied to his parents about his whereabouts, but Potts had given me his blessing on the condition that I made it to school in the morning. At six-thirty, when the traffic came through for the morning shift change and the light over the city was yellow with the pollution, the steelworkers cursed and jeered us from their cars.

The early Moravians might have been non-combatants, but in later years war became a fine old Bethlehem tradition. By the end of World War I, the steel plant in my home-town was the largest Allied munitions supplier in the world. To protest the war was to protest the very industry that put bread on Bethlehem's tables.

I didn't go into Nisky Hill at the corner of Wall and Center. Instead, I walked alongside the fence: the neat gray posts wore tiny caps of snow. Finally, at the foot of High Street, I shifted the roses under my coat, switched the umbrella from one hand to another, swung open the gate—and stopped.

The snow was falling straight down, tufting the limbs of trees, crowning tombstones, adding capes to the wings of angels. Among the graves it lay trackless, undisturbed.

I stood a while, shifting the roses under my coat. Although the graves were no more than a hundred feet from the gate, I could not quite pick out their individual stones among the crowd. I leaned against the gatepost and simply could not go in. It seemed wrong: my solitary footprints in the snow, a rose left here and here and here. A car worked its way past and I tilted the umbrella to hide my face.

After a while, I noticed the stones nearest the gate were carved in Greek. I stared a long while at the foreign letters, then looked over the acres of graves, trying to take in all the lives, all the loss, the grief, the forgetting, the walking away.

Gradually I admitted that my feet were getting wet. The roses were slipping underneath my coat, and my face was raw in the cold. Still I could not bring myself to go in or turn away.

Fine, I said to myself, as if my soul were a stubborn horse. I can wait.

We are on the way back to the barn from one of our regular Sunday rides. Vee pauses deep in the woods.

I titter. I know what's coming.

Vee detours from the ritual, raps on my helmet.

—I'll pinch your cheek, she threatens.

—Yes, ma'am, I say, feeling full of myself and fresh.

Behind me, I feel her draw herself up, inhale. I know she closes her eyes, smiles, know what she will say next.

Vee never comes to church with us, but every Sunday she says her own benediction.

In church, the pastor says:

—May the Lord make His face to shine upon thee and give thee peace.

On Hadley's back, Vee says:

—Natalie, always remember this. Throw your heart before you. Then go after it.

For a moment, she holds me tight. Then we walk on.

Back at the hotel, I thanked the doorman for the umbrella, dragged the roses from beneath my coat, and stamped my feet.

From behind the desk, Marko called: "Lovely afternoon, Miss Baxter. May I call housekeeping for you? They'll have a vase."

I studied the roses, mummified in their paper, and doubted they were still alive, but Marko was already on the phone, ordering some poor soul in housekeeping to deliver a vase, double quick.

When the housekeeper arrived, she had not just a vase but shears to cut the stems. She was wearing a neat uniform and spoke with a lovely accent. "Clean Spanish," Alec's bigoted father would have called her, with her silvering hair drawn back into a knot, her chipped tooth, and the crucifix with tiny diamonds at her neck. How provincial I'd once thought Bethlehem was. Only later did I figure out what a mix of cultures we had here.

She exclaimed over the roses, and I suspected

she was truly delighted with them, because if she'd been cleaning my room, with one set of clothes drying on hangers while I wore the others, she'd figured out I didn't have much money.

The flowers were somewhat bruised and beaten.

"May I?" she said, then expertly plucked away the outer brown petals from the roses, leaving tight fresh petals underneath.

"That's marvelous," I said.

"The inside keeps." With a quick hand she cleared away the trimmings, took the knife, wished me a good evening, and went out.

On Lucy's wedding day, Vee listens hard each time footsteps come up the stairs. She is dressed early, in an elegant dark green dress. She has never been thinner, but her hair is long enough to be coiled, powder and rouge brighten her face, and her cast is propped on a pretty pillow on a chair. Earlier, when Potts and I decorated the car, we threatened to wrap her crutches in streamers, too.

The wedding is very small. Just us, and John Casey's three brothers from Maine, and some school friends of Lucy and John Casey. Neighbors and musician friends come and deliver gifts, and at each knock on the door, I am sent to answer.

When the florist appears, I call out:

—Lucy! Flowers!

Vee startles in her chair, then calls me over, and whispers in my ear:

—Are any of them for me?

Lucy comes down the hall, barelegged. She is dressed as far as her slip. Her hair is brushed and her face is powdered, too. She examines the contents of each box.

—These are mine, she says, setting aside her circlet and bouquet.

—And these are yours.

I take the box and drop it on the floor, I am so eager.

—I'm the one who's supposed to be nervous, she says.

She lifts out my bouquet and hands it to me. I take a whiff, then stand in front of the hall mirror to admire my French braids, my pale green dress, and my bouquet.

Standing beside me, she pulls my hands and my bouquet down to my waist.

—Hold it there. People will want to see your dress.

—No, they don't, I say. What people?

Vee coughs.

Lucy whirls. She is so sweet today, so generous and mild, I think she ought to get married every day.

She unboxes a corsage and carries it to Vee.

Vee coughs, touches her hair.

Later when Lucy decides to walk to church, Vee says she'll stay behind.

Potts gives her a level look.

—You are coming, he says.

—Why not, says Lucy, scooping up her bouquet, snatching Potts and me by the arm. Why wouldn't she?

For a minute I see the hardness in my sister.

—I'll call a cab, Vee says. I couldn't walk anyway.

Later, I am scared. I sit alone in the front pew on our side of the church. Across from me are John Casey's brothers—all tall, blond, and rangy, with the same big hands and feet. Potts and Lucy and Lucy's best friend are somewhere in the back. The minister, John Casey, and his best friend come out and stand. And stand. The minister checks his watch. The door creaks open behind us. Potts sticks his head in, looks around, shakes his head.

No Vee.

After about forever, Potts opens the door again, gives a signal. The organ music changes. In comes Lucy's friend, then Potts and Lucy. John Casey's brothers stand. I sit, crying. The minister gestures for me to stand.

I do, wiping my eyes on my wrists, watching my beautiful sister and my father parade past me, see a thousand things in Potts's face. He kisses Lucy, leaves her with John Casey, scoots in beside me. He lays his arm around my shoulders, I press my wet face into his lapel.

Then we hear a small noise in the back of the chapel.

The door opens. Vee tries to sidle in, crab-wise. The door bangs hard against a crutch. She props herself against the back wall.

A signal seems to go around the room. It is clear Vee does not intend to sit.

And so the minister begins:

—Dearly beloved.

Afterward, as soon as I see Vee, I want to know:

—Why didn't you come and sit with us?

I see Potts waiting for an answer, too.

—I shouldn't have come in at all, says Vee. It's bad luck to enter behind the bride.

chapter twenty-four

On Christmas Eve, I was restless and ill at ease. Finally, although I was much too early for my appointment with Mac, I put on my coat and found myself heading east on Broad. For a few blocks, I barely paid attention, merely slipped and scuffled along the sidewalk, and every so often turned my face up into the heavy curtain of snow. Then I stopped. There on the right was the old YMCA where I had gone for swimming lessons, and across the way an old jazz club where Potts had sometimes sat in with his bass, and where, for all I knew, my wild sister had cut part of her swath, cheaping it up on the piano. No wonder Potts had been so worried. Half the club owners in the city must have called him with reports, once they'd figured out who Lucy Baxter was. So much for the big secret I'd thought I had as a kid.

Saturday morning and I am up early. I tiptoe around the kitchen, in my turtleneck and jodhpurs, ready for my lesson. I pour juice, take bread from the box on the counter.

When the front door creaks, I spin around, and there is Lucy, coming up from downstairs, carrying her shoes by the heels.

—What happened? I say, and drop the bread.

It is rare that we are alone together. There are all those years between us, and besides, Lucy has a contempt for me which is as natural as the air.

She looks at my riding clothes.

—Horse girl, she says meanly.

She is wearing a brown beanie with two white felt letters on the front: a freshman dink from Lehigh.

She sees me looking at it, gives me a cold stare, then doffs the hat.

—Lucy!

Her heavy blond hair has been hacked off. It rises in spikes, with a few longer locks drifting here and there. She runs her hands through it, and makes it stand up even more.

—Who did that? I whisper.

—I met these two boys and I dared them to. At Lehigh.

And then she is crying and laughing, too. She picks up a napkin and scrubs makeup from her eyes.

—John Casey? I say stupidly.

Lucy sits, cocks a shoulder like a movie star.

—John Casey? she mocks.

I bend down and pick the loaf of bread up off the floor.

—It's all his fault, anyway, she says. Her head goes down and she sobs some more. He asked me to marry him.

I put the bread down on the table in front of her as if she might want it.

—Marry who? I sidle near her and reach out for her ragged hair.

Lucy snaps upright, snatches the loaf of bread, and hurls it across the room.

—Listen. John Casey asked me because I bet myself I could make him. I did. I made him. Then I walked all over the South Side. Across the Hill-to-Hill, down Fourth Street, up to St. Tim's, the works. And somewhere in there I had some drinks, I played the piano, and I got this haircut.

Before I can think of something to say, her arms clamp around me. My ribs hurt, my neck is pulled the wrong way; still Lucy holds on tight. Then she sobs:

—Don't tell, don't tell.

Every Saturday after that, we spend a little time together in the kitchen. I am getting ready to go to the barn; Lucy is sneaking in from her nights out on the streets of Bethlehem. She hugs me with those slender arms of hers, or swoops behind me and gives me smacking kisses on my cheek and neck. I live for these encounters. They are exotic, they are terrifying, they are our only secret between sisters.

She knows every club that will let her in. She takes tips by the fistful when she is allowed to play. She drinks at frat parties, watches the dawn at Illick's Mill, even helps some students at Moravian College put a beer can in the hand of the statue of John Amos Comenius.

I am still young enough to consider it a treat to stay late on a summer evening at Saucon Park and watch the eastern sky glow red when the slag is dumped. I think of Lucy in the same way: dazzling, dangerous, a force beyond my comprehension. I never listen when my father explains the slag piles or what happens in the smokestacks when they are burned off at night. And I do not try to understand Lucy, either.

That first morning, we hear Potts come down the hall. Lucy lets go of me. I snatch the dink and jam it on her head.

—Girls?

Cool as anything, Lucy gets up from the table, takes the napkin with the makeup on it, walks out of the room.

I paused at the corner, above the Minsi Trail bridge. I felt as if I were caught alone on the Great Plains during a blizzard. Squinting, I could barely make out the car dealership across the way. I dawdled a moment, then turned down the hill, toward the bridge.

The bridge was concrete now, four lanes wide, with a barricade down the center and high mesh fences. I walked halfway across, stopped and looked down the river. To the right ranged the bluffs of Nisky Hill. Nearby, a flight of stairs led down to the canal banks. A train was stalled out on the tracks below. I stood

337

gawking at the dark geometric shapes of the mills running east and west along the banks, all in black and dark red, the shed roofs of corrugated metal, the stacks like the barrels of guns. Here were the mills that had drawn immigrants from around the world. Here were the mills whose need for engineers had built an entire university. Here were the mills that had fabricated the skeleton of Madison Square Garden, built the George Washington Bridge, erected the Empire State Building. Steel from Bethlehem had built the turbines at Niagara Falls, held up the great Ferris wheel at the Chicago World's Fair. And just how long had Beth Steel lasted? One hundred years? One hundred thirty? Start to finish. I laced my fingers through the fence.

One Sunday morning, Lucy locks herself in her room and refuses to come to church. Vee is writing a letter. Potts and I leave so early that we amble up Market Street, then go into the old Moravian burial ground.

Inside I hold his hand. Roots of the old spreading maple trees have tilted some of the walks and the two hundred fifty years have erased the letters from some of the stones. The Moravians buried their dead in choirs, all the children in one place, all the married ladies in another, the single men someplace else. The stones are small, flat, uniform because the Moravians believe all are equal in the eyes of God. Once my father told me that in England the Moravians buried their dead standing up, so they could get a head start rising to heaven on Judgment Day.

We stroll from section to section, and legions of round-bellied squirrels escort us, hoping for nuts and treats. At the New Street gate, Potts asks what I have on my feet.

Saddle shoes with knee socks that match my good corduroy jumper.

—They'll do, he says, and with no further explanation, he takes my hand and leads me across to Wall Street.

The narrow walks undulate beneath our feet, and grass grows up through the herringbone pattern of the bricks. The houses here are old, and odd details of them stand out: the steep slate roofs, the variety of simple elegant doors, the various shades of brick and stone. My father has a friend who lives in one of them, an old man who never wears a topcoat over his suit in winter, but only winds a scarf around his neck and covers his head with a wool beret. When I am old enough, my father teaches me to return his greeting in Czech:

—*Dobrý den, Pane Klier.*

On the far side of Center Street, we go into Nisky Hill. On the graves of children, lambs lie with folded knees. Above one tomb rises an angel with swirling skirts. Another is marked with a pillar that seems half barber pole, half rocket. Just above the bluff, a cannon points out toward the river. Around it, I learned in school one year, are the graves of soldiers from the Civil War.

We follow the path that runs along the edge of the bluff. Below us lie the canal and the poky Lehigh River. Across the river, beyond the flood dike, are the mills with their black corrugated roofs and their high brick stacks. Suddenly, rolling down South Mountain like leaden water, comes the peal of bells.

—St. Mike's, my father murmurs.

I stare across the river, over the mills, up toward the stone towers of Lehigh University and the steeples of churches as if I can see something in the air. Plumes of smoke and steam waft up from the stacks.

Then bells ring all over the South Side, and the air over Bethlehem fills with their leaden ripples and with the falling trills of carillons. The skin on my arms turns to ice.

Church by church, the bells fall away.

Potts smiles.

We do not go to church that day. Instead we leave the cemetery by another gate, then cross the river on the Minsi Trail bridge. The tires of the passing cars are like timpani on the metal grate, and the men who pass us carry black or silver lunch pails with a dinner to eat halfway through the shift.

On the South Side, iron grills are folded across some of the storefronts. People walk the streets in their church clothes, which are fancier than ours. Others sit along the counters of Dmitri's Lunch and the Blue Anchor and Tackitz Corner Store. We walk up hills through neighborhoods of houses with turrets and porches that wrap all the way around.

At every corner, I step close to my father and look with him for oncoming traffic. In time, my left foot begins to hurt and Potts keeps taking me by the hand and I keep trying to shake him loose. Finally we turn, walk down a steep alley, and come out on an avenue. We turn again, then stop in front of a Greek diner.

—Snack? he says. I should call home.

He sits me in a booth, and I look at the hand-written card that is the menu. Two little dark-haired girls in Sunday dresses and pink pastel shoes sit on stools along the counter playing a finger-clicking game and singing to one another in Greek. I pretend not to watch them.

A waitress follows Potts back from the phone.

—Coffee? she says.

—Black, my father answers.

—Me, too, I say.

The waitress's hands fly up:

—Poppa?

—Half milk, he tells her.

The woman returns in a minute. Potts leans back in the booth, sips his coffee. I can tell he is about to disappear before my eyes. I squirm in my seat and say:

—Is Lucy getting married?

He reaches across the table and takes my hand. He says nothing.

—Well, is she?

He opens my hand, studies my palm.

—Annie Oakley's getting calluses, he teases.

I am offended. Annie Oakley was a Western rider and I have had enough lessons from Vee and Mr. Detweiler to disdain anyone who must put that much leather on a horse in order to stay on its back.

—You'll never make a musician, Potts says.

I announce that I am going to ride horses.

He waggles my hand back and forth.

—Better marry a millionaire.

—Vee didn't.

Potts studies me a long moment, his face pleated with worry.

—She's thinking of moving home again. To Winding Hill.

—She can't, I say. I don't want her to.

That absent thoughtful look comes over him again.

—I'm sorry, he says. I can't say I understand.

Finally, with wet feet and very red face, I climbed the broad half dozen stairs that led to the front door of Mac's offices. As I passed between the pillars and crossed the front portico, I saw that a piece of garden statuary had been brought in under the roof for the winter. Near the door, a small, beautifully lettered card instructed: "Knock and enter." I did, rapping on a paneled door so heavy I doubted I could be heard. Hadn't there once been a knocker? Then I saw it, the heavy brow of a lion's head hidden beneath a wreath tied with a maroon velvet bow.

I pushed open the door and found myself in a place I knew well. The foyer, with its glossy parquet floor, umbrella stand, and heavy mirror, opened into a front parlor. I remembered the odd feeling of being in a mansion with attorneys camped out in it. Mac Vorhees had always done his best to modernize without destroying the place. The first floor housed the law firm, and upstairs was Mac's private residence. I stood for a moment on the heavy carpets, studied the grandfather's clock in the corner, the walls of glass-doored bookcases. The receptionist, in a dark wool suit with a bright poinsettia pin on the lapel, hurried in, took my coat, offered coffee.

I declined.

She glanced at her watch and told me Mr. Vorhees was waiting. She stood poised to lead the way.

"Is he still in his old office?"

She nodded and let me go alone down the carpeted hall into the west wing of the house.

Mac was waiting at the end of the hallway, standing square in the doorway. He was a slender man, whose bones and skull now seemed too large, and whose elegant suit was far too loose. He wore a handkerchief just so in the pocket, and a boutonniere. He didn't look happy to see me.

"Miss Baxter."

"Mr. Vorhees."

I wasn't sure if I should shake his hand or kiss his cheek.

He stepped back from the door, ushered me into yet another parlor, now a kind of outer office: carved furniture with tapestry upholstery, a baby grand piano, its top closed, a fireplace, some oil paintings, more glass bookcases, a large desk, and walls of polished hardwood filing cabinets. Underfoot lay

Persian carpets; casement doors led to a broad side porch.

"This hasn't changed," I said, delighted.

As a young man Mac had bought the building from an old industrialist. When I was a little girl, he had often walked me through the house, letting me scamper up and down the steep maids' stairs and pull the hidden bell ropes. He had told me stories of the workers and workers' wives, of ward men, mayors, bankers making their way to this very house in order to ask for jobs, forgiveness, favors. The man's son had opened the front door, taken names, seated visitors, while the old man gave hearings in the study, fair or otherwise. I'd imagined the boy in baggy trousers and a vest, half proud, half fearful of his responsibility.

"It will change," Mac said. "Soon enough."

We went into the office itself. He closed the glass door behind us, then sat at the rolltop desk.

I chose a nearby upholstered chair; it was built somewhat low to the ground, like a hearthside cricket chair.

"You look good," I said.

And he did, really. I'd braced myself for a visit with someone as pale as Potts in his last weeks.

"I've been reconstituted."

He smiled sourly, lifted the crease from one knee to save his trousers, and with effort crossed his legs. Silk socks wrinkled around his ankles; even the shoes seemed loose on his feet. But his hair was bright white and well cut and his color good.

"They've let me out of the hospital. All freshened up for Christmas with IVs." He pointed in the direction of the mills. His hand was small and wrinkled, but I remembered the discreet gold ring. "I have a growth. Hardly a surprise."

We had tracked the size of Potts's tumor in fruit: the size of a grape, the size of a cherry, a plum, an apple.

"I'm sorry," I said quietly.

"You knew I was ill. Tom Maxfield could have helped you."

I started to get up.

He gave me a sickly smile. His teeth were yellow. "Sit. He's not in from the country and you're here now. It's a progression we all know well: brain tumor, lung cancer. Whatever I say, check it with Tom later. I don't see clients anymore. When the liver fails, toxins affect the brain. Although I have as yet to make a major gaff."

"Really," I said, horrified. "I can go."

"I've upset you." His face softened. "I wish I could remember when I saw you last."

I stood, walked over to the window seat that ran under the casement windows. Outside, the gardens were muffled in two feet of snow. I took a quick sharp breath.

I'd last seen Mac at my father's funeral.

Behind me, I heard Mac say, "You proposed to me once. I do remember that."

I wiped my eyes, breathed again, then turned and sat.

"I was what? About five?"

"I should have said yes. You were a bright and fearless little girl."

345

The phone buzzed on his desk. It was a slim black model, not the heavy apparatus of my childhood.

He answered it, then asked if I would like coffee.

No, it would be too much trouble.

"I'm due for juice," he said.

In a few minutes we heard footsteps, the quiet chinking of things on a tray. I had coffee, black, in a fine Moravian cup.

"Instead, your father suggested I court your sister."

I sloshed coffee into my saucer.

"Lucy?"

He sipped his juice, delicately palmed some pills from a tiny china dish, swallowed hard to get them down.

"Vivian."

"Oh. My father's sister."

"How is your sister?" He set the juice down, patted his lips.

"She died," I said.

He shook his head. "I knew that. I'm sorry."

"Did you know Vee?"

He smiled. "She had dinner with me once."

I wanted to say: What was she like? Were her eyes the deep green I recall? Was she elegant? Glamorous? Fun?

"I was too much of an old stick." He smiled ruefully. "I told your father I couldn't imagine her here. He was so worried."

"It wasn't you," I said. "She had someone else."

"That's why he worried. He even came to

see me about legalities. Could he stop it? The man was married, or some such."

"Yes, but first he was supposed to marry her."

"It worried your dad."

I shrugged. "No wonder. In the end, she killed herself."

Mac Vorhees rolled his chair around so that suddenly his knees were close to mine and he was facing me straight on.

"The day after my sister's wedding. She left her bride's gift for Lucy, and a big bouquet of roses, and she shot herself."

Mac studied me. "And do you know why?"

I waved dismissively. "It's ridiculous, really."

However much Vee's story meant to me, I wasn't about to tell it to Mac Vorhees: the broken leg, the sheer dumb luck of Lucy selecting the same wedding day, the arguments with Potts, even Vee's anxiousness on the wedding day itself, which much later I figured out had to do with the fact that she was on pins and needles, hoping for those idiotic, weighted anniversary flowers. What had she said? For sorrow and apology.

They had been delivered, we guessed, sometime after the rest of us had left to go walking before the wedding, yet before Vee herself had made her way to the chapel.

Not that they had done a damn bit of good.

His voice turned querulous: "I asked if you knew why."

"She was…discouraged. Her leg was broken and was slow in healing. My sister was getting married." I picked over my words, felt as

347

if I were exposing Vee to ridicule, making something silly of what had been the center of her life. "I think my father may have tried to break off her correspondence."

Mac threw back his head and laughed, nastily. Then he had to wipe spittle from one corner of his mouth. The handkerchief looked like linen, as pure white as a new stock tie.

"Fairy story," he said.

I stared.

"She was dying. She came to see me."

"To see you?"

He put his fingertips together, regarded his juice, drank some more.

"Is that what your father told you? She killed herself for love?"

"He never said. I just thought—"

"You thought." He leaned forward. "Tell me. Have you ever been in love?"

I stared.

"Yes," he snapped. "Have you ever been in love?"

I shook my head. "I don't know."

Did Alec fit this category or not?

"She doesn't know," Mac said, gesturing to invisible listeners lined up on the window seat. "Well, what is love, anyway? What we have when we're not afraid to admit we have it."

I was beginning to wonder about those toxins.

"What do you do for work?"

"I ride horses."

He barked with laughter. "You haven't even grown up."

"My God," I said. "I'm almost forty."

He shrugged, smiled nastily. "Well, there's

money enough. You have no real need to. You're far from rich, but you'll get by."

I was speechless.

He leaned toward me. "Money doesn't mend the heart," he warned.

I finished my coffee. He reached over, took the cup and saucer and set them on the tray. I waited to see if he would shift gears or if I should make a run for the door.

"Your aunt, from what little I knew of her, was an admirable woman. She lived," he said quietly. "And when she found out what the future held, she stopped."

I opened my mouth to speak.

He held up a hand.

"As I recall, a doctor somewhere realized her broken bones were only a start. Her other bones were deteriorating too. No doubt, she had a cancer. She sought a second opinion. The same. She was a nurse, wasn't she? She knew exactly what was coming."

"But she came home and decided to teach me to ride. She had on that giant cast. Three days a week we went." My eyes filled with tears. "We rode the bus. All the way to Orchard Creek. Three days a week," I said again.

Mac nodded. I had proved his point.

"Time went on," he said, "and, despite our failed dinner date, she came to me for advice. How could she be certain no one was blamed? What would become of her insurance? How could she leave what she had to you and your sister?"

I frowned.

"But it was the day after Lucy's wedding."

"She had the decency to wait. Perhaps I should call up the file for you."

Frantically I began re-sorting old images: Vee's anxiety and snappishness, the large amount of champagne she drank at the wedding supper, her driving around the city afterward with one of John Casey's brothers, even her sudden change of plans, spending the night in her old apartment and packing all her things. And how annoyed Potts had been at her return trips to the hospital and her refusal to simply give up her apartment and live with us. She had grown worse, steadily worse, through that last spring and summer, and all along Potts had insisted that it was the poking and the prodding at the hospital that were doing her no good, and that if she just gave herself time she would surely heal.

"Did my father know?"

Mac closed his eyes.

"I don't know. As I recall, she didn't leave a letter. I arranged her affairs, but no one asked me any questions."

"Did you advise her to leave a letter?"

He looked right at me, then closed his eyes. "I can't remember. Perhaps I will have that file called up and summarized for you."

We sat in quiet for a while. He finished his juice.

"I'd better go," I said.

He stood.

"Don't get up," I told him.

He nodded toward the ceiling.

"I'll go upstairs."

"Still live over the shop?"

He smiled at my father's old joke.

"I miss your dad," he said simply.

Me, too, I thought, but could not get the words out.

He walked me back to the reception area, and one last time I took in all that Mac had been careful to preserve.

"We won't bill this," Mac told the receptionist. "Friend of the family."

The receptionist looked surprised.

"Leave us an address," Mac said.

I hesitated, then gave General Delivery, Shipville.

"We'll send you an accounting of assets and a list of decisions we believe you need to make sometime in the near future." His eyes glinted. "And that, Miss Baxter, we'll add to your account."

I thanked him for seeing me, kissed his hot cheek.

"You're not rich," he said quietly. "But you might get started."

"I will," I told him, although I had no idea what he meant.

The receptionist and I watched him make his way down the hall. He walked with great care, as if he might fall or drift away.

"Is he all right?" I said.

She fingered a button on her blouse. "He only has a few weeks left."

I stepped out onto the sweeping front porch, closed the heavy paneled door behind me, went down the steps to the walk, then realized I had forgotten to ask about vigil tickets.

chapter twenty-five

And so there was no point in staying—except that the snow was coming down so hard and thick that driving back to Shipville was out of the question. Soon I even regretted the great distance I had to walk back through the storm to the hotel. It was late afternoon by the time I reached Main Street. The snow was deep on the walks and remotely I thought how pleased Potts would have been to have the city closing this way on Christmas Eve. How he had muttered about people who shopped at the last minute, although, as a bow to the merchants' association, he opened the store each Christmas Eve until one.

Outside the hotel, I hesitated, then turned and waded up the sidewalk toward my old corner of the city. And there, knee deep in snow in the growing dusk, I was suddenly aware that it was almost time for feeds in the heartland. All the barns and farms would be busy with evening chores and then, except where there were births or illnesses, the stables would soon be shut up for the night. I thought of Pierce, thought of little girls dreaming of ponies for Christmas presents, thought of the animals, touched with magic, speaking over their mangers at midnight.

And somehow it made me think that I could stand once more at the foot of Broad Street, could stand in the dark and look through the snow-thickened air back through time, up into the night through our old windows. Christmas Eve magic would charge the air, and once again all would be visible: the multicolored lights on our tree upstairs, the soapsud snowdrifts I patted onto the glass of the shop door, the heavy wreath hanging from our sign. I would see Potts, too, cooking up the vile concoction he claimed was Grandma Baxter's eggnog, lacing it with rum. I would see him after Lucy and I had gone to bed, playing Santa with gifts he'd bought no more than a block or two from our own store. And Vee would be there, too, in her last Christmas, leg heavy with plaster, face chalk white, camping it up with Christmas bells for earrings. Could I now see what I had not seen then? The signs that her bones, perhaps her soul, were giving out?

How fierce she'd been when she taught me to ride, how strict and how determined. I shuffled through the snow and knew this dusky Christmas Eve what I did not know then: that she had known that she was dying and that the riding lessons had been her last deliberate gift to me.

I was halfway to the corner when I began to weep. I ducked under an awning, leaned my shoulders against a brick storefront, and muffled my sobs in the sleeve of my coat. And then I thought: I forgive you.

For what, I didn't know.

In time, I pulled myself together and turned back toward the hotel. I was just barely inside the door when the doorman rushed over with a brush and swept snow from my back and shoulders, chiding me all the while about not carrying an umbrella. Gloomily, I thanked him and, wishing myself far away from all solicitousness, I slunk toward the elevator.

Marko burst out of the office.

"Miss Baxter. Great news! Because of the weather no ticket is required. I spoke with the head sacristan."

I had no idea what he was talking about.

He looked disappointed. "That is, if you still wish to attend services at Central. Early vigils are at five, late vigils at eight."

I sniffled. When I was a little girl I had often wondered whether Zinzendorf had named Bethlehem during the early service or the late one.

"I love your boutonniere," I said, and fabricated a smile.

A bouquet of frothy red and green ribbon was pinned to his lapel.

"Simply present yourself at the doors on Heckewelder. They'll begin seating thirty minutes before the hour." He grinned, put on his concierge act, and bowed. "Compliments of the Hotel Bethlehem."

Up in my room, I stripped off my clothes. My thighs and buttocks were ice cold and cherry red. I would just pick the ice clots from my hair, throw on dry clothes and go. I opened my closet, remembered sadly that I had always loved to dress for vigils. Even my father had been more formal on that night— always a good suit, a new shirt, and tie. Usually I wore velvet or combed wool, new tights, or, as I grew older, new shoes or a straight sheath dress.

Instead of rushing, I bathed with care, then washed and dried my hair, and pulled on my lamb's-wool sweater and velvet jeans. I blinked back tears, wondered if I had what it took to go to vigils all alone. I fussed with my hair, studied myself sadly in the mirror, and then, after some thought, dialed the phone. I was desperate to talk to someone, to hear a live, familiar voice. I didn't have the home number, but I got the service and left a message.

The woman on the other end seemed miffed that I did not have an animal dying at my feet or even, for that matter, a more specific message. She pointed out that it was after five and Christmas Eve to boot.

"Just tell him I called," I said tiredly, wondering if he would have forgiven me enough to call me back.

I went downstairs. As I walked past, the dining room glittered with candlelight and there were formal diners obviously snowbound at the hotel—city folk with wet feet tucked under the long drape of the tablecloths.

In the pub, I ordered a steak and salad but could not eat. The barman, then a waiter, then another waiter wished me a merry Christmas. All at once I was truly ready for Christmas to be over, and for a little while I thought I would gladly slip them an enormous tip if they would turn off the medieval Christmas carols and take down the greens and the discreet white lights.

By the time I finished, I was still not certain I would go to church. I went over to the front door and peeked out. The doorman told me the roads were almost impassable. He was no doubt right: there was zero traffic on the street. Deep snow lay everywhere, although it seemed to be falling in a more leisurely, decorative way.

And that's what finally got me out the door. I would wade across to Central because, on a night like this, without the crowds, it wouldn't be like Central at all.

Only a small crowd gathered at the northeast doors, and we were seated, all together, in the front half of the center section of the sanctuary. Against the walls, the gaslights flickered, and overhead the Moravian star shone down on us. From the balcony came the sounds of the stringed instruments, playing the traditional chamber music. I pulled off my coat, wrapped it around my shoulders, nodded my hellos to the people on either side of me. A few rows ahead of me sat MacVorhees, dignified and alone.

With my sleeve, I daubed my face and instantly regretted it. You don't dry tears with wool. And so I blinked, then closed my eyes tight and listened. From the balcony came a Bach chorale. When it ended I felt braver, and peeked forward in the bulletin. There were all the old hymns: German, Latin, English. My hands began to tremble.

The sanctuary was perhaps one quarter full when the doors swung shut. I was concentrating on my breathing, wishing I were near the aisle in case I began sobbing and couldn't stop.

It never really changes: Christmas Eve at Central.

The lights dim and the gas jets flare in their etched glass globes. The giant star, with its twenty-six slender points, casts its light on the congregation. And from far above us, up in the belfry, blowing out into the winter air above the city, come the sweet but distant sounds of the trombone choir.

I settle into the velvet bolster on the pew. Vigils is nearly the best part of Christmas: the stringed instruments in the organ loft, the Latin anthems, the German hymns. From the balcony, a child with a trembling voice sings all alone to the thousand-strong congregation:

—Morning star, O cheering sight! Ere thou cam'st how dark earth's night!

And the congregation sings back:

Fill my heart with light divine.

We sing hymn after hymn, listen to the choir, to a prayer, to a reading of scripture. There is no sermon; the offering goes to an orphanage.

Each year I look ahead through the hymns, trying to guess the moment, but each year, I let out a little gasp when it finally happens: all the sanctuary doors, front and back, swinging open in the same instant, and there in each dark doorway stands a woman in white holding a tiny single candle, lit, and next to her a man in a black suit, offering up a tray of tender beeswax tapers, each one lit, their flames a sheet of light blazing up into the darkness.

And then they march into the church in pairs, the women and the men, and the trays of light seem to float down the aisles. I shake with excitement. Hand to hand, the candles pass until the church is filled with tiny clouds of candlelight.

—Hold it straight, I hear my father whisper.

Losing track of the hymns, I watch the golden beads of wax slip down into the ruffled tissue-paper skirt.

At the very end, the organ cascades down on us, and we begin to sing:

—With awe and deeply bowed.

The minister raises his candle over his head, and, a few at a time, candles are lifted in the congregation, then all of them go up, mine too, trembling.

The hymn fills the air:

—We our thank-offerings bring, and grateful sing.

My hand shakes, and the flame of my candle wavers, too. And then I am crying, because I am so happy and so sad and because I don't know why and because the light of the tiny candles is falling down all around us.

Afterward, I sat. The lights came up gently. Candles were blown out and the air filled with the sharp whiff of smoke. Gingerly I plucked at the skirt of my candle. I nodded when the man beside me wished me a merry Christmas. My face felt hot and sticky.

His wife leaned over the pew, wished me a merry Christmas, too, and asked where I was from.

"I grew up here."

She leaned forward and shook my hand.

"At Central?"

"In a way." I tucked my candle into my coat pocket, folded up my bulletin and slipped that in, too.

The woman spoke quietly to her husband, and after a moment he turned toward me.

"We live just over on Wall Street. Would you join us for a drink? We like to have someone in after vigils."

Perhaps they were merely being spontaneous, good-hearted. Or perhaps I was to be their once-a-year stranger, invited by tradition.

"I'm sorry," I said.

Murmuring more greetings of the season, the couple turned away.

I dawdled in the pew, studied the manger scene behind the pulpit, especially Mary's face, bowed, beaming. Who was I to forgive Vee? It seemed to me I, too, had been wrong somehow. I fingered my candle, plucked the skirt, left a fingerprint in the hardening wax.

The postlude ended, and I turned and looked up to the balcony. A choir member kissed the cheek of a friend. The organist clicked off the light on the music stand. Musicians carefully packed their instruments.

Finally, as I was pulling on my coat, I saw MacVorhees up ahead, settling his scarf inside his collar. For a long moment, he caught my eye. Then he smiled, put a finger to the brim of his hat and turned away. Tiny in his elegant overcoat, he worked his way through the small crowd, nodding and shaking hands, and then passed through the sanctuary doors and out of sight.

Back at the hotel, I shed my coat, stamped the snow off my boots. There was a wonderful gaiety about the place, but I had no desire to be chatted up or jostled or wished the best of the season.

Upstairs, I opened the door to my room, looked to the phone, and did not see what I realized I had been wishing for: the red message light, like a little beacon or a throbbing heart.

Outside my window, the snow had nearly stopped. I stood looking out into the last heavy feathers of it falling through the light of the streetlamps. Then I got into bed and, exhausted and confused, cried myself to sleep.

chapter twenty-six

In the morning I was ready to get out of Bethlehem and get on with whatever it was I had to get on with. I decided to be a grown-up and call Pierce. Since there seemed to be a twenty-year lag in my ability to understand what went on around me, perhaps when I was pushing sixty, I would figure out just what had happened to all of us on that little farm in Shipville. Meanwhile, I would call, wish him a merry Christmas, offer a simple apology for my bad behavior, check on the horses, and arrange a time to come back and get my things. Somehow I would also have to find a way to say goodbye to Mason and leave Miriam her gift.

I called at seven.

No answer.

Seven-twenty.

Seven-thirty.

Seven forty-five.

I wondered what the hotel charged for the phone.

I called again at eight.

Eight-fifteen.

Eight-twenty.

At nine, I tried Mason.

He was out on a call. A man was on duty at the service and he sounded harried but cheerful. Of course, he would take a message.

I left my name and the fact that I was at the Hotel Bethlehem, then I paced around, tried Pierce again, twice, three times. Still no answer.

An hour later, I called Mason's service again.

"I really need to reach him."

"He's out on calls."

No kidding.

"This is Natalie Baxter again."

Now the man was blunt. "Dr. Mason synchronizes his own calls."

I sighed. The script again.

"But can't you patch me through? Or give me the number in the Jeep?"

"And what exactly is this in reference to?"

"Pierce Kreitzer's horses." I took a little breath. Lied. "It's an emergency."

I hoped it wasn't, but I was willing to appear foolish if it would help me reach someone in Shipville.

"Just a minute."

I pictured Mason in someone's barn, focusing on an ailing animal as if no other creature existed or might have demands to make on his time.

The service came on again, said Mason was out of reach for the moment, but assured me they would keep trying to contact him if it were a true emergency.

I repeated the number of the hotel and sat down to wait.

It didn't take long.

"Still there, eh?" Mason said. "Did you win the lottery or what?"

"Family money," I confessed.

He didn't believe me, laughed. "Of course. Everyone with family money lives the way you do."

I decided to skip it.

"Look," I said. "I was going to say I'm sorry for—well, for whatever. But—" Then I told him I was beginning to worry about Pierce.

"It's a holiday," Mason said. "Soon even I might be done for the day. He's just gone somewhere."

"I don't know," I said. "I've called all morning. Did you ever call him? When I didn't come back?"

There was silence on the line.

"I'll swing by," Mason said after a while.

"Call me."

"Nate," he said. "Just come home."

I am home, I wanted to say.

Instead I said, "Are you mad at me?"

He paused. "I was. I don't take kindly to the way you up and leave."

"I'm sorry."

"Don't apologize." Then he laughed. "Unless you plan to mend your ways."

Now I was silent. I had no plans.

Mason spoke again, businesslike: "I'll drop in on Pierce and get back to you."

I called room service for coffee. While I waited I had the sense that I had had as a kid that the dead are with us. When I had first learned about oxygen, I had had the idea that right now, right this minute, I might be inhaling a molecule of oxygen that had passed through the lungs of George Washington, or Lafayette, or Zinzendorf. I sat on my hotel bed with my china cup and delicate coffeepot, and I thought about Vee and Potts and Lucy and how I breathed their air and lived the life they had somehow bequeathed me. I closed my eyes and wondered if I really could leave Bethlehem.

When the phone rang, I slopped coffee in my saucer.

"Come back," Mason said. "It's worse than you thought."

"What's up?"

"Just get back here. Now. Pronto. But don't go to the farm. Stop at my place first. Or go to Weirbachen's. Not the farm. Promise me, Nate."

At the front desk, I was disappointed to find that Marko had the day off. The young woman with the remarkable fingernails waited on me instead, and she asked, with some worry in her voice, if I were leaving because of a problem.

Well, yes, I said, I was, but when she offered to see if it could be taken care of, I realized she was talking about life in the hotel while I was talking about life as I had known it on the outside.

The bellboy, wearing hiking boots today instead of high-tops, took the collection of shopping bags which was passing for my luggage. For my return to the farm, I had pulled on my jeans, although I was still wearing the lamb's-wool sweater and the good city overcoat.

The bill was a good two grand. I handed over the credit card. Cheap at the price, I thought. Although there was no real telling what I had gotten.

We had almost finished the paperwork when the manager materialized and said, "The Hotel Bethlehem looks forward to your next visit. Your car is out front."

I asked them to say goodbye to Marko for me, the young woman gave me a glamorous wave, then I ran out under the marquee; the doorman held the car door. I started the car, and because I had no choice, went south on Main, tried to hang a right onto the Hill-to-

Hill Bridge, got shunted underneath the bridge instead, and was promptly lost. I swept through interchanges and intersections, making turns on sheer instinct, until finally I found Schoenersville Road. From there I clung to 22, although it was a highway known best for its terrible repair and its extremely high rate of fatalities. I passed the airport, smiled again over its grand new name of Lehigh Valley International Jetport, and knew I could find my way.

The roads weren't bad. The snow had stopped during the night, and the air was still. Ragged patches of blue mixed with high, fast-moving clouds.

I headed west, constantly checking my watch, the signposts to Harrisburg, and my speed. When I finally got off the interstate, I thought about pulling in somewhere. How long would it take? To run in somewhere, grab a sandwich and some coffee? Each time I saw a place to stop, I slowed down, then calculating the time, drove past, dreading what lay ahead. At some point, it occurred to me I had not had the chance, or taken the time, to see the back roads of Bucks County I had ridden with Vee. Perhaps they were best left to memory. I didn't know.

Shipville, as I drove through it, was decked out for Christmas. The town was crowded with Nativity scenes: legions of Wise Men, gangs of shepherds, more Christ childs per acre than I'd seen in Bethlehem.

I thought again of Central, of the sweep of the sanctuary, the greens and the gaslights.

I sang a few bars of the last hymn: *With awe and deeply bowed*. Tears filled my eyes, and despite my sorrow and my fears, I felt rinsed with peace.

On the far side of town, I had to choose: Mason's or Fred Weirbachen's. From Mason's I could call the farm, but if I drove to Fred's the road would take me past Pierce's, and although I had promised not to stop there first, I could still take a peek at whatever might be going on.

I made the last turn, and was creeping along at twenty miles per hour, craning my head to the left, trying to see. And then, for the second time in ten days, I put a vehicle in a ditch.

chapter twenty-seven

Two state police cars and a sheriff's car were parked at hasty angles. Mason's Jeep was pulled up to the barn and so were a few cars and trucks I didn't recognize.

I calculated. Two and a half hours had passed since I had spoken to Mason.

I got out of the car and a trooper hurried on foot down the drive.

"Ma'am, this area is restricted. I'm going to have to ask you to move along."

"I live here," I said. "Or— I used to."

He spoke into his radio.

While I waited, I noticed a huge pile of trash stacked at the corner for the trashman. It had snowed here, too, but not as much. Only six or eight inches covered the pile and the corners of the boxes, soaked and disintegrating, were sticking out. What with the holidays, Pierce must have missed the changes in trash pickup.

"Are you Natalie Baxter?"

The trooper's question startled me.

I went back to the car, got my wallet, and showed him my license, which was from Ohio.

"Ma'am," he said. "You do know this has expired?"

I muttered something under my breath about taking care of it.

"You're to go directly to the barn," he said.

I headed up the drive. Behind me, I heard a car, stepped aside to let it pass, saw the identification on the door, and began to run.

Up in the barn, Fred Weirbachen was crouching in the aisle with two men I didn't recognize. When I saw what they were doing to Sheila's stall, I gasped.

The rollers squealed as the door of another stall was rolled open. Galen's.

"Natalie!"

It was Mason.

I expected him to come toward me, perhaps put an arm around my shoulders, explain.

"What the hell are you doing here? I told you—"

The other men turned. They were lifting the heavy planks up out of the channels so as to disassemble the front wall of the old mare's stall. And that meant only one thing.

"Sheila's dead?"

"Just get in here," Mason ordered. "I can use your help."

I stepped toward Galen's stall. Mason's face was hard and still.

"Sheila's dead," I said again.

"Yes."

He thrust an IV bag at me. It felt gelatinous, cool, surprisingly heavy. I gripped it with both hands and looked around the stall. Galen was down. His head drooped, and his bones seemed to stick out of his hide.

"She was dead when I got here."

Mason crouched next to Galen, and was pulling off one IV bag so he could start the one I was holding.

"How is he?" I said stupidly.

The horse barely responded to my voice.

"Critical. And I keep thinking maybe I should just put him down. But I wanted to save one at least."

Pudgy Galen.

I stared at the wall, as if I could see down the length of the barn through the heavy planks.

"We've lost two others, too. The Appaloosa and the bay."

"Lawrence," I said. "And Archimedes."

"We don't know why, Nate. They were left outside."

"*Outside?* But it's been—"

Mason gestured. I struggled to hold the bag still.

"And the other mare?"

"Steady, Nate."

My hands shook harder. "And the other mare?"

Finally Mason took the bag from me, hooked it up, taped it in place. With his broad hand, he stroked Galen's neck, then lay his palm on the shoulder of the suffering gelding, spoke to the horse more than to me.

"We don't know why, Nate. Two were left outside. The rest were in. The mare must be an easy keeper. She's held up better than the rest."

"But why? It's been bitter."

"We don't know."

"Well, someone ought to ask the son of a bitch," I said.

Mason glanced at me. "We can't."

Abruptly I sat in the corner of the stall. I hid my face in the arms of my fine black city overcoat and listened to Galen's labored breathing. I thought of how I had loved the deep snow in Bethlehem, how it had settled me, and all the while my charges had been left out in it to die.

"I know," I said finally. "I saw the coroner drive in."

"But how did you know to call?"

I was crying into my sleeve. "He loved his holidays."

"Or feared them," Mason muttered.

"Where is he?" I said after a while.

"At the hospital. He was still alive when I got here."

"He had plenty of goddamn shells," I said bitterly.

Mason gave me a puzzled look.

"Well, he shot himself, didn't he? With

that damn shotgun. What did he do? Miss?"

Mason came and crouched beside me. "Maybe you should wait to talk until they call you to the house."

He wrapped his arms around me and I hid my face in his collar. Pierce had shot himself and it was all my fault. The horses were dead, dying, and that, too, was all my fault.

"Ach," I heard Fred Weirbachen say after a while. "We're ready."

I began shuddering. "I want to see her," I said. And then I was weeping.

Mason's parka was miserable for crying on, and without thought, I opened the zipper a few inches, pressed my eyes against his turtleneck, and cried my guts out. After a while, he put his hands over my ears. Vaguely I heard the chinking and banging of heavy chains.

"Fred?" he called. "Fred?"

Then I heard him say, "Can you hold off a minute? Natalie is back."

Fred came and stood in the doorway. He put his hands in the pockets of his baggy pants. A bright new scarf was wrapped around his neck. He had a hacking cough.

"We're all to blame," he said, looking at me sadly. "We all knew he was going—" And he made a loopy gesture with one hand, then let it fall. He shuffled his booted feet. "Missus has a bed for you. She said to say. You come to us."

Huddled in my city clothes in the corner of a horse barn, I began sobbing again. Dead horses lay all around me, except for Galen, who lifted his head once or twice, and for Prima, frantically chomping hay.

"We'll find her a home," Mason said quietly.

"She has one," I said. "Merry Christmas, Miriam. If she can stand it."

He said nothing then and it vaguely registered with me that he had no idea what I meant.

"Student," I told him, and lifted my head.

"And as for you, pal," I said to Galen, "pull through this and you can eat your oats out of a silver bucket."

After a while, Mason broke away from me and stood. I sat there watching Galen, convincing myself that the horse looked better. I heard Mason go down the aisle and out of the barn, then heard him come back in.

"Natalie," he said. "They're waiting for you."

"Who?"

He looked at his feet, tested the rebound in Galen's skin.

"Everyone, really. There are questions. And, well, there are only four or five more hours until dark."

I stood, thwacked clumsily at the wood shavings clinging to the long skirts of my coat. No one should have to bury horses in the dark. They would have a hard enough time, digging through the snow and the frozen earth.

Out in the aisle, I hesitated. "I want to see her," I whispered to Mason.

He took me by the arm, turned me toward the door.

"No."

I had grown to love the old mare and I wanted to stroke her face and neck one last time. I wiped my eyes.

"No," Mason said again.

At the threshold, I thrust my hands into my pockets, ran my thumb along what was left of my vigils candle. Then I squared my shoulders and breathed with care all the way down to the house. Behind me, I knew that Mason watched me go.

The trooper who met me at the door looked like a little girl in a trooper's costume. She seemed too short, too young, too perky, and when she led me into the kitchen and took off her Smokey the Bear hat, I saw that her hair was pinned back with barrettes and that a huge diamond sparkled on her left hand.

"Christmas Eve," she said, waggling her finger. "I'm engaged."

I wanted to turn her around and see if there were a key in her back. Certainly she couldn't be real.

Just inside the kitchen doorway, I halted. Over the sink, a solitary ray of light illuminated the glass sun catchers: a moon, a flower, a bright red horse, several crystals hanging from colored ribbons. The counters were spotless: no dishes in the sink or on the drainboard, no pots or pans left out. Not even the coffeemaker was in sight. A plaid dish towel lay folded next to the refrigerator, but that was all. It reminded me of a kitchen in an advertisement—immaculate and uninhabited. I glanced at the bulletin board, glanced away, then back. There I was, a few of my photos mixed with Allie's.

The little girl trooper turned into a real one. She looked from the photos to my face and back again.

"That's you," she said.

"I need to sit. They weren't here when I left."

I couldn't help noticing that, from a distance, riders look somewhat alike in their boots and helmets.

The trooper narrowed her eyes, lay a hand on my arm. The diamond twinkled. "Do you need something to drink?" she said. "They'll be downstairs in a minute."

I can't pretend I told my story in anything resembling a straightforward manner. The medical examiner was a thin, red-faced man with sharp blue eyes and graying reddish hair. He sat at the kitchen table, turned his chair to the side, and crossed his legs as if this were a social call. He did not remove his heavy overcoat. I didn't understand why, if Pierce was still alive, he had been called out. A young man in a trooper's uniform sat biting at a hangnail, ready to take shorthand, and a detective, in horn-rimmed glasses and a necktie with a reindeer on it, prompted me with questions. One of them was wearing a little too much aftershave. Probably a Christmas gift.

At first I said that the last time I had sat in this kitchen had been to talk to Pierce about

Twister's navicular. But of course that wasn't true. I had lived here, hadn't I? And so I changed my story, tried to tell of the shock of Twister's death and how afterward Pierce had taken me in and how he had been much kinder than I had thought possible. Then out of the blue I said I couldn't believe he'd actually shot himself.

The detective and the coroner eyed one another. Finally the detective spoke: "And are there firearms on the property?"

"Two," I said. "That I know of. One was the shotgun."

The coroner nodded.

The young man looked up from his note-taking. "We have that secured."

I told them about first seeing it in the closet and about Pierce giving me the shells. "And then I ran."

I was sitting at the table, too, my hands folded in my lap. I was afraid if I put them in my pockets, I would crush the remnant of my vigils candle.

"And that was all it took?" asked the medical examiner. "Shotgun shells?"

The stenographer looked at me, waiting, bit his nail. I opened my hands, lay them on the table, studied my own nails. They seemed a little blue.

"No," I said finally. "I found some pictures."

The medical examiner and detective were suddenly far too casual. The detective lifted the end of his tie, studied the reindeer. "Present from my kid," he said, and gave a funny smile.

"Mine are grown," the coroner said. Then he turned to me: "Pictures of what?"

The stenographer looked down at his pad, ready for an answer.

"Of me," I said finally. "I didn't know he was taking them. It gave me the creeps."

"Of course it did," said the woman trooper behind me in the doorway.

Everyone looked at her. Then the detective asked where the pictures were and I told him that I was just being neat, tucking in that errant sock, and there they were, months of photos, months of deception.

The stenographer got it all down.

"Weren't there pictures last time?" the medical examiner murmured.

I stared.

The detective gave him a steely look. "And what about the other firearm?"

"But he used the shotgun, didn't he? So it doesn't matter, does it?"

"Maybe you should tell us," the woman trooper said.

So I kept them there a while longer, telling about my Aunt Vee and how she got the .22 and how she used it in the end and that I'd last seen it in my bureau drawer. I left out the part about shooting a hole in the ceiling.

The woman trooper left and came back shortly.

"The apartment's empty."

"No, it's not," I said. "It's not. There's a pile of boxes just inside the door and...Oh, God," I said. "The trash."

"Check the bureau?"

The trooper nodded.

I gave her a desperate look.

The medical examiner shifted in his chair, recrossed his legs, let his overcoat fall open. He leaned an elbow on the table and gave me a confiding look. "Perhaps you don't know that we've been here before for an unattended."

"A what?"

"An unattended death. This one probably finishes the other. Not that we ever figured out the first one."

"Allie?" I said. "She died of cancer."

The medical examiner ignored the detective.

"Actually, Mr. Kreitzer didn't shoot himself. He was malnourished and he took an overdose."

"But I thought he shot himself. You were asking about guns."

The detective eyed me. "No, miss," he said. "You were telling us about them. At the very least you established that today's victim has been suicidal."

"Can he survive—?"

The medical examiner shrugged. "He seemed to have been starving himself, and it's hard to know exactly what he took. He might get off with liver damage."

I brightened.

"And he might not make it at all," the detective added in a low voice.

"But what were you saying about Allie?"

If I had been confused before about what had happened on this farm, now I was more so.

"Miss Kreitzer didn't die of cancer. This may

376

seem academic, but, although she had cancer, and certainly cancer in advanced stages, the blood screen showed some substances that were rather interesting. Certainly they hadn't been prescribed." The medical examiner pointed an index finger toward the ceiling. "He said he came home and found her sprawled in the hallway, that he picked her up and carried her back to her bed and only then realized she was dead."

Well, the girls had gossiped that there was some kind of mystery.

He let his eyelids fall, hooded his gaze. "He swore that she had begged him to help her die. We may never know. There's no clear line between failing to live and intending to die."

I lay my face in my arms. "So why did you say there were pictures?"

"There was a warrant and the search turned up some pretty sick stuff: pictures of her whole decline, even pictures of her dead on the floor and dead in her bed."

"He was a photographer," I said. "He won awards."

"You didn't feel that way about the shots he took of you."

Then I thought I knew: They'd had a deal. He could watch her through his lens, do his work, shoot her decline, her death. In exchange, when the time came, he would help her die. But he had failed her. She'd asked for help, and when he hadn't been able to go through with it, he hadn't been able to let go, either, and so he'd kept his absurd promises about Twister and the farm.

I lifted my hand, then let it fall. "Right now I feel sick. I knew something was wrong and I just ran."

"You're not alone. That old neighbor's feeling it, too." The medical examiner shook his head. "For all you know, you kept him going that much longer."

"And he still might live," said the pixie trooper in the doorway.

The detective stood, smoothed his tie. "Merry Christmas, all. Let's get out of here."

The stenographer followed, casting me one more curious glance, but the woman trooper stayed behind and patted my shoulder. "You saved yourself. That's always first."

"I don't know," I said. "Is it?"

She turned and left, her service boots like concrete blocks at the end of skinny ballerina legs.

The medical examiner and I sat and looked at one another. Then he sighed.

"The problem now is that Pierce Kreitzer is a schoolteacher. Well liked, for all we know. Even if he lives, he's put every kid in this district at risk." He shook his head with disgust.

"At risk," I echoed.

"For suicide," he said. "As you very well may know."

I closed my eyes, then realized Mason was standing in the doorway to the kitchen. How long had he been there?

"She'll be with me," he said.

"A word, then."

The medical examiner stood and they

stepped into the living room and talked for a few minutes.

"I'll stay with her," I heard Mason say. "We have a horse to nurse."

Mason used the phone, made a few calls, and within forty-five minutes someone showed up with my truck. We hooked it up to Allie's trailer, rigged one half of it with a sling, then backed it up to the barn.

Galen staggered out of his stall, and up the ramp. Mason and Fred Weirbachen slung him up so that his feet touched the floor but the canvas sling held his weight. Prima, arrogant and still hungry, dove up the ramp after a bucket of oats.

The plan was that Mason would drive and that I would ride in the back in order to keep an eye on the horses and raise a ruckus if Galen began to fail. I went in through the escape door, braced myself in the equipment hatch, and the minute the door closed behind me, I felt terrified to be alone.

Somehow I had gotten the idea that if I kept Mason, or perhaps anyone, always in my sight, I would be all right. I stroked the horses' necks, whispered to Galen, and, for the first time in the presence of horses, felt utterly alone.

At the foot of the drive, we stopped. Mason came back to the escape door, opened it a crack and asked if there was anything I wanted. No, I said. I didn't care, but when we didn't start,

I peeked out the window and in the gathering dusk saw him unloading my shopping bags and other things from the rental car. I'd thought he'd meant my pile of boxes in front of the drive.

Riding in the back of a horse trailer is harder work than it seems, and I was grateful the trip was short and that Mason was a deliberate driver. I braced myself with every turn, swayed each time we stopped. I knew why horses got off vans crazy or exhausted.

At Mason's, we pulled around the back of the house and office. A breezeway connected the house to a snug six-stall barn that reached out into a small pasture deep in snow. Mason stopped the truck, came around to the trailer.

"You stay here," he said. "I'm not quite sure how to manage this."

Before I had a chance to say much, he turned away. I stood, willing Galen to stay alive and watching Prima snatch at her hay bag. She would do well with the attentions of a young doting owner, and Miriam, I thought, might just be ready for whatever miracles the mare might bring about.

In time, Mason returned. We unloaded Prima first. Oddly, Mason had opened the outside doors to the two stalls farthest from the house. The outer doors of the other stalls remained bolted top and bottom against the weather. At his direction, I led Prima into the end stall. Inside the barn, a radio was blasting. He had spread bedding, filled water buckets, and thrown hay. Prima entered eagerly, snatching hay and pacing her new quarters.

Galen was more difficult. The trip had exhausted him. As soon as we unsnapped the belly band he sagged, and, when he was asked to back down the ramp, his hindquarters buckled.

"Pop him on the nose!" Mason yelled. "Pop him on the nose!"

I bit my lip and gently cuffed the horse. With each tap, his ears flapped and his eyes focused briefly. He got his feet underneath him and with Mason leaning into him on one side and me on the other we got him into the stall next to Prima's.

Mason rigged a sling, ran another IV line. I covered him with a wool blanket. Finally Mason put an arm around my shoulders.

"You go in."

I didn't want to, but he guided me out the back of the stall so that I had to walk around the outside of the barn to the house.

Inside, I milled from room to room, rubbing my hands together as if I were cold and not able to bring myself to take off my coat. On a big desk in the living room were piles of papers, journals, magazines, other mail. There were a few paintings, a huge fireplace with a wood stove rigged up on the hearth, braided rugs, odds and ends ranged across the mantel. Kerosene lamps hung in sconces on the wall. In the kitchen I opened the refrigerator. Not much. What was I looking for, anyway? I smiled over the four kinds of ice cream in the freezer and the giant jar of cookies on the counter. The knives were dull, and a stack of bowls had accumulated in the sink. I wondered if he lived on cold cereal and milk. Pierce could have cooked for him, I thought, and then, since I didn't know what to think next about Pierce or about any of it, I kept snooping around. Off the kitchen was a little laundry room with a stack of clean clothes on the dryer, and next to it was the bathroom. I turned on the shower, undressed, stood under the hot needle spray, and when I was finished dug through Mason's clothes and pulled on a clean turtleneck, a flannel shirt, some dry jeans and wool socks. The pants I cinched up with a belt.

When Mason finally came in, I was examining the small collection of liquor bottles on a sideboard.

"Pour me one, too," he said, and headed for the shower.

Later, he said, "I feel like the Red Cross." He had built a fire in the wood stove, wrapped me in a blanket, poured two large glasses of red wine, and scrambled eggs and thawed waffles from the freezer. "Okay?" he asked every so often.

And I would nod. I had no idea what else to do.

I wanted to sleep, but could not bear to close my eyes.

I wanted to hold still but flinched each time a log sighed in the fire.

I wanted to talk but could not. What was there to say?

Mason simply sat near me in a wing chair, put his feet up on a hassock, and gave his Labrador permission to jump up onto the chair next to him. Other than that, he held still, although I had the sense that he was ready to pour more wine, to listen, to pile on blankets, in general to keep an eye on me.

In time, he asked if I would like to see a doctor. Would I like to talk to a trauma counselor? The medical examiner had given him a name. Was there anyone I'd like to call? Sometime later he said it worried him that I'd stopped crying. And, apparently, had stopped talking, too.

"Aphasia," he said, getting up to poke the fire and add more wood. "They warned us about it at vet school."

The Labrador opened an eye, stretched its toes, sighed, went back to sleep.

Finally, I frowned at him.

"That was a joke, Nate. Aphasia? Without speech?"

I shook my head. "Twister spoke," I said. "I heard him."

He said nothing.

"That ever happen to you? Do you ever hear the animals you treat?"

"I haven't experienced half what you have."

"Oh, *Pierce*," I said, suddenly furious.

"Well, he might live. I meant your aunt. I was there when you told that part."

"Did I say that she was dying? The attorney told me. On Christmas Eve, he told me that she shot herself because she was dying."

"And is that all right?"

I stared furiously at the tempered window in the wood-stove door.

"Everyone leaves," I said, full of sorrow.

"Nate," he said. "You're pretty good at it yourself."

I glared at him. "Learned behavior," I told him bitterly.

The buzzer in the kitchen sounded.

Mason got up, as he had been every hour or so, to go out and check on Galen.

"Stay put," he told me.

Sometimes it took longer for him to come back. This time, he came over to the couch, stood over me, and said, "May I?" Then he sat beside me, put an arm around my shoulders, pulled the blanket over both of us. I pressed my cheek against his shoulder and stared at the fire. Within minutes, he was asleep. His arm turned heavy, and I thought about sitting just like this with Potts on the Thanksgiving night when the phone rang to tell us Vee had shattered her knee. Only then we didn't know all that would follow.

In a while, I dozed, too, starting violently when the buzzer sounded in the kitchen.

Mason breathed heavily and kept right on sleeping.

Gingerly I pried myself away from him, arranged the blanket over him. After a moment's thought, the dog slid down from its chair and followed me.

I kicked into my boots, pulled on a coat, took the flashlight from beside the door, and went out to the barn. From the breezeway I could see the bitter brightness of the stars.

Slipping into the barn, I found a switch and turned it on. One string of electric lights illuminated. Rich shadows threw themselves up along the hay piled neatly down the left side of the aisle. On the right, the top half of each stall door was open. The outer doors were all bolted up against the cold, and the stalls were shadowy and dark. From the first stall, I heard something bleat.

A goat. I smiled wryly. Mason has a pet goat. Who would have thought?

"Shush," I said.

The bleat came again. Not a goat, but familiar.

I leaned over the door, shined the flashlight into the stall.

Yes, there was a goat. But also, looking back at me, was a leggy black foal. It had a white snip, a couple of white socks, and it was clearly not too happy.

I slipped into the stall. The goat gave a loud bleat, but stood its ground, swinging its head from side to side and blinking in the light. The foal took two steps toward me, then stopped, snorted, and wrung its tail.

A foal. I couldn't believe it. I studied it. Maybe a week old? It came toward me again, clumsily, with the heartbreaking awkwardness and confusion of an orphan. How much they lost without their mothers. Somehow, if they

385

lived, they never quite turned into horses, never carried themselves well in a herd, never seemed correctly wired.

The little guy butted my hip, my waist, my arm. I stroked his neck, rubbed my thumbs along the corners of his mouth, bent and breathed into his nostrils, traced the fine lines of his ears.

He butted me some more. I ran my fingers through his wispy plush-toy coat.

"Look," I said, seeing the automatic bottle feeder on the wall beside the door. I walked over, squeezed the nipple, wet my fingers with formula and offered them to the foal.

He wrinkled his lip and bleated.

"You have to eat," I whispered. "Or I'll have to go wake Mason. And he's had one hell of a day."

The baby staggered toward the opposite wall and butted it with his head. I went after him, offered my fingers again. Suddenly he began to suck.

Then I heard a footstep, the creak of a door, and before I could stop myself I was screaming.

"Nate, Nate. It's me. Mason. You're all right."

I screamed again, gasped, then forced myself to stop.

The foal scampered off to the far corner of the stall and stood flicking its ears and bleating. The goat's jaw froze; it stood and stared.

Mason was in the doorway to the stall. I was too embarrassed to look at him. "I'm sorry," I said.

"You've had a shock. I shouldn't have come up on you like that."

I closed my eyes, settled myself, then inched toward the foal, hugged his neck, and again offered my fingers for him to suck.

"Imprint that colt," Mason said, "and you're staying until he's weaned. He's already had one loss too many."

He turned away, went into the house, came back after a while with a square bottle filled with warm formula and topped off with a livestock nipple. He held it up to me as if offering a toast.

"I mean it," he said. "Careful of the imprinting. I'm afraid you'll leave."

He watched me long and hard in the half-dark.

"You don't trust me, do you?"

"I'd like to," he said. "Your skills impress me. And your heart. But trust?" He smiled, shook his head.

I came toward him, hesitated. He held the bottle up, just a little out of my reach.

"I've only done what I thought I had to."

"Ever think about what you leave behind?"

"I'm learning," I said sadly. My eyes welled, and I reached out for the bottle. "Now will you check Galen?"

"Yes, ma'am."

And so I fed the foal. At first I was careful. I let him have the warm formula and simply patted him on the neck. But soon my hands began to roam, exploring the fragile baby, his eyelids, his ears, his funny dimpled chin, the baby wrinkles on his chest.

"Look at you," Mason said when he came back. "He likes you."

"How's Galen?"

"Don't get your hopes up."

"Who owns him? He's a little beauty."

Mason sighed. "If he lives, I'm afraid that I do."

"Softie," I said, and smiled. "Owners couldn't pay the bill?"

"I didn't want you to see him. I'm barely giving him even odds."

The colt finished eating, licked his lips, leaned against me, let his eyelids flutter.

"He needs a name," I said.

"Nate."

"I know, I know, but he does. Even if it's only for a little while."

I eyed him more closely. "Is he black? I can't tell in this light."

Mason was quiet.

Twister was black. We were both thinking that.

"No," he said after a while. "He'll be a gray."

I sighed with relief.

"We'll call him Zinzendorf."

"Zinzendorf? What's that?"

"And you a history buff," I said. I hummed a few bars of the hymn: *Not Jerusalem, lowly Bethlehem.*

Back in the house we fed the fire, poured more wine, burrowed beneath the blanket. Then I got up and dug in the pocket of my city coat. There in the bottom was my vigils candle, its skirt crushed. I plucked at the red pleats of paper, fluffed them up as best I could. Then I found a match in the kitchen, came out, and perched on the arm of the couch.

"It is 1742," I said. "A few days before Christmas. The Moravians have only had time to build one small building to get them through their first winter in their new settlement. People live in one half, animals in the other. And then, the day before Christmas, who should arrive but Count Zinzendorf himself. He is their benefactor, the man who bought land from his friend William Penn in order to make a home for them in the wilderness. With him is his daughter Benigna, sixteen years old. Imagine being sixteen and off to the wilds of North America with your father."

This was my kind of story.

"And halfway through the service, they are singing the old hymn: *Not Jerusalem, lowly Bethlehem. Was that gave us what would save us.*"

My eyes filled with tears. I sang the verse.

Mason smiled. "I think you're flat."

"And so they enter the barn and stand among the animals and as the vigil service ends Zinzendorf names the city."

My hands were trembling but I lit what was left of the candle, and we watched the tiny flame burn all the way down into the skirt.

chapter twenty-eight

On New Year's Eve, I drove over to DreamWeb Farm. I admit I fibbed to Mason, said I was going to town to run some errands. For an alibi, I had drawn up a grocery list.

We had spread out the feedings for Zinzendorf, who now bleated not at the sound of Mason's footfall but at mine. So that was that. At least until he was weaned from the bottle, I was staying.

"I'd suggest you stay for good," Mason said to me once, but then his voice trailed off.

I made a face. "But I'm not to be trusted."

He shrugged and I could see he had decided not to be hurt. He touched a corner of his mustache. "You're wise not to make promises if you don't plan to keep them. You don't mislead people on purpose."

Oh, but no doubt I sometimes did without intent. Myself included.

For three nights, we had huddled in the living room, trading off the couch, the wing chair, the armchair, and one or the other or both of us rose every few hours to the sound of the kitchen timer in order to check the foal. With great regret we'd had to put Galen down. There was no point in making him suffer any further, and it was not clear just how far he would ever come back to normal. We moved Prima to the stall next to the baby and often she stared through the slats, horrified, jealous, fascinated by the little nubbin of a horse in the next stall.

Zinzendorf seemed well enough, feeding noisily at every opportunity, responding to our voices, agreeing to be handled, but petting and sweet talk would not make up for a mother. He could still slip, still fail to thrive, and die. Or he could grow up into a horse who only by some miracle turned out all right.

As I approached the farm, I drove more and more slowly, then as I rounded the bend toward the driveway, I hit the brakes.

My pile of boxes was gone. Taken to the dump? Picked up by the police? By Fred Weirbachen? I sat with my foot on the brake. What would have remained? Harmonica, china, clothes, books, letters—most of it would have been ruined. Wondering where my equipment was, I found the courage to pull up to the barn.

Deep down, it was Vee's pistol I was after. As promised, Mac Vorhees had sent a rendering of her story as gleaned from his files. The type-script had pretty much confirmed what Mac had told me Christmas Eve. He added that Tom Maxfield would handle my affairs in the future, wished me a happy and productive life, and signed it himself, in a wavering hand.

I had since decided to find Vee's pistol, lay my hands on it, and walk it up to the top of Twister's hill. There I would shoot off all the ammo I had left. Was it the Scots who shot into the air for blessings on the New Year? Perhaps I would feel those old precious brain waves of prayer and perfect aim, shot after shot. Perhaps I would feel something lift from me, would finally make my peace with Vee and how she died and what she had given me before she did. I had even imagined myself climbing Twister's hill, had felt the pistol's heavy weight against my hip, had heard the rattle of the shells in their plastic case, heard the snap snap snap of the .22.

I got out of the truck and gingerly made my way up the cubby stairs. The place was bare. No pistol. Only the stripped cot, the empty bureau, the hole I'd shot in the ceiling.

What had I been thinking? That a trained state trooper wasn't smart enough to look in a drawer and find a gun?

I felt a chill: my pistol, Vee's pistol, gone. And then I realized I was the only person on the face of the earth to whom that little pistol meant a thing. And that, I thought, is what life is all about. What we make of it. What we attach.

I clattered down the stairs, then turned toward the barn. But I could not bring myself to go in. I stood outside and lay my open palm on the wood planking of the door, closed my eyes, and listened. Nothing. After a while, I went around the back. There on the edge of the field were the new graves: Sheila, Lawrence, Archimedes. I saw that Fred had taken the time to dig three separate times. A separate grave for each.

For me, I thought.

And then I knew what to do.

I went through the back doors of the barn. It was a relief to see that they had rebuilt the stall front, had almost swept up the evidence of Sheila's carcass being dragged from her stall and down the aisle to the back door.

I stood, lost and helpless.

Then I poked my head into the tack room. There were my saddles, mixed in with the rest. And Twister's bridle, neatly figure-eighted. For a minute I thought of taking it with me. All great horses are buried with their bridles.

Again I regretted the way Twister died. I should have stayed with him. I touched his bridle. There would be other horses, and if I were very lucky I would ride them with something he had given me. Then I went into the grain room and filled a bucket to the brim with sweet feed.

At each grave site, I paused, swept the ragged frozen earth with a handful of grain. I had grown up with a Russian girl who spread nuts and apples on the graves of ancestors so the birds and squirrels would feed there and bring life. I scattered the grain and cried and wished I knew which horse was buried where. I tried to think of something to say, but all I could come up with was the old riders' rhyme: "Apple core, say no more, who's your friend until the end?"

Potts dies in the spring. The leaves are out, the grass deep green in Nisky Hill. The apple blossoms have gone by. The world is rich. I stand at the graveside. Lucy is in black. Her

393

face is blanched, slashed with the color of her blush. She cries as if she will die, horrifying racking sounds. John Casey stands a little way off from her, as if afraid to touch her. His large hands hang empty at his sides. The graveside prayers are brief.

—May the Lord bless thee and keep thee and make his face to shine upon thee.

Then something about comfort in our comings-in and our goings-out.

Alec stands beside me, his arm clamped around my waist as if he alone keeps my feet nailed to the grass.

I stare down into the grave, watch my father lowered into the ground in an elaborate coffin. Lucy picked it out, ordering that no expense be spared. I picture Potts running his hand up through his hair, then offering a mild rebuff.

Lucy throws a rose onto the lid of it, sobs all the harder.

I am shredding the rose I have been handed. Vaguely I am aware of the bright petals cascading down my skirt.

Alec whispers something to me.

I hand him the flower. There is not much left to it.

—You do it, I hiss.

He looks into my face.

I stare at the ground. Petals lie around my feet. I step back in horror. Shake them free from my shoes.

Across the way two fat robins bounce across the grass in search of worms.

The minister finishes his prayers, closes his Bible. The machinery silently rolls.

I turn to Alec. My face is wet. He kisses me alongside one eye. I look at him, but cannot quite see him. I break out of his grip, turn, and walk away.

He lets me go, then runs after me.

I hear Lucy call him back.

—Oh, Alec, she sobs. Just leave her. She'll be fine.

I have done nothing but walk the city since Potts has died. Two long nights on Alec's arm, not speaking, wreaking God knows what havoc on his precious grade point average, which must remain pristine if he is to transfer to Penn, become a doctor, save the lives of strangers.

I walk toward the gate, then swing alone down to the bluff by the river. The bells of St. Mike's do not ring for me. Then I sneak out a far gate, dodge into the mouth of an alleyway of double-doored carriage houses converted to garages. I know there is a gathering, coffee and rolls, in the vestry of the church. I know they all think I will turn up there sooner or later. My sister. John Casey. Alec. MacVorhees. Reverend Nussbaum.

Half hidden, I stand and spy on them, a small clutch of people in dark clothes leaving Nisky Hill. And then I take a roundabout route back to the apartment. I do not feel the pavement under my feet, or see much of what I pass. I go up to the apartment, make my small raid: Vee's letters, the china cup, my mother's photo from my father's bedside. And then, with no sense of destination, I begin to drive: three states, five states, seven states.

It was quite the slog. The day was cold, and soon my feet were wet. The snow was shin deep and it wore me out to lift my boots with every step. I thought a few times I should have driven around the back, but there was something fitting about the effort. On and on I went, weeping sometimes, laughing once or twice, sometimes, by habit, absolutely numb. The handle of the bucket bit through my wool mittens.

When I finally reached the grave, it was nothing but a hilltop covered with snow. I stood looking out over the valley. There at my feet lay the Weirbachens' farm, where Mason and I would eat noon dinner on the New Year, sharing the traditional pork and cabbage to bring luck for the coming twelvemonth.

Beyond the next range of hills lay Mason's place. Pierce was still hovering in his coma, his future far less certain than the foal's. I had been to see him once, hooked up to machines that kept him tied to life when no one knew if he wanted to come back. What was it Mason had said? "You don't even know people get attached to you. It makes them crazy when you leave."

I swung the bucket, then reached in and scattered a handful of grain as carefully as if planting a crop.

We do not know it then, but our last ride before Vee's knee shatters is on a chill Sunday in November. She sits erect behind me. Her hands in buff string gloves hold the reins before us.

Beneath us, Hadley surges like the ocean. Dry leaves boil up around his hooves. We gallop down a shallow hill, around a bend. The coal-black tips of Hadley's ears mark the boundaries of my vision.

Vee's face comes down beside mine. I feel her soft cheek, the bristle of her curls.

—Natalie!

I jam my heels down. The straps of my jodhpur boots tighten around my ankles.

—Ready?

She slips her hands along the reins. Her arms, in the sleeves of her green hacking jacket, reach further along his neck.

Hadley flicks an ear, settles his weight.

We round another bend.

A monstrous log blocks the path.

Vee's arm slips around my waist.

In my ear she counts:

—One... two...three...!

And then we lift off the earth. Behind me, Vee comes forward with the jump, and she folds my body, too, so that our weight is up over Hadley's neck and shoulder as he sails through the air.

He lands.

We gallop on.

One, two, three: another log.

One, two, three: a small gate.

One, two, three: a stone wall.

—That's it, Vee says behind me, and lets go of my waist.

Hadley jigs, dances sideways, snatches at his bit, slows down.

Vee gives him a pat. Then, with her gloved hand, she raps on my hard hat.

Again and again, she tells me: always thank the horse for what it gives you.

I fling my arms around Hadley's neck.

—I love you, boy, I whisper.

Then I sit up, lean back, and whisper:

—I love you, too.

She raps on my helmet, kisses my cheek.

—Out here, she says, it's possible to love the whole damn world.

I stood with my bucket of grain on the hilltop near Twister's grave. Soon I would go for groceries and then head back to Mason's and feed the foal, see how it felt to make even a short promise and stick to it. One of these days I would call Alec, too, and for what it was worth, let him know what had become of me. I reached into the bucket, scattered another handful of grain, then set the bucket down, planted my feet, scooped up a double handful, and flung it high over my head. The winter wind caught the golden grain, scattered it and all my sorrows and my blessings at my feet.